I0672661

THE TRISKELION SERIES

A PROMISE FOR TOMORROW

LUNA EVERLY

A Promise For Tomorrow is available in Paperback

Copyright © 1st Edition 2024 Luna Everly

All rights reserved.

No part of this book may be reproduced, distributed, or transmitted in any form
or by any means, including electronic or mechanical methods, without prior
written permission from the author, except as permitted by U.S. copyright law.

This is a work of fiction. Unless otherwise indicated, all the names, characters,
businesses, places, events, and incidents in this book are either the product of the
author's imagination or used in a fictitious manner. Any resemblance to actual
persons, living or dead, or actual events is purely coincidental.

Cover and Interior Design © Quirky Circe Book Design

ISBN Paperback 979-8-9881075-5-2

ISBN eBook 979-8-9881075-4-5

To those who reach for that happily ever but come up empty-handed time and time again: We must trust in the unknown, embrace the in-between, and dance through the chaos.

TRIGGER WARNINGS

This book contains dark elements such as crime, violence, death, grief, drug use, drinking, cheating, memories of abduction, vivid talk and scenes of abuse/torture, infertility and loss, menstruation, light bondage, knife play, and explicit sexual content. Intended for those 18+

Time is ticking.

And it's incredibly precious.

When a family emergency forces Madison to go back to her old life in New York, she is faced with confronting her past and the people she left behind. Emotions run high as she is thrust back into the underworld with the two men who still hold her heart.

Even after all this time.

Where almost everyone is moving on with their lives, Madison remains stuck on what could have been.

A year ago she wanted simple. *Safe.*

Now, her untimely arrival home has her questioning everything she once thought she needed.

During her stay, Liam and Maddy are tasked with working together to organize a wedding for a syndicate member as Diego works to reclaim his throne—*and his wife.*

Vacillating with the familiarity of being around Liam and the desires Diego stirs within her, Madison is presented with a choice.

The man who claimed her heart in college? Or the man who taught her how to embrace the woman she is today?

The final book in the trilogy will take Madison down a slippery slope of facing her fears and letting her heart take the lead.

Will history repeat itself, or will Madison decide to leave them in her past once and for all?

CHAPTER 1

MADISON

One Year Later - New Year's Eve 2016

"*GAHHH*!" I shriek for the umpteenth time this year.

Scorpions.

Nasty, creepy, *crawly* little creatures.

We're not in New York anymore—that's for sure. I have no idea what I was thinking when I dropped everything to come live here. *An escape? A chance at hitting the reset button? Putting as much distance as I could get between me and the two men who have my head in a constant tailspin?*

Ding. Ding. Ding.

Regardless, here we are. Donning a flip-flop in one hand, and a can of scorpion killer in the other. Beady black eyes fixate on me as its pinchers spread wide, poised for an attack. A venomous barbed tail protrudes from its hairy pale exoskeleton, pulsing with agitation. This pet of the devil himself is preparing to launch itself at me—*or so I tell myself.*

As if it can read the fear in my eyes, or perhaps is intelligent enough to take in the trembling of my hands, it launches itself over the lip of the bathtub. *Scuttling. Right. Towards me.*

I release a blood-curdling scream. A scream that should've

had the neighbors in apartment 4C running over thinking something unspeakable happened. Luckily, Simon and John are used to my 'unwarranted outbursts'. The couple gave up racing over after my first few encounters with these eight-legged monsters. Now, they just opt to send a hysterical text about me being a giant baby or playfully remind me I'm not cut out for a life in Arizona. Usually, followed by an offer to go grab a drink or join them for a glass of wine in their apartment next door.

Spray foam smacks the space next to the scorpion, making it bob its tail in my direction—not that I am anywhere near the ledge of the tub. My ass is firmly pressed against the granite countertop of the vanity. *It's just a scorpion, Maddy. A small one at that. You've got this, girl. Now smack the shit out of it.* I brace the sandal, ready to send the creature back to the depths of Hell, where it belongs when the black sparkled shoe is tugged out of my grasp.

Slap.

"Jesus, Mad. I woke up thinking Diego was at our front door," Lexi mumbles groggily, handing me back my shoe. She shuffles over to the vanity, retrieving two tissues before leaning over the tub and removing the mangled, *very dead*, scorpion.

"*Pshh.* Even Diego couldn't make me scream like that," I scoff defensively.

She tosses the balled-up tissue into the wastebasket, then leans a hip against the granite, crossing her arms over her chest.

"Oh, really? So you're admitting that Diego can't make you scream?" A smirk forms on her lips as she arches a sassy brow.

"That's not what I said...I mean not like... *that*. And you're a bitch," I joke. "Can we lay off the Diego topic, please? As if today is not bad enough already. Ya know, with it being my one-year anniversary of moving here. Of course, the Universe just loves to fuck with me and had to add a nice cherry on top of my already shitty day," I groan, nodding to the trash bin next to the toilet.

2

"It was the smallest scorpion *ever*. John and Simon text you yet?" She laughs as footsteps approach from down the hall.

I snag my phone off the vanity and notice a new text in our group chat.

> **SIMON**
> That scorpion had to be the size of my nan's knickers for you to scream that loudly. 🌮

> **JOHN**
> Or maybe, she had a guest over... the kind who own private jets... 😏

Lexi's fingers fly across her phone screen, click-clacking away before my phone chimes with a new notification.

> **LEXI**
> *gif of a girl with her index and thumb finger hovering close together, indicating tiny* It was THE smallest scorpion 🦂 If it was the size of your nan's knickers this apartment complex would have already been on fire.

> **MADDY**
>

A deep chuckle radiates from the doorway. Conor is leaning against the door frame, barefoot and shirtless, sporting a pair of gray cotton sweatpants. He's biting his lower lip, holding back another chuckle while shaking his head. His giant paws hold out his iPhone, the screen illuminated, revealing a group chat we are all in. *Should have never included that asshole in our sacred neighborly group chat.*

"And you want to visit *Australia*?" He bends over at the hip with tears in his eyes as he starts to crack up some more. "Good luck with that, lass," he says between snickers.

Heat rushes to my face. *Conor reminds me so much of Liam.* If Lexi wasn't head over heels in love with him I could have just

3

as easily cut him off. *Okay–not easily.* I love Con. He was one of my first friends in the Tri-State Syndicate. My own personal bodyguard before Liam ever was. None of this was easy. Letting go of the friends—the family I had created with all of them.

I stalk his way and jam my pointer finger into his tattooed chest. "If my best friend didn't love you so much, you would have already been cut off."

His amber eyes soften as he delicately wraps his hand around mine. "Aw, Mad. I was just playing around. Look, I even set the timer on the coffee pot last night. How could ya possibly cut me off when I help supply ya caffeine addiction?"

At the mention of coffee, the rich aroma of dark roast permeates our space and the melody of the machine brewing soothes my misplaced anger.

A smile forms on my face as I stare up at him. Untangling my hand from his, I pat his cheek twice.

"Such a good bodyguard you are," I praise, the sarcasm flowing so easily off my tongue.

We both know that although he is here visiting his girlfriend, he is also keeping tabs on me. I side-step him, entering the hallway that leads to the kitchen. *And coffee.*

Lots and lots of coffee.

The cabinets clank in my search for a clean mug. Coming up empty, I open the dishwasher and grab my favorite one off the top rack. It's sparkly purple and embellished with a crescent moon and stars. The words LET THAT SHIT GO are stamped proudly below the moon. I figured if I saw the words enough they would stick.

They haven't.

Lexi and Conor's matching mugs are also in attendance. I retrieve them, placing them on the counter next to mine before grabbing the oat milk from the fridge. Lex and Con have been eating a plant-based diet for the last few months. While I agree that oat milk tastes just as delicious in my coffee, old habits die hard. I snatch my half and half from the fridge, adding it to the coffee receiving line formed on the counter. Another text notification chimes on my phone.

I swear, if there are any more jokes in the group chat at my expense, I will lose it.

Today just isn't the day.

Glancing over at my phone while pouring coffee into each mug, I notice it's a text from my mom:

MOM

Call me.

A chuckle escapes my lips as Lexi and Conor make their way to the kitchen, taking a seat on the stools at the kitchen island. *She couldn't just call me? She had to text me to call her?* I quickly finish up, placing their respective drinks in front of them before leaning back against the counter.

Lexi grabs hers, bringing the steaming cup to her lips. "What's so funny?" Her bright blue eyes search mine.

I mirror her, bringing the purple mug to my lips and savoring the smell before sipping. "It's just my Mo—" Coffee sloshes over the rim of my mug as I slam it down on the counter. "What is that?!" I point my index finger at the giant rock on her left hand.

"Oh, this?" Lexi feigns innocence, holding up the ring finger that houses her newly acquired engagement ring. My gaze remains locked on the stunning diamond ring before shifting to Conor—who is sporting the biggest shit-eating grin.

"I asked her to marry me last night," he announces proudly while gazing at his fiancée. Waves of love and devotion pour off him. *It's freakin adorable.*

A squeal leaves my lips as I run over to stand between them, pulling the love birds into a hug. "I am so happy for you both. Welcome to the family, Con," I wink at him. He returns the sentiment while taking a sip of his coffee.

Clearing his throat he says, "The two of us were going to

spend New Year's Eve with you, Simon, and John...but we..." He stumbles around with his words as Lexi jumps in to intervene.

"We were invited to celebrate our engagement in New York. Liam has plans to dedicate a special portion of the gala to us." Lexi grabs my hand and searches my eyes. "I know you want to completely separate your life from *theirs*, and I respect that one hundred percent. It's just that navigating this wedding will be challenging. I want my best friend to feel comfortable and happy...but you know Conor has an obligation to his syndicate and intense loyalty to his best friend. He asked Liam to be his Best Man, Mad. I would be honored if you would be my Maid of Honor—and possibly consider joining us in New York tonight?"

"I...of course, Lexi! Yes! I'll be your Maid of Honor. I can handle Liam for a few interactions. We are adults, after all. But New York... tonight... I..."

"Lass can't handle a little scorpion yet claims she can handle Liam," Conor mumbles over the rim of his mug.

My eyes slide over to his with venom way more potent than that of the *'little scorpion'*.

He leans back with his hands raised in surrender.

I was about to explain that it has been over a year and I am perfectly capable of keeping my feelings separate from my duties as a Maid of Honor...when my phone vibrates against the kitchen counter, rudely interrupting me.

"Hey, Mom. Sorry, I meant to call you. I just got some exciting—"

"*Madison.* I need you to come home tonight, sweetheart." My heart drops at her tone. "Your father, so typical of him, has been hiding the severity of his heart condition from all of us. He called to let me know that the surgeon has him scheduled tonight for a triple bypass surgery at NewYork-Presbyterian Hospital. The surgeon spoke with me after I demanded I talk to him. He told me to—" her voice cracks, "*prepare*. This surgery has a thirty percent chance of being successful. If he doesn't go through with it, he will most likely suffer another deadly heart attack—which is what led him to the ER in the first place."

"Why is he in the city?" I ask, my voice quivering with anxiety.

"He was stable enough to transfer to where his surgeon does his open heart surgeries."

I cup a trembling hand around my mouth. "Oh my God, Mom. Okay. Yeah, I'm coming home. I'll book something right now."

"I love you, sweetheart. I have to run and call Mikayla. Call me when you land."

CHAPTER 2

MADISON

"FUCK." I can't get any last-minute flights. Tonight is the busiest night of the year to travel." I let out an aggravated sigh of frustration.

"I just got off the phone with customer service. They won't let me transfer my ticket over to you this soon before boarding. I even explained the severity of it," Lexi growls from her seat at the kitchen island. Her laptop is there with about twenty different airline tabs open on her browser.

"Fucking gobshites," Conor sneers. A hesitant look crosses his face as he takes a moment to look at me. "I have an idea. I'll ask Killian if he will lend me the jet. Then we can all head to New York together."

I chew on my thumbnail, not wanting to ask him for anything. After a pregnant pause, I nod my head. *What choice do I have left?*

Time is ticking.

And it's incredibly precious.

He dials Killian, pressing the phone to his ear. A few seconds go by before he shakes his head. He didn't answer. *Damn it.* Conor looks back up at me, seemingly thinking the same thing.

"Call *him*," I confirm with a sigh.

This time he doesn't hesitate. Con places it on speaker. It rings twice before Liam's husky voice fills the line. "Hey, brother. Have you decided if you are using those tickets to come to New York tonight?" His excitement over seeing his newly engaged best friend has my heart beating faster beneath my ribs.

"About that...Maddy's father is at NewYork-Presbyterian Hospital. He had a major heart attack and is scheduled for a triple bypass later this evening." Before he has the chance to continue explaining, Liam interrupts.

"What the fuck? Is she okay? Is she on her way to New York?" Anxiety laces his tone.

Muffled conversations are going on in the background. It's hard to make out who else is whispering.

"We've been trying all morning to get a flight out there for her. We even tried to swap our tickets for her, but the airlines won't allow it. Which is why I was going to ask if—"

"Yes. It's done. The jet is all yours. Take the flight with her so she isn't alone," he demands.

I let out a sigh of relief which does nothing to slow my frantic heart.

More hushed chatter fills the line, this time way louder.

Then my heart feels like it stops entirely.

"You know my jet is faster than yours. It will get there in practically half the time. Give me the phone, I'll set it up," a voice like whiskey offers.

"Let go of my phone, Diego. Christ, you're fucking overbearing sometimes," Liam chuckles in the background. *Huh? What the hell is this semi-friendly relationship between them?*

My phone buzzes in my hand, starting my heart back up. I glance down at the text—*scratch that last part—it just stopped again and took a massive nosedive dive into my stomach.*

UNKNOWN

Mariposita, I'm sorry to hear about your father.
What kind of husband would I be if I didn't
send you one of the fastest jets in the world?
Please don't be your stubborn self and deny
the help. The jet is still yours and it's preparing
to pick you up in Arizona. Tell Conor and Lexi
to keep their flight. The hospital won't allow
anyone beyond family in the waiting room.
They may as well enjoy the Gala and their
engagement celebration.

UNKNOWN

If your Dad is anything like you, he's strong.
He's gonna pull through this, baby.

"It's done, Liam. Tell Conor we'll see them later and congratulations," Diego's baritone voice registers through the haze in my brain.

"You heard him, Con," Liam says almost defeatedly. "I'll send ya the details shortly."

Lexi's worried gaze lands on me before I meet her eyes. Clasping my hands together I turn on my heel.

"I'm going to go pack."

MY KNEE BOUNCES up and down as I wait for my flight in the small waiting area of the private airfield. Against her better judgment, Lexi and Con took their original flights earlier this morning. She wanted to come with me to the hospital, but I told her they were strict on having family only in the waiting room. Plus, the two of them should be able to enjoy the evening that was planned for them. She finally agreed and demanded that if I needed her at any moment, to call her.

A staff member places a hand on my shoulder, alerting me

that my flight is ready to board. They silently direct me, walking a short distance towards the airstairs of Diego's jet.

"Welcome back, Mrs. De La Cruz." Amy, the flight attendant with a warm smile greets me at the top. She reaches out and collects my overnight bag slung over my shoulder. I try my best to return the smile but my married name shocked the shit out of me, temporarily paralyzing my facial features.

On bated breath, I enter the cabin and let out a sigh of relief, noticing it's empty.

The leather groans as I plop my ass into a seat and plug my headphones into my phone. I prop my elbows on the table in front of me and scroll my Kindle app for a good book to read. Amy makes her way towards me, realizing I am about to check out. At the same time, the engines fire up, slightly rumbling the space.

"Can I grab you anything to eat or drink before we take off, Mrs. De La Cruz?"

My cheeks heat as I shake my head to decline. "You don't need to call me Mrs. De La Cruz. Maddy is fine."

"Damn, *Mariposita*. I am shocked you didn't want a coffee from your favorite machine."

Amy smiles that warm smile again at me before shifting her gaze to *The Bone Breaker* behind me. Hints of coconut, salt, and mint caress my sense of smell as he approaches. Apparently, they are a deadly combination of aphrodisiacs because my heart beats wildly in my chest.

"Mr. De La Cruz, can I get you a coffee before we take off?" the flight attendant asks him. I can just barely register what she's saying over my pulse whooshing in my ears.

"Not right now. Thank you, Amy. I'm sure mid-flight my wife will change her mind." He stifles a laugh before taking a seat directly across from me.

My tongue is lead in my mouth. There is so much that sits

between us. So many unspoken words. Yet, neither of us says a single thing as the jet takes off on the runway.

We just stare.

Unabashedly taking each other in.

He looks good. *Okay, he looks fucking delicious.* Just the same if not more muscular and toned than when I last saw him. Certainly too good to be sitting in front of me right now with that cocky smirk on his face.

The man is supposed to be *dead.* And here he sits, casually resting against his seat, exposing his identity—*for me.*

Finding the courage to speak first, I lean over the table and whisper, "You shouldn't have taken the risk of being exposed like this for me."

"I would *die* for you," he rasps, laughing at his own joke. *Very funny.*

He leans in closer and rests his elbows on the table between us before extending a hand and taking mine captive. Diego strokes his thumb over the empty space where my wedding rings once sat.

I try everything in my power not to look into his eyes. If I do, I'll surely break. I am too vulnerable tonight to fend him off. Traitorously, my eyes glide up from his hand on mine to his broad chest before climbing higher. They trace and reacquaint themselves with the shape of his smooth lips, then follow the curve of his cupid's bow to the bridge of his sturdy nose. Slowly, they glide up until two piercing blue eyes stare right back at me.

And then I'm drowning.

"I missed you," he whispers. Gone is the sarcastic bravado nature I am used to. Desire and longing replace it, brewing like a storm beneath those eyes.

Tears fill my own to the brim, threatening to cascade down my face in rivers. I take a steadying breath through my nose, attempting to keep them at bay.

Diego is out of his seat in a second, nudging me aside to sit and then pulling me into him. He cradles my head against his warm chest. It's then that I allow the tears to fall.

And fall.

And fall some more.

I'm not sure how long we stayed like that. The rhythmic rise and fall of his chest and the soothing sensation of his fingers massaging my scalp was like a lullaby. The safety of his arms and the pure comfort of him had my eyes fluttering closed.

His chin remained resting on the top of my head. Only when his lips brush against my temple do my eyes pop open.

"You know the surgeon doing your father's surgery is the same cardiothoracic surgeon who helped me? Dr. Angosta. Trust that if that man can kill me and bring me back, he'll take great care of your dad."

I lift my head off his chest and swipe at the remaining tears with the sleeve of my sweatshirt. Uncertainty fills me hearing this information, unsure whether to be hopeful or worried by it.

"What? How do you know that?"

"Sweetheart, I may be *dead*," he air quotes, "but I still have plenty of connections. In fact, I have such *wonderful* connections, that even if the Feds discover our little story, I have a man in my arsenal who could help wipe the entire case clean. Hell, I may even decide to rise from the dead with an official statement and claim my throne. I've been quite busy this last year."

I shake my head, attempting to rid myself of the confusion while rubbing my eyes. *Any chance this whole day has been a dream?* When I still see Diego sitting there next to me, I sigh heavily and lean back into my chair.

"Hey, Amy?" I spot her sitting near the small kitchenette. "I'll take that coffee now—*please*."

She walks over to the beautiful stainless steel machine that I've without a doubt missed and starts prepping it. "What would you like to drink?"

"Quad espresso over ice with some of that sweet cream foam you have," Diego interjects.

I glare at him, narrowing my eyes and pursing my lips.

"Tell me I'm wrong." He shrugs, folding his hands on the table. The glint of his black wedding band catches my attention.

He still wears it.

Bastard.

CHAPTER 3

DIEGO

SO. *Fucking. Stunning.* That anger of hers riles the beast in me. The one impatiently salivating, waiting to get a taste of her. There's nothing better than watching the heat behind her eyes ignite and those chestnut orbs crackle with invitation.

To keep going.

To keep pushing her.

If it means keeping her distracted from her family emergency, by all means, allow me to take the heat.

Amy places our drinks down before us along with a few pastries. Madison's eyes widen with excitement seeing her favorite lemon tarts amongst the spread. She plucks two from the tray, popping one in her mouth and placing the other on her plate. Moaning her contentment and making my cock twitch, she washes it down with a healthy sip of her espresso.

"What made you choose this color?" I play with a strand of her curled hair, twirling it around my finger and wishing I could wrap all of it around my wrist. It's luxuriously soft and dyed the deepest shade of purple. So deep it's practically black, shimmering with an aura of violet. It certainly suits her. In my eyes, Madison has always been a queen. Adding purple to her hair only enhances that regal look she often pulls off.

Trembling fingers raise her cup as she pulls the straw between her pouty lips, buying herself time to answer me.

Fuck. This woman is perfection.

Her eyes scan mine, those thick lashes fluttering as she looks me over. My little butterfly is completely unaware she's checking me out again just as I am her. A smile forms on my face and it feels good. *Damn good.* It's been too long having this woman out of my sight.

The way we left off was not at all what I had anticipated. *I mean honestly? I don't know what I was expecting, but her up and leaving all together wasn't it.* I've spent the entire year focusing on ways to make it right.

To her. And my people.

My syndicate needs me—and not the ghost version where my cousin leads the organization. I am ready to step into my role and take my seat back for all to see. Thankfully, I found a way to do so.

We've got enough evidence to prove Geraldo was to blame for all the atrocities that were stacked against me. There is a strong possibility that my guy in the Feds can rewrite the details of that night, completely removing the death certificate along with the interviews with my wife and anything else revealing my death. If he can pull that off, we may stand a chance at getting back to the way things should have been. I will publicly resurface and there won't be any written details of our stay in Greece other than our marriage certificate.

That we can leave.

"I've always loved the color...and I needed a change of pace," Madison finally admits. "Dying my hair makes me feel in control, especially when everything around me becomes chaotic. It's something I get to *choose*. A constant if I wish it to be."

Her eyes stray from mine and she tucks a lock of hair behind her left ear, clearly uncomfortable continuing. That's when I spot it. The smallest tattoo I've ever seen...with such *incredible* detail. Her artist did a fantastic job with the fine lines.

My heart pounds wildly in my chest as it did when I said *I do.* My exquisite wife inked herself with a permanent reminder of me.

A delicate blue butterfly adorns her skin right behind her ear.

All this tension building inside of me is poised and ready to reach out and touch her.

Reclaim her.

I strike like a snake, clasping her throat. Forming an O, her mouth pops open and a gasp slips from her lips. My hand slides up the soft skin of her neck, fingers wrapping around her delicate jaw. I tilt her head towards the window, needing to take a closer look at this *mariposita*. The pad of my thumb skims over the now goosebump-ridden skin of her neck.

Her chest rises and falls against my forearm and her hand has come up to grip my wrist—but she's made no attempt to remove it.

And I know she can.

Liam helped train her all those months I couldn't. With that knowledge—and because I just can't fucking help myself—I lean down and place my lips over the blue ink. A buzz runs across them as she shivers beneath me, inhaling sharply through her nose.

"*Ocean Eyes...*" she exhales breathily.

The grasp I have around her jaw tightens as my cock turns hard as steel in my jeans.

I nip at her earlobe, my teeth grazing the soft skin before whispering, "You never stopped being mine, *Mariposita.* And by inking yourself with a constant reminder of me...it appears I never stopped being yours either."

Too impatient for a response, I swivel her face back towards me and kiss my sweet girl senseless. She kisses me back with such fervor that I become lost and found in the same moment.

All that exists in this moment is *her*.

Her soft lips, her tongue dancing with mine, our hands roaming as much surface area of each other as we can get.

I drag her on top of me so that she straddles me, my erection pressing firmly into the sweet spot between her legs. Heat radiates beneath her thin black leggings, siphoning a growl out of me.

Fuck. I need her.

Desperate hands find the back of her head, my fingers clenching the curled purple strands at the scalp. With a yelp, she inhales against my lips and grinds down harder on my pulsing cock pressing at her core.

These goddamn leggings need to be gone. *Now. Where's my knife? Shall I remind her of the last time I stripped her leggings off her?*

"I need to be inside you, baby." I nip at her tattoo, eliciting another delicious moan from her.

Poor Amy. She's too sweet of a woman to witness the reunion I have planned with my wife—otherwise, I would have just taken Madison's tight cunt right here and now.

I stand, cupping my hands around her delectable round ass. She wraps her arms and legs around me, continuing to kiss me as I walk us to the bedroom at the back of the cabin. Blindly reaching for the handle, I grasp it, shuffling us inside before slamming the door shut with my wife's back against it. Releasing my hold on her, I let her slowly slide down my chest and over my painfully hard erection. When her feet land gently on the floor, she places her palms flat against my chest, steadying herself.

Her chest rises and falls with anticipation.

Those gorgeous eyes have grown wide, even her pupils have dilated with lust. Loose curls cascade around her, framing her heart-shaped face. The tip of her tongue darts out to lick her swollen lips as her eyebrows scrunch together.

No... no... I know that look.

Don't overthink this, Madison.

It's not just the physical act of sex that I *need*. That I *crave*. I am an extremely sexual creature—*that won't ever change*. Sex has always been just that—*sex*. A way to tame my needs. But I have done that countless times with faceless others.

What I crave right now is *Madison*. There has been a void inside of me that only *she* can fill. She was the only one I have been with who sees me for me. Not *El Rompe Huesos*. Not the son of the ruthless Basilio or the heartless fuckboy.

Me. *Diego De La Cruz.*

The man who isn't this monster everyone makes him out to be.

Well, not to the innocent, that is.

My fingers itch with the desire to feel her skin against mine, to hear her breathy little moans as I kiss every precious inch of her body. I want to feel her heart gallop wildly as I slide into her and spend the rest of this flight worshiping her.

Stepping a few inches back, I reach between my shoulder blades and pull my t-shirt over my head, tossing it to the floor. She doesn't skip a beat before she's back in my space, skating her fingers over the tattoo I got last year.

The pad of her index finger traces over my chest and the black ink etched into my skin. My artist created the visual of exposed bones, showcasing my ribcage and sternum. The artwork portrays where my heart would be.

Except, there, underneath the cage of ribs, sits a blue and black butterfly.

I grab her hand and hold it over my heart. "The only cage you belong in, *Mariposita*, is the one right here beneath my ribs. You are the other half of my soul and the organ that's been missing all my life. A beacon of light breaking through my darkness. The gentle and delicate beauty that compliments my twisted nature. You, sweet girl, have given me the freedom I never knew I would have. No longer am I a prisoner to my line of work, to my father or my uncle, or their followers. You broke the chains of my dark reputation and encouraged understanding and compassion to the people under my syndicate's protection."

Two lone tears roll down the apples of her pink cheeks. I swipe them away with my thumbs and cup her face, tilting it to greet her glossy eyes.

"I love you, Madison De La Cruz. I was wrong for not telling you about my fake death. I did it for you. For us. But I was an idiot. You can handle anything, and although I knew that, I still tried to shield you from any repercussions of my past. Of who I am. That is a regret I'll have for the rest of my life. Because it took you from me and ended up pushing you right back into Liam's arms."

"Diego...I made my choice..." I stop her, gently placing a finger to her lush lips.

"Regardless of whether you actively chose to stay away from us—we both knew eventually you would come back. Your best friend is marrying his best friend. You were coming back into this life one way or another. Just a lot sooner than you may have anticipated. Which is why I am begging you to give me another chance. Before you hop back on the Liam train. Give me a chance to be your husband. If at the end of the day you choose him, I'll get our marriage certificate erased from existence too. That tattoo can be a reminder of your resilience and strength," I sigh, tapping the space behind her ear twice. "A reminder that you are and always will be a queen."

CHAPTER 4

MADISON

HIS WORDS, *that breathtaking tattoo*, the sincerity in his eyes. Even the way he kissed me...As if the world was ending and there was no tomorrow.

It has me questioning *everything*.

Every word I ever told myself about why I left. All the reasons I couldn't possibly forgive him. And not only leaving him but completely cutting Liam and Killian off as well. I didn't like who I was becoming, but look at me now. Afraid of a damn scorpion when I have faced death in the face one too many times. There is no question that I was stronger around them. Even with all the looming threats.

Simplicity and naivety is what I longed for. But other than working my shift at the local coffee shop, taking my frustrations out at the gym, or enjoying a night out with my favorite neighbors, it felt all so lonely and mundane.

And that felt more like a cage than ever being around Diego or the Kennedys.

It started to become clear that what I was craving might have been a bit more wild and a little less traditional.

I didn't want a lazy river.

I wanted the whole damn ocean, chaotic and unpredictable.

Thanks to Lexi, I was able to figure my shit out while living with her—well, *sort of.* God totally granted me an extra sister when we became friends. *That's for damn sure.*

Last year, the night of the New Year's Eve gala, she didn't even bat an eye when I told her I needed an escape plan. She simply handed me her keys and told me to stay for as long as I wanted.

It was fucking amazing the first few months. We got to spend time catching up and having girl nights. We went out drinking with Simon and John, coming home drunk off our asses and eating all our favorite snack combinations while watching trash reality TV. Our Thursdays always consisted of homemade pizza, wine, and *The Vampire Diaries.*

Carefree, genuine, fun.

Over time, those nights became less and less frequent. Her studies and clinicals for PA school started getting more intense, which occupied a lot of her time. If she had a spare minute, she was either at the gym or seeing Conor. Which I totally understood. He's an amazing guy and truly makes her happy, always trying his best to make his way out to her every few weeks. Usually staying for the weekend.

Lexi and Conor swore they would keep my whereabouts and activity to themselves, not sharing it with Liam or Killian. I was the one who couldn't keep Con in that position. He is viciously loyal to the Kennedy brothers, especially Liam. It wouldn't be fair for him to lie for me.

About a month or so later, on a drunken emotional night of sitting around the coffee table drinking tequila, I told him it would be alright if he let Liam know where I was.

He obviously did.

Yet, I must give props to Liam—he respected my wishes and never once reached out. Never sent me anything. Maybe it's due to the fact he gets tidbits of information from Conor.

Lexi's man may claim he isn't my bodyguard any longer, but

there is a silent understanding between us. He most definitely relays my day to day back to Liam—at least while he's here. As much as that's frustrating, at the very least it's comforting, knowing Con would never let any harm come my way while he's around.

Conor, trying to gain back a level of trust and respect, recently let me in on a little information. Information I would have been better off not hearing at all.

Christmas Day to be specific.

I had stayed in Arizona, not ready to see my family and have to finally discuss my ridiculous life.

As far as they knew, Killian and I spent some time in Greece before traveling more of Europe. We both realized we weren't as compatible as we had once thought and ended things on New Year's Eve. Lexi offered me a place to live and I decided a fresh start was in order.

Mom is under the impression I accepted a nursing job there —little does she know I am a barista at the local coffee shop.

I actually prefer it that way.

It brings me so much joy being able to socialize with my customers and get to know them. Plus, the unlimited free coffee —that's always a perk. *Yes, that was a stupid coffee pun.*

After a few months, I befriended a few of the regulars, becoming an active participant in their juicy gossip. I tried my hand at baking, which is a work in progress. My thirst for knowledge even led me to researching the different regions coffee is grown, including the different types of rich soil it requires to prosper.

The new experience continued to inspire me, encouraging me to venture out and take a few baking classes. Which was actually ridiculously fun. *Especially when you get to eat your treats after.*

My mind has started to conjure up ways to open up my own shop one day. It's what has kept my mind off of Diego and Liam.

Well, the majority of the day. Night comes rolling around and it's a whole different story. Majority of the time they are sleepless and contain a few good cry sessions.

Anyways...we were all celebrating at Simon and John's, baking Christmas cookies and drinking Prosecco. Which was followed up with some really good whiskey Conor had brought. Killian granted him a few days to spend with Lexi for the holidays. Being the ever doting boyfriend, he even joined us in wearing an ugly sweater—it was absolutely hysterical.

So as we were rolling out the dough, and drinking our whiskey on the rocks, he tells us the story of the time Lainey and Liam got into a flour fight while baking Christmas cookies. Apparently, flour was all over the kitchen and each other. Both of them spent the remainder of the night cleaning it up. That part I handled...well...*ish*...even though jealousy worked its ugly serum into my veins.

He proceeds to spill the beans that Kieran had just sent him a picture of them reenacting that *said* flour fight. Of course, being the divas and shit stirrers they are, Simon and John beg to see the picture. Conor is halfway through the bottle of whiskey at this point, so he willingly shows everyone his phone. I told myself not to look.

But you should know me by now, right? Of course I did.

*Liam has his arms wrapped around Lainey—who kept her dark locks of hair—*in case you were wondering. *Flour is coated all over their faces and lashes. Liam is sporting the biggest smile. Lainey is organically laughing with her hand cradling Liam's face and a palm full of flour in the other. Killian, Selena, and the rest of the guys are in the background with looks of laughter and tears in their eyes.*

I ended up smiling and laughing at the picture along with everyone else in the room. Lexi shot me a sympathetic look before I excused myself to the restroom. And that pretty much summed up my Christmas. All I could think of before bed was if

Liam was happy. And if he was, then I wanted him to be. He didn't deserve for me to have ended things the way I did.

I was so ready to give us another shot... that is... before Diego rose from the dead. And then I just threw his heart on the ground at the airport drop off. Even after all he did for me and how patient he was during my period of grief.

Grief over another man.

Another man that's my husband.

My husband that wasn't in fact dead.

He deserves better. So much better.

Relishing that last sip of my second coffee, I glance out the window. The New York lights are twinkling up at me from below.

We must be close.

Earlier, after being tongue-tied, I left Diego standing in the bedroom with the excuse that I needed to call my mom. *Which, I did.*

But it was his closeness, his pouring his heart and soul out to me that had me running. He remained back there for the majority of the flight, watching TV. I couldn't bring myself to join him. Too nervous to lie next to him on that bed.

Maybe he fell asleep? Just as I consider checking on him, the bathroom door clicks shut and the shower turns on alerting me he's up.

I guess he's getting ready for the gala tonight. *I wonder if he had a date prior to my untimely arrival? Maybe she's waiting for him now.*

THE FLIGHT LANDS around 7:00 PM. It feels like so much time has passed–considering the three-hour time difference. Mom let me know that Dad had just gone in for surgery. They moved him up from his original scheduled time at 8:30 PM.

27

Diego managed to take his seat only a few minutes before we landed looking refreshed and smelling divine. He hasn't said anything to me since our little show-and-tell moment in the bedroom.

With haste, I grab my bag from Amy and sling it over my shoulder, quickly thanking her and descending the stairs. Diego reaches out and snags the strap, pulling me backward into his chest.

"Give me this. And stop rushing. I don't need you falling down these stairs and breaking your goddamn neck," he practically growls, before slinging my bag over his shoulder and lacing our hands together.

I chance a look at him, but can't decide what's going on in that brain of his. Black sunglasses shield his beautiful eyes from me. Seems he's still keeping a low profile—*at least for now.*

He steps in front of me, guiding us down the remaining stairs. When we reach the bottom, a blacked-out Escalade pulls up. The door opens and my heart drops into my stomach. Liam, in all his masculine glory, jumps out of the passenger seat and jogs over to us.

He has on his signature leather jacket, black jeans, and a black v-neck. His beard is just as scruffy as it was in the Christmas cookie picture. The dark strands of his hair are all messy and disheveled...most likely from running his hands through it one too many times. He's even filled out more— looking broader and more defined, if possible.

I wonder if Liam and Diego have been hitting the gym together? Wouldn't that be a sight to see.

Diego releases my hand and steps forward to clasp Liam's, pulling him into a back-slapping hug. If my mouth wasn't already hanging open, it is now. *What the actual fuck is this bromance?* Liam returns the sentiment, slapping his back in exchange, except his eyes are glued to mine.

Butterflies assault my stomach, the intensity of their swarm making me dizzy. It's probably just my ears popping and my body regaining a sense of equilibrium. *Riiight, Maddy. That's exactly it.*

"I told you my jet is superior," Diego taunts sarcastically.

My eyes roll at their banter. *Or I think they did.* It's hard to tell if I am still in shock or not. Liam pulls back from Diego, shooting him a playful sneer. He takes a step my way, but before he can get anywhere near me, *The Bone Breaker* shoves my overnight bag into Liam's chest.

"Be a good lad and take my wife's luggage. We are in a hurry," he demands in the worst attempt at an Irish accent I have ever heard.

Liam flinches but recovers so quickly, I almost miss it. "Fuck you. Next time you get shot twice and are bleeding out on a yacht that is about to blow up, I won't be there to help."

"I don't plan on having history repeat itself, asshole," Diego says cryptically.

Liam slings my bag over his shoulder, turns on his boot, and walks us to the car. Diego places a hand on my lower back but I increase my pace, forcing him to drop it. As Liam is placing my bag in the trunk, Diego opens the back door, gesturing for me to get inside. Even going as far as to bow. *Fucker.* He only did that because I denied him the ability to keep touching me.

Heat builds inside me, replacing my haze of confusion with anger. I spin around as he cages me in, one arm resting above me and the other against the door of the SUV.

"You know, I didn't come here for this. I'm here to see my dad, not here to play games," I whisper-shout.

He hesitates a second before picking me up like a child and placing me in the middle seat of the Cadillac. Leaning over, he grabs the buckle, gliding his hands over my thighs and buckling me in.

"Let's get you to him then, *Mariposita*."

His muscular frame slides in next to me, slamming the door

shut. Liam hops in the passenger seat as Kieran turns around in the driver seat.

"Hey there, love. Long time no see." He chuckles before turning his attention to the road.

"Hey ya big bastard. I see you haven't changed a bit." I laugh, despite my irritation with the two other men in this car.

Liam still hasn't acknowledged me.

Music replaces the awkward silence as we make our way towards the hospital.

AS WE APPROACH the front entrance, my phone vibrates with a text message from my sister Mikayla.

MIK

Are you almost here? I'm outside smoking a cigarette. I'll wait for you to go up.

Fuck. I don't need her seeing Liam or Diego–it's not like she knows who Diego is... but I don't need him running his mouth about us being married—or any other detail he may be inclined to share. Kieran pulls up to the entrance and I spot my sister right outside. *Thank God for tinted windows.*

"Nobody get out of the car," I announce frantically. "I don't need my sister asking questions."

Liam chuckles before speaking. "She is quite the investigator. She'll without a doubt know something is up if *I* get out of the car. I planned on coming in with you, is that not alright?"

My hands grow clammy. I slide them over my leggings to absorb the moisture.

"No, that's okay. I appreciate that, really, but I think it'll be best if I go spend some *alone time* with my family." It's hard to ignore the shakiness in my voice. *Damn these men.*

30

Diego stirs next to me, seemingly annoyed at my request. "I'm your *husband*. I can be there with you."

I turn to look at him while unbuckling my seatbelt. "Please, can we drop the husband act for now? I need to get to my dad, and I need to digest the fact that not only am I back in New York, but I am back here with all of you."

This time both Diego and Liam flinch as if I slapped them. Diego purses his lips like he wants to say something, but stops himself. I slide over the bench and pull the door handle but it doesn't open. Trying again, I get the same response.

"Oh shite, we had little Kian in the car the other day and put the child lock on. I can get out and get ya," Kieran offers.

"No!" I shout, knowing my sister has a keen eye and will remember him from the club and my graduation dinner. "Just pop the trunk, I'll grab my bag."

I scramble back down the bench and awkwardly straddle-climb over Diego. Our noses practically touch at how close we are. The sunglasses he was wearing now rest on top of his head. Those sapphire eyes of his flash with a fresh round of lust before dulling out. Sturdy hands come up around my waist, giving me a gentle squeeze before he opens the door.

"Your father will pull through, *Mariposita*."

My emotions climb higher as I clamber out of the SUV.

This is all too much.

Just before closing the door, Diego adds in his final two cents. "Tell the surgeon I said hi." He shoots me an antagonizing wink. The desire to smack that look off his face has my hands trembling.

Opting for a less violent approach, I slam the door in his face and flip him off for good measure. Liam rolls his window down, biting back a cackle. Luckily, the car and fully tinted windows shield my sister's view of us.

"Hey, do ya have a place to stay after? I'm sure your family got a hotel room. But if they don't, call me, I'll come grab ya. You can stay with us if you want... no pressure or anything. I know you weren't planning on coming back." He smiles sweetly at me but his eyes hold a touch of sadness.

Maybe even regret.

"Thank you. I'm sure that won't be necessary... I've got to go. Thanks again!" I wave before walking to the open trunk to collect my bag.

Mikayla spots me and starts walking my way. I scramble to shut the trunk and meet her halfway, pulling her into a tight hug.

"I've missed you," she sighs, rocking me back and forth.

"I've missed you, Mik. Jeez, it's been too long."

CHAPTER 5

LIAM

DIEGO SAID to be at the private airfield at 7:00 PM. I stare at the dashboard clock: 6:30 PM. I couldn't risk being late. Madison needs to get to her father. That's the only reason she's here. Although, part of me is curious if she would have come back tonight had this not happened. For the engagement celebration that is...

Conor and Lexi arrived at the 5th Ave penthouse an hour before I left. I didn't have long to catch up with him. Between the designers and staff prepping for the gala and traffic all over New York City tonight, I didn't have time to chat. Which leaves me wondering where Madison will be staying tonight.

Shit. What a fucking turn of events.

I realized when Conor asked me to be his Best Man this morning that meant Madison would be Lexi's Maid of Honor. Hope fluttered in my chest at the idea of seeing her again. But then I remembered my promise to her and the situation I put myself in.

Lainey and I remained friendly as we always have right after Madison left. That all changed these last couple of months leading up to Christmas...when she and I got drunk together.

It was after the Halloween party Selena hosted at the

33

penthouse. Lainey had been cooking all day and I had been mingling with some of our friends and a few suppliers Killian had invited. By the end of the night, I was in bits. Lainey approached me with a bottle of tequila and a mischievous smile.

Entertaining the idea of swimming drunk with her could lead to crossing the line, but I did it anyway. I hadn't slept with anyone the entire time leading up to this night with hopes I'd have heard from Madison. After not even a whisper, I knew it was time to get back into the dating world.

But saying and doing are two very different things.

Lainey always showed interest, increasingly so since Madison left. It was refreshing and something I had seriously started to consider.

But I never caved.

Stupidly, I held on to that sliver of hope that Madison would reach out.

From what Conor had told me, it seemed she was doing okay out west. Of course, I knew where she was. I knew the day Conor went to visit Lexi for the first time after Madison left. Yet, I refused to check up on her. She asked me not to. Which meant I had to respect it. Conor did share information here and there, but I never questioned him further. I took what he was willing to offer, knowing his friendship with Maddy was just as important.

So... back to Halloween...

After a few too many tequila shots turned into body shots, we both jumped into the pool on the upper level. Steam swirled around us on that crisp autumn night. Lainey was feeling bold and frisky and removed her bikini top, flinging it in my face.

So. Fucking. Cheeky. *"You're fucking plastered," I laugh, tossing her top onto the pavers and spreading my arms along the edge of the pool to hold myself afloat.*

She swims around me for a while, tits out on display to the starry sky above before diving under the water and breaching the surface right in front of me. Her hands grip my forearms, using them as leverage to pull herself flush against me and my growing erection.

"I want you, Liam. Not want you for just a heated, drunken moment... but want you want you. I always have since we were young. I was just too afraid to tell you. You were always so closed off to everyone around you. So... soo...grumpy," she whispers as her lips brush against mine.

My arm slinks around her, craving physical touch more than anything in this moment. Her lips part invitingly as my tongue darts out to taste her. Her breasts press firmly against my chest, rubbing against my nipple rings. Lainey wraps her legs around mine, gyrating her hips over my now very hard and throbbing cock. Meanwhile, my other fucking head keeps shouting at me to get out of this fucking pool. The memories of having Madison in here are starting to tarnish this moment.

If I am to commit to this idea of me and Lainey, I need to take her out of this pool.

So, I do.

I break our kiss and swim us over to the shallow end. Do you know how fucking hard it is to swim with a hard on and a lass around your waist?

Not fun.

I help her out, slapping her ass and tossing her over my shoulder before dropping her back down onto the sun bed lounger. She giggles excitedly as she arches her back, stretching out on the cushion. Her nipples have hardened to peaks from a combination of lust and the cool air. They are beautiful and pink against her ivory skin. Those gorgeous breasts of hers are perky and round and looking fucking edible all wet like that. I drop my swim trunks and step out of them before removing her turquoise bikini bottom. She bites her lip while watching me in all my naked glory.

It's wild that the woman before me has been in my life since I was a lad, and here she is, all grown up and spread out naked before me. I lower a knee to the cushion between her legs and press

35

my palms on either side of her. My tongue darts out to lick the salty water off her neck, trailing lower to circle around each goosebumped breast, then even lower to circle her belly button. I place kisses on her stomach and then back up to the space between her breasts until I latch onto her neck.

She lets out a breathy moan of approval, wrapping her legs around my hips and inching her warm pussy closer to my cock. My lips find hers as I enter her slowly. She adjusts to my size, remaining still before lifting her hips and encouraging me on.

"Show me you're with me," Lainey purrs.

I kiss her again, letting that hesitant part of me fade away—at least for tonight.

My hand finds her hip and the other grips the hair at the nape of her neck as I pick up my pace, thrusting into her. The sounds of our wet bodies slapping against each other fill the patio space. Her nails scrape my back as I deepen my angle and find that sweet spot inside of her.

"Fuck, Liam....fuck, fuuuck," she moans her satisfaction.

I'm grunting like an animal, ready to explode and holding off as long as I can for her. It's been too damn long.

"I'm close... so close," she mewls.

"Touch yourself, come all over my cock, lovely."

Her hand slides between us as she circles her clit and her cries of pleasure become staccato. I savagely slam into her two more times before her pussy grips me, making me see stars. Luckily, I still have half a mind after all that tequila to pull out. A second later, I'm gripping my cock and showering my cum all over her stomach.

Since that day we have spent plenty of time getting to know each other—*more intimately.* Growing up together meant we already knew plenty about each other. Still, there are nights we have laid in bed talking about the things we never knew or would still like to know. She rarely asks about Madison, usually avoiding the topic altogether. But I know how women are, always so curious about the exes... which leads me to believe she hasn't asked out of fear of the new information we all received this morning.

Con is engaged to Madison's best friend.

So what does that mean for our future? Because, *fuck*... if I am being honest, I was just starting to fall a little harder for Lainey...

Even if my heart refuses to let go of Madison completely.

Kieran breaks me out of my reverie, indicating with his index finger that Diego's flashy jet just landed. "They are taxiing in now. Ya gonna be alright, brother?"

I clear my throat. "Yeah, Kier. I'll have to get used to seeing her. She's Lexi's Maid of Honor. *Matron of Honor* if we are getting fucking technical." That detail tastes sour in my mouth as the words pass my lips. *Madison married Diego.* Legally, although all fuck sorts of complicated, she is still his wife.

This past year, Diego has stayed with us more in New York than he has at his home in Miami. *I guess when you're 'dead', you can do business for the underworld from anywhere.* He's been spending time with his sister and our nephew Kian—who is freaking adorable, by the way. Tomorrow is his first birthday and Sel has been going crazy planning his celebration. The party planners have blocked hotel rooms a few doors down so that they can be ready to retransform the space in the morning.

I can't say *The Bone Breaker* and I have much beef between us any longer. After saving his arse on that yacht, we sort of... bonded in a way. With Madison gone, and neither of us really belonging to her, we've grown closer.

What started out as constant jabs at one another turned into a sort of brotherhood. He and I go out for drinks from time to time at the shitty bars the Feds have no place snooping around. We'll even workout together if my schedule allows for it and I'm not staying at my home in Connecticut. I guess being around him has softened me up.

Misery seeks company, if you will.

He's a damn good uncle, too. Kian loves spending time with him. Even Killian has warmed up to his brother-in-law. The two have found ways to form a tighter alliance between the syndicates than ever before. Our gun and drug trade has even benefited quite a bit.

"Are ya gonna tell her?" Kieran asks cautiously.

I know what he means. "No. Not now. She needs to focus on her father. Knowing won't change a damn thing anyway. If anything, it may make her want to stay away even more. I can't do that to Con. Lexi needs her best friend at the wedding."

"Alright, mate." He claps my back and puts the Cadillac into drive, slowly approaching the jet just as the passenger door opens up.

The airstairs descend and my gaze darts straight to her as she comes into view at the top. Nervous hands find my scalp as I tug my hair at the base of my skull. *Fuck.* She looks good. *Tan as fuck too.* That Arizona sun is treating her nicely I see. She's wearing a cute pink sweatshirt, black workout leggings with mesh cutouts, and a pair of black sneakers. Her Vera Bradley overnight bag is slung over her shoulder.

If that is all she brought, she must not be planning to stay long.

Being the arsehole I know him to be, Diego pulls the strap of her bag, tugging her backward into him. She scrunches her face in disapproval as he pries the bag off her shoulder and swings it over his. Grabbing her hand, he shuffles around her and heads down the steps first, guiding her down like a child. I let out a chuckle, knowing I'd have done the same damn thing.

She can be clumsy at times. It's safer that way.

I open my door and step out, jogging my way over to them. The cold air nips at my skin, causing my eyes to water. Diego greets me, pulling me into a handshake and then slapping my back. As my palm claps the arsehole's back twice, my eyes raise to meet Madison's.

Damn.

You couldn't tell before, but her hair isn't black. It's the deepest shade of purple—like the iridescence of raven feathers.

Stunning. Any color is gorgeous on her, but this one may just be my favorite.

"I told you my jet is superior," Diego goads sarcastically, making me cluck my tongue.

He is right—but his ego is inflated enough. *No need to add more to the collection.*

I take a step forward, about to tell her that I am sorry to hear about her dad, when Diego shoves her overnight bag into my chest.

"Be a good lad and take my wife's luggage. We are in a hurry," he says in his best Irish accent. The prick should be fluent in it with the amount of time he spends around us.

My heart skips a beat at the mention of 'wife' but I shake it off, taking my frustrations out on *The Bone Breaker.* He can certainly take a few jabs.

"Fuck you. Next time you get shot twice and are bleeding out on a yacht that is about to blow up, I won't be there to help."

"I don't plan on having history repeat itself, asshole," Diego says derisively.

Over this bullshit game already, I turn my back on them and head off to the Cadillac.

I am placing her bag in the back of the trunk when I hear aggravated whispering coming from the back right passenger door. Straining my neck to get a look over the back of the seat, I see Diego has Maddy caged in.

Seems they haven't gotten off to a great start either. Looks like the two of them are bickering or perhaps having a lovers quarrel.

Who the fuck knows right now?

Diego never clued me in on whether or not he had heard from her all these months. I mean, I suppose I never did either. Not to mention, he's seen Lainey and me together, which might have ended that mystery for him. *I wonder if he told her?* She

39

didn't seem to direct her anger at me... more so, she seemed shocked to see me.

Diego picks Madison up and places her stubborn arse in the middle seat, leaning over to buckle her in like a toddler. I stifle a laugh, knowing it'll only make matters worse. Whatever the hell is going on—should stay between them.

I make my way to the front passenger seat and strap in. Diego has slid in next to her, legs spread open wide, taking up as much of her space as possible. Out of my peripheral, I spot Kieran looking like a puppy waiting to see its owner again after a long holiday. You can practically see his damn tail wagging, tongue flopping out of his goofy mouth.

"Hey there, love. Long time no see." He releases a hearty chuckle before turning his attention back to navigating us out of the airfield.

"Hey ya big bastard. I see you haven't changed a bit." Her sweet voice fills the small space, breathing life back into all of us. It embraces me like a familiar hug and shimmies its way through the cracks in the wards I have up around my heart.

Damn, the power this woman has over us all... *and without even trying.*

Silence settles in around us, prompting Kieran to turn some music on. The rest of the ride is awkward at best.

It surprisingly doesn't take us very long to get to the hospital —considering it's New Year's Eve and everyone is trying to get to their events.

Madison's phone vibrates against her clasped thighs and she releases a heavy sigh. We just pulled into the main entrance... and there, smoking a cigarette in the designated smoking section, is her sister Mikayla.

Seeing her smoke has me itching for one now. Lainey has me weaning off them...but today is not a day I can refrain. Certainly not with Madison's sultry jasmine and amber scent flirting with my senses. *I'm on fucking edge, okay?*

"Nobody get out of the car," she demands. "I don't need my sister asking questions."

I let out an approving laugh. *Been there. Done that.* Mikayla doesn't fuck around. As if Madison's graduation dinner didn't prove that enough...The lass caught onto me and Maddy almost immediately. Chewing my ear off until I confessed that her sister and I had a secret relationship.

Christ. Awful memories of that night and regret for not being with Madison when she was taken try to force their way to the forefront of my mind. None of this would have happened had I just been with her and Selena outside. Definitely not with her sister doing those disgusting green tea shots. Old anger towards Diego threatens to resurface, but I take a few calming breaths and put them back where they had been buried.

Can't change the past now.

I finally find my voice. "She is quite the investigator. She'll without a doubt know something is up if *I* get out of the car. I planned on coming in with you, is that not alright?"

"No, that's okay. I appreciate that, really, but I think it'll be best if I go spend some *alone time* with my family." *Ouch.* I guess that means coming back here is strictly for her father. Even Diego seems pissed. Perhaps some of that anger is directed at me for offering to go with her.

"I'm your *husband.* I can be there with you," he grits through clenched teeth, clearly bothered by her lack of needing our support.

"Please, can we drop the husband act for now? I need to get to my dad, and I need to digest the fact that not only am I back in New York, but I am back here with all of you," Madison huffs out while unbuckling her seat belt.

She's anxious. It's written all over her face. We are only prolonging her from seeing her family.

Diego purses his lips, looking ready to demand he go in with her. When he notices her frantic face, he eases off, keeping whatever he meant to say to himself. *Good.* We respected her wishes this time last year and we need to do the same now.

Nothing has changed.

Maddy slides across the leather seats. She tries to open the door, then tries again, looking to the front of the SUV when she is unsuccessful a second time.

"Oh shite, we had little Kian in the car the other day and put the child lock on. I can get out and get ya," Kieran offers, reaching for his own door handle.

"No!" she all but shouts. It occurs to me that her sister will notice Kieran and put two and two together. The lass is a clever one. "Just pop the trunk, I'll grab my bag."

Without wasting another second, she glides back down the opposite side of the bench and awkwardly straddles Diego, attempting to climb over him and exit through the other door. Her head is bent towards his so that their noses practically touch. He takes full advantage of her position, gripping her hips before opening the door for her.

"Your father will pull through, *Mariposita*," he soothes as she climbs out. She's about to close the door when he adds, "Tell the surgeon I said hi," while shooting her a wink.

As sassy as ever, she slams the door in his face, flipping him the bird through the tinted windows. Diego chuckles deeply, clearly amused– and knowing him—probably aroused.

I roll my window down, needing to make sure Maddy will be alright tonight.

"Hey, do ya have a place to stay after? I'm sure your family got a hotel room. But if they don't, call me, I'll come grab ya. You can stay with us if you want... no pressure or anything. I know you weren't planning on coming back." The somber tone of my voice probably gave me away.

It's not like I actually expected she would come home and suddenly end up staying with us. I just thought... *Fuck.* I don't know. Perhaps she would want to reconnect with everyone—even just platonically—while she's here.

"Thank you. I'm sure that won't be necessary... I've got to go. Thanks again!" She waves at me before collecting her bag from the trunk.

Her sister meets her halfway, embracing her in a loving hug. The two of them sway back and forth, relishing in the emotions of their reunion. Apparently, Madison hasn't been home at all since she left.

Not even to see her family.

Not even for Christmas.

Which is strange.

The love she has for her family runs deep. Staying away from them couldn't possibly have been because of us...

Could it?

CHAPTER 6

MADISON

"MADISON, SWEETHEART." Mom pulls me into a hug while Mel comes up from behind, wrapping herself around us. My arm curls around my younger sister. I've missed her so much. I miss our coffee dates and rides in the car. Even the damn teenage gossip. God, she looks so much more mature. Where has the time gone?

What was I thinking not coming home for over a year? Family means *everything* to me. I let myself isolate and wallow across the country over two men. Three if we want to get technical–but Killian and I no longer share anything romantic. Selena has been and always will be his true love. That doesn't mean I didn't need the distance from him as well. He and I were fine until the night Diego took me. He hasn't been the same since.

Certainly not the man I once fell for.

"Come sit down. How was your flight?" Mom pats the seat between her and Mel.

I take a seat, placing my bag on the small coffee table in front of us. Mikayla claims her own, crossing her arms over her chest. Like a hawk, her eyes have narrowed and zeroed in on me, waiting for my response.

Fuck. She knows something. However, that look on her face

tells me she'll keep my secret. I bet she is just dying to get as much evidence as possible before she approaches me on it.

"It was fine. Screaming babies, lots of flatulence, and a bit of turbulence. Typical flight."

Mikayla holds back a snicker and shakes her head, redirecting her attention to her phone.

Looks like we are in the clear for now.

"Madison, that is so unladylike," Mom scolds.

I shrug innocently. "Just stating the facts."

Mik's blue eyes find mine. "*Facts.* What airline did you take?"

"Our favorite. *Obviously.* Who doesn't love extra legroom?" I laugh as casually as possible.

"Lucky you to have found a last-minute seat. *Especially* on New Year's Eve," Mikayla adds dramatically.

"*Very* lucky. Speaking of luck," I swiftly change the subject, "how's Dad?" I ask my mother.

"The surgeon said he would let us know the progress about halfway through."

MAD, WANNA GRAB COFFEE FOR EVERYONE?" Mik whispers.

I stand, too eager for a coffee and a break from all the catching up with my mom and Mel.

"Yes. The usual?" I ask, glancing between the two of them.

Mom nods her head as Mel places her headphones in, drowning us out with her music. Mik links her arm through mine as we head for the elevator. She presses the button and tugs me closer.

"Mom may believe that you flew commercial, but we both know you flew on some fancy private jet. How's Liam? Surprised he's not here. Bet that behemoth is pacing out front, chain smoking." She laughs at herself and I can't help but laugh as well. That is spot on for Liam. If we were still together and... Lainey wasn't in the picture... he probably would be doing just that.

On a sigh, we step into the elevator. With the lack of conversation, the eerie hum of the gears fills the space between us.

"A lot has changed, Mik. I'll get into it. But right now, Dad is my main focus."

She pats my arm. "I know. I'm your sister. Sun and Moon remember? We may be miles apart, but I will always know when something is off with you. Moving to Arizona isn't like you. Even having your best friend there, nothing could have kept you from your family or your man. You're too much of a romance junkie for that. So, what did *he* do?"

A ding signals our arrival at the main floor. As the doors open, we step out into the brightly lit main lobby. Mik leads us to the cafeteria, still keeping our arms securely linked.

"It's *so* complicated. Even saying it out loud won't do it any justice. So I'll give you the Cliff Notes—you're good at that." I elbow her playfully in the ribs.

She releases me, rolling her eyes. "Cliff Notes are the reason I still got A's on all my exams while maintaining a healthy social life, thank you very much! Please, continue. I'll catch on."

I place two cups beneath the coffee machine before hitting the button to dispense questionable coffee into mine and Mel's. Mik makes her own and Mom's.

"The night of my graduation dinner," I look around, making sure to keep my voice low. "I was taken...by someone close to Liam and Killian. Someone in the same line of business as them."

Mik swivels her head, eyes wide. "I knew something was up. *Taken*? What the hell Mad? That's why Liam left our little green tea bonding moment abruptly? He ran outside looking savage as fuck and completely stressed—he never came back. Killian had

47

told everyone you weren't feeling well and that Liam had taken you home."

"Liam and Killian are involved in... Let's just say that the club we went to—*The Triskelion*—it's all part of the life they live."

"*The life.* As in... the mob?" She lowers her voice, peering at me sideways as she pours cream and sugar into each of her cups.

"Yes. Killian is the leader of the entire syndicate for New York, Connecticut, and Jersey.

"Well. *Fuck.* And goody two shoes Madison thought dating the head of it and then his *brother* was... smart?"

"Yeah. I guess I did. I've never felt more alive in my life. But after some...complications...I needed a break from it all. I thought leaving that world behind would make me go back to being a goody two shoes but it didn't. It made me crave the risk, the unknown, and the kind of love I've always dreamed of even more. I became a stronger woman through all of this."

Mikayla puts lids on all the coffees and places them in a cardboard carrier. We check out, making our way back to the elevator. I'm surprised she's remained so calm about what I just told her.

"So back to this *taken* thing. Were you actually with Killian in Mykonos? Or were you a hostage?" she questions, her voice trembling.

"It started out as a prisoner situation. But the man who took me never once hurt me. He helped me. And then in return, I helped him." I smile at the memories of Diego and me bickering over my desire to help him. I release a small chuckle thinking back to his cheerful Post-Its and motivational quotes.

"What the fuck are you smiling over? *Madison*...you can't be serious," she hisses appallingly. "Which floor is neuro on? We need to get your brain checked. *STAT.*"

"Liam and I reunited. It wasn't so cut and dry or as bad as it sounds." *I'm downplaying it for her sake.* "I was always safe with

Diego. But to answer your question—*no*. I wasn't in Mykonos with Killian. He was there eventually to handle business. I was with Diego, Selena's brother."

"Holy shit. You fell for your captor. Of course *Beauty and the Beast* was your favorite Disney movie. All makes sense now. Tell me the truth. You fell for him, didn't you?"

The doors open to the surgical waiting room. I shoot my sister a look to zip it. In silent understanding, she nods.

"Yes," I whisper in confirmation.

A woosh of air leaves Mik's lips. "And now you're with no one. All alone in Arizona. *Madison...*" she chastises.

"Yup," I pop the p, all the emotions gathering thickly in the back of my throat.

MY FATHER'S GIRLFRIEND, Diane, joins us a little while later. She is such a sweet woman. Dad certainly adores her. We do too. She fits in perfectly with our crazy family dynamic.

"I'm so sorry it took me so long to get here. I was in Florida visiting my sister when I got the call."

"No worries, Diane. We were all scattered around when we got the call too. He's doing okay. The last time the nurse came out, she said the surgery was going well and that it should only be a little while longer before they close him up."

"Thank God," she lets out a sigh of relief, sagging back into her chair with her hand over her heart.

Just as we all fell back into our respective texts, emails, and music, the surgeon comes out. He spots me first, walking over to our little group.

"Mrs. De La Cruz?" he asks incredulously. "I didn't realize I was performing your father's surgery. It's a surprise your husband didn't give me a ring."

My mouth must be hanging open like a fish because my sister steps forward before my mom gets the chance to overhear.

"She prefers to go by Madison." She shoots the surgeon the 'shut the fuck up' eyes in her kindest voice.

Thankfully, understanding crosses his features. "My apologies, Madison."

I nod gratefully as Mom, Diane, and Mel reach us.

"How is Vinny doing?" Diane asks with concerned eagerness.

"The surgery went well. He is extremely lucky. We expect that he will live a much healthier life moving forward. Of course, that comes with the responsibility of making sure he maintains a healthy diet, adding in low-strain exercise when fully recovered. He is in recovery now. I can let you see him briefly. Unfortunately, only one person may stay overnight. Hospital policy," he states. His conflicted eyes flick to mine.

I turn towards Diane. "Diane should stay. We will part ways after and reconvene in the morning."

"I agree," Mom and Mik say in unison.

CHAPTER 7

KILLIAN

"SIR, Madison just arrived. She just got out of an Uber and is on her way up," Colin whispers, pulling me aside.

The kaleidoscope of lights from the stage dance across his face. His eyes are lit with genuine excitement. All of us have missed her presence. I squeeze his shoulder before kissing my wife's head beside me.

"I'll be right back, love. I have to greet a guest of ours at the front entrance." She tilts her head in concern. My hand comes up to smooth away the elevens between her pinched eyebrows before sweeping down her cheek. "Nothing to worry about. See you in a bit."

Maneuvering my way through the drunk and lively crowd, I find my way to the door. Standing at the entrance is a beautifully tired Madison. As she spots me heading her way, a small smile creeps onto her face.

"Well, well, well. Look what we have here. You look good, Mad."

"Thank you, Killian." She looks around, admiring the entrance. "The place looks incredible as usual," she beams, a smile gracing her face. "I wanted to call, but I didn't want to chicken out. Grabbing an Uber and heading straight here was the only way I wouldn't. So... would it be okay if I crash here for the night? I didn't want to crowd my sisters and mom at the hotel."

"Of course. You are always welcome here, Madison. You know that. Here, let me take that for you." I grab her bag off her shoulder. "I'd say I'll take you to a guest room but..." *Fuck.* This is uncomfortable. I need to clear the air with her. It shouldn't be this way between us.

"Mad!" Lexi shouts from behind me, her heels clicking against the marble as she makes haste towards us.

Her arms wrap around her best friend, protectively pulling her into a warm embrace.

"I'm so glad you're here. Dad's okay?"

"He is. They expect him to make a full recovery. Thankfully, there were no complications."

"Thank goodness," she says relieved. "You want to get cleaned up? Maybe join us for a drink if you're up for it?"

Madison plays with the strings of her sweatshirt. "I don't know. I'm not really dressed for all this. I may just get to sleep. I need to be back at the hospital early."

"Whatever you need, just let me know," I offer. "We are pretty much at full capacity on extra bedrooms. Kian's first birthday is tomorrow, so we have a few people staying the night for the festivities."

"Shit. I should have called. I can just go," she says remorsefully.

Her hand reaches out for her overnight bag. I take a step back, denying her. *No.* She needs to stay. This will always be her home. We will make it work.

"She can sleep with me. Con can stay with the boys in the bunk room," Alexis offers.

Mad shakes her head. "Lex. It's your engagement celebration. You aren't forcing your fiancé to sleep in a bunk bed when he should be sleeping next to you. I'll just sleep on the couch. It's no big deal."

Liam approaches us from the kitchen. His demeanor changes instantly upon seeing her. *Immediate concern.* Madison has yet to realize him as he reaches us.

"What's wrong, beautiful? Everything okay?"

"Hey, Liam. Yeah. Yeah. Everything is fine. I didn't realize you had a full house tonight. I should have just stayed at the hotel," she rambles, brushing him off.

He reaches out, gently cupping her elbow. "I told you I'd pick you up. You should have called me. And no, you can stay in my room. I'll sleep on the couch or...find somewhere to sleep. Don't worry, love."

Like a goddamn sitcom, Lainey joins our little gathering. Her arm slinks around her man, forcing him to release Madison and wrap his arm around her. His tattooed hands find their place at her waist. She lays her head on his chest—*clearly tipsy*—not even realizing that Madison is present.

"Liam. Where have you been? Since the ball dropped you've been MIA." Her hand comes up to caress his face.

Madison steps forward, placing her delicate hand on my shoulder. Disheartened eyes look up at me.

"Is Diego staying here tonight?" Her voice wavers as she whispers, her eyes searching mine for the answer she desperately seeks refuge in.

"Yes." I spin her, shielding her from the whispered conversation Liam and Lainey are having. Lost in their own little world. Lainey still hasn't noticed Madison. Perhaps we should keep it that way—*for now.* Madison doesn't need the added drama on top of her already hectic night.

"Come, love. I'll take you there." I collect her soft hand in mine, guiding her up the stairs and away from the love birds. Alexis shoots her best friend a concerned look, but she returns it with a faux smile in typical *Madison* fashion. Always trying to reassure everyone she is okay—when she most definitely is not.

Not at all.

Reaching the second floor, I direct us to the bedroom next to the elevator. The same one that Selena occupied while she and I were working on our shit. *Quite ironic that it now belongs to her brother.*

Rapping my knuckles against the wood, I knock twice. When no one answers, I turn the knob and open it a crack, confirming the room's vacant. *Diego must be downstairs at the bar. Hopefully not with a woman. I'm not sure Maddy can take much more tonight.* I place her overnight bag on the chair at the base of the bed.

"I'm sure Diego won't mind if you help yourself to his shower. I can imagine you're exhausted—but perhaps you have it in you for one drink? Tea even? Lena would love to see you just as we all are. It's good to have you back... for as long as that may be." I linger at the threshold of the door like an awkward eejit.

"Thank you, Kil." Her eyes roam around his room, likely looking for clues as to what he's been up to in here. It's neat and tidy–not much to analyze.

My hand cups the back of my neck as the awkwardness increases tenfold. "Listen, Maddy. I owe you an apology. I wasn't myself after we broke up. I became a version of myself I never imagined I would become. Christ, I was no better than the ones we took out. Fatherhood has reminded me of my priorities and that power is not designed for everyone. Especially me. I let my emotions and need for revenge override my logical thinking. You, Diego, and Liam should never have been pawns in the fucked up decisions I made. I was too harsh on Liam. I let you go off with Diego when I should have fought harder for you to stay. I did awful things to Diego out of the desire to seek revenge. He's a good man. I see that now. I've made my peace with my brother and him. Perhaps I don't deserve your forgiveness, but I could use it. I've missed you, Madison. Life around here just isn't the same without your bright personality."

Her hair shines with a purple hue as she steps towards me in the dimly lit room. It's a beautiful shade. She sucks in a breath before placing my hand in hers.

"I forgive you. We were all forced to make some crazy choices. No one person was to blame for everything that happened. I think we've all had space and time to move beyond what transpired. Kil, I understand why you acted the way you did. It took me a while to realize it, and for some time I wasn't even able to be around you—for what you did to Liam. More *specifically* for what you did to Diego. But, I can see how our history and the way Diego went about it... could have created this need for revenge. Time has taught me that some things fade while others linger. The anger I held towards you no longer exists. I forgive you, Kil. I'm not sure if I'll be here long, but moving forward, you and I are good."

She pulls me into a hug and instantly I melt. Her touch is soothing. Like aloe on a sunburn. There is this immense feeling of relief having her here in my arms. This isn't anything remotely sexual. It's just how Madison makes you feel. Calmness curls around me like a weighted blanket, relieving all the anxiety built up over her this past year. Her forgiveness is everything I needed and more.

As she pulls away she murmurs, "I'm not sure I'll make it down. I'll see how I feel after my shower."

"Okay, love. Anything you need just press 2 on the phone." I gesture with my hand to the phone on the end table.

Her nose scrunches up. "Isn't that going to call the kitchen?" she asks warily.

I let out a chuckle, understanding what she means. "Yeah. Lainey is off tonight, she's spending the night...enjoying herself."

Madison purses her lips at my verbiage. I wouldn't say there is jealousy there, but she's definitely unnerved by this situation.

I don't blame her. *It has to be uncomfortable. Been there.*

I'll let Liam deal with this one.

God only knows what those two are. Not sure my brother ever really made it official with the lass. Meanwhile, she's absolutely smitten with him. Quite frankly, she always has been.

"Alright. Thanks again, Kil. I'm off to go shower." She juts her thumb out behind her in the direction of the en suite .

"See you soon, love."

"WHY DIDN'T you tell me Madison is here?" Selena whisper-shouts at me from her spot at the bar.

Everyone is doing a round of shots in honor of Con and Lexi. Lexi is steaming drunk and so is Con. The two of them are doing karaoke on stage singing "Marry You" by Bruno Mars.

"I didn't want to overwhelm her. I knew if I told you, you'd have made a beeline straight to her."

She links her fingers through mine and lays her head against my shoulder. On a sigh, she says, "Yeah, I would have." A laugh slips past her gorgeous lips. "Make sure those two don't go sneaking off to elope tonight." Her head turns towards the stage where Con and Lexi are spinning around while finishing the chorus.

"I'll make sure Liam keeps an eye on him."

"Mind if I join?" Madison's voice carries over the awful singing.

Unable to help herself, Lena wraps Madison up into a hug. Tears drip over my wife's cheeks as she tells her how much she has missed her.

Maddy rubs gentle circles over her back. "I missed you too, Sel. I'm sorry I've been such a bad friend. I should have reached out more. I could have Facetimed you and Kian or came to visit.

It's awful I only got to see him through the phone a handful of times."

"It's okay. You needed the time to figure out what you wanted. What you went through, Mad. A break from it all was needed. I don't blame you for anything. Our friendship is still here and just as special and solid as when we last left off."

Fresh tears roll over Madison's cheeks and drip down onto her simple black cocktail dress. She isn't wearing a mask, but she doesn't need one. Plenty of our guests refuse to wear theirs. Even Lena took a break, complaining it was too hot.

For someone who wasn't planning on coming here, Madison certainly made sure to have a dress on hand. I'm glad she did. We all needed this. Perhaps she'll come back tomorrow for Kian's birthday. Maybe Selena and Liam can even persuade her to move back.

She belongs here.

Her departure was directly caused by our actions or lack thereof. Madison should never have felt forced to run away from her home.

Her family. Friends.

"We have a lot to catch up on," Maddy affirms with a sniffle.

Selena clasps both of Maddy's hands in hers. "Will you consider coming back after seeing your father tomorrow? I would love to catch up then." She leans in close to whisper, "I'm sure my brother would, too."

Madison and my wife giggle together. Just like they used to. I'm thrilled they have reunited. Lena is glowing with happiness.

"I could use a drink," Maddy declares contentedly.

"Let's get you one," Selena beams, already dragging her best friend towards the front of the bar.

CHAPTER 8

LIAM

"YOU'RE BEING DISTANT, Liam. What's up, baby?" Lainey caresses my face as we sit at the bar watching the hilarious future Mr. and Mrs. Hayes. They are drunk off their arses, singing along terribly to Marry You by Bruno Mars.

I finish off my whiskey, buying myself some time to explain the events of today. It's inevitable that Lainey will discover Madison's return. I'm surprised she didn't recognize her earlier when Mad was standing there in the entrance.

My gaze darts over to Sel walking towards the bar and I nearly choke on my drink. Madison is with her and they are heading directly our way. She looks beautiful in her black dress. One of my favorites. The one that hugs her curves in all the right places.

Fuck, this is going to be complicated.

Lainey and I have had such an amazing time together these last few months. I was just starting to move on...yet, I'm not certain I ever would have been able to. Madison was always there. Her memory alive and well in my mind.

"Hey, guys," Sel announces their presence. Her smile is radiant as she glances over at her best friend. The woman is glowing now that Maddy is back in the picture. I've seen just how much it affected her not having her friend around to go through the adjustments of motherhood with. Especially with her mother not around. She could have used Maddy's nurturing touch to keep her calm. Don't get me wrong, Kil did an amazing job. But there's nothing quite like witnessing the power of friendship between two women.

Lainey swivels on her stool to greet Sel and almost immediately her posture becomes rigid. She straightens her spine and throws her shoulders back, bracing herself.

"Madison! I didn't know you were home. Liam didn't tell me." Her eyes blaze with hurt and frustration as she slings her head over her shoulder to glare at me.

Maddy shifts on her feet, gripping the edge of the bar for support. This isn't what she came here for. The goddamn drama.

"It wasn't exactly planned. My dad needed emergency surgery here in New York."

The bite of jealousy Lainey was sporting subsides as she releases her shoulders, sagging back to lean into me.

"I'm so sorry to hear that. I hope he makes a speedy recovery." She plasters on a smile.

"Thank you," Madison says sweetly, returning the sentiment.

"So, Mad..." Selena breaks the awkward tension hovering between us all. "What are you drinking?"

"I think the question is what are *we* drinking," she laughs, draping her arm over Sel.

"Well... I *would*... but I can't. Kil and I are expecting again!" she beams.

That's news to me. But *damn*. Good for them.

"Oh my goodness, Sel. That's amazing! Congrats!" Mad pulls her best friend in and rests her cheek against her head.

Selena's chocolate eyes scan between Lainey and I before saying, "I didn't mean to spoil it. Kil was going to tell all of you tomorrow. Tonight was for those two love birds." She wears a warm smile, pointing towards Lexi and Con—who are now cuddling by the stage.

"I'm good at acting surprised," I laugh, promising her I'll keep her slip up to myself.

"I can see that," Lainey grumbles snarkily. "Madison, do you think I can talk to you for a moment after you get your drink?"

Madison raises her eyebrows quickly before recovering her features. "Sure." Her perturbed eyes briefly dart over to mine before returning to her friend.

Sel shoots me a 'good luck with that one' look, knowing this is about to be fun. I sigh out my agreement and subtly nod.

"What'll it be, sweetheart?" The bartender asks while approaching our area. I'd like to rip out his fucking eyes for lingering too long on her cleavage. Knowing I can't, I choose option B— which is to inhale a calming breath through my nose. *Fuck that.* That's not working either.

Brushing her violet locks behind her shoulder, Madison leans forward to request a blood orange margarita. Lainey hops off her stool and lowers her elbows onto the bar, sticking her arse out for me to admire—or as a reminder of what I could lose if I stray. *Noted.*

"Make that two, please," she flirts, winking at the now drooling mess of a bartender. *Be fucking professional, mate.* That'll be the last time we hire this clown for an event.

Having Lainey lean over the bar like that while using her bedroom voice should drive me insane—it doesn't. And that's saying something. Considering how much of a selfish and protective prick I usually am.

A firm hand grips my shoulder from behind, temporarily distracting me. "Hey, asshole. Have you heard from Madison? Is she okay?" Diego saunters around me, coming into view.

I shake my head and pinch the bridge of my nose at the fact that Lainey definitely heard that. Without a shadow of a doubt, she can now confirm I purposely chose not to disclose that

Madison was coming home. So not only am I in the fucking dog house, but I am also lying in my own shit.

There aren't any words at the moment. My mind is a vortex created by the two women currently occupying it. Don't get me started on who is occupying my heart. With my index finger, I motion to my favorite bartender, who nods their understanding and starts preparing me another refill.

It's going to be a *long* night.

God knows if I don't pace myself, Lainey will be force feeding me another disgusting smoothie later on.

Diego brushes past me, placing a possessive hand around Madison's waist. My molars grind together seeing them interact. She doesn't shy away either. If anything, she leans in closer to him. Madison retrieves her drink and takes a step back from Lainey, grateful for the reprieve.

Lainey retreats towards me instead of instigating things further to take a seat on my lap. Manicured fingers raise her glass to her lips as she joins me in watching their interaction.

"How's your father?" The concern in *The Bone Breaker's* eyes is palpable.

He lowers his head so that they are as close as humanly possible. Madison raises her chin to stare up at him. Her cognac eyes dart back and forth, ensnared in his penetrating gaze.

Once-a-fucking-gain, jealousy works its way into my system. I inhale deeply causing my nipple rings to brush against Lainey's back through my shirt. Granting myself another sip of my drink helps simmer the fire blazing through me. The one that was once just ash and ember while Madison was gone, is now a full blown, raging inferno. Ya know how it goes... she's a breath of fresh air.

That's all my fire needed to reignite.

Oxygen.

She is the oxygen we all were lacking in our lives.

"He's doing well. Surgery was successful—thank God," she simpers before taking a healthy sip of her citrus drink. Flecks of sugar dust her lips and I suddenly want a taste of it. Bringing the rock glass to my lips I swallow another healthy portion, but my favorite whiskey dulls in comparison to my current craving.

The 23 year old bottle is sure as shit not tequila and Madison.

Diego's hand comes up to caress Maddy's pinkened cheeks and rubs his thumb along the delicate skin below her ear.

Wait a fucking second. Is that a butterfly tattoo? She got that for him?

"That's amazing news. Stay with me tonight?" he asks enticingly, his thumb still stroking the ink.

She nods her head, her cheeks now a cherry red. "I already had Killian take me to your room when I arrived. That is, if you don't mind bunking with me tonight. I would have stayed at the hotel, but the girls would have been super crowded and uncomfortable."

Diego leans his head down further so his forehead touches hers. "Where you sleep, I sleep, *Mariposita*. Remember that."

Madison inhales sharply as her pupils dilate. *Fuck.* I can't sit here and watch this shit anymore.

I shift Lainey over to get up but the little vixen grinds down on my lap and wraps her arms around my neck, subjecting me to this torture.

"I'm getting tired, Liam. I have a big day of cooking ahead of me for Kian's birthday. Come to bed?" Her intentions are clear as she continues to shift on my lap.

Her fingers curl under my chin and her lips meet mine. My lips part, inviting her to deepen the kiss—which she takes full advantage of. I need to lose myself in her tonight. I was doing fine. Just fine...Until a certain someone came crashing back into my life like a hurricane.

"Dance with me?" Diego asks at the same time as Selena.

Madison's sweet laugh has me breaking the kiss and abruptly tugging Lainey back toward the house.

"Goodnight, everyone," I growl, barely able to get the words out of my mouth.

Lainey complains about her heels and that she can't walk that fast. My arms come down as fast as possible to scoop her up. I carry her the rest of the way through the house until we reach my bedroom.

On a bounce, she lands on the bed, giggling while stripping her dress off her in record time. I lower myself down onto the mattress, caging her body under my thighs.

Angry hands wrestle my tux off before tossing my black mask onto the carpet.

"Fuck me like you fucked her," Lainey begs as she presses my head down to her core.

"Lain... I'm sorry I didn't tell you. I didn't want it to ruin your night." I attempt to ease the anger rightfully coursing through her.

"Prove to me that it doesn't bother you. That she no longer means what I mean to you now."

She's glaring down at me as I hover over her glistening pussy. French nails tug my hair with unleashed desire. When I don't make a move to devour her, she releases her grip on my head and scrambles back until she's able to pull the sheets down and slide beneath them.

"You can't, can you? *She* comes back and you go right back to wanting her," she whimpers while tucking her face into the pillow.

Releasing a frustrated sigh, I run my hands through my hair and lean back against the headboard.

"Lain, we never really discussed what we were. I know we've been moving in the direction of a relationship, but I think we haven't crossed that line because, yeah...Truthfully I've not been able to fully let go of Madison. I'm working through all of these emotions. I was so close to embracing this connection between us. Madison coming back today definitely derailed me a bit. It hurts. Seeing her and seeing her with *him* is stirring up some ugly shit. Shit I thought I moved past." My hands come up over my face and drag back down as a frustrated sigh leaves my lips.

Lainey turns back to face me, laying her cheek on her hand pressed to the pillow. Red-rimmed eyes and fresh tears greet me. Those jade eyes of hers shine with so much hurt. I feel like such a dick for ever getting involved with her before I was truly ready.

"Do you want to stop seeing each other, Liam? I know you loved her, I know it takes time to recover from those emotions, and seeing her tonight stirred up old feelings... but I am asking you what you want from me? How do you feel about *me*?"

Sliding down the bed, I get under the covers and pull her into me, cradling her head and twining my fingers through her soft curls. My chin rests on her head as I let out a massive breath. The one I feel like I've been holding since Madison got off that plane.

"I am starting to fall for you, Lainey. Hard. You are kind and sweet and always know how to brighten up my days. You're always encouraging me to do better with my health and my anger. Spending these last few months with you has been so healthy and healing. I found solace in your arms and my heart started to mend. But I'd be lying to you if I said I no longer felt anything toward Madison. That's not fair to you, Lovely. You deserve a man—"

She stops me by lifting her chin and pressing her soft trembling lips to mine.

"I don't want other men. I want *you*. I know what you're capable of giving in love. I've seen it. You would do anything for the woman you love. I can only hope that one day you will feel that way about me too. I thought...maybe...you already did. But, I see that I was wrong. I love you, Liam. I think I always have since we were kids. I'm willing to wait. I'll give you the space you need to process this. I don't want to hear about what you're doing behind closed doors. I don't want to see it blatantly in my face. Just promise me you'll try to work through how you're feeling and let me know when you figure it out."

Fuck. I couldn't ask for a better possible outcome. She's an angel, this one here in my arms. The damn organ in my chest beats harder as my lips crush hers.

"I hope I don't hurt you through all of this, Lain. You don't deserve that. I feel like I am already letting you down."

"You're not," she promises between kisses. "This way gives you closure that I am not sure you ever had. I know you'll be back in my arms when the time is right."

She finds her confidence again as she slides her hand down my chest. Her fingers glide down further until they wrap around my cock, pumping it until it's throbbing.

I deepen our kiss. Our tongues dance as our hands roam and explore each other's skin like it was our first time. Lainey moans her approval as my fingers slip through her wet folds.

"Do you want me to stop?" I ask as I nip and suck at the base of her neck. I roll us until I am above her, adding pressure to the hand between us.

"No. Show me what I've been missing. Give me what you've given her," she pleads.

Replacing my hand with my cock, I shove my hips forward, entering her in one swift move. Her head leans back against the pillow in bliss. My hips swivel, grinding down my pelvis to rub her clit while fucking her. Her legs widen inviting me to go deeper.

Our lips meet again as I show her what it could be like to be mine. I had been holding out. This kind of intimacy is what I wasn't giving Lainey.

So, I spend the rest of the night showing her and myself what this could really be like if I just let go of the past. All while trying not to think of what this means for tomorrow.

Single.

CHAPTER 9

MADISON

HOW CELEBRITIES ARE able to wear sky high heels to every event, even to just grab a coffee, is beyond me. I've only had these bad boys on for a few hours and my feet are already throbbing. The little toe on my right foot may even end up with a nice blister tomorrow. *Fanfuckingtastic.*

"I can't believe you are sleeping in Diego's bed tonight. All my bets were on Liam...but I see now that he's a bit...pre... preoccupied," Lexi hiccups.

A giggle escapes me at how cute she is leaning against her man for support. Con shoots me a look letting me know he's about to steal my friend away for the night. Well, practically morning.

It's 3 AM.

We all collectively spent the night enjoying the live band, dancing, even doing some karaoke. I had a few too many shots, which I will regret in the morning. *Oh well.* There is a lot to celebrate. For one, my dad is going to be okay. And my best fucking friend is getting married to a man who is literally perfect for her.

I catch Diego studying me from his seat at the bar. The

corner of his lip lifts as he notices me staring back. He needs to stop looking at me like that. *God, he's gorgeous.*

"Yeah. Well, he deserves to be happy. It's not like I gave him any reason to wait for me."

I mean those words, but I'd be a damn liar if I said it didn't bother me seeing him with Lainey. Conor pulls me into him by the back of my neck and kisses the top of my head. It's brotherly, and the first time he's shown me this much affection. Shifting me over, he snuggles Lexi in closer to him.

"You lot are the most compassionate and selfless women I have ever met in my life. Mad, I'm not saying this because Liam is my boss or because he's my best friend. Give him some time. I don't think that Lainey and him are official. He hasn't been right since you left. Healing? Sure. Complete? Not at all. I know Diego is going to try and get back under your skin like he did in Greece —and if that's who you want I'll always support ya. Promise me you'll at least be open to seeing what Liam still feels for ya."

I snuggle in closer to Con, embracing him and my bestie whose eyes are shut with a huge smile plastered on her face. *Plastered* being the key word here. She's such a cute happy drunk.

"I'll do my best, Con. I wasn't expecting to come home and end up right back where I left off, but here we are. I have been planning on coming back for some time now. The process was just going to take a bit longer. Dad needing surgery expedited that. So let's rip this bandaid off and find out where my heart is leading me."

"Hear, hear," Lexi slurs, holding her heels up to the sky.

Con cackles and releases me, swooping Lexi up into his arms. "You gonna be alright, love? I'm gonna take the princess here up to bed."

"I'll be fine. I've got *The Bone Breaker* watching me." I nod in his direction.

Conor rolls his eyes before giving me a gentle smile. "Have

fun with that one. He's been a pain in my arse since he's arrived."
With those parting words, he walks through the dissipating
crowd towards the sliding glass doors.

My eyes retreat back to Diego who is already making his way
over. The band announces that this will be their last song. Like a
classic romance movie, Diego outstretches his hand.

"Dance with me, *Mariposita*."

"Fine," I sigh as our hands connect and butterflies assault my
stomach. Amazing how he can make me feel like a ball of
nerves, yet so completely comfortable in his embrace at the same
time.

Warm, strong hands find my waist as he guides us to the
center of the dance floor. It's just us. Killian would normally be
out here enjoying one last dance before announcing the end of
the Gala—but he's not around. Sel looked exhausted and she has
a big day tomorrow. I bet the two of them snuck away earlier.

Diego pulls me flush against him and claims my left hand.
His index finger traces where my wedding rings once sat. We
start to sway and my body relaxes against his. The addictive
scent of mint and coconut wraps around me, bringing me
temporary peace. Those tired and tipsy eyes of mine flutter shut
against his chest, allowing him to guide and support me.
Naturally, I relax further into him. The soothing beat of his heart
acts as a sound machine, slowing the pace of my own.

Just like the ocean, just like him, our bodies ebb and flow to
the music like a lullaby.

"Tell me this doesn't feel right," he whispers into my ear, his
chin resting at the crown of my head.

"Mhm," is all I can come up with at the moment.

The rumble of his deep chuckle vibrates against my face.
"You'll see. We didn't get much time to get to know each other.
I'm sure there are things you'd like to know about me before you
decide on forever with me—*which you will. Again.* Until that day
comes, I'm here to show you all of me. All the ugly, awful parts

of me. And all the monotonous parts too. Like the fact that I enjoy watching baseball on my down time or eating shredded wheat cereal for breakfast," he laughs in such a boyish way.

The kind of way I only ever experienced a handful of times.

The rough pads of his fingers lift my chin to greet his gorgeous eyes. *Sapphires on fire.* For a second, I am breathless. Lost in the depths of them and in awe of how he's baring his beautiful soul to me. *Again.* For the second time today.

"*The Bone Breaker* version of me and the Diego you fell for. I want you to see both. That way if you can love both monsters, you'll never find a reason to leave me again. I know why you ran." A painful expression carves his usually smooth features.

My hands come up as the song slows down to a close. They cup both sides of his face before pulling him closer to me.

"I ran because I was scared. Scared of who I was becoming. Of how much I enjoyed it. When in reality, I was never designed to be part of a life full of violence and chaos. I'm a rule follower, Diego. Not a rule breaker. Yet, how addicting it was to have that risk come with the kind of love I never could have imagined. Certainly not one I would have experienced in the medical field or in my hometown. This adventure...the constant push and pull, the heightened risk of actually losing the person you love adds a certain *charm* to the chaos. Living in Arizona, *now that* is mundane. I want adventure, I want the unknown. And most of all, I want to stop overanalyzing everything."

With force, I tug his lips to mine, opening up to quench the craving I've had all night. Mint tingles on my tongue as his runs along mine.

"Don't go back to Arizona. Stay," he insists breathily between kisses. His fingers find my hair and twine through it, holding me hostage between his powerful hands. "Let's go back to Miami. Wait, fuck that. How about we take the new yacht they built, that's currently waiting for us at the island, and travel the world?

Spend time with me the proper way. Get to know me. Your husband."

I don't know what to say. That sounds amazing—completely out of a fairytale, and perhaps even unrealistic, but amazing nonetheless. I want to. *I really. Fucking. Do.* But I need to at least start by moving back to New York. Spend some time with my family. Be around for Sel and Lexi for all the wedding events. I need to get my plans in order to open up the coffee shop....

The microphone gives off a high-pitched frequency before Liam's deep voice fills the speakers. I glance over at him on the stage. His mask is off and his shirt is unbuttoned to reveal the black ink of his ravens tattoo. One tatted hand remains in the pocket of his tuxedo pants as the other grips the microphone with white knuckles.

"I wanted to thank everyone for your attendance this year. Your generous donations to this year's organizations and charities are deeply appreciated. With the Gala coming to an end, I wanted to make sure to inform those of you who are not yet aware, that my brother and I have decided to switch roles. With the blessing of the other members of our family near and far, I am now the official leader of the Tri-State Syndicate. My brother has stepped down but will continue to help with decisions moving forward. Anyone who has any questions—or any *issues*," he chuckles deeply, "Can take it up with me. Have a great night, everyone. Please get home safely."

He returns the microphone to the stand without breaking eye-contact with me. *What the fuck?* Killian always said he didn't want the power, that he wasn't cut out for it like Liam. I guess fatherhood and the events of last year proved that to him. *Should I go up and congratulate him? Did Diego know about this?*

In question, I twist my body to look at him. The man doesn't even seem the slightest bit surprised. He knew. It's not like I was owed this information. A heads up would have been nice. Diego notices me staring and shrugs.

"I personally feel Liam is a better fit. I've got two bullet holes in my body to prove that."

"I should go congratulate him." I look down at my feet.

Why do I feel so awkward right now? Diego and I were just having a moment and along comes the Universe adding a bit of zest to my already fucked up fairytale. *Oh, shit.* I'm bleeding. Bright red blood is smeared down the side of my foot.

Goddamn heels!

Diego realizes at the same time I do. "Christ, baby. Let's get you cleaned up."

I risk another glance at Liam before allowing Diego to guide me through the crowd and up to his room.

"Wait. *Madison*, wait up," Liam's voice echoes behind us.

We are halfway up the flight of stairs as Liam catches up with us. I grip the banister and spin around to see him taking the stairs two at a time. The heat radiating off him absorbs into my body as he closes the distance, stopping a step below me.

"I know it's late. Do ya think after you get cleaned up," he nods to my foot, "That we can talk? It'll only take a few minutes."

"I'll meet you in our room, *Mariposita.* Take your time. But if that foot becomes infected, there will be punishment." Diego shoots me a wink while smirking as he continues his ascent.

"I'm a nurse, asshole. I think I know how to take care of a blister. But thank you so much for the reminder of your wavering sanity."

"You love it," his amused baritone voice carries down the stairwell. He clucks his tongue. "And before you think to lie to me, remember how I feel about it."

I whip around angrily to see his back still to me and his index finger motioning back and forth horizontally.

Ugh. Why does that turn me on? *Maybe I should be more concerned with my wavering sanity than his.*

My cheeks flare with heat and my core tingles with desire.

Liam notices. His strong jaw works and his face turns red for other reasons. Trying to calm down, he inhales deeply before releasing it.

Hmm. That's new.

"I can find a bandaid for you. Let's get that foot cleaned up."

I nod in response and follow him toward his bedroom, coming to an abrupt stop. *Is he fucking insane? He's going to bring me to his bedroom where Lainey is probably sound asleep in the bed? No fucking thank you.*

"She's not in here. Lainey and I aren't together at the moment. We never really were, but it's...it's complicated, Mad. Please come in? I'll explain it all."

He opens the door and guides me inside our old bedroom. Memories come flooding back like Polaroids in a scrapbook. Every good moment right up to the one where I found out Diego was dead—which he wasn't.

Aaaand I'm right back to the day I left here.

CHAPTER 10

LIAM

MADISON REMAINS quiet as she sits on the lid of the toilet with her foot in my lap. I run a cotton ball with alcohol over the broken blister on her pinky toe. Don't get me wrong, I appreciate Madison in a pair of heels, but seeing what it did to her feet and what all these women endure by wearing them has me irritated. Once more, I dab a fresh cotton ball and wipe the injury.

Air hisses through her clenched teeth and she places her hand over mine.

"I can take it from here."

Tilting my head up, I raise an eyebrow at her. "Let me help you. I know you are fully capable of taking care of yourself, sweetheart. I *want* to help. There's a difference."

She cocks her head and bites her bottom lip, clearly holding back what she was going to say. Which is sexy as hell, but also allows me to continue. Those chestnut eyes study me as I retrieve the antibacterial ointment and place it over the raw skin with a Q-tip.

"I was never trying to dictate your life, Maddy. Or make you feel trapped by an overbearing, overprotective arsehole like me. I just wanted to lighten the weight you keep on your shoulders at all times. Weight that isn't yours to bear, but you do it anyway."

I open the seal of the Lion King bandaid and remove the plastic tabs. Gently, I wrap the adhesive around her pinky toe before running my thumb up the arch of her foot.

"All done," I rasp, patting the smooth skin of her bronzed calf. "Sorry, Lion King was all I could find. The house has changed to a baby-zone since you left."

She lowers her foot off my lap as I stand and clean the garbage up. I rinse my hands and walk out of the en suite to change into something more comfortable. Entering my walk in closet, I grab a pair of gray sweats and a shirt, knowing Madison will complain about me being topless. *Although...*

Fuck the shirt.

A minute later, I find her sitting at the edge of the bed looking around. Narrowed eyes briefly take me in before landing back down to her lap where her hands are clasped together.

"I used to feel that at times you could be overbearing, but not an asshole, Liam. Your need to protect runs deep, anyone can see that. Especially for the ones you love. Or loved in my case."

"I never stopped, princess." My feet carry me to her until I am standing directly in front of her. I gather her trembling hands in mine. She's so strong. Today was intense and I'm sure this place and all of us bombarding her with our affection is taking a toll on her. "Lainey and I started this past Halloween. We got drunk after Selena had hosted a party here. I was hoping you would have reached out—had you still felt something...anything for me. But...you never did. I hated myself for not having the courage to tell you how I felt. I kept reminding myself that you asked for space and I'd be disrespecting you by contacting you."

"I'm sure Con gave you a daily update," she jabs, crossing her hands over her chest. There's that fire. This is the Maddy we have all been missing. The sassy little spitfire. *When did she become so timid? So unsure of herself?*

"Trust me, Con never spied on you while he was there with Lex. That doesn't mean I didn't soak up any scrap of information he would willingly share. But I never asked. It killed me not knowing how you were. Or if you were safe. Over time, and very slowly, I moved on from completely numb to feeling the sensations of life again. I enjoyed spending time with my nephew. Hell, I even enjoyed getting to know Diego better. We found ourselves hitting the bars and gym together. And in a weird, fucked up way, his presence reminded me of you. That constant reminder was like a fix. Then Lainey showed interest in me that night at the party and I caved. I wanted to *feel* again. She showed me I was still capable of it."

The comforter wrinkles as I take a seat next to her on the edge of the bed. A sad smile spreads across her face while she studies me, her eyes lingering on the tattoos at my neck before dipping lower to my chest.

"I'm not upset with you, Liam. Lainey is a sweet girl. I had my moments of jealousy over her in the past only because I knew she liked you. But I knew you would never entertain her while we were together. Now that we aren't, it doesn't bother me. You had every right to move on. When you told me on Valentine's Day that she's always shown interest in you, I knew that she wanted you. I mean, *shit*. You two grew up together. She probably knows everything about you."

A small chuckle slips out. *She's not wrong.* Lainey could definitely give you a spreadsheet of my whole life leading up to today. Doesn't mean she knows my heart though. That's really my fault for not opening up enough.

For being guarded.

See, that's the thing about love. So many different forms. Lainey loves me. I do believe that. The thing is, she loves what she *knows* of me; what she's experienced with me over the years. She doesn't know the full extent of my heart.

My biggest fears.

My soul.

Whereas Madison, knows the depths of my soul. All the

darkness that encompasses it. Yet, miraculously, she still loves me. *Least, I hope so.* She may not know every single thing about me since birth, but she knows my soul. And that is more than enough.

It's not that one love is more precious than the other. They are just very different.

With Lainey, this thing between us is simple. It's carefree, uncomplicated, and natural.

With Madison, it's deep, it's enthralling. *Reckless,* even. Always twisting and turning and begging for more than we can give at times. Yet, we always find a way to burrow ourselves deeper than we had before. It's something we had to work hard at every single day—even if it felt as easy as breathing. The love we shared was as complicated as all those systems working in tandem, reminding you to breathe. That constant tending to each system is what kept our love as strong as it was at the time.

Emotionally, mentally, physically.

"Lainey and I hooked up that night. That was the first time I had been with anyone since you."

Madison worries her lower lip, prompting me to grip her chin and loosen her teeth from it with my thumb.

"I figured that. It would be hypocritical of me to feel differently, considering I had slept with Diego the night of my wedding. It's not like I expected you to stay single and celibate."

Her warm hand tugs my hand off her face and places it in her lap. She doesn't release it though, which is a good sign. It means I get to explore this further. See where my head is at. I don't want Lainey feeling second best. And again, she's not. I just need something. A sign that this thing burned out between Madison and I. Or... perhaps she wants Diego. Hell, maybe she wants none of us at all.

"Don't play with her heart, Liam. I left. I said goodbye. She's lucky to have you. And she would make an amazing wife for the new leader of the Tri-State Syndicate. Congrats by the way." A beautiful smile spreads across her face. I'd give anything to keep it there.

"Thanks, baby. It was for the best for everyone involved. Kil wanted to spend more time with his family. He realized his mistakes last year and asked me to take over. Everyone was agreeable with the decision because we are the same age and Jack trained us equally. I didn't even need to go to Ireland."

"Kil always wanted that family life. I'm happy for him."

Her smile broadens at the mention of a family life. I know how desperately she desires a family of her own. It kills me that we were headed that direction before everything took a massive shit.

"If we were still together, you'd have been back in the spotlight again...the way it was with Killian."

Mad tosses her hand out, waving it to the side. "Yeah, what a headache that was. I'm sure Lainey is more equipped to deal with that, being she grew up around it." Her eyes have settled on my raven tattoo. That reminds me...

I tuck her purple hair behind her ear and caress the space where the delicate butterfly is inked into her skin.

"Nice tat." I raise an eyebrow.

"It was a reminder of my decisions in this life and where it led me. To freedom, to change, to strength, and finding myself through a rebirth of sorts."

I run my thumb along her bubblegum tinted cheek. "It doesn't remind you of a certain someone with a matching tattoo?" Bastard had gone all out getting that chest piece of his. The artwork is incredible, but I knew who it was for. Was forced to see the damn thing every day at the gym.

"I mean of course it reminds me of Diego. He's the one who calls me *Mariposita*. In a way, what happened with Diego in Greece, it pushed me to become stronger. I grew a spine. It encouraged me to chase the dreams I've always wanted and not the ones my family set out for me."

"You didn't want to become a nurse?" I ask, genuinely curious.

"Don't get me wrong. I've enjoyed helping people. Becoming a nurse wasn't something I was ever against. I just...I don't know. I also enjoyed having a choice. It was more of a set plan my parents laid out for me rather than a personal choice."

The moment her confession rolls off her tongue, I realize how badly I had fucked us up last year. Where I saw doing whatever it took to protect her as something good, even heroic... she saw it as removing her choice. That was why she was so adamant about staying to help Diego. She wanted to help. We were so focused on saving her and doing what we felt was right, that we ended up completely ignoring her choice. *Well, I did.* Killian tried to show me that.

Fuck. What a damn fool I am.

"Christ." I run the hand that caressed her cheek into my hair, tugging at the back.

"Sweetheart, I'm so sorry if I ever made you feel you lacked a choice with me. Especially in Greece."

"It's alright, Liam. I knew you weren't doing it to be malicious. You did it to protect me. I see that now. I'm telling you this because it explains the tattoo. It explains why things turned out the way they did with Diego. And I'm sorry, too. For any moment I made you feel like our love wasn't enough. Diego was just the thing I needed after everything I went through. He understood my desires more than I did at times. That feeling of releasing control—but willingly—was *everything* I needed to mature. To become a stronger version of myself. You and Killian coddling me all the time was sweet, and it made me feel secure, but it didn't help me grow."

I release a massive sigh. "I get it now, Mad. I just couldn't bear it if something ever happened to you and it was because Killian and I brought you into this life."

"I actually missed it," she admits, giggling more to herself. "I missed how strong and cherished I felt around you all. I felt like going to Arizona backtracked me in some ways where it supported me in others." She leans in, her seductive jasmine and amber perfume awakens my senses and has all my blood flowing south.

"Can I tell you a secret?" she asks softly.

I lean in, mesmerized by her eyes and the long thick lashes that grace them.

"Mhm..."

"I'm terrified of scorpions," she whispers.

I can't help myself. I lean back and grip my stomach, letting out a hearty chuckle.

"Sweetheart, you have better knife skills than some assassins I've met. A scorpion should be afraid of you, not the other way around."

"That's my point. I went from feeling and acting my strongest to a complete wimp!" She hangs her head. "I want to come home," she mumbles. The defeat that courses through her is something I need to change. *Fuck*, I hate seeing her like this.

I pull her into my chest, cradling the back of her head and rubbing gentle circles into her hair. "I've been staying at my place in Connecticut a few nights a week, to give some space to Killian and the family. You are welcome to stay there while you figure things out. As you've seen, I have a spacious guest room with an en suite. You could have your own space, *and* you'll be close to your family. They'll only be a ferry ride away. Just knowing you're there and knowing I can protect you will ease my worries. You know being involved with us carries a risk."

"I do. I'm ready to come back. Not to mention, Con and Lex could use a little space of their own. No better time than now with the wedding coming up. She told me tonight they want to get married this spring. Things are going to move quickly and they'll probably need our help..." She is chewing on her thumbnail, contemplating her options. "Can I let you know soon? I want to talk to Diego and Lexi before I commit to anything."

"Of course, love."

"I don't want Lainey to feel pushed to the side. If—*If*—I decide to move in, *temporarily*, I want you to continue to date her. Just because I came back doesn't mean you forget about the life you had before my return."

"She already discussed with me tonight that we are not going to keep seeing each other. At least not until I figure out you and I."

"That's really big of her. Is that what she wanted to talk to me about earlier?"

"Not sure. Perhaps she wanted to try and lay her claim, but after our talk earlier tonight, she understood where my head is at."

The light of Madison's phone glows between us. She bends her head to look at it and releases a sigh.

3:45 AM.

We all have an early start. I'm sure she wants to see her father in the morning. Hope blooms in my chest at the thought of her coming back tomorrow. I'm sure Sel invited her to Kian's first birthday. It will give me more time with her—assuming Diego doesn't go off gallivanting with her.

"We should get some sleep. I want to be able to see my dad during visiting hours tomorrow before Kian's birthday." *Ahh, she is coming.* "Lexi also mentioned dinner to discuss the wedding. I believe you are invited as well."

"That so?" I play with my beard while moving to stand. Madison hops off the bed and retrieves her heels from the floor.

"That's what she said." She shrugs, a smile creeping onto her face before it turns into the cutest yawn. "Excuse me. Sorry, that was rude."

Her tired feet stumble to the door. She cracks it open but lingers, turning around to glance up at me. I hold the door open, giving my hands something to do so I can stop touching her like she's still mine.

"It's late, you've been running around all day. And that wasn't rude, it was cute as fuck." I wink.

As if my good intentions were going to fucking last long, I reach out and stroke my knuckles along her bicep. Satisfaction fills me seeing the goosebumps spring up in their wake.

"Goodnight, Liam."

"Goodnight, Madison."

CHAPTER 11

DIEGO

THE DOOR CREAKS OPEN SLOWLY. She's being careful not to disturb me. It's dark in here, the room only illuminated by a small night light in the bathroom. I'm relaxing on the couch—but she can't see me. Madison creeps towards the end of the bed where she left her bag and comes up empty. Confusion slaps her in the face knowing she left it there earlier. Watching the gears turn in that beautiful mind of hers, she starts to tiptoe to the walk-in.

A small gasp echoes the space as her hands come up to rest against her lips. All her clothes are neatly hung up or folded on top of the dresser below. Even her few pairs of shoes are lined up nicely on the shoe rack. *Courtesy of yours truly.*

A smug smile forms on my lips as I approach her. Quietly as a panther, I creep towards her. It's almost 4 AM. Unpacking her luggage would allow her to get some rest before another busy day tomorrow. I made it my priority when I got back.

I'm about to sneak up behind her and sarcastically reprimand her for being out all hours of the night like some rebellious teenager when she starts to undress.

Fuuuuck, this woman is testing my control. I purposely took the couch so she would feel respected and not pressured to sleep with me. On the other hand, I desperately wanted to hear her invite me to bed.

And if she didn't, I'd find a way in it.

The feeling of her body wrapped against mine is not a memory I could ever forget. Every morning I wake up craving her, wishing I could reach out and run my hands over the curve at her waist or over the swell of her perfect ass. My palms itch to run through her silky hair. I want to be the one stirring her from sleep. Starting with a stolen kiss before having the privilege of watching her eyelids flutter to greet a new day.

But she's been gone for a year and I'm sure this night was a huge trip down memory lane. My sweet wife might just want space.

From me.

From Liam.

From this whole clusterfuck of a day.

Black fabric cascades down her back as she slips it off her beautiful body. A nude strapless bra is next to go, followed by a strappy black thong. *Coño.* My wife is a fucking goddess. I send a silent prayer up to my mamá. *Please help keep this woman in my life. I know I asked it once already, but I'm good at pushing my luck. So I'm asking again.*

The exquisite view is quickly replaced by a pair of drawstring fleece pajama bottoms and her oversized university t-shirt. Either sensing my presence or needing the bathroom, she spins on her now bandaged foot. A squeak leaves her lips at the sight of me.

"You don't *look* like a pumpkin..." I glance down at the skin where my watch normally sits.

Heat swarms her eyes and that one sassy eyebrow of hers arches. The soft palm of her hand lands flat against my chest as she shoves me back out of the closet. "Very funny."

I step out of her way, allowing her to pass me. Only to follow her as she shuffles to the bathroom. Madison takes her place in front of the vanity and I lean against the doorframe, crossing my arms over my bare chest. Discovering her cosmetic bag, she retrieves her toothbrush and toothpaste and starts to vigorously brush her teeth.

"How is prince charming?" I snide.

The amber in her chestnut eyes always shines brighter when she's mad. And right now? They are glowing like some ethereal being. The toothpaste foam coats her lush lips as she lets out a dramatic faux laugh.

"*Ha.* If you ever consider switching careers to become a comedian—*please* don't."

She rinses her mouth, gathering her hair to one side of her neck before spitting into the sink. Isn't it amazing how when you love someone, something as trivial as them brushing their teeth can become a beautiful work of art?

I want this moment captured and framed.

"How about I keep my title of *El Rompe Huesos*? Would that suit me better? Or would you run if you actually saw me in action?" I tap my lip with my index finger.

Dabbing a white hand towel at her lips she retrieves a makeup wipe and begins cleansing her face.

"I've seen you in action." She shrugs indifferently.

"That was *nothing.* However, if you'd like to reenact that scene where I strip you of your clothes with my knife while you are suspended from the ceiling—I'm *absolutely* game."

Her face is now spotless and completely bare. *Beautiful.* Shuffling through her bag, she retrieves a serum bottle, pumps a few drops into her hands, and rubs them together before slathering her face.

"After the shock wore off and I realized you weren't actually going to do anything, I really enjoyed it. Same goes for our wedding night."

"Did you?" My voice has deepened with lust at her admission. "So you enjoy being restrained?" I ask, now intrigued.

"Yes. Because for the first time in my life, I actually put my full trust into someone. And that felt freeing. I always have to have control in my life, but with you, I don't know what it is, I just trust you with my body...among other things."

She always shocks me with how sassy she can be one minute and then a complete open book, vulnerability and all in the next. It has me reaching for her and pulling her to my chest. My fingers thread through her soft hair that she's tossed into a messy bun. I tilt her head up by gripping her hair tighter. Cinnamon eyes light with desire as a moan slips off her succulent lips. I lick my own as I press my throbbing cock against her body—that's now flush against mine.

"I want to kiss you again." The gravel in my voice is not hard to miss. "But you could use the sleep. I'm sure you're exhausted."

"Then kiss me once and let's go to bed." It comes off as an invitation *and* a threat. *I fucking love it. I love her. She knows exactly how to stare down my beast.*

Skimming my nose along her collar bone and then up her neck, I tease her. My teeth graze over her tattoo before nipping her earlobe.

"I would, but you smell like *him*. And in order to erase that, I'd need to do far more than kiss you, *Mariposita*." She inhales sharply as a shiver races through her body.

"What would that entail?" Her fingers trace the tattoo I got for her, making my cock swell even more than it had watching her undress.

I snake a hand down the front of her pants and drag a finger through her soaking wet slit. Sliding up, I find her clit and circle the little bud until it's blooming. Madison grips my bicep as she moans out her pleasure.

"I would need to lick, suck, and bite every inch of you before you got on your knees and took my cock in your mouth like a good girl." Her breathing intensifies as I slip two fingers into her opening. Thrusting in and out, she starts to mewl and buck against my hand. Her fingers grasp my triceps as her legs start to shake. Delirious with need, my tongue licks a path from the neckline of her t-shirt to her tattoo.

"After you swallowed every last drop of my cum, I'd taste you, spread out right here on this bathroom counter, before fucking you until the sun comes up. There would be so much of *me* inside *you*, it would drip down your thighs the rest of the day. And as you socialize with the man whose scent once lingered on your beautiful skin, you'll not only reek of me, but be sorely reminded of who you belong to."

Removing my hand, I place a gentle kiss on her forehead. "I told you I was going to show you both of my monsters. If I'm not the man you fell for, not who you thought I was, I'll let you go for good this time. Liam may desire you as well, and he deserves a fair chance, I guess... but—"

Madison slams her lips against mine, effectively shutting me up. That's all the permission I need to rip her damn clothes off.

"Fuck, baby," I manage to get out before she shuts me up again and drops to her knees.

Impatient hands drag my black sweatpants down my thighs as my cock springs free, pulsing in anticipation. She wastes no time licking me from base to tip, swirling her tongue around the crown. My head snaps back as I grip both hands on the molding of the door frame above me.

"*Madison*," I whisper her name like a plea. A plea to stop teasing me with her talented tongue and to take my fucking cock into the back of her throat.

Like the damn mind reader she is, her mouth wraps around my full length. I watch through lust hazed eyes as she takes every inch until I hit the back of her throat. My hips thrust forward, causing her to gag, but she quickly regains control. Her throat relaxes around me as she starts to bob her head. Determined hands caress my sensitive balls, dealing me a new wave of ecstasy. Watching my cock disappear between her pink lips has them tightening in her grip. The sensation is *intoxicating. I'm going to fucking explode.* Like a damn teenager getting head for the first time, I can't hold back. My wife smiles coyly as a few tears roll down her cheeks. She knows if she keeps this pace up— I *will* lose it.

"Fuck. Fuuuuck, *Mariposita.*"

Removing my hands from above me, I grip the back of her head and savagely fuck her mouth. She gags again but continues to take it.

"I want you to swallow every fucking drop. Do you hear me?" I grunt out.

She nods as I continue to thrust faster into her mouth.

"Such a good fucking wife," I growl.

Stars erupt across my vision as my cum paints the back of her throat in multiple spurts. She moans out her approval as I slowly release her head and pull out of her mouth. Leaning forward, she licks my cock like ice cream off a spoon before licking her swollen lips.

Holy. Fucking... this is my wife? *My wife.* I have got to be the luckiest motherfucker on the planet. *No.* The whole goddamn universe. *Please let her stay mine.* I can't lose her to Liam. He's a good man, and I consider us friends, but he can't give her what I can. I know she knows that. Regardless, I'll let her explore this with us until she figures it out.

Madison stands, tidying the hair that's now falling out of her messy bun. Not that it's really even in a bun at all. Her hair tie is hanging on by a thread.

"It may not have been 'mile high club' worthy, but I'd like to think you enjoyed that," she states as she sashays by me to our bed. My pants are still at my ankles and I'm coming back down to Earth after that mind blowing orgasm, so I'm not as quick to move and grab her.

Kicking the fucking sweats off me, I stagger over to her. She's already climbing into bed. I reach out and grip her by the bicep, flipping her onto her back. The light reignites in her eyes at my nearness. The wood bed frame creaks as I lean over her and press my knees to the mattress between her thighs.

"That was far *better* than the mile high club. Because during 'said' mile high club, I imagined your face. And, baby? The real deal, couldn't light a candle to my imagination. *Christ, Madison.* You are perfect in every way."

I kiss her hard, tasting myself on her tongue. She relaxes into the bed, soaking up this moment just as I am, her eyes darting back and forth, lost in mine. That moment of bliss comes to a screeching halt when her hand slides up my chest and she pushes me back.

"I've got to get some sleep. You've seen me cranky and it isn't pretty. Between you and me, the espresso machine here just isn't as good as the one on your jet." She winks before shimmying her perfect body up the bed and sliding beneath the sheets.

"That will be remedied *immediately.* And if you think for one second you are going to bed unsatisfied, you are about to be *sorely* mistaken. That's not how this works, *Mariposita.*"

On a growl, I throw the sheets back, my stomach rippling from the laughter pouring out of me. She makes me feel so fucking carefree and wild. Not being able to help myself, I start to tickle her. Madison's sweet laughter joins with mine as she tries to wiggle her fingers under my armpits.

"Diego!" she reprimands squeakily.

My hands grip her by the ankles, dragging her down the bed. Spreading her thighs wide, I dip my head until my tongue finds her clit. Her eyes slam shut as she arches her back off the bed. Pink nipples harden to peaks as her full breasts press towards the ceiling. *Exquisite.* This is another moment I need photographed —because she is devastatingly beautiful.

Add it to my growing art gallery.

Slipping a finger into her channel, I collect her arousal and use it to rub a circle along her other entrance, which puckers at my touch. Ever so slowly, I increase the pressure until my finger slinks in. After a bit of resistance, the muscle relaxes and allows me full entrance. Adding two fingers to her cunt and replacing my mouth back on her clit, I begin to suck and lick in intervals.

"Wow. Oh. My. Goddddd, *Ocean Eyes*," she mewls as her asshole and pussy clench down on my fingers.

"That's it, baby. Just wait until you take my cock here." I pump my fingers in and out of her, dragging out her orgasm. Like an exorcism, trembling thighs lift her ass off the bed as she rides out the euphoria.

"Yes...*Ocean Eyes*. Fuuuck."

Her ass falls back onto the bed and her body goes slack as it tremors with aftershocks. I pull my fingers out and give one last swipe to her delicious pussy, swirling my tongue around her opening to collect every last drop of her sweetness.

Lazy fingers rub circles through my scalp as she catches her breath. She looks down at me with half-lidded eyes.

"You were the first person to...to take me there like that," she stutters, still breathless.

"I'll have to do it more often if that's what it does to you," I smirk, more than satisfied with how this night ended.

"Mhm..." she mumbles. Her eyes are closed and her breathing has started to slow.

I hop off the bed and clean up in the en suite. Even though I want her smelling like me, I decide to rein in the animal. Using a warm wash cloth, I clean Madison up and tuck her spent body under the sheets before sliding in next to her. Possessively, I pull her to me, keeping my left hand secured around her.

Placing a kiss to her shoulder blade, I close my eyes and drift off to sleep knowing my heart is back where it belongs.

CHAPTER 12

MADISON

I STIR awake to Diego's erection saying 'Good Morning' to my ass cheeks. He's still asleep, so I take a moment to stretch, still achy from last night's adventures. His arm falls off my body as I twist and turn. Instantly, I feel cooler. He's like a fucking sauna at night. And I thought I slept hot.

Sheesh.

I reach across to the nightstand in search of my clutch. There, next to my plugged-in phone, is a glass of water. I take a few sips, smiling over the rim at the thought of him taking care of me last night. After the incredible orgasm he gave me, I was spent. It didn't take much to fall into a peaceful slumber.

Squinting my eyes, I tilt the phone to read the time. It's hard to tell with these blackout curtains.

8:33 AM.

Grrr. Guess I should get showered and ready. I need to visit Dad before the visiting hours end at 11:30 AM.

"Can we stay like this a little longer?" *Ocean Eyes* mumbles against my shoulder. He wraps his arm around me again, tightening his hold. The cold metal of his wedding band presses into my stomach, right over the scar I have from the car accident.

"Honestly, I wish," I sigh, clasping his hand and removing it from around me.

"Can I ask you something before this moment disappears and Liam tries to swoon you?"

Laughter threatens to escape but I bite it back because his voice is adorable in the morning. Definitely not *Bone Breaker* intimidating. More like the sexy lead singer of a band who just spent the night serenading his fans.

Or worshiping my pussy.

Regardless...

"Go on, *Ocean Eyes*. What's up?"

"Did you sleep with anyone while you were in Arizona? I won't be upset. I'm just curious if another man pleased you," he rasps, pulling me back down so that I lie on my back.

He's leaning his head on the hand he has bent against the pillow. Looking all God-like, staring down at me with those sparkling blue-topaz eyes and messy untamed hair. They are so stunning I almost forget what he asked me.

"Um...no...no. I didn't. I spent my days working at the local coffee shop or going to the gym. Occasionally, I'd meet someone out at the bar. My favorite couple, Simon and John would always try to encourage me to go home with one of the guys who tried to grab my attention, but I never did. It just didn't feel right. Did you?"

He smiles like the Cheshire Cat at my admission and shakes his head back and forth, a loose curl falling over his forehead.

"As if my performance last night wasn't proof enough... No, I haven't slept with anyone. A few of my past flings heard through the grapevine that *El Rompe Huesos* was still alive and tried to reconnect, but I wasn't having it. There was only one woman I craved—and she was two thousand miles away. Wanting nothing to do with me."

His hand finds my face as he lowers his lips to mine. "Does

she want me now?" The vulnerability in his voice has my heart rate spiking.

"I'm not sure what I want. I need time, Diego. Can you give me that? Time to figure this out? Time to decide what I want... or...possibly who I want?"

My heart slams against my ribcage when he remains silent.

"I won't keep you from being with Liam if that's who your heart longs for. If dating us both is what you need to figure it out, then fine. I'm not going anywhere."

"Thank you for understanding. I actually have an important question. Are we still legally married?"

"Fuck yes, we are. So I suppose we are agreeing to an open marriage for now?" He chuckles, rubbing his left hand up his sternum. His ring catches my eye. I wonder where mine are now? I left them with Lexi the day that I left. She gave them back to him.

"Right. Guess so."

I sit up and slide off the bed, not even bothering to hide my nakedness from him. He's seen it. The man pulled a damn tampon out of my vagina and had his fingers up my ass a few hours ago... Pretty sure any ounce of anxiety or embarrassment I had over my body has gone out the window.

Entering the en suite, I turn the shower on to almost scalding and then step in. The hot water soothes away any of the achiness I obtained from the plane ride, dancing, and early morning extracurricular activities.

The glass door slides open and Diego enters, taking up all of my space. "I have request."

"Request?" I ask incredulously. This is going to be rich coming from him.

"Okay. A *demand*. You know me too well," he laughs as he slathers shampoo into his hair.

"What's that?" I ask, washing my body with his coconut body

wash instead of my own. He notices and smirks before shifting behind me to rinse his hair of the suds.

Cobalt eyes swirl with the intensity of a Category 5 hurricane. He hooks a muscular arm around me and tugs me forward. Our bodies slap together on contact as his hand trails down my tailbone and over the swell of my ass. The palm of his hand comes down hard, the sting of the hot water adding to the potency of it.

"This is mine and mine *only*," he growls.

He stalks towards me until my shoulders hit the tiles and his right hand lands flat against the space next to my head. Getting nose to nose with me before kissing me senseless, he releases an exasperated sigh.

"I want to fuck you into oblivion right now," he groans. The promise lacing his voice has me clenching my thighs together to ease the ache of desire.

"I think I want you to fuck me into oblivion right now," I laugh, staring at his frustratingly handsome face.

"You *think*? Gee, *Mariposita*. That wasn't what it seemed like last night when you were swallowing my cock or when you arched your back so far off the bed you nearly snapped your spine." Diego slides his hand off the wall and wraps it around my neck. He lowers his lips to my ear. "Do you need a reminder of how much you wanted me last night?"

Holy. Shit. My core throbs at the words coming out of his dirty mouth. His vulgarity has me turning into a puddle of need at his feet and circling the drain. This man will be the death of me.

Yes! I need a fucking reminder.

I also need to get to the hospital, to the toy store, and then back here for Kian's first birthday. All while trying to keep my wits about me. That is, if I am going to get through the rest of the day with both Liam and Diego. Oh, and let's not forget the talk I need to have with him about potentially moving in with Liam.

Today is going to be fun. *So much fun.*

I need espresso. *Stat.* And maybe another orgasm...

"Maybe later," I shrug, acting uninterested as he releases me to finish up his shower.

"*Definitely* later," he sneers, placing a chaste kiss to my lips.

He steps out, leaving me alone with my thoughts. And in a whirlwind of emotions.

I let out a shaky breath.

Get it together, Madison.

TURNS OUT, Dad won't be allowed to have any visitors. The hospital has a bad virus going around and is just now limiting the visitors to one person—typically, the spouse. You will be required to gown up before entering the room each time. Luckily, they anticipate him to be heading home in the next two days. I can visit then.

On a brighter note, I was able to talk to him for a while. He sounds like shit, but I guess that is to be expected when they break open your ribs and bypass three of your major arteries.

He's one of the strongest men I know, my father. I can guarantee you in a few days he'll be asking to go back to the gym —even though we all know he can't. Try telling him that. This is the same man that pulled his breathing tube out when he woke up.

Before anyone in the house could see me, I snuck out, grabbing an Uber to my favorite coffee shop a few blocks over from here. They have the best pastries and their espresso is smooth and rich, barely acidic. *Still not Diego's espresso... but a top five.*

The barista recognizes me. She hands me my coffee, and her

and I get to chatting a bit. Apparently, the owner is selling the place.

"A month ago he sold it to a 'mystery buyer'," she air quotes. "Some billionaire from Florida."

"Are you able to stay on?" I ask, knowing how much this job means to her. She's been working here full time, trying to pay her medical bills that racked up from a bad car accident she had a few years ago.

"I'm not sure. I hope so. I love it here."

We exchange numbers and I wish her well before taking off down the block. I am on a mission to find the cutest boutique or toy store for my nephew. I want something unique.

I walk a few more blocks, admiring the holiday decorations. New York City is always magical this time of year. My phone starts to vibrate in my pocket. I toss my empty cup into the trash can next to me and retrieve my phone.

"Hey, Lex." I press a finger to my exposed ear.

"Where are you, girlfriend? Liam is losing his shit over the fact that one of the guys didn't drive you to the hospital."

"I never went. Hospital is on a visitor restriction due to a virus running rampant."

"Oh, damn. Are you okay? How was the rest of your night?"

I bundle my scarf tighter around my neck as a bitter breeze blows down the avenue.

"It was *interesting*. We can talk more about it over dinner. Are you still planning to talk about your wedding tonight?"

"Yes. That's also why I am calling. Conor and I aren't able to attend Kian's birthday. We are on our way to Connecticut. Con needs to take care of some shit at *The Triskelion*. Are you willing to come out with Liam tonight and have a few drinks with us at the club? Liam agreed to it. He said he'll drive you guys there."

"Umm... yeah, I don't see why not."

"Awesome. Thanks, girl. I gotta run. I love ya! See you tonight. I want every detail!"

A laugh carries along the wind before I hang up. She really means it—*every* detail. Heat spreads to my cheeks at the memories of what we did last night.

Suddenly feeling like I'm being watched, I turn around, but find no one behind me. *Weird.* I look left and right before entering the cute baby boutique. Already, I spot the cutest gift. A wooden coffee machine with numbers and fun shaped gadgets. There is even a set of colorful coffee mugs that comes with hand carved and painted donuts and pastries. Yes. *Hell, yes.* It's the perfect sensory and educational gift. Beyond all that, it's straight up adorable.

Of course, his auntie would get him his first coffee machine.

Maybe it'll even make his Uncle Diego crack a smile.

THE HOUSE IS BUZZING with some of the syndicate members and their families. Sel was careful who to invite from her play groups, wanting to keep it more of an inner circle party. The party planner did another incredible job. It went from a Vegas themed party last night to a fully functioning zoo.

I kid you not.

There are animal tanks and exhibits lined up. A petting zoo is out on the patio in the heated tent they left up. Face painting and a craft station is over in the dining room. Cotton candy, popcorn, gummy candies, and ice cream stations are spread out throughout the main floor. There is a man outside with a headset microphone, dressed like Steve Irwin, directing an animal show-and-tell. From what I can hear, they are exhibiting a baby kangaroo.

Oh my God. I need to be out there! I want all the baby animal snuggles.

I crane my neck, trying to get a peek of the cute little joey when a familiar hand lands on my lower back. Liam chuckles next to me.

"Ya want me to ask how much they cost?"

Playfully, I slap his hand away. "No. They shouldn't be someone's pet...but I wouldn't mind heading out there to take a look."

"Come on, princess. I'll come with you."

As we walk towards the patio, I spot Lainey in the kitchen prepping kid-friendly finger foods. My stomach growls just looking at the mini cheeseburger sliders, Dino nuggets, mac and cheese cups, and the cute little grilled cheese dunkers with a side of tomato soup. They even have pizza in the shape of crocodiles.

My kinda food.

Liam must have heard my stomach growl.

"Hungry?" he asks amused.

"Yes. I can just grab something later." I'm not trying to bring attention to myself. Lainey is working, she doesn't need my hunger, along with Liam trying to feed it, ruining her concentration.

Or breaking her heart.

"I'll be two seconds. What do you want? Lainey won't mind. She feeds me before everyone else all the time."

He goes to leave and I grab him by the forearm, lightly digging my nails in. "*Don't.* Lainey may have given you the space you need for all of us to figure things out, but that doesn't mean she's okay with it. She's probably hurting, Liam. I would be. I'll wait until the waiters come around with the food."

His demeanor changes as he takes in what I just said. "You're right. I wasn't trying to hurt her. I just wanted to feed you." Shame replaces his cheerful features.

My thumb rubs away the crescent marks I unintentionally left on his arm.

"I know. Sorry for hurting you. I didn't mean to dig my nails in like that." Now *I'm* the one feeling shame.

We continue to walk out through the glass sliding doors. "Oh, sweetheart. You can dig those nails into me anytime you want." He wiggles his eyebrows forcing a laugh out of me.

Idiot. I just told him not to flaunt us in front of Lainey and here he is making innuendos.

"Please never stop calling me out for being an arse. Where everyone just accepts it from me, you call me out on it. Not only that, but you correct me in a way that's not condescending. So, thank you."

"No problem. Oh maa God, he's sooooo freakin' cute!" I squeal my excitement, skipping over towards the stage. A few children and their parents are surrounding the adorable baby kangaroo.

Liam follows me, leaning against the bar where they have chocolate milk, lemonade, and soda fountains. He grabs himself a lemonade, sticking his cup up in silent question. I decline, shaking my head, far too preoccupied with the baby animals to worry about a drink.

The director comes up to me and offers me the joey. My eyes actually fill with tears of joy at the fact that I am currently holding a baby kangaroo. The soft fur of his coat tickles my fingertips as I run them over his ears and down his back. Liam comes up and snaps a picture of me.

His fingers click away on his phone. "I'm sending this to you. You may want to make it ya dating profile pic. It screams animal lover." He rolls his eyes for good measure.

I adore this side of Liam. The playful, sarcastic man I fell for.

"You're an asshole," I laugh before checking myself. I'm surrounded by kids. They don't need me cursing.

"Alright, everyone. Our next special guest has two claws and a stinger. They are part of the arachnid family. Can anyone guess what it is? The kids are seemingly stumped. I raise my hand shakily.

"A scorpion?" I practically squeak.

"That's right." The animal caretaker removes the blackish-blue scorpion from the tank. "This is an Emperor Scorpion. Right from the rainforests of West Africa, they are one of the largest scorpions in the world. These arachnids are usually docile and not very aggressive. The males tend to be even less aggressive than the females. I have a special pair of gloves for one lucky parent. Would anyone like to hold him?"

"She would." Diego strides down the stairs leading to the tent, pointing right at me.

"No," I whisper, horrified. I grind my teeth and glare at him. *What is he thinking?!*

He takes a step between Liam and I. I shoot Liam a desperate look, silently begging him to back me—but he doesn't.

"It might be a good thing, love. To get over your fear," he concedes, rubbing his fingers over his chin.

"Oh, go to He—Heck." I recover myself before the little kiddos can hear my potty mouth.

The assistant hands me the thick gloves as Diego sits behind me on the floor, bending his legs at the knee and pressing his front against my back. I sit cross-legged on the ground, my hands shaking violently.

Strong, confident, *bare* hands cup around mine.

Steadying them.

Lending me some of his confidence.

"Let's get our girl back," he whispers over my shoulder. He lowers his chin to lean on it. "I overheard Liam talking to Conor about your fear of these little guys."

Anger simmers under my skin knowing Liam was talking about me to Con. What I confessed last night wasn't really a secret, but my words meant more than just fear over a scorpion. I'm sure it wasn't malicious in intent. Still hurts all the same.

"Okay, try to stay still. He shouldn't sting. I'll be right here in case he tries to make a run for it. I just ask that you remain calm," the Steve look-alike requests.

"You are trained to take down a full-grown man. This scorpion isn't a threat unless you threaten it. It can sense your movements. Deep breaths, *Mariposita*," he encourages. "Most times, fear becomes irrational when we let our minds create unlikely scenarios."

The man in the tan khakis places the scorpion into my gloved palms. It twitches and crawls a bit, getting acclimated. Thankfully, it doesn't make a move to scurry away.

Diego tightens his hands around mine, "Even if it does sting you, it feels like a bee sting and its venom won't kill you. You've endured plenty worse than that."

He's right. I have. I study the creature in my hand, feeling slightly sympathetic for trying to kill its friend. At the thought of its kin, the scorpion reacts, bobbing its tail and opening and closing its pinschers.

Fuck. It's like it knows what I was thinking.

Diego inches his body closer to mine, pressing his solid chest against my rigid back and pulling his arms in so they press firmly against mine.

"Don't let your fear control you. *You* control *it.* Remove the spiraling thoughts and you can wrangle it in. Then you *conquer* it."

With caution, he removes his hands from around mine after they cease their shaking. The scorpion doesn't move. It stays completely still, as am I. All the tension I was holding starts to dissipate. This isn't as bad as I had imagined.

After a few moments, the caretaker collects the scorpion and places it back in its enclosure. "How about a round of applause for this brave young lady."

The tiny claps of the kids and the loud whistles Liam is giving off have me feeling proud of myself.

I did it.

Thanks to Diego.

And I guess Liam, too—for not babying me and letting me chicken out.

"Alright, everyone. We are going to take a fifteen-minute break and then we will be back with more animals for you to hold."

Diego extends a hand and helps me up. He tugs me forward, slamming me into him and pressing a kiss to my temple. "I'm proud of you, *Mariposita*."

The sweetest of smiles graces his face to reveal a dimple on his cheek. Which is something I only now noticed. He releases me from his embrace but his hand drops down to claim mine. Liam joins us as we head inside for some food.

"Did you know that scorpions spiritually represent embracing your fears in order to overcome them?" Diego starts. "It aids in your personal growth and serves as a reminder of how resilient you are. Your year in Arizona wasn't a waste, Madison. It was your *scorpion*. You may have felt bored or lonely, but it was all part of your journey. Part of rediscovering yourself. Coming home and embracing what you were running from— that shows how strong you are. Try to remove all the bullshit that's enhancing your fears and focus on conquering it. When you do that, you'll have the answer you're looking for." He shoots me a devastating smile, followed by a knowing wink.

I can't help but stare at him in awe.

Hot and philosophical?

Swoon.

When we enter the kitchen, he kisses the top of my hand and releases it. "After the party, I have to fly to Miami. I have some *business* to take care of," he says vaguely.

"Will you be back tomorrow?" I ask, but it comes out whinier than what I was going for.

The Bone Breaker chuckles. "So eager for me to return?"

"Just curious," I retort, a smile creeping onto my face and calling me out on my bullshit.

Heat spreads to my cheeks and my pulse spikes knowing he's right. I will miss him.

He shoots me an amused look before mouthing, *"Liar."*

"If all goes according to plan, I should be back by tomorrow night. Will you be here?"

Liam answers for me. "We are heading to Connecticut tonight. Conor and Lexi are meeting us at *The Triskelion* to discuss our wedding duties over drinks."

"Ahh. I take it you'll be sleeping at Liam's?"

I turn towards Liam, unsure.

"I have a guest room. She is welcome to stay there while she sorts out moving back home."

Goddammit, Liam.

"You're moving home?" Diego asks astoundedly.

"I want to be closer to my family."

"So, Miami is out of the question? But staying at Liam's is okay? *Right*. Got it." The bitterness in his tone has me wincing.

"Diego..." I touch his arm. "I haven't decided on anything yet. Tonight we may stay there... but that doesn't mean I'll be moving there."

"I need to kiss my nephew goodbye. It's fine. I'm not mad you'll be spending the night with him. I'm disappointed you didn't tell me you were considering moving there. Anyways..." He places a fleeting kiss on my pouting lips. "Be safe tonight. My phone will be on if you need me... or if this asshole bores you to death," he laughs, playfully slapping Liam's back and retreating towards the dining room where Kil and Sel are with Kian.

Feeling a bit let down, I go off in search of some food before joining my sweet little nephew.

CHAPTER 13

LIAM

MADISON'S RESPONSE to Diego leaving tonight was expected. Seeing her pout over him was like a swift kick to the nuts. She never said she *wasn't* comfortable with sleeping at my house tonight...so perhaps we'll get a chance to talk again.

Lainey has all the finger foods being sent around. She's moved on to work on the dessert display. Naturally, I want to be by her side. Yet, my eyes refuse to stray from Madison. The purple-haired goddess is in the dining room with everyone. Those enchanting curls drape around her face as she leans down to help Kian paint a giraffe.

He's one, so not much real painting is getting done, but he's enjoying himself. Giggles and babbles fill the room as he smiles, revealing two little front teeth. Maddy holds his tiny hand in hers, guiding the yellow tipped brush along the ceramic giraffe. Killian and Selena are chatting with Diego—whose eyes keep darting over to Mad. A smile tugs at the corner of his lips watching her engage with the little lad.

Grief hits me like a punch to the gut.

I wanted a family with Madison.

We could have had that by now if everything didn't happen the way it did. Madison must feel me watching her. Sad eyes connect with mine. Moisture pools in her lower lids as Kian open mouth kisses her cheek and pulls her into a hug. Her arms come up to wrap around him, gently cradling his head. Her gaze finds mine again, this time filled with uncertainty. She wipes the tears from her eyes and smiles wistfully.

What if that pregnancy test had been positive? We could have had our own little one running around right now. Diego would have never been given a chance for Maddy to fall for him — because she never would have even made it to Greece.

Why does life have to fucking suck so bad? Madison wants to be a mom more than anything. And yet, she struggles with infertility. I want Madison and a family with her, but it's looking like she wants Diego.

I mean, *shit*. What am I doing here?

Do I even stand a chance?

Deciding no one needs to witness my spiraling pity party, I go off to have a smoke. I pass by Lainey who is adding animal face cupcakes to the top tier of the dessert display. Her hand reaches out to cup my elbow.

"You okay? What's wrong? You seem upset." The nurturing concern in her voice eases the tension building in my chest.

"I just got emotional seeing little Kian, that's all." I smile down at her. No need to burden her with my shit.

"Madison has you all messed up. Doesn't she?" she pushes.

"No. It's not her. It's me. I'm working through a lot of emotions right now, Lain. You look beautiful by the way. The food was awesome." A frown forms on her face as she realizes that's all the interaction she'll get from me.

Placing a brief kiss to her temple, I step away, needing that cigarette now more than ever. My mum would be so ashamed of me for selfishly holding the hearts of two amazing women.

After taking the elevator, I find my way out to the top deck. Steam swirls in ribbons around the pool which is gradually changing colors. I focus on it, slowing my heart rate down and breathing in and out through my nose. *Ahh.* I feel like I can breathe again. *Why not light up that cigarette?*

Reaching into my jeans pocket, I retrieve my lighter and pack of menthols. The flame of my Zippo ignites as I light the end of my cigarette and pull the nicotine deep into my lungs. I lean over the balcony railing, watching the busy New York City streets. It serves as a great distraction from my racing thoughts.

The grating sound of the sliding door has me turning back around. Madison wraps her sweater tighter around her as she slides the door shut.

I reach into my pack and pull out another cigarette, holding it out between my thumb and middle finger. "Still smoking, lass?"

That familiar statement has her smiling through her own tears as she saunters my way.

"I could use one. I haven't had any in a while," she sniffles, wiping under her eyes with her sleeve.

Handing her the cigarette, I hold out my lighter as she leans in to light it. She inhales briefly before blowing her smoke to the sky. "Thank you."

"Anytime, love," I sigh, placing the lighter back in my pocket before pulling her into me. "That could have been us."

She nods, taking another drag. Circling her back with my free hand, I take a drag of my own. We stand there for a while not saying a word, just comforting one another.

This feels different.

It's sadness over what we may never have together.

Acceptance in a way.

I snub my cigarette out in the ashtray on the cocktail table and she does the same.

"You'll have that family, baby. Even if it's not with me."

"Yeah, maybe one day," she agrees morosely. "What time did you want to head to Connecticut?"

"Can you be ready in an hour?"

"Yes. I'm pretty much ready, I just need to freshen up and change."

AN HOUR LATER, I'm knocking on Diego's door. Madison swings it open a few seconds later, looking incredible. Straight white teeth form a smile under her dark purple lipstick. Her hair is in waves around her shoulders and dark smokey makeup enhances her gorgeous eyes. Madison laughs in reaction to my staring—she's absolutely radiant.

Definitely in a far better mood than earlier.

An overnight bag sits at the entrance of the door, sparking hope in my chest.

Guess we are staying.

Perfect.

She does a little twirl in her form fitting black dress. Leather pointed pumps wrap around her feet. They are sexy as fuck. My eyes trace up her muscular calves, then thighs, all the way up to her round arse. It takes me back to the night we went to *The Triskelion* for her surprise party. I had to shove my fists into the pockets of my slacks to prevent myself from reaching out for her. She wasn't mine. She was Killian's. What a turn of events that night ended up being.

Madison is the only woman I have ever taken back to my house in Connecticut.

A small leather wristlet hangs off her wrist as she opens her arm to scan her body up and down. "You like? Selena lent me one of hers. It's a little snug, but it works."

"You look incredible, Madison." I grasp a strand of her hair between my fingers. "I love this color on you."

"Thank you. I was actually considering dying it back to black soon. Believe it or not, the purple is hard to maintain. Plus—it was sort of a phase. I tend to change my hair color during major changes in my life."

I grab her overnight bag and sling it over my shoulder. Fidgeting with the strap, I try to distract myself before I do something crazy, like pull her face to mine and kiss the hell out of her. *I don't think she's ready for that.*

"I see, so that's why you went red when I first saw you at the gala?"

She suppresses a laugh as I guide her to the elevator. "That was all the stylist. But I did give her free range. I needed a change. Plus, I was really conflicted on my feelings at the time—similar to how I feel now."

"And when you dyed it back to black before we went to *The Triskelion* for your surprise party?"

"I knew then I wanted to go back to my roots. I wasn't that girl. The one in the lavish gowns and jewels. I wanted to be the Madison you met at the college bar." *My heart soars knowing the truth. She dyed it back for her and for me. I knew it.*

"Shit, do you need a jacket?"

"I'll be fine. The car is heated and we'll be going right into the club."

"Take this," I shrug out of my sports jacket and place it over her shoulders. "I don't need you catching a cold. You need to be able to see your father in a few days."

Madison smiles up at me as her hands close the jacket around her exposed chest. That's when I spot my necklace. How I hadn't noticed it until now is beyond me. *Oh right, I was admiring the body I've kissed every inch of.*

Black diamonds of the raven sparkle between her clasped hands. The pendant, proudly perched between her collarbones.

"Nice necklace," I smirk.

"I was feeling nostalgic."

"I see that," I shoot her a dazzling smile, my mood significantly changing for the better.

The elevator takes us to the lobby where my Audi R8 Spyder is waiting out front. There is not even a chance of snow in the forecast and we haven't had any precipitation the last few days. Tonight is the perfect night for a ride in my new toy.

I take her hand and open the doors to the building, revealing the shiny chrome car idling at the curb. Kieran is there watching it for me. *And probably jerking off to it.* He was more than willing to pull it around for me.

"Have a safe trip." He pats my back and takes a step back.

Pulling the handle, I hold open the door and help Madison in before shutting it. I toss her overnight bag in the trunk and eagerly slip into the driver seat. Madison notices my excitement as we buckle in.

"New car?" she guesses with a shy smile.

"Yes." I rev the engine for emphasis. Maddy's smile widens as she waves to Kieran and we enter into traffic.

AN HOUR and a half later we are pulling up to the back door of the club. Madison and I talked the entire ride about her time in Arizona. I learned how much she enjoys working at the coffee shop and her dreams of owning her own. It's pretty fucking cool that she took some classes on how to bake pastries. If it wasn't going to be weird as hell, I would ask Lainey to teach her a thing or two. Lainey's pastries and baked goods are fucking amazing.

I step out of the car and Madison does the same, not waiting for me to open her door. *Stubborn woman.* I'm trying my best to impress her tonight. I'd like to be the perfect gentleman she always said I was. The one that perhaps I lost sight of after losing her.

"Here." Her hand glides across mine as she hands me back the jacket.

The static between us is like a live wire. Where earlier I thought the breaker was completely shut off...

Now, I'm not so sure.

"We can't have the leader of the Tri-State Syndicate looking like a slob," she teases.

"Oh, sweetheart...I was this close," I hold out my fingers in reference, "To wearing my jeans and leather jacket. I fucking miss working the college bar. You know how much I hate wearing this damn fancy shit."

"I like you rugged. But...I'll admit, I do enjoy seeing you dressed up." A blush spreads across her face as she walks to the entrance. Ryan opens the door for us and his eyes widen as he notices Madison. "Hey, Ry. Good to see you again."

"The same to you, Madison. Welcome back, he says astonishingly. He turns his attention to greet me. "Sir, Conor is here and waiting for you in the VIP lounge."

"Thanks, Ryan," I respond, gripping his shoulder.

The metal door clicks closed behind us as we enter the elevator. Madison is fidgeting with her wristlet and struggling to get her lip gloss out. When she finally manages, she coats her lips with a shiny gloss, adding a shimmer to her already darkened lips. Pressing them together with a *pop*, she places the tube back into her wristlet and leans against the back of the elevator.

I can't tell if she's toying with me. The sexual chemistry in this elevator is sizzling. So, I settle on testing the waters. Claiming her hand in mine, I lead us out of the elevator and down the hallway to my office. Her brow raises in question.

"I forgot something." *I didn't.* But perhaps the memory of me finger fucking her on this desk will decide how our night is going to go.

Eyes like melted chocolate widen as I close the door behind us. The black of her pupils expands as she takes in my oak desk.

CHAPTER 14

MADISON

THIS ROOM. *This desk.* My heart rate picks up until it's punishing my ribs. The night we came into this office changed our course. It changed *everything.* Being back here right now has my breasts pressing against the tight fabric of Selena's dress.

Liam casually strolls around his desk, digging through his top drawer for God knows what. Part of me feels he brought me in here to toy with me. I guess I've been toying with him, too. My little lip gloss stunt was something I used to do around him. It worked like a charm, always invoking passionate kisses that led to *more.*

Lifting my chin, I watch as he collects a roll of condoms and tucks them into his pocket.

He strolls back around the desk and leans against it, crossing his arms over his broad chest. A tattooed hand comes up to pinch the bridge of his nose as he lets out a frustrated sigh.

"What are we doing, Madison? Because right now, I want to rip that fucking dress off you and fuck you right here on my desk. I want to cross the line we never got to the last time we were in here together."

I bite my lower lip as my hesitant eyes meet his. Lust ping pongs between us, waiting for one of us to stumble first.

"We..." I say shakily, sliding my tongue over my lips to wet them.

He takes one determined step forward.

"Lex and Con..." I look behind me at the door.

When I turn around he's in my space, smelling of lavender and cedarwood.

And *destruction*.

His hands come up to cup both sides of my jaw. Lowering his scruffy face to mine, he inches closer until our noses touch and his lips are a breath away.

"I miss you, baby," he groans.

"I miss you, too. But... Liam... this feels so... *foreign*. It's not like I've dated two men before. If that's what we are doing here. I don't know how this works. I'm *married*. And until I get a divorce that title feels binding. It feels wrong to want to fuck you," I ramble, listing every excuse in the book.

The truth is, I want to see if my feelings for Liam are still alive. I just feel extremely guilty for doing so. For Lainey's sake and for Diego. Even though both men let me know I am free to make my own choices, it feels like I'm cheating on them both.

"Stop overthinking. Follow what you're feeling in this moment. Let your heart lead you. Diego knows what we are up to tonight. Just feel, baby." His soft lips brush against mine as he says it.

Liam walks us back until I hit the door and cages me in like he always does. It feels so good having his firm body pressed against mine. Those muscular arms act like blinders on either side of me.

All I can *see* is him.

All I can *feel* is him.

Like the familiar ridge of his erection grinding into me.

My nipples harden under the thin fabric of this dress. I opted to go braless, considering the dress is a little tight. You can see every edge and strap outline.

Rough hands slide up the side of my thighs and grip my ass.

Oh, fuck it.

I jump up and wrap my arms and legs around him. The black satin fabric rides up as he presses his hard length further into the apex of my thighs. As I moan he claims my lips and devours them like a starved man. His tongue fights with mine for dominance as groans leave both our mouths.

"Mmm, baby. Look how easy it is to fall back into us again."

"Stop talking. I don't want to think. I need to feel, Liam," I beg.

I shut him up, kissing him hard as his hand slides my lace panties over, slipping his fingers through my arousal.

My head slams back against the wooden door at the feel of his fingers breaching my entrance. They slide all the way in up to his knuckles. The fullness leaves me breathless. Tattooed fingers curl inside me, hitting my G-spot just right. I start panting as his lips lick and suck on my neck. Chest rising and falling, desire and passion sweep over me. The sound of his metal belt unclasping warns me of what's next.

I want this right? I want to see what this is between us. We've always had an amazing sex life. God. When was the last time I actually had sex?

It couldn't have been my wedding night...

His fingers pump in and out of me as I feel the outline of his cock pressed against his boxer briefs.

He lowers me to the floor, removing his fingers and grabbing the roll of condoms. "As much as I'd like to fuck you raw, it's probably best we use protection."

"Yeah. No, totally," I say breathlessly.

He stares at me and then the condoms. The frantic moment of lust dissipates. Now it just feels interrupted and forced.

I slide my underwear back over my hips and tug my dress down. He doesn't object, placing the condoms back into his pocket and tucking himself into his pants before rebuttoning and buckling them. He runs a hand through his hair and blows out a breath, careful not to make eye-contact with me. I do the same, walking over to his private bathroom and fixing my hair. Thank you, Jesus for a twenty four hour lip stain. It didn't go anywhere.

When I come back out, he has the door opened and a hand in his pocket.

"Let's continue this later? Somewhere a little more... practical?" he laughs, breaking the period of silence we just had.

"Yeah. Let's see where the night brings us," I nod, suddenly feeling shy around him.

It's not that I didn't want to have sex with him. I did. I was more than turned on. But that pause to wear a condom had me reevaluating. It gave us a minute to look beyond the haze of lust and realize we may have been falling back into old habits.

Because it was how things used to be.

Not because we thought this moment was right.

Having attachments to others doesn't help the cause either. Where Lainey was a thought in his mind, Diego was a thought in mine.

Makes for one awkward moment.

"HOLY... HE DID WHAT?!" Lex whisper-shouts as we chat alone in the bathroom. Liam and Con are back in the VIP lounge. The two of us are a few martinis deep.

"He took out a roll of condoms, Lex."

"I mean smart, yes. Can't blame the guy for wanting to be safe for everyone involved. But what a way to make it awkward. He knew what he was getting going into his office."

"Yeah...*God.* How do people date multiple partners at once? I can barely keep my emotions in check around the two of them."

"Back to Diego...you gonna lose your back door virginity to him?" She waggles her eyebrows suggestively.

"I'm going to need a lot more time for that... Diego is huge!" I emphasize with my hands.

Lexi giggles and grips my arm as she leans over. "Girl, you need to get laid. It's been too long. I have an idea, why don't you just fuck the both of them at the same time?"

"*Lexi.* Be serious," I admonish.

"I am. You have two men willing to let you fuck the other. Take full advantage, girl. You know once you choose, they are gonna go all cave-man protective and that window for threesomes will be *poof.* Gone. Probably forever."

I shake my head, partially turned on by the idea. Just think about what a disaster that would be. Fucking the two most alpha possessive men I have ever met.

I can't see them sharing nicely.

As we leave the bathroom and head back towards the suite, gunshots go off. Ice runs through my veins as I shove Lexi behind me and search for Liam or Con.

Shit. The suites are sound proof.

They probably can't hear the commotion. It sounds fucking close, too. Jostling Lexi through the crowd, I hurry her and I into the nearest room. It's one I haven't been in before. The lights are off but there is a dim red night light on either side of this massive bed.

Lexi is violently shaking next to me. I search for a lock on the door but there isn't one.

What the fuck?

"Who has a room in a club like this without a lock?" I vocalize my thoughts.

"It's for BDSM, ya idiot. People like to watch." Lexi manages to throw sarcasm my way even in a tense situation.

This is why I fucking love her.

"Go hide in that closet. I'll keep watch at the door," I whisper-shout at her.

"I'm not leaving you, Mad."

"Liam trained me. It'll be okay. Go. *Please*, Lex," I beg.

I can barely see her eyes but understanding crosses them as more gunshots go off.

"Okay. But if I hear anything I'm coming out."

"Fine. Now, *go*," I demand through gritted teeth.

The popping sounds closer, making me wince.

Then it stops completely.

The door handle jerks as the outline of a person comes into view through the frosted glass.

I press my body as flat as possible against the wall behind the door. If they open it, they may not see me, which will give me the advantage to take this fucker out.

Just as predicted, the door slowly creaks open. Hysteria and yelling fill the space from the level below. My fist clenches as I prepare to go down with a fight.

As the intruder shuts the door, I pounce, knocking him to the floor. The position allows me to come up behind him. I wrap my thighs around his neck, cutting off his air supply. The guy is good, he manages to roll us over, getting me under him. I pray he doesn't have a weapon. Liam trained me to disarm someone—but not in the fucking dark!

I can barely see.

My fist meets his jaw as I get in a good punch. *Yes, Maddy!* His hand clamps down on my throat, squeezing. I throw my knee into his ribs, trying to knock him off me.

"Fucking, bitch. You should have been dead by now."

"Sorry. I'm not that hard to kill," I snarl, refusing to give away my nerves.

His fist slams down across my lip, splitting it. Pain ricochets across my jaw as blood drips into my mouth and down my chin. I use that to my advantage and spit into the fucker's face. It gives me a second to move—and I do, throwing my fist into his nose and hearing a satisfying crunch. I use the full force of my body to roll him off me and scramble back to my feet. Then doing what I was trained to do, I kick him in the temple with my heel. He falls back, hitting the floor with a thud. Not wasting another second, I dash for the door.

He's here for me. If he wakes up, he won't go after Lexi. At least, I hope I am making the right decision. Please, God. Let her be alright. I need to get to Liam. He's only a few doors down.

Sending up a silent prayer, I make a run for it. Except, the prayer doesn't reach very far. I trip over my heel and crash at the threshold of the door. Black shoes catch my attention as I lift my head. It's pounding from the adrenaline and the punch the dickhead landed.

My eyes scrunch closed with anticipation of the man in front of me attacking. But it never comes. I peek one eye open. Liam's tattooed knuckles come into view as he pulls me to him. Ryan and Conor rush in to restrain our attacker. Noticing he's knocked out, Con looks at me conflictingly.

"Lexi! She's in the closet. I told her not to come out," I scream as blood splatters Liam's shirt.

Liam cradles my head as Conor leaves the unconscious asshole with Ryan and goes to get his woman. She comes out trembling like a leaf and clinging to him.

"Madison, are you okay? I couldn't see or hear anything in there. I was worried sick. If you didn't come get me in another minute I was coming out with this cane and a whip. The closet is full of all sorts of freaky shit." With a clank, she drops the sex toys to the floor and wraps her arms around Con.

"Wish I knew that sooner," I grumble. "I'm okay."

"No you're not," Liam growls. His fingers brush over my split lip. "Restrain that fucker in here with those chains. Use the metal cuffs. I don't want him going anywhere. There are too many high end clients here tonight. We don't need a show. As it is, we pulled the fire alarm upstairs and cleared all the college kids out. I'm not looking for a headache with the cops."

"Yes, Sir," Ryan confirms.

121

Liam starts dishing out commands. "Con. I'll take Lexi and Madison back to my place. Ya mind talking to the Chief of Police? I know you and him have a good relationship. Meet me back at the house when this is all settled. I want the fucker moved to the shed behind my house. I'll take it from there."

"Of course. Don't worry, boss. This one is easy to clear up. It would seem he's working alone."

Con kisses Lexi roughly before heading out of the room. He must have been a ball of nerves coming in here. *Poor guy.*

"Come on, ladies. You're safe." He nods to the man now suspended from the ceiling, "This one will be dealt with after you girls get cleaned up and are situated."

It's then that I recognize my attacker. "Liam, that's the bartender from the gala. The one that served Lainey and I our margaritas."

He glances back and his eyes narrow to slits. "I knew that clown was off. I need to talk to Kil about our security measures. How long has he been employed by us?" he mumbles under his breath, more so to himself.

We walk to the car in silence, surrounded by a bunch of Liam's men from *The Triskelion.* Lex and I hold hands the entire time. Liam leaves his R8 and takes the Range Rover they keep here at all times. The windows are bullet proof. Not to mention, there is a ton more room for the both of us.

I slide into the backseat with Lexi, hugging her to me. She isn't used to this. I shouldn't be either, but I am. It comes with the territory of dating a man in the underworld.

Liam glances back in his rearview every few minutes as he navigates us to his home. Lexi lays her head on my shoulder, releasing a massive sigh.

"I can stitch up your lip when we get back to Liam's. It might not require it, but I'll need to take a closer look," she offers.

"Better do a good job, can't look botched in my Maid of Honor photos," I laugh, trying to lighten the mood.

Liam chuckles from the front seat as Lexi joins him. "*Matron of Honor*," they say in unison.

"Ugh. Guys, come on. That title makes me sound so old," I complain.

"That title makes you sound so *married*," Liam growls.

Guess the moment we had earlier is gone.

"Lay off, Liam," Lexi stands up for me. "She just knocked out a man twice her size. The least you can do is show her how proud you are. Who gives a fuck about her marital status. We both know that isn't the problem here. Your jealousy and control issues are."

Shots fired. And this time by Lexi.

Damn, Lex.

We arrive at Liam's at the perfect time. Lexi and I hop out and follow the lit pathway to his front door.

"Thank you," I whisper.

"Welcome. You're a badass and he's being a pussy. If he wants you he'll prove it. If not, you know where you stand. It's okay to let that relationship die out if it's not there, Mad. Although, I still think a threesome could help you decide..." she suppresses a giggle as Liam unlocks the door for us.

He looks down at me as he holds the door open, questioning if what he just overheard was true.

Feeling ballsy and full of adrenaline, I just shrug and wink. *Ow.* My face must be swelling.

They would never agree to that.

But the way Liam is looking at me right now says otherwise.

CHAPTER 15

LIAM

AFTER A QUICK SWEEP of the house, I meet the girls back in the entryway.

All clear.

"Lex, help yourself to the guest room shower. It's right down this hallway here," I extend my arm, gesturing to the door at the end of the hall. "Madison, I'll help you get cleaned up in my room. You can use my shower. I want a look at your injuries."

Lex looks at me, wondering what move to play here. "Alright. I could use some tea to calm down after all the events of tonight. I'll get cleaned up and meet Maddy in the kitchen in a half hour. If she needs stitches, come and get me, please."

I tilt my head slightly, encouraging her to start moving. Maddy is looking pale and ready to either vomit or lose it.

"Con has some of his clothes in the closet. He stays here when he's working the overnight at *The Triskelion*. Grab something warm. I'll get the fire going, you girls can warm up by it with your tea."

Remembering her way around, Madison starts walking towards my bedroom. It's a few doors down from the hall bathroom, two other guest rooms, and my office. With haste she books it down the hall. The fire can wait a little longer.

Madison needs me.

I follow her, she's already trying to undress. The bedroom door was left open and I can see her struggling to get her dress off. The zipper snagged a quarter of the way down. As it is, the dress fits her rather snugly. Frustrated hands tug at the material, hoping it will give.

It doesn't.

"Ugh!" She stomps her foot, kicking her heels into the air to get them off.

That's my cue, I jog over to her, dodging a flying heel and take in her disheveled, pre-melt down. In an instant I've got her curled into my arms as I cradle her head.

"It's the adrenaline hangover. It's like a panic attack, sweetheart. You're okay. I'm right here."

"Get this fucking dress off me right now. I can't breathe, Liam. *Please*, I can't fucking breathe," she sobs. She's hyperventilating. Her breathing has turned staccato.

Spinning her around, I rip the dress at the zipper seam and pull it down her body. She steps out of it and backs into me as my arms come back around her, my head resting on top of hers.

"Breathe, baby." I inhale deeply, having her mimic my movements. Tremors shake the both of us as her body tries to calm down.

"Breathe. I'm right here. I'm not letting you go," I say soothingly.

Her head bobs against my chin as she nods. Slow, even breaths replace the erratic, panicked ones.

Good girl.

Christ. I hate seeing her like this. She did good. Lexi is absolutely wrong. I am proud of her. But this is where Madison and I differ. If she still wants to be my woman, as I want her to be, she needs to be protected at all times.

She is always going to be a target.

It's unfortunately the nature of our lives. Even in our own damn club it can happen. It happened in our home last year.

From here on out she will have someone with her. I was lenient tonight because she's been asking me to trust that she can handle herself.

And she can, I know she can—*I fucking trained her.*

That doesn't mean in situations like tonight she won't end up traumatized and physically hurt. Seeing blood on her skin and redness around her neck has my hands balling into fists around her.

"Let's get you in the shower. I want to take a look at that lip, baby." I clench my teeth with enough pressure to snap my jaw, just barely able to get the words out. *Cue the tension headache.*

The anger coursing through me is like a pressure cooker. At any moment it will blow. It needs a release, an outlet.

Con better get that son of a bitch to the shed soon.

Dropping my arms to cup her under the legs, I carry her feeble body to the shower. It's a walk-in, there is no glass. I place her down on the bench and turn the water on, testing the temperature. Like most women, she prefers it practically scalding, so I crank it up a notch until thick steam permeates the room. Completely zoned out, she pulls her legs up and wraps her arms around them, laying her head on her knees.

Fuck. Not giving a damn about my clothes, I walk under the spray and sit next to her. Steam swirls around us as she tilts her head to look at me.

"He said I should have been dead by now," she mumbles groggily, her voice horse from nerves and asphyxiation.

The organ in my chest skips a beat causing my own adrenaline to momentarily spike. *This was personal.* It wasn't a threat towards me or Diego. This was a direct threat towards Madison.

Godfuckingdammit.

The girl comes home for a few days and already she has a threat against her.

"Did he say anything else?" I ask, my voice coated with too much ire.

I'm trying to reel it in. Trying to control it. My hands shake as I tilt her head up to look at her lip. It is going to need stitches. Definitely way too deep and the blood is still having a hard time coagulating. I grab a wash cloth and gently wet it, pressing it to her lip.

"No. He didn't have time. I spit blood in his face." Although it comes out monotone, there is a hint of pride there. Her quick thinking definitely gave her the upper hand.

"This is going to need stitches, love. I'll get you cleaned up and into fresh clothes. Lexi can stitch you up in the kitchen."

She nods, removing the washcloth from my hand and holding it to her lower lip.

While she tends to the wound, I shampoo her hair, gently massaging her head and scanning her scalp with the tips of my fingers for any further lacerations. Seems okay.

"Anything else hurt?"

"No," she clips.

Grabbing the detachable shower head, I rinse the suds from her purple locks before moving on to add conditioner. I leave it in, letting it work its magic on her thick strands while soaping up a loofah and cleaning her body. Madison uncurls, allowing me to clean her properly. Her body is still limp with exhaustion.

With legs like a newborn calf, she stands and walks herself beneath the spray to rinse out the conditioner. Suds from the body wash run down her beautiful breasts and over her stomach. After a bit of a struggle to remove my wet clothes, I finally reach out to her, clasping a hand behind her back. She reaches for the loofah, adding a bit of soap before scrubbing my body with it. Her eyes won't reach mine, purely focused on the task at hand.

"That's good, baby. Don't worry about me. I'll need another

shower after what I have planned for later," I try to bite back a growl. That fucker is going to wish he never stepped foot in my club. Never laid a hand on what is mine.

And she is mine.

She always will be—even if it ends platonically, Madison will always be part of my syndicate and family.

Dainty hands replace the loofah, running up my chest to clasp my face. "I'm sorry, Liam. For earlier."

Lacing my fingers through hers I bring them to my lips, kissing them. "Don't worry about that now, baby. I'm just glad you're safe."

I reach behind her and turn the water off, grabbing two towels off the vanity. I secure one around my hips before bundling her in the other, helping her onto the bath mat.

Shock is always the result of moments like these. I'm so far past that feeling now, it no longer phases me. Madison has had her fair share, but this was different. She fought back and won. That hand to hand combat, that rush of adrenaline, it's a lot to come down from. When you finally do, you end up crashing. I need to get her warmed up and in bed.

The chill of my bedroom hits us as we exit. She stands there by the bathroom door looking broken and lost. I dig through my drawers until I find a pair of sweatpants with a drawstring and one of my sweatshirts. I place them on the dresser and toss on a fresh pair of boxer briefs. The sensation of her eyes on my body has my anger easing and lust filtering in.

When I turn around to dress her, the white fluffy towel is now forgotten about on the floor. This goddess is standing with her hands on her hips, stark naked. Her pink nipples are pebbled and the bronze skin around them is dusted with goosebumps. Wet violet hair clings to her arms and over the swell of her breasts leaving water droplets dripping down the center of her chest. I want to lick each one, tracing my tongue over each nipple before climbing higher to lap the water at her neck. My cock pulses, tenting my boxers which directs her gaze to the V at the elastic waistband.

I can't.

Not now.

She needs her lip fixed and some rest.

"Liam..." I know that tone. God, I fucking love that tone. It's sexy as hell and has my patience wearing thin. If I don't change this ship's course soon, I'll end up inside her the rest of the night.

Grabbing the thick navy blue sweatshirt, I hold it out in front of me.

"Arms up, love."

Rejection clouds her eyes. She wants me. We have always helped each other through our tough moments by being as physically close as possible. Not being able to give her what she needs right now is killing me.

Her right hand grips the sweatshirt while her other retrieves the sweatpants on my dresser. She dresses quickly, shielding her perfect body from me before heading back into my en suite. Drawers slam open and closed as she searches around.

"I need a brush," she snaps.

I reach around her to pull open the top drawer, handing her one.

She tugs at the handle, avoiding my skin touching hers. Anger courses through her as she aggressively combs through the knots. It sounds fucking painful—yet she hasn't even flinched.

"Mad. It's not that I don't want to..." I say hesitantly.

"Save it," she snarls, pointing the brush at me before continuing her task. Fiery eyes meet mine in the mirror before continuing. "That's twice tonight you stopped. In our past we *never* would have stopped. Because *nothing* could have prevented me from being with you. Especially after moments like that. It's how we heal each other." Her voice is raspy and full of fire.

"Don't you remember the night at Declan's pool house? Our shower?"

She flips her head forward as a few drops of blood drip onto the tile. Securing a hair tie around her messy bun, she side-steps me into the bedroom and out the door.

Goddamnit. She's absolutely right. Why am I being so cautious around her? So gentle.

This isn't me.

And this certainly isn't *us*.

The real reason is because she doesn't feel like mine anymore. *My woman.* Certainly not in the romantic sense. She's the woman I wanted to spend the rest of my life with. The same woman I fucking proposed to before she married another man. That fact has me scrubbing a hand down my face and releasing a sigh before heading out after her.

SNIP.

Whistle.

Crackle.

"There. All done. Only needed five stitches," Lexi sighs her satisfaction.

"*Only.*" Madison rolls her eyes at her best friend. "That's one too many."

"It'll heal. The mouth heals pretty quickly." Lexi says, dabbing antibiotic ointment onto it.

My eyes drift off the two of them to the kettle on the stove. I grab the handle, pouring water into the two mugs on the counter. Shuffling over to the refrigerator, I hit the ice button, dispensing two cubes and placing one in each mug. It crackles like the fire, taking the heat out of the beverages.

A man can only hope to do the same with Madison.

She's currently fuming.

The ladies are sitting by the fire. I can only see Maddy's profile, but her body language screams pissed. Thankfully, the anxiety attack has subsided to be replaced with hatred towards me.

Ya know what? I can't even blame her. Here I am catching the Hail Mary she threw, only to fucking fumble it, just to watch Diego recover it and regain possession.

I approach them, placing the mugs down on the brick by the fire. "Make sure you both drink up. Your bodies need to warm up."

"Thanks, Liam," Lexi says gently, smiling up at me.

Madison doesn't say a damn thing, she just takes a sip, scalding the taste buds right off her tongue—*as usual.*

"Con is on the other end of my property. I have a shed where I take care of...situations like tonight. I'm going to head over there. I'll be gone for a while. At least a few hours."

As if snapping out of a trance, she looks up, placing her mug back down. "Okay. Can I come?"

Lexi looks as appalled as I am.

"Abso-fucking-lutely-NOT. Stay here. You need rest, sweetheart."

"No. Stay with me," she demands, her voice holding a hint of neediness to it. And trust me, I want to. I can't think of anything else I'd rather be doing right now.

Confliction hits me hard.

I need to extract information out of this guy.

He was after Madison. We need to know why and if he is working with anyone else. I don't want to scare her, so I don't say any of those things.

"I...Madison, I can't. Things have changed now that I've become leader. I need to go, I'm sorry, love," I say with authority.

Avoiding the pained look in her eyes, I spin on my heel and head to my room to change.

This is my favorite sweatshirt— it still smells like her.

CHAPTER 16

MADISON

CALLOUSED fingers run over my hip, pulling me back into a firm body.

"I'm so sorry, baby." The scent of whiskey and lavender wraps around me like a scarf and helps loosen my eyelids.

They crack open as I spin around in his arms. "Liam? What time is it?" I ask groggily.

"Just after 3 AM." His voice is rough as his thumb skims over my still numb lip.

"Did you get what you needed from him?" My vision adjusts to the dark, taking in red-rimmed eyes and the broken skin around his knuckles.

"No. The bastard won't break. Usually by now they would have—1 don't want to risk killing him without the information we need. So I called in *reinforcements*." Resignation coats his words.

Why did he say it like that? Is Killian coming? Does he feel like he's failing as a leader by calling in backup?

His arm curls around me, pulling me in closer. "I handled this whole night like an eejit. I've been walking on eggshells around you, Madison. I'm so terrified of fucking this up with you, that I am quite literally fucking this up with you. I was so damn terrified when one of my men came in to alert me of the active shooter. All I could think of was that you weren't next to me. I couldn't protect you. I couldn't shield you from a fucking bullet. I may have trained you well, Madison, but you're not bulletproof. When my search came up empty after checking the restroom and then the two rooms before the one I found you in, my heart sunk. I couldn't handle the possibility that you had been shot or killed. The moment I got to the third room and saw you laying prone there at the entrance, and that *bastard* on the floor behind you—I shut down. My brain just kept reminding me of what *could* have happened and not fully comprehending that you were safe in my arms. That you had taken him down yourself."

"I'm okay, Liam. You trained me well," I try to reassure him, still groggy.

His chest rumbles against mine as he lowers his forehead to mine. "I can't lose you, Madison."

"You didn't," I whisper, looking up into his worried eyes.

"No, I didn't." His hands cup my face before he lowers his lips to mine. He's gentle at first, careful of my stitches. My eyes close, savoring this moment. When we break apart, I lower my head to his chest as his arms lock around me. I'm not sure how long I stay like that, listening to the steady rhythm of his heart, the calming rise and fall of his chest. Lavender and cedarwood are a deadly combination, finally bringing some peace to my racing mind.

My nails comb through his hair before I pull him closer to me. Featherlight strokes of his fingertips tickle my skin as they lift the hem of my sweatshirt. Hesitating a moment, his eyes search mine, asking silent permission to continue. I reach down and help him lift it over my head. Next to go are my sweatpants. Torturously slow, he unties the string that keeps the oversized pants clinging to my hips. I shimmy out of them, kicking them down to the bottom of the bed. I'm left naked and bare for him under these sheets.

The tips of his fingers glide down over the swells of my breasts and circle each nipple, which hardens at his touch. Each of his palms cups around them as he reacquaints himself with my body. After giving my breasts attention, he moves on to trail his hands down the curve of my waist and over my ass, squeezing it before tugging me closer. All I can feel is the heat between our bodies and the massive erection he has pressed to my center.

"These need to go," I sigh breathlessly, tugging off his sweatpants. He kicks them to the bottom of the bed near mine.

I find my courage, gripping his cock in my palm and running it up and down. Pre-cum beads at the tip, encouraging me to rub it around the swollen head. His fingers circle my clit at the same pace I've set with him. Teeth nip at my neck before his lips find the base of my throat.

Two fingers slip into my throbbing entrance. I hook my leg over his hips before rolling on top of him. He continues to finger fuck me, letting me ride his fingers as I grip his cock from behind, pumping it.

A moan slips out as I toss my head back. My walls clench around his fingers as his cock twitches in my hand.

"Get the condoms. Now," I huff out. "I need this, Liam."

His hand slides away from my core to reach into his end table drawer. The crinkle of plastic opening shoots waves of anticipation through me.

Liam lifts his hips with me on them to sheathe himself. His hands land back on my waist, gripping it tightly as if I may disappear.

I rise and line myself up, sinking slowly down onto his cock. A hiss leaves my lips at the twinge and fullness I feel. It's been over a year since I've had sex. My hips move, remembering how easily we fit together. He meets my thrusts, lifting his hips as mine come down. Our sighs and moans mixed with the sound of slapping fills the room. As my pace picks up so does my blooming orgasm. Liam's cock swells inside me—he's close.

Eager fingers grip my hips almost bruisingly as his jaw clenches. The door to his room creaks open. Liam slams into me over and over again, ignoring whoever is there. As an orgasm is ready to tear through me, I somehow manage to force my head towards the door.

Diego is there. His shadowy figure leaning against the door, arms crossed over his chest, *watching* us. Amused. Turned on.

That should have been a bucket of cold water on my libido. Instead, it makes me moan out.

"You like him watching us, baby?" Liam growls as he continues slamming into me unrelentlessly. "Show him how good you are at riding my cock."

Another moan rips up my throat as my pussy clenches around his pulsing length.

Diego comes up next to us on the bed and grips my neck, curling his fingers around my jaw. Coconut mixes with the smell of lust and lavender as he leans down to kiss me roughly. His tongue runs over the stitches. His other hand dips between my folds, circling my clit. Stars blur my vision, the edges an aurora of changing colors.

My body explodes with pleasure.

Screaming my ecstasy into his mouth.

"*Mariposita...*" he sighs.

"*MARIPOSITA...*" Soft, minty lips brush against mine as the feeling of his fingers register around my neck. It's not rough. He's ever so gentle, just enough to stir me from sleep. I open my eyes to find Diego sitting at the edge of the bed.

"*Diego?* What..." I look around the room in a daze. Sweat

beads on my chest under my sweatshirt. I'm in Liam's guest room bed. No one is here but the two of us. A very *clothed* Diego is looking down at me with a mixture of amusement and anger. Those ocean eyes of his have me wanting to pick up right where I left off in that dream.

A dream.

Fuck. Was any of it real? What Liam said to me. He was here, I could have sworn he was here.

Knuckles caress my cheek as his gaze drops down to my busted lip and then my neck. The muscle in his jaw pulses, taking in the bruising that has started to bloom there.

"He's going to wish Liam ended his pathetic life once I get started on him. But first... care to tell me what you were just dreaming of?" His lips twitch and heat flares in my cheeks.

"I... uhh...was I talking?" I stammer, full of embarrassment.

"I wouldn't say you were talking...more like moaning and some names were mentioned." Lust coats his words, making them come out raspy. Warm fingers graze the hem of my sweatpants where the sheet sits. His thumb paints invisible circles over my exposed skin.

"Is that something you would want? The both of us at once?" His voice is like gravel, rough and full of curiosity.

"I'm... I'm not sure. I think maybe it's just the idea of it that turns me on."

"I may be one kinky son of a bitch, but I don't share. For you, I would be willing to make an exception. If that's something you would want to explore."

He stands, throwing the sheet off me, and extends a hand.

"But first, I need you to see this, see me—*The Bone Breaker.* You'll witness the worst parts of me. That way, when you decide, you will know who truly lurks under this skin."

I place my hand in his and slip on a pair of Liam's slides. *I'm not afraid of him.* We head in the direction of the backyard, I'm assuming to the shed Liam had mentioned.

"Why didn't you answer your phone? I called you a few times. Liam rang me earlier to tell me what happened and that he needed help interrogating. I was done with my assignment early. *Thank fuck for that.* Had the jet ready to take me right to Connecticut."

"My purse is back at the club. I must have dropped it during the commotion," I rasp, my voice groggy from sleep.

"Ahh. Speaking of... I heard you took that motherfucker down, knocked his lights out." A smile is spread across his face, revealing his straight white teeth and adorable dimple. "I'm fucking proud of you, *Mariposita.* So fucking proud, baby. I'm sorry you got hurt. I absolutely hate seeing you like this. But trust me, they *will* pay. You'll see that," he snarls.

It's a promise. Without a shadow of a doubt, he'll be serving his own version of justice.

We walk hand in hand through the woods at the back of Liam's property. The sun is rising, the first set of rays are starting to peek through the trees.

"Thank you, *Ocean Eyes.* I'll be alright. It's only a few stitches," I say, attempting to pacify him by downplaying my injuries.

"It's five. And your neck? Does it hurt? I'm sure it brought back some unpleasant memories."

"It did—briefly—but then I remembered what you told me. To not let my fears control me by spiraling out of control. This wasn't Geraldo. I wasn't back in that cell."

His arm tightens around my waist as he kisses my temple. "It's okay to have felt that way. That doesn't make you weak, baby. I just wish I was here. Coming down from an adrenaline spike is rough. You feeling okay now?" he asks, rubbing his palm up and down my arm.

"Yeah. I actually feel much better."

"You're welcome," he teases smugly.

I elbow him in the ribs. "Cocky, bastard."

A deep laugh echoes through the woods as we approach the opening to a field. A decent sized shed sits there. It's more like an old stable than a shed. Conor and Ryan are guarding the front. Liam is sitting by the door in a folding chair. Blood is caked all over his fingers as he sits there smoking a cigarette. His head snaps up at our approach.

"Why is she here, Diego?" he snarls.

"She's here because she needs to see this. She needs to see what we are all capable of. Stop shielding her from it. Let her get the full picture so she can decide what she wants."

Liam's eyes widen at Diego's suggestion–well, I wouldn't call it that. We all know Diego isn't asking for Liam's permission. His eyes drift over to me.

"You sure you're okay with this?" His eyebrows come together in confusion. *Understandably.* I was just sleeping after having a major panic attack, and now I'm here, about to witness torture and death.

I straighten my spine. "I'm sure."

THE MAN who attacked me is chained to a chair in the middle of the room. All sorts of tools and knives are hung throughout. *The only thing missing is the horror music.* Liam is leaning against the door, arms crossed over his chest and wearing an angry sneer directed at Diego.

Diego could give two shits, his back is to Liam anyway. *The Bone Breaker* is inspecting all the tools dangling from hooks along the wall, getting familiar with the inventory. Already, he has shifted into the man the underworld fears. Even his body language screams *run the fuck away.*

It's slow. Calculated. Lethal.

Every step he takes makes the semi-conscious man twitch.

"I assume you know who I am?" Diego states casually, continuing to check his inventory.

The man's mouth is bound. He doesn't speak regardless. Those eyes however, scream with recognition. I noticed that the second Diego sauntered in.

Clinking fills the space as the man I married collects his tool of choice. It's some sort of plier. *Oh, God.* Like a predator playing with his prey, he circles the man, repeatedly throwing the plier in the air and catching it.

Then suddenly, like a snake, he darts out, leaning over the chair and getting face to face with my attacker. "Who are you working for?" he barks.

Silence.

"Can you hear me?" he bellows, cupping his hand over his mouth like a megaphone. When the man doesn't even blink, let alone respond, Diego continues his mental fuckery. Shrugging he says, "If you aren't going to listen, I guess we won't be needing these..."

Gripping the tip of the man's ear with the pliers, he tugs while pulling a sharp knife from the back pocket of his jeans and slicing his ear clean off. My attacker screams behind the gag. Tears drip down his face and onto his bloodied torn shirt.

It hits the floor and I feel light headed.

Jesus Christ.

Liam takes a step towards me. The heat of him registers at my back.

Diego circles again before leaning over and lowering his voice to a whisper. "Luckily, you have two...Can you hear me now?" he teases into the man's remaining ear. When the guy nods vehemently, Diego laughs to himself. "Good." Cleaning his knife on the man's shirt, he places it back in his pocket.

"I think we got off on the wrong foot." *The Bone Breaker* slams his boot down onto one of them. A crunching noise fills the space along with a groan of agony.

"Again, good thing you have two..." Diego chuckles cryptically. "You see the trend here, Mateo? Or would you prefer I call you MJ? Hmm... maybe just *Junior*."

Mateo? Junior? As in Mateo—Geraldo's right-hand man...This must be his son...

"Fuck you," Mateo seethes behind the gag.

Diego's fist flies out, plowing into the man's jaw. Blood sprays all over him and Diego. Normally, blood doesn't bother me—or gore, for that matter.

Right now, I feel like gagging. I turn my head away from the gruesome scene unfolding before me.

"Hmm.. now what would Mateo's son want with Madison? *Revenge*... That's why you're here. I'll ask one more time. Are you working alone?"

When Mateo continues with his silent act, Diego strolls over to the tools and claims a sawzall. My heart beats harder in my chest wondering what he'll do with it.

I can't turn away, needing to see this through.

Unintentionally, I step back, feeling Liam's rigid body press against mine. Whether he knows it or not, he's giving me the strength I need to continue standing here.

"My bad. Here, let me help you with this," Diego says like a bro.

The saw clicks on. As the serrated blade pulses, Mateo's eyes widen, registering just how much pain he's about to experience. *The Bone Breaker* slices through the fabric of his bindings and further down his lip until he reaches the bottom of his chin. Excruciating screams echo through the small space, encouraging me to close my eyes and lean further into Liam.

"That's *much* better." Diego drops the saw to the floor, prompting me to open them again. He's leaning over Mateo, gripping his face between his clenched fingers. Blood pours over them and runs down Mateo's chin and neck. Crimson stains his shirt and the floor below them.

"My wife needed stitches to close the wound to her lip. The wound *you* gave her. Was only fair to repay the favor. But they don't call me *The Bone Breaker* for nothing, Mateo. I've actually taken quite an interest in teeth these days. Perhaps I should become a dentist. My wife told me comedy was out. Apparently, she doesn't like my jokes." He looks at me and winks before turning back. "Better stick to what I know."

Shoving the pliers into Mateo's mouth, he wiggles it around until he starts gagging on his own blood. "For every stitch my wife needed, you will lose a tooth. And I hate to break it to you, *asere*, but she needed five." After another strangled scream pierces the air, Diego leans back to admire a molar clasped in the plier.

"I'm working alone. You killed my father and cousins. That bitch had you switching teams so fast. It wasn't until *she* showed up that you let a little pussy get in the way of your duty. My father had big plans. She ruined it all," Mateo mutters malevolently over a mouthful of blood, before hanging his head and sobbing through the pain.

Diego slams his fist into Mateo's ribcage, making his head jerk back. The sound of cracking assaults my ears. I inhale sharply. Liam's hand comes up to my shoulder to grip it firmly.

"We can go. You don't need to see the rest, sweetheart," Liam whispers urgently.

I should run the fuck away.

Update: I don't.

Diego issues a vicious kick to Mateo's chest causing the chair to collapse backwards from the force. His head slams against the metal frame, causing more blood to pool on the floor beneath them.

Surprisingly, he's still conscious.

Leaning over him, Diego pulls the pliers back out. One by one he rips the remaining teeth out through agonizing screams.

My breathing has intensified and shallowed. Liam rubs up

and down both my arms now as my body shakes under his touch. *"Madison..."* he begs for me to leave.

"What plans did he have, *Mateo*?" Diego growls, his voice deep and menacing.

"I was going to be leader. My father was going to eliminate both you and Geraldo. But then this pretty little *puta* came along and disrupted those plans. I was going to enjoy your wife and make you watch as I claimed her *and* your kingdom. For what you did to my father and cousins." Mateo laughs and coughs, spitting buckets of blood onto the floor next to him.

Diego goes deathly still.

Only his fingers twitch.

"Liam, take her out of here, please. I'm afraid Madison will never look at me again after what I am about to do." He says it so calmly and with so much conviction, it leaves no room for negotiation.

Anxious anticipation ripples through my body in the same way it has to be zipping through Mateo's.

"Come on, love. Let's go." Liam tugs at my waist, trying to get me to move, but my feet literally can't. It's impossible at the moment to get my brain to get my goddamn feet to move. I just stare at the man I'm married to.

I'm not afraid of him.

And I really fucking should be.

CHAPTER 17

LIAM

"ARE YOU ALRIGHT, love? You're shivering," I say apprehensively.

I tug her to me, our shoes crunching over the dead leaves as we make our way back to the house. Where earlier her feet had been glued to the floor watching Diego dismantle Mateo, now she is nervously scampering back to the house. My hand curls around her arm to stop her as we approach my back deck.

Wide glassy eyes greet mine as the sunlight catches them, changing her irises from warm brown to honey. Her bronze skin glowing in the morning light has me itching to reach out and run my fingers over its softness. I raise my hand, ready to do so, but then stop myself. Maddy is on the verge of having another breakdown.

Fucking, Diego. I knew sending her in there was a mistake.

"Did you come to my bed before you went to the shed? Around 3 AM?" The desperation in her voice has me on edge.

Why is she panicking about the answer to that question and not what she just witnessed?

"I did, I wasn't there long. We talked, remember? You were pretty much half asleep, but we talked, we cuddled, we kissed.

You fell asleep on my chest before I left to go back to interrogating. I had some time before Diego got here."

Releasing a shaky breath, she turns to walk up the three steps of the deck, crossing it and pulling the sliding door open with force. This woman has no idea what is going on in her mind right now. She's spiraling. And the worst part is, I don't know how to help her.

"Madison. What's going on, sweetheart? Talk to me." I follow her, picking up my strides through the kitchen and down the hall to the guest room.

"I just need some rest. I...I don't understand what I feel right now. You were here...earlier. And then Diego... he... I woke up to him and *you*...we were...I was dreaming of..." She throws her hands in the air exasperatedly. "It doesn't fucking matter!" she shouts. "It was just a dream..." she quietly trails off.

I lean against the door frame and cross my arms over my chest. "What did you dream of, Madison?" My voice grows deeper, downright huskier with the need to strip her naked and remove all of her anxiety—and quite frankly—*mine*.

Her only focus would be me.

I would take away all the chaos swarming her beautiful mind.

"So your speech earlier, about wanting to protect me and feeling defenseless when you couldn't find me in the club. Your apology for not staying with me. That was all real?"

She sits at the edge of the bed, kicking off my slides that are way too big for her sexy feet. The ones I can't stop thinking about hanging over my shoulders.

"Yes. That was all real." I slowly approach her until I am standing between her legs that are draped over the bed. "What am I missing here, Maddy?"

She lifts her head to stare up at me, gnawing on her lower lip. "I must have fallen asleep after. I had an interesting dream and it made me question whether parts of it were real or not."

I place my bent index finger beneath her jaw and press the pad of my thumb to her chin.

"Ya wanna talk about it?" I ask hoarsely.

Cherry red paints her cheeks as her eyes dart from mine to land on my lips. I hover over her as she leans back on her elbows, my arms extended on either side of her head.

"No," she whispers in the most agonizingly sultry voice.

I lower my body until there are only inches between us, her warm breath fanning my face, her breast pressing against my chest.

Adrenaline always does this to me. I can imagine she's looking to escape in the throes of passion. I would be fully invested as well, no questions asked, if she wasn't just freaking the fuck out. Not to mention the fact that she's injured.

Warm hands run through my beard and up higher until they are tangled in my hair. Her thumbs rub the apples of my cheeks as she lowers my head the rest of the way.

The second our lips touch, I know we aren't going further. That usual spark we always have isn't there. It's flickering, but there isn't any wick left to burn.

Madison must notice, too, pulling back as she recognizes her fantasy or that dream she had isn't comparable to this moment. I roll over and land next to her on the bed, lying on my back. My hands come up to wipe over my face as I release a massive sigh the same time she does.

A good long shower is in order. The fact that she even kissed me with another man's blood caked on my skin is traumatizing in itself.

"*Liam.*" She doesn't look at me as she says my name, drawing it out, eyes focused on the ceiling. There is a wobble to her voice that I don't like.

Not one fucking bit.

I tilt my head to watch her.

This is it. I feel it down to my bones.

The end of her and I.

The words she is about to say are going to have a ring of finality to them. After the night she had, I should be the one to do it. Make it easier on her. She is struggling to get the words out, I can see it in the way her eyebrows are scrunched together; the way her lower lip trembles.

But all I can whisper is, "*Madison*."

Because I am a fucking pussy and don't want to let this go. Let her go. Doing so would only give her a reason to really end this.

"This isn't working," she says solemnly, her voice breaking.

"I know, baby." I grab her shaking hand glued to her stomach and bring it to my lips, kissing it gently before entwining our fingers and laying them between us.

We lie there for a while. Sniffles fill the space as my thumb rubs the back of her hand.

"When you once promised me forever, you meant it then, ya?" I barely recognize the sound of my own voice as it breaks with grief.

Of what could have been.

Of what we had at one time.

"Of course I did. I never expected for my feelings to ever falter for you. I love you, Liam. I really do. I just don't feel that we are ever going to go back to who we were. I'm never going to be that girl you met."

"Tell me why. I'd do anything for you, Madison. You're my fucking soul, don't you see that?" I beg, my chest tightening with each beat.

"You're more protective of me than ever. Being the leader of your syndicate is going to make you even more on edge, caging me in...and I can't have that. I can't breathe when you are like that. The night I got taken, everything changed for us. I wanted to get back to us more than anything. Those months leading up to last New Year's Eve, I wanted to try again. Had Diego not showed up and thrown off my equilibrium, I would have asked you if we could have had a fresh start. *But he did.*"

I shake my head against the mattress in denial. "You left us *both*. Doesn't that say something? We could have hit the restart button. You could have told Diego to fuck off."

"I could have. I'd be lying if I said that the space from the both of you wasn't important. I needed that time to get my head on straight."

"The chemistry we can get back. We just need time. We don't have to rush this. It can go at a slower pace." I grasp on to anything that will keep her here. Even if only for a little bit longer. Perhaps I really am just clinging to desperation at this point.

A lone tear slips down her cheek as she maneuvers her whole body to her side to look at me.

"It's not there anymore. I know you felt that confirmation just now. You felt it in the shower and you felt it back at your office. There are two people we share that flame with that we can't forget about. That is what is preventing us from taking this further. The hesitancy is why we can't do this."

"Fuck, baby." I turn to my side to get closer to her. She's right. Doesn't mean I want her to be. My heart beats frantically against my sternum as I prepare to agree with her. We will always be in each other's lives. Just not how we had once imagined it.

"You are my soulmate, Liam. Maybe in this lifetime we just weren't meant to be together. I want to thank you for always being there for me, always protecting me—even if you can be over the top with it. Thank you for always loving me until there wasn't anything else to give. You were so fucking patient with me, especially after Diego died...You even respected my wishes while I was gone. You're an extraordinary man. Inside and out, Liam. Lainey or whoever you end up with is going to be a lucky girl."

A tear trickles over my lower lid, curving over the bridge of my nose and onto our conjoined hands. I sniffle and clear my throat, trying to get it the fuck together, but it's been a hell of an emotional twenty-four hours.

"I love you, Madison. Always and forever. This life or the next. I can promise that. I'm not sure I'll ever be able to give Lainey this side of me. You're the only woman I have ever truly been this vulnerable with. So thank *you*, princess. For teaching me how to lower my guard for those I care about. I've lived a miserable existence up until your beautiful face came waltzing into my bar." A laugh escapes me, elevating the moment from somber to reminiscent.

A little sob-laugh slips past her lips, which are attempting to form a melancholy smile.

She shimmies over to me and I lift my arm so she can snuggle in closer. Her face presses into my neck, probably the only place that doesn't have blood on it, as my hand holds the back of her head. I place a gentle kiss on the top of her head. Her delicate hand clamps my back between my shoulder blades, gripping my sweatshirt. Tears land one by one onto my neck, dripping down my chest as our erratic breathing slows.

"Promise me no matter what happens now, we stay true to who we are. I will always protect you, Madison. If you are in danger, you bet your pretty arse I'm jumping into action."

"Fine. But promise me in return that you'll give your all to your relationship with Lainey. I want you to be happy. You deserve love and someone who brings you joy, Liam. Open up. Let her get close to you. You need to let me go."

Placing another kiss to the top of her head, I nod. "Okay, sweetheart. I promise."

I'm not sure if I really do plan on letting her go, but I have to try.

Madison's breathing becomes steady, her back rising and falling under my hand. The warmth of her exhales tickle my neck.

She's asleep.

Poor thing is exhausted from these last few days. Last night and this morning have been intense. I wrap my arms around her more firmly, adding this moment to my memories, for it is the last time I'll ever get to hold her like this. Our hearts beat in sync like they always do.

Soulmate. Lover. Friend.

I'll always be hers. Doesn't matter what category she puts me in. I'd still jump in front of a bullet for her. I'd still empty my bank account for her. Where Lainey will have my love, my passion, respect, and honor, Madison will always have me as her protector.

And now she'll have Diego to love her.

I've seen how they are. There's no denying it anymore. He brings out a side of Madison that is dripping in regality. An absolute queen when she's around him. She's courageous, strong, and determined. I could never take that from her. She deserves to feel that way. If Diego is what makes her happy, then I'll bow out.

That's all I want.

To see Maddy smile.

From the moment I met her, she never fully smiled. Doubt and anxiety always plagued her. Seeing her smile while with me had given me hope I could keep it there. Seeing her with Diego —I can't compete with how radiant that smile has grown or the confidence she imbues being in his presence.

At the mention of her husband, he materializes, shirtless and quietly standing at the threshold of the door. The man is only donning a pair of boxer briefs. His clothes must have been discarded and burned back at the shed. Like a peacock showing off his feathers, he puffs his chest, proudly sporting his tattooed chest. A thick coat of blood covers his face, making him look fresh off the scene of a goddamn horror film. His broken knuckles are saturated as well, all the way down to his nail beds. The majority caked onto his forearms and neck.

Relief courses through me knowing Madison is still asleep. My arms tighten around her protectively. She shouldn't see this. It's gruesome as fuck. Even I found it hard to stomach Diego's torture. The fact that she lasted as long as she did is impressive. But that was child's play compared to what Diego had planned next.

He was only getting started...

"Well isn't this *cozy*," Diego snorts before passing us and heading into the en suite. He barely spares a minute to glance at Madison curled up on my chest. *Talk about dissociation.*

The soothing sound of the shower turning on drowns out the array of emotions slicing through me. I attempt to leave, giving them the privacy they need and the space to get myself cleaned up. Maddy clings to me like a goddamn koala bear. She's still asleep, so I cradle her closer until her knuckles relax and my sweatshirt goes slack.

Our flame may have burned out, but there's no doubt our souls don't yearn for the comfort of each other.

Unfortunately, that's not enough.

And we both know it.

CHAPTER 18

DIEGO

MAHOGANY WATER CIRCLES the drain before slowly transitioning to pink. Pumping a healthy portion of shampoo into my hand, I begin to scrub the fuck out of my scalp. This is the part of the night I yearn for. As savage and grueling as my job can be, and as thrilling as it feels in the moment, reality sets back in and all I want is this fucking blood and viscera off me. Where some men of the underworld wear it like a badge of honor or a goddamn trophy, I see it as another reminder of a life I can never escape.

Even if I wanted to, it runs deep in my veins, this need to end those who have wronged me or my family. To draw out their agony as they have to countless others.

And it just so happens that I'm the best in the game at it...

They don't call me *The Bone Breaker* for nothing. I've earned that title. It's one I'm willing to maintain—be it everything goes right with my resurrection. Everyone I've ever tortured and killed, deserved to die.

Mateo was no different. For his wrongdoings and plot against not only my life but my wife's as well. Beyond that, he was just as corrupt and evil as his bastard father and my piece of shit uncle. Men like that will never make it far. Power drives them to extremes and at some point that need for power makes them sloppy. Tonight proved just how sloppy MJ had become. I mean, *really*? Entering a heavily armed club? One man. No back up. What did he expect? It's a miracle he even made it far enough to get Madison alone.

I scrub at my skin with body wash, letting the loofah scratch my skin raw, before I step under the spray. My fingers sift through my hair as pink suds drift down my body and are discarded down the drain. Eventually, the water runs clear and so does my mind.

Thoughts of my wife soothe me as I inhale a deep breath. Safe and finally asleep in Liam's arms. It doesn't appear the two of them had done anything sexual—considering Madison is clothed and Liam still has dried blood caked onto his skin.

Even if they had, I'm not bothered.

Liam is able to offer Madison solace during tense situations like tonight. He provides her with a type of comfort I may not always be able to.

Coddling isn't in my name.

That doesn't mean I don't want to offer her it when I can. I've grown softer with Madison. She has access to the side of me no one other than my baby sister will ever have. A gentleness only they hold the biometric key to. In my *humble* opinion, not always coddling Madison has made her grow stronger. And it's a fucking beautiful sight to bear witness to.

My cock grows hard just thinking about how she stood up to Mateo tonight. And that's not the only thing swelling. Immense pride blooms in my chest knowing she took that asshole down all by herself.

Anxiety riddled me when I couldn't get in touch with my little butterfly. The phone just rang and rang and kept going to voicemail. I planned on coming home regardless. I missed my woman. Whether she admitted it or not, she missed me too. But it was that nagging feeling something was off that had me boarding our jet with haste.

When Liam called me, explaining what happened, and asked for my help, a sense of reassurance slithered its way in, buffing out the sharp edges of my anxiety. Madison risked her life to come back on that yacht to help me. She stayed with me on the island even when Liam was there to save her. My incredible woman braves any challenge. That fucking fortitude of hers inspires me every time I see her in action. The second the words left Liam's mouth, I knew she was safe. That she handled it.

Fuck. What I wouldn't give to have seen her take him down.

On the other hand, I don't hold *that* much restraint. *Only* when it comes to her. The second Mateo's fingers so much as touched her perfect skin, I would have beat him until he was unrecognizable. *No one* touches what is mine and gets away with it—as clearly proven tonight.

Mateo paid for his sins in more than blood.

I could have drawn it out a lot longer. The mental fuckery was way more thrilling than breaking as many of his bones as I could before ending his pathetic life. The intense desire to get back and hold Madison in my arms is what ended my interrogation prematurely.

Seeing her handle my form of torture was sweet relief. She could have fled. Part of me, the fucked up part that knows she's too good for me, wanted her to. Shock hit me when she stood her ground—even when I amped it up. I drew a line when Mateo voiced what he wanted to do to my sweet little butterfly. The red-hot anger that coursed through me warned me to get her out of there.

I wasn't holding back.

I wasn't dragging it out.

I was going all in.

Every blow to his body, every slice with my knife, I saw her beautiful face. I saw what is so fucking precious in my life. Never seeing her again, never hearing her beautiful laugh, or being on the receiving end of her quick-witted comments had me in a monsoon of blood.

Mateo was a dripping, mangled mess when my fury finally eased up. Had Madison seen that, she would have ran. And I would have let her. Liam was right in some ways, wanting to shield her from this side of us.

It's selfish, really.

While I agree she absolutely should not have witnessed my savage meltdown, seeing my handiwork allowed her to form her own opinions about the monsters lurking under my skin. They may have only breached the surface while she was there, but it was enough.

She proved she can handle me.

It was the trauma she would endure from the rest of my techniques that was *not* necessary.

And between us— I think Liam was happy to take her away... he was looking a little green.

With one last rinse, I shut off the water and step out onto the mat. I search around for towels but come up empty. Looks like I'll be using a hand towel next to the sink. I claim it, making quick work of drying my body before realizing I have no extra clothes in here. My suitcase is on the bench at the edge of the bed.

Eh...Fuck it.

A few lingering water droplets cling to my naked body as I parade out into the bedroom in a swirl of steam. I'm sure Liam's view is comical at best. My cock sways between my legs as I saunter over to my luggage. Liam's eyes bug as he cradles Madison's sleeping body to him before shifting her back down to the mattress.

"Christ, Diego. Ya couldn't spare me the goddamn visual?" He stands, huffing out his irritation.

I let out a boisterous laugh knowing damn well he's

comparing the size of my cock to his. Madison stirs. She moans crankily before sitting up disorientedly.

Beautiful. Stunning. Mine.

She touches her cheek, where the bruising is worsening before looking between the two of us. Half-lidded chocolate eyes widen like saucers as she takes in my now jutting cock. I'm tempted to grab it and stroke it with the look on her face. Except...that may prompt her to reenact her dream. And selfishly, I want her all to myself tonight.

Of course, Liam's dumb ass is still standing by the bed, arms crossed looking at her like she hung the moon. Madison's gaze volleys between the two of us until her attention lands on my chest and then gradually dips lower.

Lust courses through me, my cock twitching with a carnal need to have her. To take her right now. A delicious blush creeps up her cheeks before she crosses her legs at the ankle. Don't think I didn't notice the little squirm that followed.

"Diego. What the actual fuck? Why are you naked? She points her index finger my way before directing her attention back to Liam's lingering presence. Pointing her finger his way, she asks appalled, "And what the hell are you still doing here?"

"I was just going to shower. I wanted to make sure you were okay, love. I tried to give you two...*privacy* when Diego came in. You clung to me like a pair of wet jeans. I couldn't leave ya like that."

She nods, biting her lower lip and running her tongue over the stitches at the corner. "Thanks, Liam. Please, don't let me keep you any longer." Her nervous fingers lace together before she says, "Go get cleaned up. Sorry I kept you hostage."

"Not a problem. Anytime. I mean it, Madison. Everything we talked about earlier. If you ever need me. I'll be there." He winks. A small smile tugs at his lips before he stomps out of the room like a dark cloud, clicking the door shut behind him.

Shiiiit. What'd I miss?

I dig through my black leather bag in search of a pair of sweatpants. The heat of Madison's stare penetrates me like a tanning bed. It takes great dedication to continue my task of pushing my feet through each leg before pulling the waistband up. Blood rushes south, tenting the crotch. My little butterfly slides off the bed, her bare feet molding to the floor as she plods over to me. Warm arms wrap around my ribs as she lays her head against my chest. Her cheek rests over the butterfly tattoo as my heart beats steadily against her face. A deep breath rattles her chest when she releases a built up sigh.

Instinctively, my arms wrap around her, pulling her flush against me. I lower my chin to rest on the top of her head.

"Want to talk about it?"

She shrugs in my arms. "Which part?"

"Any of it? All of it?" I shrug as well.

"I'm not afraid of you, Diego. And I should be. I should run... far...*far*...away," she whispers.

"That's a valid statement. I can be a scary motherfucker. Yet, here you are," I confirm, tightening my arms around her and pressing my cheek firmly to her head.

A small giggle breaks the tension between us. A symphony to my ears, clearing out all the phantom screams. Like ghosts, they linger around after a tough assignment or interrogation session.

"Yet, here I am. Kinda hard to run when you have a loaded gun pressed to your stomach." Her one eyebrow arches in challenge.

Mmm. Feisty. I love her like this.

I slide my hands up the curves of her body, lifting the sweatshirt she's wearing and stripping it off her. My fingers dip into the waistband of her sweatpants, pushing them to the floor. They are Liam's anyway. I don't need my girl in his clothes.

A streak of desperation hits me as my hands find her face, fingers fanning out around her ears and clinging to the nape of her neck. Soft lips find mine, the prickle of stitches nudging against my skin before I even lower my head. Her hot, needy tongue glides over my lower lip before tangling with my own. The tips of her fingers press against each of my shoulder blades, digging in and pulling me tighter against her body.

I lower my head pressing kisses to her neck, over each bruise formed there. A shiver races up her spine as goosebumps spring up over her bare breasts. My greedy hands cup each one, toying with the puckered nipples. Madison releases a pleased moan, throwing her head back, giving me better access to the column of her throat.

My teeth graze over the space at the base, before my tongue licks up the gorgeous length of it. As my lips find hers once more, I pick her ass up, her legs finding their place around my hips. Her arms circle my neck as I hold her with one hand, tossing the comforter and sheets to the bottom of the bed. My knee finds the mattress before I lower us down onto it. I hover above, admiring those sparkling eyes.

"I'm not running anymore, Diego. I'm yours—*only yours*—if you'll still have me. I don't want to be anywhere else," she confesses breathily.

Like the Grinch, my heart feels like it just grew three sizes larger.

Twice more, I kiss her, leaving the both of us breathless. "You, *Mariposita*, are not only etched into my skin," I say, placing her hand on my chest, "But are etched into my very soul. Not having you would mean this erratic heart beating beneath your fingers has ceased."

A radiant smile spreads across her face. I'd kill anyone who threatened to take it away from me. Her determined hand slides down my chest, dipping below the waistband of my sweats. I stop her, cuffing her wrists with my fingers.

"I would love nothing more than to hear my name sung from this beautiful mouth. But, I refuse to fuck my wife in her ex's house. An ex I have come to respect." I shift the both of us until we are vertical and drag the covers back over us. My arms drape around her center, pulling her back against my chest. "Tomorrow is a new day—and I plan on ravishing you. So sleep, beautiful. You are safe, you are mine, and you are loved. *So. Fucking. Much.* I love you, *Mariposita.*"

Her body snuggles in closer until there is nothing between us but the heat of our bodies. "I love you, *Ocean Eyes.*"

It's the first time she's actually said it. Madison loves me back. Nothing could have prepared me for what it felt like hearing those three little words. Five, if you add in the nickname she gave me. The one that drives me wild. *My wife fucking loves me back.* Damn. I sit here in awe and elation knowing she's mine in every sense of the word.

Legally, spiritually, and romantically.

A few heartbeats later, silence fills the room. Her breathing has slowed and shallowed. Just when I think she's fallen asleep, my sassy woman says, "I'm holding you to that."

A deep laugh rumbles my chest, shaking her and I. I place a kiss on her shoulder blade.

"Go to sleep, gorgeous. You're going to need it."

CHAPTER 19

MADISON

I SLEPT the entire day away. Lexi and Conor left at midday to head back to New York. They had a flight to catch back to Arizona. With everything going on, Liam gave Con a bit of time off to spend with her while they prep for the wedding.

Diego woke me up with lunch earlier this afternoon. He brought in a tray of sandwiches and some soup Liam had prepared for everyone before they hit the road. I didn't realize how hungry I was until I devoured two sandwiches and half a bowl of soup. Which led to the *itis*. All I did was close my eyes to digest and ended up falling asleep again. It barely registered that Diego had snuck out of the room shortly after.

I stretch my arms over my head, curling my toes against the soft sheets. My hands sprawl out on either side of the mattress, coming up empty. Diego must be with Liam, sorting out everything that happened last night. *What a crazy night.* Not one I wish to remember, but one that I *need* to remember.

This will be my life now.

If I want to remain part of Diego's life, and call the Kennedys my family, I need to always remember the risk.

But with risk comes reward, right? It's one I am willing to take. I've explored the alternative and tried living away from them.

It's just not possible.

The buttery soft material of Diego's t-shirt clings to my body. *Damn.* I really must have been in a food coma not to notice him dressing me in not only his t-shirt but a pair of sweats as well. Thank goodness I feel well rested. I should be—considering it's almost five o'clock.

I shuffle over to the en suite to brush my teeth and wash my face. One look in the mirror has me gasping. The bruising looks downright awful. Dark purple and green splotches cover my jaw line, climbing up towards my cheek. Similar bruising has formed like a necklace around my throat. My fingers glide over the markings in frustration. *How the hell am I supposed to visit Dad looking like this?*

Diego enters the bathroom, spooking me. I jump as our eyes meet in the mirror. Sneaky bastard is as light on his feet as a panther.

"It's winter. It's not unusual to wear a scarf. Don't worry, baby, your father may never catch on. I know you have amazing makeup, it'll cover the bruising. The stitches can be explained by a fall."

"I don't want to lie," I grimace, wincing from the pain in my jaw.

He steps into my space. The warmth of his body pressing against my back and his hands gripping the counter around me send delicious shivers down my spine.

"So don't," he whispers, his minty breath tickling the shell of my ear.

With that knowledge, I swivel around in his arms. His forehead meets mine as he places a gentle kiss to the tip of my nose. Sapphire eyes ignite with fire as he takes in my flushed cheeks. My gaze lingers on his lips and the tongue he runs along the bottom one.

"I can't tell my dad your real career. He'd never let me see

162

you again," I scoff, ignoring the overwhelming desire to close the gap between us.

"You plan on lying to your family the rest of your life?" he asks amused.

"Not lie...maybe just omit that I am married to the most terrifying criminal the underworld has ever seen?"

He takes another step forward, pushing my ass against the granite countertops. "Don't forget the most dangerous." Heat pools in my core as those eyes of his swirl with mischief. "Do you want me to talk to him?" he asks in a more dignified tone.

"The man just had a heart attack. Let's not give him another one," I glower.

On a heavy sigh, *Ocean Eyes* steps back. Cool air rushes between us, dousing my libido.

"I understand. But someday, I'd like to not be your dirty little secret, *Mariposita*. Maybe down the road I can meet your family the proper way. Even ask your Dad if I can marry you."

"Kinda late for that," I snort.

His blue orbs narrow. "You *will* have the wedding you deserve. This time we are doing it right. Can't change the past, baby, but we sure as hell can have a do-over. Let's make this one the day we think of years down the road when our kids ask us about our wedding. It won't be tarnished memories and chaos, but a beautiful day. Surrounded by true family and friends celebrating the love between two souls who met through a twist of fate."

I do my best to hold back a snicker. "Twist of fate? You make it sound like we were epically brought into each other's lives. You did the twisting of fate's arms by kidnapping me!" Now, I can't help it. I brace the granite behind me and toss my head back in a giggle fit.

Diego joins me, a radiant smile forming behind his lips. "I'd do it all over if it meant meeting you again for the first time.

Except this time, I wouldn't follow through with my dumb ass plan."

I shrug. "Like you said, you can't change the past. I honestly believe it had to happen that way for our love to have formed the way it did. You taught me so much about myself I never knew existed. Because of that, I gained strength and courage I never had before. *You saw me.* Not as a damsel in distress, but as someone who is powerful. Someone who is a fighter. If it wasn't for you, I may have never discovered this side of me."

"She's beautiful, isn't she?" he growls, abruptly spinning me around and snaking his hand down my sweatpants. "Just watch how beautiful she is when she comes," he pledges.

His tenacious fingers split my folds, sliding through my slickness and dipping inside. After my head hits his shoulder on a drawn out moan he adds a third, pumping in and out of me. Diego's other hand gently wraps around my neck. I watch us in the mirror, as he does. Mesmerized by the sight of us. The sight of his powerful hands, the knuckles split, gripping one of the most delicate parts of me. Not once have I ever felt fear while they are there. Oddly enough, it gives me a sense of security knowing I am his.

His to pleasure, his to own, to love, to fuck, to protect.

This man has helped push me to grow, he's strengthened my mind and heart. I wouldn't have chosen him if it wasn't for the tidal wave of emotion that comes with how right it feels to be with someone who knows you better than you do.

Ecstasy builds inside me as my walls clamp around the fingers that stretch me. He increases his pace, thrusting them inside and curling to activate my g-spot. My emotions climb along with pleasure as tears spike my eyes, realizing exactly how much I love this man.

How thankful I am for him.

"Such a remarkably strong woman," he praises in my ear. He

pushes us up against the vanity so that the palm of his hand adds pressure to my clit. "And all mine."

Silver stars spark across my vision as my chest heats. I close my eyes when his hand curls tighter around my throat. Muffled moans carry around the room as I prepare to lose it. My legs are like Jell-O. Surely, they would have given out if he wasn't here supporting us.

"Fuck, *Mariposita*. Open your eyes. Look at what I see every time I make you cum."

It takes a serious amount of effort to force my eyes open as bliss like no other detonates inside of me. Diego's hand glides from my neck to cover my mouth, stifling my screams. His name falls from my lips on repeat, being chanted over and over behind the cover of his palm.

"Stunning. You, my sweet wife, are absolute perfection."

His arm, thick with visible tendons, moves to hold me up as his hand slips out from my pants. He places all three fingers in his mouth, sucking the evidence of my orgasm off them.

"Fuck. That was hot." I laugh, unabashedly checking out my husband. *Husband. Damn.* That reminds me... "Where are my wedding rings?"

As if he couldn't glow any brighter, his smile broadens, exposing his dimple. "Ahh. I thought you'd never ask. I have them. They are safe. You'll get them back when the time is right," he says cryptically, his lips twitching with the secret behind them.

"What are you up to, *Ocean Eyes*?" I spin in his embrace, linking my arms around his neck and narrowing my eyes at him.

"You'll have to wait and see." He smirks. "Patience, *Mariposita*."

DIEGO HANDS me my coffee while getting back into the black Range Rover. We made a pit stop at my favorite coffee shop near Killian's before heading out to Long Island. He offered to go in, saying he knew the owner. I'll have to remember to ask him if he can talk to the owner about Kira, my favorite barista. Maybe he can help keep her employed.

Knowing Diego, he'll make it happen.

Ten minutes later, he's on the phone booking us a hotel. Mr. Romantic thought it would be best to grab a cozy hotel by the water. I'm familiar with it. The one overlooking the Long Island Sound and ferry terminal. What's better? It's not far from Dad's.

I tried to suggest he stay back at the hotel while I'm gone, but with everything going on, he refused to leave my side. Secretly, after everything that's transpired, I don't want to be alone. Which means he'll drive me and wait in the car before we head to the hotel for the rest of the night.

Diego remaining in the car isn't up for debate.

He has to.

It's bad enough Mikayla is already on my case. What a shitshow it would be to have to introduce him to them. Could you imagine? *"Hey everyone...this is Diego, my husband. He's currently hiding his identity as he is the underworld's finest."*

I'm sure that would go over well.

"What's got you all worked up over there?" Diego interrupts the hypothetical scenarios running rampant through my brain. My face scrunches at the visual of my father turning all different shades of red. His hand lands on my thigh as he traces circles with this thumb.

"Just thinking of all the things that need to get done in Arizona. All the loose ends I need to tie up in order to come home for good." My teeth clamp down on my bottom lip, knowing it's a concern of mine but not the current one.

"Lexi already agreed to pack your stuff and Conor is going to help her ship everything here. What are you worrying about, baby?" He removes his hand to collect his coffee, taking a sip. I can't help but stare at his throat, watching it work as he swallows.

It's hot as fuck.

Everything about this man is hot as sin.

"She's got a lot going on with the wedding planning and wrapping up PA school. She doesn't need to be burdened with cleaning up my stuff," I admit.

"Why is it so hard for you to let anyone help you, Madison? You help everyone all the damn time. At what point will you allow people to do the same for you?" The frustration in his voice is clear as he sips his coffee. The aromatic scent of dark roast mixes with that of leather. His coffee sloshed over the lid as he was placing it back in the cup holder.

"I guess if it was a problem she wouldn't have offered," I concede, sopping up the liquid with a napkin. I bring my steaming cup to my lips and take another generous sip as we speed down the highway.

"There we go." His hand lands back on my thigh, fingertips toying with the inner seam of my yoga pants. "Such a strong-willed woman," he tuts. "Let people help you. There is absolutely no shame in that. Let go of that need for control once in a while."

I take another healthy sip, savoring the feel of his strong hand on my thigh and the delicious coffee evoking life back into me.

"I offered Conor and Lexi the island to host their bachelorette and bachelor party. Liam was talking with them over breakfast. They seemed pretty confident about wanting a Jack and Jill. Will it be triggering for you to head back there?" he asks cautiously.

My hand wraps around his, giving it a reassuring squeeze. "Not if I'm with you. Plus, I lived there for six months after your little Houdini trick." I roll my eyes at him and he catches it in his peripheral.

His grip on the steering wheel tightens until his knuckles turn white. "After you get back to the hotel, you are going to regret rolling your eyes at me. You know *exactly* what that sass does to me. I'm beginning to think you do it on purpose, *Mariposita*. Like you enjoy provoking the monsters under this skin," he rasps, arching his eyebrows suggestively.

"And so what if I do?" I goad before taking a sip of my coffee in the most nonchalant, bratty way.

"Baby, you have *no* idea what you're unleashing."

"You want me to let go of control? It's all yours tonight," I state boldly while throwing in a flirtatious wink. My core clenches in anticipation. If my orgasm this morning was any indication of where my head is at, I am more than ready to hand over my control to him. In fact, I'm looking forward to the kind of pleasure I've yet to experience—the kind I know he is capable of drawing out of me.

CHAPTER 20

LIAM

I STEP out of the shower back at the penthouse. Lainey was out of the house when I got back. Her project of the day was to shop with Selena for ingredients to make some organic teething biscuits for Kian.

Towel drying my hair, I take a seat at the edge of the bed and unplug my phone from the charger.

RYAN

Cleaners and landscapers have thoroughly taken care of the property. It's all set for your next arrival, boss.

I send out a quick reply of thanks, knowing not a trace of what went down will be found. My thumb scrolls the screen as I check out more of my messages.

CONOR

Hope you're holding up okay, brother. Lex told me that you and Madison had a heart to heart last night. She isn't coming back to AZ. We are packing up her stuff to be sent home. Just thought you'd like to know.

We did. It's how it should be. I was foolish to think we stood a chance with Diego still in the picture. And putting my immediate jealousy aside, he's the better choice for her. I can't give Madison what Diego can. I'm too much of a protective prick. I can't help it—especially around her.

CONOR

And what of Lainey?

She and I need to talk. I want to take this slow. At our own pace. Maybe give the relationship more time to grow. But I promised Madison I would give it my all. So, I am going to try. Lainey has been extremely patient with me already. I just hope she's willing to continue.

CONOR

I'm sure she will. The lass has been head over heels for you since we were kids. Also, heads up, Lex and I agreed to do the Jack and Jill in Miami.

Lovely. It's honestly a beautiful island. Spending time there last year was peaceful. You know Maddy and I will make sure it's a great week for everyone.

CONOR

Looking forward to it. I'll see you in a few weeks when I get back. Gonna try to spend some quality time with my woman 😊

I scrub my palms down my face. I need a fucking cigarette. I'm tempted to grab my pack and head out to the upper deck. Lainey's beautiful face comes to mind, reminding me I was making healthier choices around her. She hates the smell of it, always reminding me. Which made cutting back a hell of a lot easier.

My thumb hovers over her contact in my favorites list. I select it, sliding the phone to my ear.

"Liam?" Her tentative voice fills the line.

"Hey, Lain. Are you gonna be home later?"

"Yeah, why? What's up? Are you back already?" The excitement in her voice summons a smile to my lips.

"Yes. Just got back a little while ago. Would you be interested in a dine-in movie night with me? I'm fucking exhausted, but I miss you. I'd like to talk as well. I have a lot to get off my chest and you deserve to hear it."

"Sure. I just have to bake some teething biscuits for Kian and then prep dinner. I'll have Sarah finish up the rest for me. Did you want me to grab something sweet for later? I'm at the supermarket now."

"You mean two pints of Ben and Jerry's?"

"Mhm." I can almost see her biting her lower lip.

"Hell yes. I'll order us food from that little Italian restaurant we love with the sourdough bread. And I'll make sure to get your favorite handmade gnocchi truffle alfredo."

"Mmm... yes! That is my all time favorite. It's a date... well if that's what you want." The uncertainty in her voice guts me.

"It's an absolute date, Lain. Madison and I chose to go our separate ways, we just weren't fitting anymore."

"Really?" Her voice raises an octave with hesitant excitement.

"Really," I confirm.

"Wow. Okay, well I've got to run, I should be home soon. We can talk more tonight. I'm sorry it didn't work out between you two, Liam. On the other hand, I'm also secretly thrilled. That's awful, I know, but I was hoping we could get a real chance."

"I know, lovely. I didn't give us the proper chance to get off the ground. It was my fault. I've been the one keeping us here.

I'm not holding back anymore, Lain. All I ask is for some patience. We go at a pace that feels comfortable."

"I agree. See you in a bit."

I end the call, placing my phone on my chest while resting my head on the pillow. There is this calming sense of peace surrounding me. A few days ago there was uneasiness and even downright dread for having to conceal my feelings and emotions involving Madison. Today, there is clarity. Excitement for what's to come rolls off my shoulders. We can get through it together.

I just need to open up.

THE ZIPPO SPARKS, lighting the final candle placed around my bedroom. It's a fucking fire hazard with the amount of candles I have lit. The ambiance is set, my mood is brighter than it has been in days, and my appetite is voracious.

The smell of the Italian food wafts through the air as I begin taking the containers out of the paper bags. I set up two bed tray tables with plates and cutlery. A bucket of champagne is on ice between us. The television is already set to our favorite show. All I need to do is press play.

"Liam, this is beautiful." Lainey looks around, admiring my attempt at a romantic date night.

"I tried," I shrug, a bashful smirk tugging at the corner of my mouth.

"It's perfect," she sighs her contentment as her hand lands on my thigh.

We have our backs against the pillows propped up on the headboard. I press play and the theme song of *Sons of Anarchy* fills the flickering space. Lainey dives into her food, moaning her contentment. This is her favorite dish—which I had discovered the night after our first hookup.

She had come to my room for another quick round. Four

orgasms later...and it was safe to say we were starved. I placed the order after she ranted and raved about how amazing the gnocchi was. And I have to agree. It has easily become one of my top five favorite pasta dishes.

Every Thursday after, it turned into a routine thing we did together. That was our Friday, considering I typically was called to spend the weekends in Connecticut. Lain and I would watch *Sons* and enjoy our sourdough bread and pasta dishes. Always finishing off with dessert and a few orgasms. The nights we worked late she would slip into my room, cuddling up for one episode before we passed out from exhaustion.

It meant more to me than I gave it credit for at the time. We fell into a beautiful routine that ended abruptly because I needed to explore my feelings for Madison.

"Lain." I press pause on the show, swiping a napkin over my lips. I angle my body towards her.

"I'm sorry for putting you through all this. I never meant to make this feel like a trial run or that you were being pushed to the back burner... but it seems like it came across that way. Madison and I deciding not to try again definitely gave me the clarity I needed to see just how special this is between us. I may not have given our connection the proper credit it deserved a few weeks ago."

Tears pool in her lower lids. "Liam, it's okay. Really. I told you to do this. To truly figure out your feelings. Can I ask what made you realize the two of you weren't going to work out?"

I release a heavy sigh, fearful of her reaction. Her sage-green eyes greet mine with gentle concern. "We had a few moments where things got a little sexually charged. We never actually crossed that line, but we came close a few times. Each time we would, it was like this invisible barrier was forcing us apart. Maddy and I both felt that way, which led us to a collective conclusion that it was because of our other connections. I couldn't get beyond it, always thinking of you and how it would hurt you—and how I didn't want to fucking hurt you. Madison, she realized that what was stopping her was Diego, her feelings for him overpowering any chance of us rekindling our flame."

Her dainty hand grips my bicep, giving it a sympathetic squeeze. "I'm so sorry, Liam. I'm sure it wasn't easy accepting that."

I bow my head, too much of a coward to look her in the eyes, knowing the raw pain of that truth would be seen reflecting back at me.

No. Madison said to let down my walls. I promised her. *Godfuckingdammit.*

My head snaps up, eyes peering into Lainey's teary ones. When she notices my discomfort, she clasps my chin, letting her tears fall freely.

"Hey," she soothes. "It's okay. That's life, Liam. It's messy and complicated, but it's beautiful all the same. You loved Madison. There is history between you two that no one can ever deny or replace. It is a deep wound that will heal over time. Look at Killian and Maddy now. They've moved past it over the years. You will find your way, at your own pace. All I can ask for is that you do what you just did there." She gestures between us with her index finger before pressing it to my chest. "You give me *you*. Even your vulnerable side. The one you have a hard time showing me. I'm here. Right here. And I'm not going anywhere."

I lower our trays to the floor beside my side of the bed before pulling her to me. She snuggles in close, placing her hand on my chest before raising her chin to search my eyes. Lowering mine, I brush my lips against hers, softly claiming them. It's a voiceless promise that I'm not going anywhere either.

I want to be here.

Right here where the world seems to slow, even for just a little while.

Rubbing her warm tears away with my thumb, I tuck her against my chest and press play.

CHAPTER 21

DIEGO

MY FINGERS TAP along the steering wheel as I wait for Madison. She wanted me to drop her off down the block but that wasn't fucking happening. I dropped her sexy ass right off at the front of her father's apartment complex. Her sister Mikayla peeked out the front window when we arrived like she had some sort of sixth sense of our arrival. Even though the windows are tinted, I felt her eyes directed on me the entire time.

The playlist I've selected has almost cycled through. It's been about an hour and I'll be honest. I'm becoming impatient. I've already gone through every scenario of how I want to take Madison tonight, and if I keep thinking about her, I'm going to need to cut her little get-together short.

But fuck...I can't wait...

The feel of her silky smooth skin against mine... the little moans that slip past her lips as I slide into her... how her pussy clenches my cock... fuuuck. It feels like a lifetime has passed since I've had her.

My brain doesn't catch up to my feet until my knuckles are rapping against the door.

Madison is the one to swing it open with wide eyes that turn serpentine.

Fuck. Me. This woman is about to have me dropping to my knees just to worship her right here.

So. Fucking. Alluring.

My hands tremble with the desire to grab her by the neck and kiss her senseless, but the stares of her family have me dowsing that lust real fast.

"What the hell are you doing?" Madison growls low through her clenched teeth.

Mikayla makes eye contact with me, her mannerisms so similar to Madison's, it's actually quite scary. She raises a sharp blonde eyebrow before resting a hand on Madison's tense shoulder.

"Maddy, it's okay. He shouldn't have to wait in the car all night. I think Dad would like to meet your new boyfriend. You guys met in Arizona, right?"

The clever little fox tilts her head as she requests my response. Madison looks like she's about to slap her sister, so I claim her hand in mine, stepping around my girl and over the threshold.

"Sorry to interrupt. I know it's been an overwhelming and eventful last few days. I just wanted to make sure Madison was alright. I know she's been so worried about you, sir."

Maddy gives my hand a squeeze as she pulls me closer to the living room where a woman, who I'd assume is her father's girlfriend, sits on the couch next to Madison's younger sister. She tugs me along to the recliner where her father sits. It's that exact moment when my heart drops to my stomach—and I must admit, it takes a lot to shock me.

I've seen it all.

Her father Vinny Marrone—as in *Vincenzo Marrone*—stares at me with as shocked a face as I. This is what I fucking get for not doing my due diligence like I do any other person I've ever been involved with. I didn't do it with Madison because she is different. I didn't want to know every detail about her. I

176

wanted to discover those things myself. Like unwrapping a present.

One designed just for me.

Layer by fucking layer.

Of course, I had Selena give me as much detail as possible about her before kidnapping her, but I never once had my men look into her history. There's no file in my office on Madison Marrone. How did I overlook the last name? *Fuck. Fuck. Fuck... This is so bad.*

Madison stops a foot away from her father, her hand slightly trembling in mine. I tighten my hold on her to reassure her, but it's me who needs reassurance right now. To know her father wont whip out his piece and shoot me between the fucking eyes.

"Diego De La Cruz," Vinny chuckles. Madison stiffens next to me. "Care to explain to me how you of all people are dating my daughter? I heard you were dead."

"Wh...at?" Madison squeaks, looking at me and then to her father. "You two know each other?" There's a bite of betrayal to her voice that I don't like. But damn, *Mariposita*. A fucking heads up would have been nice.

I clear my throat before speaking. "I didn't know your father was Vincenzo Marrone."

"Sweetheart, *girls...*" Vincenzo starts, he reaches out his hand to clasp Madison's. She quickly releases my hand to go to him. "I know you girls may have suspected over the years...that I was part of the Mafia...And you were correct. I never wanted to get you involved. The less you knew the better." He pats the top of Madison's hand. "Your old man is an executor for the Italian Mafia. But this has to stay between us. As you know, this kind of information could be extremely dangerous." The warning is clearly written in his facial expressions.

Mikayla and Madison let out an incredulous laugh while her younger sister whispers, "I knew it." Vincenzo's girlfriend doesn't even blink. Of course she doesn't. She's known.

His eyes, so similar to Madison's, reach mine, prompting my little butterfly to swivel her head over her shoulder to look at me.

"I wasn't stupid when she was dating Killian. We had a nice conversation at her graduation party about keeping my daughter safe. There was a mutual understanding. Man to man. But you... *The Bone Breaker*... Never in my lifetime did I expect to see my daughter anywhere in your vicinity. The underworld treats you like a ghost. *A rumor.* I thought that's what you were until I saw a picture of you on the FBI's most wanted list."

I force a smile to my numb lips. *What the fuck do I say?* Her father isn't me, but damn he's got quite the reputation in his section of the underworld. The Italians treat him like a king because he is one in his own right. He may not be the leader of the syndicate, but he sure as shit holds just as much honor and respect as Lorenzo Caruso.

"So... you didn't meet in Arizona?" Mikayla adds sarcastically. Her father shoots her a knowing look.

"No. We didn't," I sigh, running a shaky hand through my hair. *Fuck.* I've never 'met the parents before'. Not only is this new to me but her father is *Vincenzo fucking Marrone*. "Mind if we sit?" I ask him, eyeing the space on the couch next to the recliner.

He nods. "Mikayla, do your old man a favor and grab Mr. De La Cruz here a glass of my Pappy Van Winkle." My brows raise, appreciating his taste in bourbon.

"Straight up son, or neat?"

"Neat. Who would want to water down such a beautiful bourbon?" I relax my shoulders, letting out a chuckle.

Vincenzo offers a small smile while rubbing his gray chin hair. "I still want to hear the entire story, but I'm starting to approve, Madison," he laughs, wincing and holding a pillow to his chest. I could tell he tried to avoid showing his weakness in front of me, *but fuck*, his ribs were sawed open and wired shut. Any man would be wincing.

Me included.

An hour later, I am shaking her father's hand. Respect is written all over his face. Vincenzo's girlfriend Diane drove Madison's little sister home, allowing us to talk more candidly about our past events. I left nothing out. Admitting my original plan in kidnapping Madison, to us falling in love in the most exhilarating way, to me faking my own death. Madison added her own thoughts and perspective as her father and Mikayla listened along carefully.

There were a few moments I was slightly worried her father would have me executed the second I stepped foot out his front door. Especially when we told him we had gotten married. Vincenzo remained relatively quiet. Eerily quiet if you ask me.

My mind eased a bit when Madison explained her account of my proposal and our wedding. That's when her old man started chuckling. Both our eyes remained glued on her, admiring how her eyes lit up and cheeks reddened while she explained our connection.

I place a kiss to Madison's temple. "I'll meet you in the car. I have it warming up."

She leans into me, placing a brief kiss to my lips before blowing a kiss to her father one last time. "Goodnight, Daddy."

"Goodnight, sweetheart. I'm glad we sorted this out. Don't let me see you with any more stitches or bruises again, you hear me ?" He's talking to her but looking at me.

"As I told you, I handled it, and then Diego *really* handled it. Anyways, I'm glad you are on the road to recovery, Dad. I need you around to watch the grandkids one day," she says gleefully.

It's as if a weight has been lifted off her chest. She's free. Free to continue being mine. No secrets. No lies. It's all out in the open. And *goddamn*. Hearing her talk of having my children has me ready to get back to the hotel so we can practice.

I've got one more thing I need to do before we leave. And this one is strictly between me and her father.

"Slow it down there. I just heard about your wedding today. Give me some time before you start announcing babies." Vincenzo holds a hand to his chest.

Madison laughs some more on her way out. She lets the screen door slam, announcing her departure. I turn to her father, taking a deep breath.

"I know I didn't do it the right way in the past, Sir. I would like to remedy that. I want to do it the right way. I am asking permission to remarry your daughter. I promise to always protect her, to encourage her goals and dreams. I love your daughter very much. She is an incredible woman. I'm a very lucky man to have been given her trust and love in return."

He remains silent, studying me behind his glass of water before taking a sip. He reaches out his hand to shake mine. I place my hand in his firm grip. He tugs me close. *Maybe I misjudged his lighter mood?*

"You have my blessing, Diego. *However*, there is one thing I need you to understand. No matter how much she may hate you, no matter how much it will ruin everything you've created with her... If the feds come to take you down, you leave her the fuck out of it. I don't want her being dragged into this. I know they usually don't pull wives into it, and having a good attorney will prevent that as well. But if by some freak chance they come looking for you... You do what you did in the past. You protect her reputation and future first. My daughter will not be dragged through courts and prison because of you. Is that understood?"

"Yes, sir."

"And I shouldn't have to mention it, but if you hurt her... I end you. *Capisce*?" He releases my hand as I nod and start to walk towards the front door.

For once, I am actually speechless. This man has invoked the fear of God into me.

All because of who he is to Madison.

"Oh, and Diego?" Vincenzo rasps.

"Madison seems smitten with you. I've never seen my daughter this happy before. Even with Killian's brother. She's glowing and confident. It's absolutely refreshing to see." Pride filters out of him.

"Your daughter is extraordinary. Her drive as a woman, a sister, a friend... a *spouse*...inspires me every single day." I tap the molding next to the door before leaving.

Well...that went exceptionally well.

As I round the driver door, I hold my breath. Now would be the perfect time for a sniper to take me out. I get in and shut the door, releasing that breath and grinning from ear to ear.

Looks like I'm still alive.

CHAPTER 22

DIEGO

"ARE YOU MAD?" I ask hesitantly, as we walk hand in hand through the hotel lobby.

Madison was awfully quiet the whole ride here. That damn phone had been going off every two seconds as she crafted a response to each message almost immediately. I'd be lying if I said I didn't glance over to see who she was texting. She was going back and forth between her sister Mikayla and Lexi.

Women. Always debriefing.

Her beautiful face finally looks up at me as we navigate the lively crowd by the downstairs bar. There isn't any sign of disappointment or anger.

Thank fuck.

I hit the button for the elevator, the ring around it lights up red. She raises my hand and places it over her shoulder, leaning into me. Her warmth immediately wraps around me like a heated blanket. With it comes a wave of comfort and peace.

That's what my little butterfly does to me. She is the eye of all my storms. A place where I can protect her. A place where any enemy will deal with my wrath before ever taking away her light. If she chooses to stay, she'll always remain safe.

"I was at first. I was fuming, Diego. But then, when my dad

showed his approval, showed how much he respected the two of us...all that anger fizzled out and was replaced by relief."

The elevator arrives. I guide us inside, still keeping her tucked tightly against me. The doors close, filling the space with a quiet hum as we ascend the few floors to the top presidential suite.

"Do you think we'll still have the same chemistry now that I'm not your dirty little secret?" I goad.

Inertia sets in as we reach the top floor. She plucks the key card from my hand and dances down the short hallway to our suite.

"I don't know," she sing-songs. "Let's find out..."

God, this woman. I chase after her, laughing and smiling as she holds the door open for me. Is this what happiness, genuine happiness feels like? Cause if it is, I want this feeling to last forever. I want to keep that beautiful smile on my wife's face for the rest of our lives.

Madison spins on her heel and stops dead in her tracks. Candles are lit throughout the space, bringing a coziness to the room. The gas fireplace only adds to the warmth and charm. Her booted feet carry her to the bedroom, where a king-sized bed sits central and the jacuzzi tub in the corner is filled to the brim with rose petals and bubbles. Delicate fingers trace the soft cotton sheets where an ice bucket with champagne and a tray of chocolate covered fruit sits at the edge.

I come up behind her to wrap my arms around her center, then gather her hair to one side and place kisses along her neck. She tilts her head, granting me better access while melting into me.

"I didn't know you did romance..." she sighs her approval.

"I don't. I hope this isn't cliché as fuck...but I'm trying here, *Mariposita*."

Spinning around in my arms, she circles her own around my back. Her head tilts back as her eyes ignite with sparks of amber.

"It's perfect. Thank you," she whispers as her eyes drop down to my lips.

I lower my head until our noses and foreheads touch. Her breathing increases as her breasts press up against my chest.

"You deserve far more than I can give you. But damn, baby. Hearing your father's approval of me made me feel a tiny bit worthy of your love."

"Diego...how could you ever think you don't deserve me? You've helped mold the best version of me. That's like saying the chef who created all these amazing recipes doesn't deserve the credit. Doesn't deserve the praise or the Michelin stars. You don't have to keep trying to earn my love. I've told you once and I'll tell you again... I love you, *Ocean Eyes*. I loved you when you were my dirty little secret, my captor, and my salvation, and I love you now. I. Love. *You*." Her pointer finger presses into my peck to get her point across.

I bow my head, unable to stare into those intense eyes of hers. Her father's warning has been circling my brain the whole ride here. Am I doing what's best for her? What if that day comes again? Will I be able to hurt her? Either way, I'm fucked. Her father would end me.

And I'd welcome it.

I never want to hurt my little butterfly again. Shame hits me like a punch to the jaw.

Madison curls her index finger under my chin, lifting it until my watery eyes meet hers. "Don't. Don't doubt us now when I finally have you without any restrictions. To be perfectly clear, it was never about the rush of no one knowing. Or the rush of our relationship being reckless. Or even the knowledge there was an end date. I want you. And more than want, I *need* you, Diego. Being in Arizona, there wasn't a day I didn't think about you. About what we could have been if we had only a little more time and a little less chaos."

I extend my hand to sweep around the room. "Is this what

you imagined? Sweet, romantic gestures like this?" I let out a pathetic laugh, feeling like a fool for setting this up. *It is cliché as fuck.* But I wanted her to see a version of a normal relationship. Someone gentle and extravagant with their love language. Big gestures and sappy shit. Most of all, I wanted her to see what would have been if I wasn't the man I am.

"I already told you. I thought I wanted *normal. Simple.* You want to know what I've really been craving?"

Her ringless left hand grips my sweater and her lips slam against mine. It shocks me and takes me a second to respond. Her lips are fierce, her tongue sliding against my bottom lip, demanding entry. The pinch of her stitches sends a shock of electricity, like a neuron, rushing through me, reminding me of what she's endured to remain at my side.

My little fighter.

At that moment, something inside my soul clicks into place. My eyes slam open, staring at my own reflection through her amber woven eyes. She is everything I have ever needed. All the parts of me I was running from, all the parts I never knew I was missing until I had her in my arms. She is my vulnerability, my weakness.

Men in my line of work don't need weakness. They certainly don't do vulnerability. I don't give a flying fuck. Her arrival into my life was exactly when it was supposed to be.

Right on time.

Not a minute late.

We had to go through all of the trials we did for our relationship to grow and blossom the way it did. For us to discover ourselves together and apart. And here we are, back together. Her father, the hitman for the Italian mafia, gave me *his* blessing.

This beautiful, breathtaking woman has given me all of her by choosing me. And here I am just wasting fucking time...

My mouth drops open as my hands grip both sides of her

face. I devour her, careful of her stitches as I show her how much I fucking love and adore her. I pour every feeling running through me into this kiss. Madison moans her response at my shared receptivity and enthusiasm.

She wanted *crazy*, but her fine ass is going to have to wait on that. We'll have plenty of time for crazy, downright filthy sex. That's my forte.

Tonight, I'm going to be completely vulnerable, completely open, and give her slow. For every minute she is in my arms, I will worship her. Savor her. Take my time on her. Leaving no part of her body unmarked by my lips, my fingers...my tongue.

I tug her sweater over her head and toss it to the side. The pads of my fingers trace up her spine, leaving goosebumps springing in their wake as they work the closure on her bra. When the clasps are undone, I lower her bra straps down her arms until it drops to the floor.

Gorgeous perky breasts greet me. I want to twirl my tongue around them, suck and bite—but I don't. Lowering myself down to one knee, I place her foot on top of it. Her hands land on my shoulders to steady herself. I remove her Ugg boot, and then her sock before swapping feet and doing the same. Those black yoga pants are next to go. I hook my thumbs into the waistband on each hip and lower them excruciatingly slowly, until they are at her ankles.

Fuck, she isn't wearing any panties. My cock swells and throbs as it presses against the zipper of my jeans.

She steps out of one pant leg and I take the time to grip her thigh, raising it up. I start from her toes, kissing the pad of each one, moving to the inside of her ankle and up her calf. I run my lips and hands up until I reach the apex of her thighs.

It takes everything in me not to bite the inside of her thigh.

Not to push my nose into the soft curls at the top of her slit and inhale before plunging my tongue into her wet cunt.

Instead, I lick her bikini line and drop her leg back down. My tongue skims across her stomach and over to the other side. It continues its pursuit down her bikini line again and over her inner thigh as my fingers grip her calf, pulling it up and kissing my way down to her ankle and toes. When I tug her pants out of the way and add them to the rest of the pile, she whispers my name.

"Diego." It's a gentle plea.

Rising to stand, I bring her face back to mine. Our lips crash as I claim them. My fingers twine into her hair as I walk her backwards towards the jacuzzi tub. When we reach the two small steps to enter, I break the kiss, feeling breathless and euphoric. A smirk carves my face as I point to the tub.

"In."

"So bossy." She rolls her eyes.

My cock swells even more. I want nothing more than to fuck the ever-loving shit out of her. I know that's exactly what she wants me to do.

But again, I refrain.

In no time, I'm naked, adding my clothes to the growing pile before laying towels out in front of the gas fireplace. *That's next.* For now, I saunter over to the bed and grab the bottle of champagne. *Fuck the glasses.* We won't be needing them.

She leans forward, making room for me to slide in behind her. I press a kiss to both her shoulders before placing one over the small butterfly tattoo. Madison hums her approval as she closes her eyes and leans back against me.

Pressing both thumbs to the cork, I pop the champagne, sending it flying across the room. Madison jerks forward out of fright, causing some of the water to slosh over the edge. Her head tilts as she peers up at me giggling and biting her lower lip.

"Gets me every time. Even when I'm prepared for it." Her giggles continue, filling me with adoration.

I press another kiss to her temple, unable to keep my lips off her. Knowing I need to slow it down, I take a swig of champagne. The bubbles burst across my tongue like Pop Rocks. I tilt Madison's chin up.

"Open," I command, unable to ease that side of me completely.

Her jaw releases, as she forms an O with her lips. I tilt the bottle, letting a small stream flow into her mouth, before replacing my own over hers and whispering against her lips, "Now swallow."

The black of her pupils expand as they stare up into my own.

"Good girl. Would you like some more?"

She nods her head, her eyes glowing with the reflection of the candles surrounding the tub.

I tilt her head back against my chest and grip her jaw. She opens immediately. Tilting the bottle again, I pour more into her mouth until it overflows and she's forced to gulp it down. Her neck works under my fingers that are pressed there. The excess drips down her chin and over her neck before disappearing into the water.

I drop a kiss to her lips before taking another swig. Then my head is lowering into the crook of her neck, lapping up the rest from her skin. Lowering the bottle to the steps with one hand, my other releases her neck as it trails down over the swell of her right breast. Cupping it in my palm, my thumb circles the pink bud. My left hand catches up, repeating the process. Sinking them both beneath the bubbles and rose petals, one claims her hip, while the other dives between her legs.

"Yes," Maddy purrs.

"You're going to come on my fingers, *Mariposita*. And then I am going to clean you up before I slide my cock inside you by that fireplace." She shivers in approval against me.

As my fingers part her lips and find their way inside, she is already moaning my name. Her head rests against my shoulder as her hips move, gyrating against my hand and cock pressed against her ass cheeks. Water sloshes over the rim of the tub as we increase our momentum.

Her walls clench around my fingers as I work them in and out of her. I grip her hip, holding her to me and preventing her from sliding down the tub.

My teeth graze her neck over her tattoo. "You are mine, *Mariposita*," I growl. "I take care of what's mine. Now, come for me, beautiful."

Those trembling muscular thighs press together as her back arches against me. A melody of screams and moans ring out around us. Her orgasm detonates through her, her body melting back into me as the water levels out. The feel of her heart thundering steadily against my chest has me pulling her closer to me and wrapping my arms around her sated frame.

Mine.

CHAPTER 23

MADISON

A PILLOW CUSHIONS my head as Diego lays me down on towels he arranged by the fireplace. Warmth replaces the brief chill zipping through me as he lowers himself over me, caging me in between his two extended arms. Goosebumps litter my skin—for reasons other than being cold. Like blown glass, those sapphire eyes of his ignite with the light from the gas fireplace. I am mesmerized by the way it makes them sparkle and shine. His body molds with mine as his lips crash against my own. And once more, we can't keep our hands from roaming.

My still trembling thighs come up to circle his waist as his tongue traces my butterfly tattoo. I'm in awe of the reaction it has on him. Just the look in his eyes when he catches a glimpse of it has me squirming. It has my pulse skyrocketing, not only in my chest but between my thighs.

That look is absolutely feral.

And it makes me feral. Bat shit crazy with need.

Except, tonight, he's more reserved than I have ever seen him. We may have only had a few sexual interactions, but from what I have learned about him, along with what I have heard through the grapevine, he isn't one to hold back that animalistic nature.

With fervor, his lips meet mine, parting to whisper my name. "*Madison.*"

Powerful fingers grip my thighs, pulling me closer and adding pressure to where our hips meet. The head of his cock presses into my entrance, but instead of driving home like I expect him to, he stops himself from going further. *It is driving me crazy. Can't he see that I need him now?*

"I love you, Madison. I don't know what I did to deserve you, but I sure as hell don't plan on ever letting you run again."

I stare up into those penetrating blue eyes. They hold a promise of forever.

"Then don't lie to me ever again and I won't. From this moment forward you have to be honest with me. I can handle it. Don't leave me out of your plans."

He nods his head in agreement before placing a chaste kiss to my swollen lips. "I promise. And if I ever do, know I deserve the punishment." He winks.

I can't help but roll my eyes at him.

"Ahh... I was hoping you would do that..." he snickers, the corner of his lip coming up to reveal the pointed edge of his canine. The monster inside of him never too far.

Diego pulls out, causing me to groan my disapproval. "Diego... *please...* I need you right now."

"And you will have me. Over and over and *over* again. But for now, you will behave and accept your punishment like a good girl. No squirming. Stay perfectly still."

He leans back on his heels, gripping my ankle and bringing it to his lips. The warmth of them presses against the inside of my ankle and up my calf until they reach the apex of my thighs. Anticipation builds inside me. My core aches, clenching with the need to have him place those lips where I crave them most.

But of course he doesn't. Bastard.

He swaps ankles, repeating the process until he is back,

breathing warm air between my legs. I lift my hips, desperate for his face to make contact.

Before I have a chance to register what happened, he's gripped my waist and flipped me to my stomach, smacking my ass. The sound bounces off the walls around us. Pain and heat spread across my cheeks before they are soothed by his hands massaging the skin. If my pussy wasn't throbbing already, it's pulsing now. His lips replace his hands, trailing lower until his tongue darts out to lick a trail through my parted legs.

"*Ocean Eyes...*" I sigh out, hoping more than anything that he'll continue.

But once again, he refrains.

That sexy mouth of his chuckles before working its way over the swell of my ass, up the curve of my spine, and landing at the crook of my neck. A wave of ecstasy hits me as his cock presses into me. *Yes. Finally.* Shifting the two of us, he lowers himself down next to me so that we are spooning. Diego slides my hair away from my neck and leans his head there while lifting my thigh up and driving all the way home.

My core clenches around him, more than ready to accept my punishment. Ready to have him drive into me over and over again until my vision dots with stars.

Except, once again, he doesn't.

With extreme restraint, he works himself in and out of me, building a pleasure that starts off in a small ripple. The fire before me and Diego pressed up behind me has me scorching with need. *So much fucking need.* That ripple crescendos to a wave as does his pace.

Leaving my leg resting on the knee he has bent between my legs, he reaches around and begins to toy with my clit.

My eyes close as he brings me to the edge.

This giant tsunami he's created is starting to crest.

I'm about to crash.

Demolishing anything in my path.

He lets go completely, pistoning into me while sucking my neck and pulling the sensitive skin between his teeth.

"You are perfect, Madison," he grinds out before swiveling my head to look at him. "Marry me again. Tell me you want this just as badly as I do," he pants between thrusts.

I want to answer him. I want to shout it to the rooftops—but I can't. My vision goes all sparkly and my orgasm slices through me. My soul leaves my body as the word 'yes' gets stuck somewhere behind a garbled scream. Diego joins me at the same time, covering my mouth with his as we both ride out the ecstasy we feel when our bodies collide.

After a moment, he slides out of me, spinning me around and pulling me close. My head rests against his chest, his heart beating erratically behind his butterfly tattoo. His fingers mindlessly play with my hair as we both catch our breath.

"Is it just the sex for you then?" he asks defeatedly.

"What? *No.* Oh my God, *Ocean Eyes*. You literally took my breath away. I wanted to tell you when you asked. It was nearly impossible to get the words out..." I look up, giggling and kissing the scruff dusting his chin. A giddy smile forms, stretching wildly across my face. "Yes. Yes. I will marry you again... On one condition."

His palm cups my face as his thumb rubs the apple of my cheek. Worry etches his face as his eyes dart back and forth between mine, searching for any hint of the answer.

"I want my rings back. The same ones. I don't want you to recreate everything. Some of those memories should stay exactly as they are."

He chuckles before kissing me twice in succession.

"Deal."

Diego rises to his feet and walks over to the small leather overnight bag he brought. I take a moment to admire the inked artwork on his back. A reminder of the two sides to this man. The ones I equally fell in love with. I honestly don't believe I could do one without the other. My eyes shamelessly drop lower to admire his tan sculpted ass. *I'm the lucky one here.*

The Bone Breaker reaches inside and retrieves a small velvet box. Pivoting on his heel, he makes his way back towards me. Eyes determined as ever and sparkling with appreciation, they scan me from head to toe.

I do the same, admiring the tattoo he got for me before my gaze drops lower. I lick my lips at the sight of his abs that form a cobblestone pathway to a deep V. His cock glistens with a combination of both our releases. *It's hot as fuck.*

Diego marches his way towards me all confident, cocky, and totally *mine*. The light from the fireplace dances over his skin making him appear like some sort of God. Just like the ones from the fantasy books I read.

My cheeks heat as my core greedily clenches with the need for round two. Like the true predator he is, he picks up on my sudden shift. His cock twitches in response. The wild look on his face tells me he's more than ready to comply with my desires.

When he reaches me, he sinks down onto one knee, opening the box and reuniting me with my gorgeous engagement ring. The ring he got with such limited time, and yet, was still able to perfect—*just for me.* The blue sapphires sparkle just like his eyes right now.

"Madison De La Cruz..." he smirks. His lips curl up revealing that dazzling smile I have come to adore. "Marry me again?" He holds out the ring, placing the box on the floor beside him.

"Yes." I smile, holding my left hand out for him to slide the ring on.

As the cool metal finds its home back on my ring finger, I release a sigh of relief before his lips are on mine and I'm engulfed in his embrace, tumbling back down to the floor.

"Where is my wedding band?" I ask curiously.

Diego places a kiss to the tip of my nose. "You'll have to wait for that one."

My eyebrow raises in question as his lips claim mine, effectively ending that conversation—*for now.*

CHAPTER 24

MADISON

A NEON PINK, penis-shaped shot glass is shoved into my hand. Tequila sloshes over the rim as Lexi slams her own glass against mine.

"I want to thank my Matron of Honor and Conor's Best Man, Liam for planning this incredible bachelor and bachelorette weekend!" she shouts over the music bumping through the speakers. The beach at Diego's private island is crowded with our close family and friends.

Tiki torches line the pathways and surround the white furniture placed aesthetically throughout. Warm Edison string lights glow above us, making the space cozy and romantic.

This moment feels anything but.

There is a buzz in the air that crackles with mischief and uncertainty of what's to come.

My eyes shift to Liam who is laughing with his shot glass held high in the air. His other arm is wrapped around Lainey's waist, keeping her tucked into his side. She too, has her glass raised along with the rest of our crew.

"We are honored to have been given the responsibility to plan this," he boasts. His dark eyes briefly flicker to mine before saluting me with his glass and tilting his head back to take the shot.

I return the sentiment, tossing back my shot. "We are only just getting started," I add, raising my voice to be heard over the cheers.

Liam's eyes meet mine again before he and Lainey head towards the bar. Since we all arrived here yesterday evening, Liam has kept his distance. We have done most of our planning over the phone these last few weeks. Our dynamic has drastically changed. I mean, we knew it would. We chose this.

Still, the tequila burns a bit more than it used to.

Diego surprises me. He comes up behind me, his arms wrapping around my center as his lips press against my butterfly tattoo. "Hello, *Mariposita*."

I spin around in his arms to circle my own around his waist, raising up on tiptoes to kiss him. "I missed you," I confess against his lips.

"I missed *you*. I'm sorry it took me so long to get back to you." He lowers his forehead to mine.

"Did you get any closer to sorting out your 'big' return?" I ask, curious as ever if his trip to Greece with his cousin went as planned. He left a week and a half ago to retrieve any ounce of information he could get his hands on. His source in the Greek Coast Guard was working alongside them. Sticking to his promise, he told me his plans and kept me informed every step of the way. He and Antonio had been working hard this last month, getting much closer to proving Geraldo was to blame for the explosion of Pontus.

"The Greek Coast Guard has limited evidence about the events of that night. Which helps my case. The only thing standing in the way of completely pinning it on my uncle is the statement they have from the officiant....I'm not worried. He will no longer be a problem." The corner of Diego's mouth curves up revealing his dimple.

"Diego...You *didn't*." I place my hand on his chest, staring up into his eyes for confirmation.

"No. No. I didn't *kill* him, *Mariposita*," he laughs heartily. "He's a man of God for fucks sake. I may have a laundry list of reasons to head straight to Hell when I go, but I'd like to at least try to get a pass to where you're going."

I shake my head at the man before me. His logic is awful.

"Where you sleep, I sleep. That means if you don't make it in, I'll rip off my wings and take a skydive straight down to you. Better catch me, asshole." I slap his chest before tugging him along towards the tiki bar where our friends are gathered.

"The hell you will," he growls as I tug him along to the edge of the bar where Lexi and Con are.

"Madison! Get your ass over here and do another shot with me," she sings. "Oh, *Hey*, Diego. Welcome to the uncensored fun. Doesn't your wife look absolutely *edible* tonight?"

Diego tilts his head down to look at me before licking his lips. His eyes roam the exposed skin playing peekaboo through the cut outs of this hip-hugging peach dress. "She does. In fact, I may have to steal her away for a moment after this shot."

"Wait up! I want in." Liam booms, making his way towards us. *Wait, what?!*

When he reaches us, he claps Diego on the back. "Glad you're back. Madison has been unbearable lately. So snippy. You know what she needs to curb that attitude." He breaks out into laughter while grabbing shots off the bar and handing them out to us. *Oh...he wanted in on the shots...*

"Oh, please," I scoff. "I wasn't *that* bad.

"Who are we talking about?" Killian joins us, seemingly amused. Liam hands him a shot glass.

"Madison when she's cranky. You know what she needs."

"Yeah...*this*." Killian takes the pussy-shaped shot glass and licks the salt off the slit before slamming his shot back.

My jaw drops. *Okay*, fuck these men. *Oh right, I already did.*

That's why I am standing here as they discuss my sex life. *They aren't wrong.* A good dose of vitamin D always makes me feel better. So, sue me. But for fucks sake. Do they need to be so vocal about it?

Diego is the first to speak. "I respect you all. I know you have a past with Madison, but if I hear any of you talk about her sex life again, you won't be able to talk about it ever again. Your jaw will be wired shut so tightly..." he starts to growl. I intervene by gripping his bicep and dragging him to one of the private cabanas along the beach.

The white linen curtain swooshes shut behind us as I push him down onto the wicker couch. I straddle him, grinding myself down onto his hard as stone cock. My fingernails rake into his curled hair as my lips devour his. He reacts immediately, roughly cupping my ass beneath my dress and pushing me down onto his length. Needy fingers slide the matching lace thong to the side before he sinks one through my slickness.

"Baby, you are soaked," he groans against my lips.

"That was so fucking hot. How you stood up for me," I pant between kisses.

His lips find my neck as he murmurs, "You aren't the only one who gets cranky. A week and a half is too fucking long. I need to sink so far inside you right now, *Mariposita*. I can't be gentle with you right now."

"I don't want *gentle*. I need you to fuck me, Diego. Don't foreplay. Don't tease..." My voice shakes as I struggle to get his belt and buttons undone.

Finally, I free him, running my clenched fist up and down his length. He growls in response, lifting my ass and entering me swiftly. I cry out, my walls cinching around him. We move together, desperately grinding into each other. His fingers grip my hair at the scalp, holding me in place as his cock pounds into me.

It's too much and not enough.

His grunts ricochet around the tent, not giving a damn who hears us.

"Yes! Christ, Diego, I missed you."

"Me too, baby. So much. I promise you I am so close to clearing my name. You will have the life you deserve. No more hiding in the shadows. I want the whole fucking world to know you're mine."

As if he wasn't already practically splitting me in half, he pushes into me harder, tearing an Earth shattering orgasm right out of me. I scream out my release into the crook of his neck as tears work their way down my face.

"In the dark, in the light. I'm yours." I place a kiss to his collarbone.

"Feel better?" The palm of his hands skim up my back.

"Much," I giggle, resting my head on his shoulder.

"You?" I ask, tracing my index finger up the button of his collared shirt.

"Definitely." He lifts my head, gently clearing the remaining tears off my face. "I didn't hurt you, did I?"

"Not at all. It was just really intense—in a good way. That's why I cried," I confirm, shooting him a smile as I sort out my dress and stand.

He tucks himself back in, situating his clothes before standing. Firm hands reach out and angle my head up, his lips press against mine in the most delicate way. "It was like that for me too, *Mariposita*. Shall we get back to the party?"

"Yes. Lexi is probably looking for me. You think they heard us?"

"I think the astronauts on the International Space Station heard us," he chuckles. "Come on, beautiful." His hand twines with mine, guiding us out of the cabana and back towards the rowdy crowd.

LEXI AND CONOR are dancing under the Edison string lights. Her brother and his husband are there too, dancing to the lively EDM music blasting out of the speakers. A kaleidoscope of colors paint Lexi's smiling face. She is staring at her betrothed lovingly. It makes my heart swell. I couldn't be happier for them.

Diego spins me around, leading me into the crowd. Lexi swivels her head to greet me and squeals a tone I know all too well.

"Maddy! Let's dance." She hugs me tightly, brushing my hair behind my shoulder while swaying with me. "Seriously. Thank you for planning this." Her eyes scan the crowd and the beach. "This is incredibly beautiful."

I squeeze her tightly. "You're welcome. You both deserve to be celebrated before your big day. I can't believe you'll be married in a few days," I gush.

"I know it was a lot to plan, considering we moved it up, but we just couldn't wait any longer." She releases me to collect both my hands in hers, raising them between us. "Who would have thought two goody two shoes would marry hot mobsters?" She laughs before her eyebrows push together then raise to her hairline. Her thumb skims over my engagement ring. "He proposed again?" she shouts giddily.

A warm smile grows on my face as my cheeks heat. A few of our syndicate members along with Diego, Liam, and Killian turn to look at the commotion. Diego winks at me from the bar. This is why I love him. Without asking, he's given me the space to chat with my bestie. Sel is with him, smiling up at her brother who is looking at me like I hung the moon.

"He did," I sigh contentedly. "I'm sorry I didn't tell you. I didn't want to take away from your time to shine. Lex, I finally feel like my heart isn't wandering. This feels so right. He's it for me. I know I may have been unsure in the past—okay, one too many times—but this feels different. He's different than anyone I've ever known."

"I'll be honest, I wasn't sure about him from the beginning. Because of how you started off. He seemed like he always had a hidden agenda..." she trails off before we both break out laughing and quoting Ms. Ungermeyer from *The Lizzie McGuire Movie*.

"'Sneaky little brown noser with a hidden agenda'," we mimic her voice, perfectly in sync.

This is exactly why we are friends. She gets me. We can't help but bend over at the hip, holding our stomachs and cracking up as tears leak out of our eyes.

"But in all seriousness, from what I see on your face, and how that man is currently looking at you—as we act like complete weirdos...I'd say you are right where you belong." Her smile broadens and she pulls me in for another hug.

"Alright, alright," I sniffle, wiping a tear from beneath my eye. "Enough of the sap. Let's get this party started!" I holler.

The two of us will always be thick as thieves.

At the thought of friendships, Lainey comes up to us. *I should extend an olive branch.*

"Hey, Lexi. Congrats, again! Can't wait for the wedding. I've never seen Conor so happy."

"Thanks, girly," Lex says smiling at her. Her eyes shift to mine before Lainey turns to me.

"Madison, would you mind talking with me?"

"Yeah, sure," I murmur hesitantly. I nod my head to the giant bean bag chairs around the bonfire. "Let's sit," I suggest.

We walk through the lunatics—as in my favorite men of the Tri-State Syndicate—now dancing and hugging each other in typical drunk male fashion. When we make it to the chairs, I plop down on one and she does the same. Lainey shifts so that she faces me and I awkwardly do the same. *Get it together,*

Madison. You have nothing to feel awkward about. It's not like you are fucking Liam.

"I wanted to thank you," she starts. "Liam told me that you both held off in reuniting...sexually...and it could have gone in a completely different direction. I wouldn't have been angry with you if it had, but it showed me that you and him really do respect Diego and I."

"Oh. Yeah, of course. I mean we came close...but it just didn't feel right anymore." I spin my engagement ring around my finger, anxiously giving myself something to do with my hands.

She notices, eyes like a hawk. A genuine smile crosses her features. "Does this mean you are back to being Mrs. De La Cruz?" She nods her head towards my ring.

I look down at my ring for a moment before looking back up at her. "It does. Liam and I always thought we were going to do this one day. But he and I never realized how toxic we were. How we only fed each other's fears...or how we brought out the worst sides of each other... It wasn't always the best. Certainly not sunshine and rainbows. He's an incredible man, Lainey. Since you've been dating him, I've seen him calm down with his temper. He's smoking less, drinking less. You are so good for him. I hope you know that I am no longer trying to be in the race. I accepted Diego's proposal again because we help each other grow. I need that kind of partner. I truly wish you guys the best."

"I can see that you and Diego have that connection the way Liam and I do. And I trust that we are going to keep the lanes parallel and not let them intersect. But I am not stupid. Liam may have chosen me, and I can tell he is serious in his words and his actions...but there is always the past that will haunt him. It's moments like today that I worry he shows his cards too much. About how you still hold on to a piece of him—even if you don't mean to."

I shrug, not knowing how to respond. "I can't help that. I

don't think anyone can. Life is fucking messy, Lainey. Breaking up is like trying to mix iced tea powder into a glass of water. At first it all settles to the bottom, sitting there and heavy. It takes time mixing it for the majority to dissolve. And that's what this is. Dissolving our past relationship. I can't control anymore than he can the few granules that will always sit there at the bottom and never go away. That's just life."

"Damn. Using a drink analogy to explain to a chef that her man will always have lingering feelings for his ex." She giggles and places her hand over mine, giving it a sympathetic squeeze.

Looks like we are in the clear.

"I get it. You both had an incredibly chaotic past. I also think had Diego never come into your life, you would still be with him. However, I do have one request, to ease my worries. If Liam gets all sentimental and even flirty with you, can you tell him to stop?"

"Uhh...Yeah? I mean he shouldn't be doing that. If he does, I think you need to evaluate where you stand."

"I want him so bad, Madison. It sounds pathetic. Since I was a kid, I have always had a crush on him. He never noticed. Not until a few months ago. I don't want to lose him. We really are good for each other. I just fear my love for him will never be enough."

My lips purse as I contemplate my words. "Would you like me to talk to him? I won't say you said anything," I offer politely.

"Could you? I don't want to have to break things off with him. I was willing to wait while he figured out his feelings for you. It's already been a few weeks and he still has moments where he is cranky for no reason. Or he just got off the phone planning things with you and he's got a smile on his face that wasn't there before you called. I guess I sound like a jealous, paranoid girlfriend. I just don't want to always be dealing with your ghost. No offense." She shoots me a fake smile that makes me uneasy.

"None taken," I laugh, holding my hands up in surrender. "I'll talk to him," I stand, hinting that this conversation is over.

I can't talk about this anymore.

Liam needs to stay in my past.

He's not helping by making his current girlfriend insecure about where I stand in his life.

CHAPTER 25

LIAM

I WATCH Madison and Lainey head off towards the bonfire. *Fuck.* What could they possibly be talking about other than me? They sure as shit are not talking about nails and hair. I should intervene... but after seeing Madison go off with Diego to the cabana, and hearing her climb to ecstasy, I can't bring myself to do it.

Jealousy is such a cunt.

I wish it wasn't there. I wish I could forget about her. Move on with my fucking life like I said I would. I promised Madison I would try. *And I am trying.* It's just not that fucking simple.

Lainey has been extremely patient with me, but I know it hurts her. She showed me her frustration every time Madison and I talked about the Jack and Jill. She's been on edge since the moment we got here. Anytime I was around Madison, she would be extra clingy.

I know I need to cut Madison out of me. I'm just struggling to make the final slice.

My vision wanders over to Diego leaning against the bar. He's chatting with his sister. Her smile is as big as the Empire State Building. One hand lingers at her womb, the other rubs up and down her brother's bicep. Tears are pooled in the rims of her eyes.

Curious as to what they are talking about, I saunter over there. When I reach them, Sel swipes the tears away with her index fingers. Diego spins around to greet me.

"You alright, Sel?" I ask, placing a hand on her shoulder.

"I'm fine, Liam. Thanks for asking. *Gah*," she fans herself. "It's these pregnancy hormones that are making me a total emotional mess." She laughs sweetly, leaning forward to place a kiss on her brother's cheek. "I'm happy for you, *Hermano*. Mamá would be too. Anyways, I'm off to go find Kil." She sniffles again before excusing herself.

"Listen, I am sorry for what I said about Madison earlier. You were right to have threatened me. I deserved it." My attempt at an apology is put on hold as we both direct our attention to the woman we both fell in love with.

The one making her way towards us with purpose. *Fuck. What did Lainey say to her?* The expression on her face is not good. Not good at all.

She is a woman on a mission.

Diego chuckles, leaning against the bar and taking a sip of his blood orange margarita.

I look at the bartender in desperation. My expression must have sold her. A rock glass with two fingers of my favorite whiskey slides in front of me not a breath later. I take a healthy sip as Madison reaches us.

"Godspeed," Diego snorts facetiously behind his glass.

I glare at him, knowing he knows this woman's wrath when she's mad.

Madison makes herself known, clearing her throat as she stands between the two of us. We direct our attention to her—and like the coward I can be around her—I keep my mouth shut.

"Have a nice chat?" Diego eggs her on.

Arsehole.

"Excuse me..." She gets the bartender's attention. "Can I please have what he is drinking?" Surprisingly, she points to my glass. *This is bad.* Madison loves her tequila. She even has a thing for gin or vodka. When she drinks whiskey you know she's deep in her feelings.

The bartender pours her drink, handing it to her. Maddy takes two large swigs. My fists clench seeing Diego's amused face.

"*Fuck* that burns," she rasps pressing her left palm to her sternum. That's when I spot her ring. *How could you not?* The thing is huge.

A perfect diamond nestled between two radiant sapphires slaps me square in the face.

Literally and figuratively.

I step back in shock. *Madison just slapped me.*

"*That's* for talking about my sex life in front of everyone." She grips my shirt and tugs me forward by the collar, getting close to my face. "I need you to get your shit together and get over me, Liam. I know it's not easy. We shared something special. There is no denying that. But I have moved on. You need to do the same. Diego proposed again and I said yes. We plan on building a life together. There doesn't need to be awkwardness or even tension between us all. I'd like to keep our friendship if you can handle it. But, *apparently,* you can't. Don't tell her I said this, but Lainey is deeply hurt by your actions as of lately. Especially when it comes to me. You can't continue to keep her at arms length. She deserves better than that. Either claim your woman or let her go. I refuse to be the reason you two have issues." The anger radiates out of her like steam coming off a hot spring.

Her white knuckled hand releases my shirt as she takes another sip of her drink. Diego drapes his arm over her shoulder and places a kiss to her temple. I expect another jab, but he remains quiet, letting Madison have her moment.

I know what you're thinking...Oh my God, she hit him. Stop.

209

Just stop right there. Welcome to the underworld. We handle things differently here. Red flags are green flags in our world. Hell, I trained her to do that.

I'm actually quite proud. She's grown a lot. Stood up for herself.

Anger and lust simmer under the surface of my skin. The sting I feel on my face is turning me on. Had this happened a year ago, I would have tossed my woman over my shoulders and fucked the sass right out of her. *But she's not.* And that's the problem. Perhaps I should stay single. I need to focus on being a good leader. Shit like this, *the drama.* I don't need it. Madison was the exception. Quite frankly, she is the only one who can ever really penetrate my walls.

This. This person. It's who I am to my core. I am an arsehole. Madison and I not working out destroyed what was left of my heart. It was stupid of me to ever consider replacing her.

I finish my drink, slamming the glass onto the tiki bar. "I'll handle it. I never meant to offend you. You're right. I have a hard time erasing the past. Congrats to the two of you, by the way. I see your ring is back where it belongs. Cheers." I raise my refreshed glass to the two of them before storming off towards the bonfire where Lainey is.

Lainey spots me headed her way. She pats the space next to her on the oversized bean bag chair, but I remain standing. Her brows come together in concern at my dickhead behavior. Her bare feet hit the sand as she stands, stepping into my space. A shaky hand grips my bicep.

"I take it you and Madison had a chat." Her tone gives her away. She's hurt and she's pissed.

"I can't do this, Lain." I spit it out, getting right to the point.

"What did she say to you?" Her voice raises an octave over the bass of the music.

"It doesn't matter. Leave her out of this." I bark before inwardly cringing at my behavior.

A scoff leaves her lips before she storms off. Over her shoulder she shouts, "Fuck you, Liam."

I hang my head. I really am an arsehole.

Lifting it again, I track Lainey. She's headed straight towards Madison.

Fuck.

My feet are moving, jogging my way back to the bar. I reach out to grip Lainey by the bicep, but she's already in Madison's face.

"What the fuck did you say to him?" she screams, pointing her index finger in Madison's face.

Diego angles his body between them as I try to wrangle Lainey back.

"I told him to get over me. Exactly what we talked about, Lainey. What the hell are you getting in my face for?" Madison asks bewilderedly.

"He just broke up with me. I asked you to talk to him, not convince him to break up with me!" she screams. Her voice carries, directing a few heads our way.

"Lain, come on. Let's talk inside," I encourage. The last thing I want is to ruin Con and Lexi's day.

She spins around to glare at me. "I want nothing to do with you, Liam. We could have been great. But you just can't get over her. What is it about Madison that has all of you men unable to keep your cocks in your pants?"

Madison visibly cringes, retreating a step.

Lainey shifts her anger towards Diego. "Keep an eye on the two of them. That fire is still there. You'd be a fool to trust they won't burn you in the process of sorting out their feelings." With those parting words, she stomps off to the main house.

I release a massive sigh, scrubbing a hand over my face. When I remove my hand, I notice Madison walking away from us. Diego turns on his heel to go after her, but stops himself and lets her leave. He turns back to me, his face paler than usual.

"Are we going to have a problem, Liam?"

I don't have an answer. I won't try and get between them, but I can't help my feelings. Instead, I walk away in search of a cabana to sort my shit out.

I SLIP inside one of the cabanas and stop short. Madison is there, sitting on the couch with her head in her hands. Sobs rack her body. She hasn't looked up, which means she hasn't heard me come in. I could turn around right now, give her space.

But I can't.

My feet sink into the sand as I make my way over to her. I quietly sit down on the couch next to her. The wicker creaks and groans as I get comfortable. It reminds me of our night at the club. The day I recognized my true feelings for her. It was her friend's twenty-first birthday.

Madison lifts her head, mascara is splotched beneath her eyes. I want to run my fingers beneath it, but I hold back. I can't be that man for her anymore. She has a man. It's time I really come to terms with that.

"Am I the biggest slut for having been with all of you? For sharing my body, my soul, my trust with you?"

I can't help it this time. I reach out and pull her to me by the shoulder. She settles against my chest. "No, sweetheart. You aren't. No one thinks that. Not even Lainey. She's just hurt. I guarantee she didn't mean that. Believe it or not, she's really a girl's girl. The drinking mixed with the emotions tonight had her saying things to hurt me. It wasn't meant to hurt you. I'm sorry it went down like that. I handled it poorly."

Madison sniffles against my chest. "I should have been more responsible with all of your hearts. You, Killian, Diego." Her voice cracks on a sob, her chest vibrating against me. "I'm to blame for this mess. Maybe I should just leave like I planned to."

I gently push her back to look at her. My thumb and index finger grip her chin. Beautiful glassy brown eyes stare back at me. "Is that what you really want?"

Her head swivels back and forth between my fingers as she bites her lower lip.

I move my hand to cup her face, rubbing my thumb along her cheek. Moisture collects along it.

Through my peripheral, the curtain draws back and Diego enters. His lips form a thin line.

I ignore him. "What do you want, Madison? Fuck all the noise. What do you really want?"

Diego crosses his arms over his chest, seemingly waiting for her response.

She trembles as fresh tears cascade down her cheeks and onto my hand.

Her head spins to look at *The Bone Breaker*.

"It's him, Liam. I told you this. You just weren't *really* hearing me. I *need* you to let this die here. We don't have to hate each other, but this dies right here and now. Whatever you feel for me needs to go. I am not the girl for you. We are toxic. Can't you see that?" The agony in her voice guts me.

I release her, nodding my response. She's absolutely right.

She stands, letting my hand fall to my lap. Diego sends me a sympathetic half-smile before wrapping his arm around his woman and guiding her out of the tent.

Single. Unless I sort out my issues, I am remaining single.

And on that note, I pour myself a drink and head back out to party the night away with the rest of the bridal party.

What is the expression?

"It is better to dance in the rain than to sit under a leaking roof."

CHAPTER 26

DIEGO

DAY one of the festivities is complete. *Honestly—thank fuck.* A few stragglers are down at the beach, coupled off and stargazing. Madison has kept her distance from me. Intentionally or not, it's concerning me. The logical part of my brain knows she feels bad for participating in the drama at her best friend's bachelorette. The part only she drudges up from the depths of my blackened soul, fears she could be having second thoughts. It took everything in me not to react the way I initially felt walking into that cabana and seeing the two of them holding each other.

Liam and I have had a decent friendship this past year. I wouldn't say we are able to confide in each other about anything, but we share a mutual respect. At least I thought we did... tonight proved he isn't willing to stop himself when it comes to Madison. Typically, I'm not the type to be fazed by jealousy or insecurities. A real take it or leave it kind of man. Seeing Madison in distress over her ex, and her thinking she was to blame for all the drama between them, had stirred the monsters inside of me. They wanted to obliterate anyone or anything hurting her—including Liam. He was a fucking prick tonight.

I will say, hearing my woman choose me had me feeling all

215

sorts of elated. Yet, this nagging feeling she is still unsure keeps digging its claws into me. Her distance speaks volumes.

We parted from the cabana and went right to the crowd. A few raunchy games and a lot more drinking led to sloppy kisses —but they were brief. It was as if she was afraid to show any PDA. Far from how we were at the beginning of the evening. She was ravenous, wild, and one hundred percent mine. Now, I'm not so sure that's true. Her words say she is all mine, her actions... they confuse the fuck out of me. This is exactly why I never did relationships. If you keep the lines drawn in bold, no feelings get involved.

With Madison, every fucking red line is crossed. Hell, every red line is sprinted over with no desire to stop. *I'd do anything for her.* There is no fucking line, barricade, or obstacle I wouldn't cross for her. Which is why I am standing here in the small end of the pool nursing an espresso and sobering up. If we are going to talk later, I want to do it free of the influence of alcohol.

Can't say the same for my wife.

She's still banging back shots with Lexi at the Tiki Bar.

Adorable. When she lets loose like this, all her worries are saved for another day.

She's currently sensually swaying her hips to the music. Her dark violet curls are wavy from the salt in the air. They touch the top of her ass as she leans her head back. Manicured fingers clasp her drink which is extended above her. Lexi and my wife dance parallel to each other, enjoying the company but vibing independently. Lost in their own minds and the music.

It's moments like this that remind me just how young she still is. How in the short time she's known all of us, she's had to mature in ways most wouldn't. As much as that makes me proud as hell to have the privilege of seeing that transformation, it breaks me, knowing she won't always experience this.

As if she could sense me staring at her, she opens her eyes and locks in on me. A radiant smile spreads across her face as she places her drink down and hugs her best friend. Madison takes a few steps my way before stopping abruptly. *What is she doing?* I watch in amusement as she turns around and steals the sombrero they used for drinking games off of Lexi's head.

I expect her to stumble her way over here. Surprising me as always, she makes a running start. The sombrero flutters in the wind atop her head. Fully clothed, she jumps in, sinking beneath the cool water. I'm soaked, my espresso now blending with the salt water. I toss the cup to the side as my wife resurfaces. She is radiant. Her hair is slicked back, makeup pretty much intact, minus some smudged mascara. The look on her face has me cracking a smile. A confused chuckle leaves my lips as she plops the wet sombrero back on her head.

She leans in to whisper, placing a hand beside her lips like she is telling me a secret. "Can I have your wedding band, please?"

I raise an eyebrow, but am starting to catch on. So, I play along. I remove my ring and place it in her cupped palm that's waiting before me.

She tugs my left hand forward and slides the ring back onto my finger. Her fingers linger there, playing with the metal as she looks up at me. I inhale a breath. She's always stunning, but right now? It's like I am peering directly into her soul.

And it's fucking breathtaking.

"Diego De La Cruz. I once stood like this with you in your swimming pool as you proposed to me. Well...*technically*...you *told* me I was marrying you." Her voice is captivating. There is a hint of lust and bit of frogginess from all the singing and drinking.

I laugh at her memory of that day and rub the mascara from underneath her eyes with my free hand.

"I'm sorry about everything that's happened in the last year. *Especially* these last few months. Tonight was exceptionally awful. I doubted myself for a while, wondering if I can be the woman you deserve or if my past was going to affect our future together. I spiraled, questioning my worth. Questioning if you were the next victim on my list of people I left destroyed. That's why I was distant."

"Baby, I don't think that about you."

She places her finger over my lips to hush me. "I don't want to live my life without you. I once told you I could give you my heart but not my soul. I was wrong... Because you are my soul. Without it, I'd be an empty vessel, always wandering until I found it again. Found you again. Since I met you, you have helped me become the strongest version of myself. I have truly discovered who I am. Liam made me question pieces of myself. You make me figure it out on my own, always encouraging me and stepping in when I need it. *Please*. Please tell me I didn't fuck this up. Please tell me you'll marry me again. I love you, *Ocean Eyes*." She takes the damn hat off, frisbeeing it to the deep end.

Filled with an abundance of emotion, I pull her face to mine and kiss the hell out of her. Her little surprised yelp has my back vibrating with laughter. This perfect woman makes me feel so full, so happy. So incredibly loved.

"Yes, *Mariposita*. I'll marry you again. I never doubted you. I may have felt insecure tonight, definitely a little worried. But I never questioned your worth or if you still loved me. From the moment I chained you up in that cell and you gave me your trust, I knew that we were something more."

That playful eyebrow of hers arches and her eyes light with the memories of that day. She enjoyed it. That was the start of our budding attraction.

I kiss her again, stealing her breath away. We are both left panting. Goosebumps coat Madison's slick skin. *Time for bed.* Guiding her out, I wrap a towel around her and rub her arms to warm her up.

Madison breaks out giggling. I tilt my head to figure out why as she nods towards the sombrero floating in the center of the pool. "I'll never look at oversized hats the same way again."

"Let's get dried off. Tomorrow is a new day. And I heard through the grapevine you have an early morning?" I ask it as a question because I have no clue what they are up to. I caught a glimpse of Madison's spread sheet on our bedroom desk. 8-11 AM is blocked out, highlighted, and has a purple devil emoji sticker next to it.

We ascend my private staircase to the master balcony. "Yeah...That one is a surprise."

Cryptic little thing.

I slide the glass door open, letting her enter before me. "I could always find a way to retrieve that information."

She swivels her head on her neck to look at me over her shoulder. "That actually sounds fun. I can promise you this— you will benefit from this surprise..."

"That so?" I rasp, pulling her to me by her towel.

"Mhm."

Her mouth is only inches from mine. When I lower my head to claim those delicious lips, she inhales sharply and bolts from the room towards the en suite.

Gagging travels my way and I know she's hugging the porcelain. I follow her in. Her towel is dropped at her knees and she's clinging to the bowl.

"Ugh, Diego. Get out of here. I don't want you seeing me like this," she groans with embarrassment.

"Sweetheart, I've seen it all. Your bodily functions will never make me disgusted with you. Let me help," I encourage as I approach her.

She responds by handing me her rubberband off her wrist. I collect her violet hair into a bun and secure it with the rubberband she offered.

The palm of my hand rubs gentle circles around her back as she continues to empty the contents of her stomach.

"Did you eat tonight?" I ask concerned as she continues to gag but nothing comes out. *That has to be the worst feeling in the world.*

"I didn't really get a chance," she says shakily.

"Christ, Madison. First, let's get you cleaned up and in bed. Then I'm going to grab you some food."

She stands, stripping off her wet clothes. Snagging her toothbrush from the holder, she enters the shower. "I'm alright now, *Ocean Eyes*."

"Okay..." I say hesitantly. "I'll be back in a few minutes. If you feel dizzy, sit down. I don't need you cracking your head open." The sternness in my voice has her rolling her eyes. *The sass on this woman.* Madison shakes her head back and forth in awe, insinuating I am being doting.

Which, I guess I am.

I adore this woman.

My wife.

I ENTER my kitchen expecting it to be closed up for the night. All the lights are on. Pots and pans are on the stove. Containers and food are scattered across the surfaces of the counters. *Strange.*

My chef isn't expected here until tomorrow morning. Lainey and her are collaborating on the catering for this weekend.

Speak of the devil...Lainey comes out of the pantry, looking frazzled. Boxes of food and ingredients are stacked high, obscuring her view of me.

Excellent.

With deliberately quiet steps, I pad over to her, grabbing a few items off the top of her pile.

"Need a hand with these?" I boom, causing her to drop and fumble a few of them.

"Dddiego! I didn't see you there. Can I help you with something?" she stutters, lowering her supplies to the island.

Perfect. She should be on edge around me.

"Well...for starters, I need you to make my wife something to help cure her hangover. Except, I don't think I trust you not to *poison* it..." I start to circle the island, playing with my prey.

"I...I would *never*. Tonight had nothing to do with Madison. I was mad at Liam."

"*Liar.*" I smack my palm down onto the granite. Lainey jumps, clearly afraid of me.

Good.

"This will be your one and only warning. Speak to or about my wife the way you did earlier, and you will no longer be able to use that sharp tongue of yours. I know you grew up in this life, so you know I don't play around. I especially don't play around when it comes to Madison."

A lone tear drips down her cheek as she toughens her skin. Straightening her spine she looks at me. "You are all blind. Liam included. That's all I'm going to say. I will bite my tongue moving forward."

I narrow my eyes at her. "Bite your tongue, Lainey or you won't have one. It is very simple."

She nods silently, moving toward the blender. With her back to me she says, "I can make her a smoothie that will help her with the hangover."

Leaning back against the counter by the sink, I cross my arms and ankles, watching her every move. I don't trust her, but I'll give her the benefit of the doubt. If Liam and her reunite, I don't want bad blood between us. Not everyone handles jealousy maturely.

"*Fantastic,*" I drawl.

CHAPTER 27

MADISON

THE INCESSANT SOUND of an alarm rattles my skull. *Goddamn hangover.* I fumble around on the end table for the source of the alarm. Is it my phone or Diego's? *Regardless, it needs to shut the fuck up.* As bad as my head feels, at least I'm not nauseous. The smoothie Diego brought me last night worked wonders. I felt so much better. Right now? Not so much. My head is pounding.

"Urgh."

A container of Ibrophen knocks over in my blind attempt at retrieving my phone, followed by the water bottle next to it.

"Ugh!"

Diego's deep chuckle reverberates next to me. Warm arms embrace me, pulling my back to his front. His lips lower to his new favorite spot over my tattoo.

"I woke up thinking we had some sort of creature in here..." His morning rasp sends shivers down my spine. "Turns out, it's the deadliest of them all. My gorgeous wife with a hangover."

He chuckles again, leaning over me to shut the alarm. In his retreat, he grabs the ibuprofen and water bottle.

I sit up and he mirrors me, leaning back against the

headboard. My sweet husband empties two blue pills into the palm of his hand and removes the cap from the water bottle.

"Open," he demands.

Getting used to him taking care of me, I oblige. He places the pills on my tongue and raises the water bottle to my lips. I cover his hand with mine, still struggling to let go of my need for control.

I swallow the water and pills, lowering the water bottle. "Thank you."

His smile broadens as he releases the bottle to recap it before placing it between us on the comforter.

"Any chance you'll tell me what the surprise is?"

I angle my body to face him as his hand comes up to cup my face. "Nope," I say, popping the P.

"Brat." He taps my nose with his index finger before placing a chaste kiss to my lips. Lucky me, gets the best visual of his beautiful backside as he rises from the bed. This delicious beast of a man knows I'm staring. Muscles and tendons ripple as he stretches his arms above his head. The Kraken tattoo comes alive as he moves, turning me on even more. *Mmm.* I take a quick glance at my phone: 7:45 AM.

Dammit. No time for a quickie.

"YOUR HAIR IS GORGEOUS! You look like some warrior princess or a dragon slayer," the stylist doing my hair gushes.

"Right? My Matron of Honor is not only hot but she's a total badass," Lexi chimes in from her chair next to me.

They are curling her freshly highlighted blonde hair into delicate waves. A makeup artist is applying lashes, wrapping up her sultry look. *Damn, she looks phenomenal!*

"Mad, this was such a good idea! The men are going to lose

their minds over these raunchy books," she says appreciatively, taking a sip of her coffee.

Thank God we had quad espressos delivered to the room along with some greasy New York style egg sandwiches.

Ironically, we are only a few doors down from the master bedroom, not having to have gone very far. Diego is none the wiser. I slipped out while he was showering. It's not like he can't get the information of my whereabouts. It's *his* home. However, I do think we've reached a point in our relationship...*marriage*... where if I ask for trust or boundaries, he respects them.

And I love that about him.

"It's so good to see you again, Madison," Rebbeca sing-songs, entering the room with her assistant behind her.

"I hear we have a bride in the house?" Ellie smiles sweetly at Lexi. "Congratulations."

"*Ohmaaagod*, Madison. You flew these two here for me?" Lexi claps her hands together like a child on Christmas morning.

"I did, they are the best in the business."

The ladies blush as they approach us, opening up two large suitcases filled to the brim with gorgeous, delicate lingerie. I crane my neck to take a look at the pieces they are setting up on the bed. Some are just straps of black lace, leaving little to the imagination. One set in particular catches my eye. A black satin bow top that barely covers your nipples along with a mesh and lace thong.

My makeup artist spins my head back around to finish. Stepping back to admire his work, he shifts to the right so that I can take a look at myself in the mirror.

"Oh, *wow*." My eyes widen in delight at my own reflection. *I look fucking hot.*

"Alright ladies, the photographer is ready for the bathtub pictures. We'll start with the nude shoot now. That way, the makeup artists can add body shimmer and oil for the other shots you'll take on the bed and around the room," the photographer's assistant states, holding her clipboard out in front of her.

"Have you done a boudoir shoot before?" Phil the photographer asks the two of us as he messes with the settings of his camera.

"Can't say I have..." Lexi trails off, clinging to the tie of her bathrobe. She's up first. The nerves are trickling in.

"No. This would be my first time taking pictures...em... in the nude," I confirm.

"Well, no worries. I bat for the other team, so as gorgeous and stunning as you ladies are, you're not quite my type. My husband and I have been happily married for twelve years now. I can promise you this...These pictures will make your men go absolutely feral. I remember my first boudoir shoot..." He winks, hitting play on the bedside speaker.

Dirty Talk by Wynter Gordon starts playing and immediately Lexi and I look at each other.

Let the fun begin!

Nervousness? Gone. Shyness? See ya later.

"PERFECT...LIKE that. Arch your back a bit more... I need to see titties and perky nipples playing peekaboo with me through the bubbles. YES! Stay right there. Tilt your head a bit towards me... yes, don't move. Give me your bedroom eyes...*excellent.* Bite that lip and don't you move!" Phil has brought his A game.

I have never felt more proud of my own body than I do now. I feel sexy, confident, and beyond excited for Diego to see these. I'm even more excited for what happens *after* he sees these.

"Okay, let's grab a towel. Someone please help Madison out of the tub." Phil snaps his fingers at his assistant, as she is the only other person in the room with Lexi and I.

A warm fluffy towel is wrapped around my body as I exit the

bath. Phil places a hand at the small of my back, navigating me over to the sink. He picks up a brand new tooth brush and hands it to me. A makeup artist shuffles over to add oil and highlighter to my skin with a spray bottle.

"Lean over the counter. I want you to brush your teeth while looking in the mirror." He tosses a few curls of mine over my bare shoulder. I position myself so my cleavage presses firmly against the knot in the towel there. Really getting into it, I flutter my eyelashes and loosen my eyelids, giving the visual I just woke up.

"Madison! You are a natural, sweetheart. Work that toothbrush!" Phil praises.

Lexi giggles from the threshold of the door. She already did this part, except she did it in a satin white lingerie set and a short 1950s veil. What a stunning bride she is.

"Such a natural. That's the money shot right there. I only needed one! *Incredible.* You are incredible. Let's move on to the window." Phil claps his hands in excitement, putting a little pep in my step.

I pad over to the sheer curtains. Phil's assistant lifts it and I slide in behind it.

"Drop it like it's hot," Phil sings in regards to my towel.

I crack up, as does Lexi. The assistant collects it and walks back towards her boss.

"Sit your ass at the edge of the windowsill. I want one hand beside you gripping the edge...arch that back. *Yes.* Now, let your hair cascade down your back, lift that chin, and spread those legs slightly. Just enough to give me a tiny show. Exactly, Madison. Close your eyes and stay like that," he directs, snapping pictures.

A knock sounds at the door, making my eyes pop open.

"*Madison.* Are you in there?" Diego's voice carries over the music, a tinge of irritation in it.

I brush the curtain back. The assistant hands me my

bathrobe and I don it promptly. When I reach the door, I crack it open a hair.

"Hi."

Diego cranes his neck to see over me, but I shut the door even further.

"Was someone telling you to spread your gorgeous legs?" There is humor in his voice, not jealousy. Maybe a hint of playful curiosity.

Which is a relief.

"Uhhh... yeah. But it's not what you think. It's the surprise I was talking about. You trust me, right?" I bite my lower lip as my false eyelashes flutter while looking up at him.

His hand reaches out through the crack in the door to cup my face. "I do. You look beautiful. How's the head?" he asks as his thumb rubs a path over my cheek.

"*Much* better. The pain relievers and quad espresso really helped." I smile, leaning into his touch.

"I didn't mean to interrupt, I just so happened to be heading to my office when I heard someone tell you to spread your legs..." He smirks.

"I would have bust the door down if roles were reversed. I'm impressed with your self-control," I laugh.

"There wasn't much. Trust me, I wanted to. But marriages are about trust. After you confessed your love for me last night, I realized I've got nothing to worry about." He shoots me a wink, sending butterflies straight to my core.

Raising up on my tip toes, my lips claim his. It takes everything in me to break off this kiss. *Fuck*. I'm so turned on right now...

"Remember, we are all meeting for lunch poolside today," I remind him.

"I'll be there, baby." He knocks twice on the molding of the door before walking down the hallway towards his office.

"Wait!" I shout down the hallway. He spins on his heel. "Do

you need your office or can you do your work from somewhere else?"

A dark eyebrow raises in question. "I don't *need* it. Why?"

"I need to borrow it."

"What's mine is yours, *Mariposita*. Have at it." He shakes his head, amused. Those perfect straight teeth bite down on his lip as he strides past me, whistling as he goes.

The door closes with a *click*. I spin around and lean against it, looking up at Phil. "I want to wear that..." I point to the black bowtie lingerie Rebbeca had laid out earlier. "On his desk."

"Girl, you can have my job. I am no longer worthy..." he jokes, retrieving the set and tossing it at me. "Get dressed."

CHAPTER 28

DIEGO

I STEP out onto the bathroom mat, wrapping a towel around my waist. A chuckle leaves my lips at the thought of my chaotic, beautiful wife waking up this morning. How I wished we could have had a few more minutes for me to ravish her in the shower. That would have gotten rid of that headache of hers...

After drying off in the bedroom, I walk over to my closet and dress in a pair of board shorts and a white short-sleeved henley. Being back here has me dressing the way I like. There is nothing worse than having to dress in business attire—*scratch that*—winter clothes are the fucking worst. You're either overheating or freezing cold.

I make my way down to the kitchen in desperate need of a coffee. Liam and Killian are deep in discussion at the kitchen island. Lainey is nowhere to be seen.

Looks like she and Liam have not resolved their issues.

"Morning," I grumble, passing them en route to the espresso machine.

"Good Morning, Diego," Killian swivels on his bar stool to greet me.

Liam grunts his hello. *Today is already off to a great start.* Not

231

only did I *not* get to sink myself inside my stunning wife, but I now have to deal with not one, but two of her exes.

"Where's Madison?" Liam finally asks over the sound of the beans grinding.

"She and Lexi had some special event booked. I couldn't tell you." I shrug, not caring to turn around. My focus is on getting this espresso running through my veins before I deal with his mood swings—*or mine.*

"Lena knows something. She acted all coy this morning. You won't see her for a while though, she's sleeping in until lunch," Killian announces, standing and taking one last sip of his coffee. "I think I'll take a run on the beach before then. Cheers."

I finish prepping my drink at the same time my head chef approaches me. "I could have made you one, Sir. Sorry, I was in the back room preparing lunch. Are you finished with the machine? Mrs. De La Cruz just rang and requested quad espressos be sent up."

The corner of my lip raises, knowing my wife needs this more than I do. "It's all yours." I step aside. "Can you please make sure to send up some food as well? My wife tends to run on coffee and no food."

She smiles in response, knowing all too well how us coffee addicts function. "Of course."

Needing to address the elephant in the room, I take a seat in Killian's vacant chair.

Raising the coffee mug to my lips, I take a sip before sighing loudly. "What's up, Liam?"

He runs a hand over his face, scrubbing the sleep from his eyes. It appears he had zero last night. The question is, what kept him up? Madison or Lainey?

"Lainey won't talk to me. I slept on the living room couch last night. She locked me out of the room. And for good reason. I was a complete arse." His lips dip, forming a scowl.

"Can we be honest with each other? No bullshit. What's holding you back from Lainey? Is it Madison?"

He looks at me, owning his emotions. "It is. You know how incredible she is. I'm having a difficult time letting her go. I won't interfere. She chose you. I understand it. I'm just having a hard time digesting it, that's all. Lainey has been great for me. And as much as I wanted us to work... I realized I'm not really ready."

"She is incredible, that we can both agree. I am sorry, Liam. If roles were reversed I'd be feeling the same way. I will say, after last night, I don't know if I trust Lainey. I believe her true colors are shining through. You have known her longer than I have, so you may be the better judge of character here. There is just something about how she reacted to Madison that stems far beyond jealousy."

Liam lowers his elbows to the granite and lowers his face into his hands. "If you asked me this a few weeks ago, I would have laughed in your face. After last night, I sort of agree," he groans. He lifts his head to look at me. Pain clouds his eyes. "Honestly, staying single seems like the best option. I've got too much shit on my plate to be dealing with the drama. No one will compare to Madison. That's a fact I am coming to terms with," he sighs.

I pat his back twice, giving him my sympathy before standing. "I've got a few calls to make. I'll be in my office if anyone needs me."

Liam spins on his chair as I retreat. "*Diego.*"

On a low sigh, I turn back around. Here we go...

"Promise me you'll take care of her. I finally understand that Madison doesn't need our help. She's extremely independent. I fucked up by coddling her. Regardless, there will be moments when she burns herself out. Just promise me you'll be there to catch her when she does." His demand is full of raw emotion.

"I promise," I state simply. I don't need to tell Liam how

much that woman means to me, or the lengths I would go to protect her.

He already knows.

And with that, I make my way towards the staircase.

"SIT your ass at the edge of the windowsill. I want one hand beside you gripping the edge...arch that back. *Yes.* Now, let your hair cascade down your back, lift that chin, and spread those legs slightly. Just enough to give me a tiny show. Exactly, Madison. Close your eyes and stay like that..." A chipper male voice is carrying down the hall as I approach my office.

Excuse me? My feet stop dead in their tracks. So that's where they are. And who the *fuck* is coaching my woman, telling her to spread those gorgeous thighs?

Don't do it... Don't do it.

I try convincing myself to respect her boundaries. She said this was a surprise for me... I need to trust that. Kind of fucking hard to do when a man is telling your woman to spread her legs behind closed doors... *Fuck it.* A little check-in never hurt anyone.

My knuckles connect with the wooden door.

Footsteps approach before the door swings open. Barely enough for me to reach my arm in.

"Hi," my wife chirps, acting all shy. *Cute.*

Madison looks drop-dead gorgeous. She's always beautiful—with or without makeup—but whoever dolled her up today has her looking like a bombshell. A fluffy white bathrobe wraps around her body, hiding what is beneath—or lack thereof. I crane my neck over her to investigate the source of those words I heard. The ones only I should have the privilege of commanding.

"Was someone telling you to spread your gorgeous legs?" I

smirk, giving off the vibe of relaxed yet intrigued. Deep down, I am actually the opposite, vibrating with raw possessiveness.

I can just barely make out a bunch of lingerie lining the bed as well as studio chairs set up. Makeup and hair products are scattered all over the table. Studio lights are set up in the corners of the room. *Ahh.* Unless they are shooting a porno, this appears to be one of those scandalous photoshoots. A *dirty* one.

My fists clench knowing another male is seeing my woman naked. I take a soothing breath through my nose. She agreed to be mine last night.

This woman is mine, I remind myself.

I *trust* her.

"Uhhh... yeah. But it's not what you think. It's the surprise I was talking about. You trust me, right?" Thick Disney Princess eyelashes flutter up at me as she bites her full lower lip.

My little butterfly is nervous, and it's cute as hell.

Unable to help myself, I reach through the crack of the door and cup her face. "I do. You look beautiful. How's the head?"

"*Much* better. The pain relievers and quad espresso really helped," she raves as she smiles up at me. Without hesitation, she leans into my touch as my thumb skims the smooth skin beneath her eye.

"I didn't mean to interrupt, I just so happened to be heading to my office when I heard someone tell you to spread your legs..." I can't help but smirk at this woman. She knows how possessive I can get.

"I would have bust the door down if roles were reversed. I'm impressed with your self-control," she giggles. And I know my little butterfly would. You saw how she was with Red.

"There wasn't much. Trust me, I wanted to. But marriage is about trust. After you confessed your love for me last night, I realized I've got nothing to worry about." I wink, watching her eyes glaze over.

She's totally swooning.

And looking incredibly fuckable right now.

Raising up onto her tiptoes, she leans over the threshold and kisses me. This kiss is all sorts of needy. And greedy. And *dirty*.

Christ, who am I? Dr. Seuss? This woman has me so giddy, I'm now rhyming. So fucking be it.

I welcome her enthusiasm, opening my mouth and granting her tongue access to dance with mine. I groan internally. *Any chance I can steal her away right now?*

"Remember, we are all meeting for lunch poolside today," she reminds me after breaking our passionate kiss. Her statement leaves me feeling like a true married couple.

"I'll be there, baby." I knock twice on the molding of the door before walking down the hallway to my office.

"Wait!" Her voice echoes down the hallway. I spin on my heel to greet her. The look of excitement lights up her face. "Do you need your office or can you do your work from somewhere else?" she questions as mischief dances in her eyes.

My eyebrow raises in question, curious what she is up to. "I don't *need* it. Why?"

"I need to borrow it," she states, a poker face sliding into place.

"What's mine is yours, *Mariposita*. Have at it." I shake my head, extremely amused. I stride towards her, biting down on my lip. She sways back and forth on her feet, eager to get back to whatever she's planning.

I start to whistle on my way to the staircase.

Make it quick, *Mariposita. I need to taste you.*

CHAPTER 29

MADISON

THE LIVELY CHATTER grows louder as I approach the pool. With my beach bag slung over my shoulder, I stride over to my man who is glistening with sweat and splayed out on a lounge chair. The sun is warm at my back as I stop directly in front of him, casting a shadow over his body. A deep baritone chuckle leaves those delicious lips as he recognizes my arrival.

"Hello, gorgeous," he says smiling while adjusting his sunglasses so that they sit on top of his head.

I place my beach bag at the end of the chair next to him and lean over to kiss him deeply. His hand comes up behind my head, holding my face there and swirling his tongue over my bottom lip. A groan passes his lips like he's been in agony all morning. *Trust me, I feel the same way, Bone Breaker.*

"That bathing suit should be illegal, *Mariposita*," he tuts, tugging me forward by the metal hoop between my cleavage. Warm lips press against the swell of each of my breasts. *The Bone Breaker* shows me no mercy, licking a path up my chest and wrapping his lips over my neck.

"Diego..." I warn.

"Get a room!" Lexi teases, splashing us.

She and her future husband are in an extremely competitive match of pool beer pong. Con uses her moment of distraction to sink a ball into the front cup.

"Hey! That's not fair," Lexi pouts. "I was distracted." She pulls the cup from the rack and sips its contents.

"It is fair. That white bikini you're wearing has had me distracted the entire game," he reasons.

I get situated, leaning back against my lounge chair.

"Would you like an umbrella?" Diego asks.

"No, thank you." I wave him off. "I love the sun."

He winks at me. "I can be your sun. Warming that sexy body of yours. Making those cheeks turn red as sweat beads on your skin. Fuck, I can even make your head spin. You'll be dizzy from just being in my presence for too long."

I turn to look at him, narrowing my eyes behind the designer shades he got me. "You are *so* cocky."

"You know it's true," he brags.

My legs close in an attempt to settle down the ache there. "Nope. Not at all." I try for nonchalant.

He rolls his eyes at me, standing and stretching his arms high above his head. Rows of abs clench and his board shorts sink low, exposing the V I'd like to sink my teeth into. I bite my lower lip at the lust zipping recklessly through my body. He grabs the bottle of sunscreen, squeezes some into his hand, and starts to massage it into my shoulders, down my arms, and over my breasts. His fingers sink beneath the cups of my top, rolling each nipple. I gasp, allowing him to take full advantage.

Warm lips claim mine. Just as we are about to become lost in each other, he tosses the bottle into my lap.

"Madison and I call next," he announces before diving into the deep end.

I shake my head, ridding myself of the haze. A waitress comes over at the same moment. I shield my eyes from the sun with my hand and look up at her.

"Can I grab you a drink, Mrs. De La Cruz?"

"You can just call me Madison." I smile sweetly at her.

"In our home, you'll be addressed as Mrs. De La Cruz, *Mariposita*," Diego shouts from the pool.

Asshole. My smile widens. Being addressed as his wife always has a nice ring to it.

"Ignore him. I'd love a blood orange margarita." Diego smirks at my wittiness.

"That is Mr. De La Cruz's favorite as well. I'll get right on that." She walks away, heading towards the bar.

Liam passes her, spotting me first before shifting his gaze over to Diego.

"This seat taken?" he asks, pointing to the lounge chair to the left of me.

"Ummm... I think Lexi is sitting there," I lie.

"Come on, Mad. Don't be like that." He places his hands on his hips. "I said I was sorry."

I growl under my breath. *Insufferable man*. "Take a seat. I'm just about to play beer pong anyway."

"Goddammit! I can't believe you won again!" Conor groans.

"Madison and I will *always* be the champions. This is *our* game," Lexi taunts.

"Damn right!" I holler.

"Madison, we're up," Diego declares.

I stand, shimmying out of my skirt and removing my flip-flops. When I bend over to place them in my bag, I can feel more than one set of eyes on my ass.

"Told you that bathing suit should be illegal," Diego complains.

"Well, I like it." I stick my tongue out at my husband, who is leaning his arms on the pavers, looking up at me. His hair is slicked back. Water droplets cling to his tan skin.

Imagine a model for a cologne ad. *You know the type.* Guy in a pool, low cut bathing suit...wet skin. *Yep. That's my man. Mmm.*

I waste no time sitting down on the pavers and throwing my legs over the edge of the pool. Diego slides between them, gripping both of my thighs. Tilting his head up, he claims my lips.

"I never said I didn't *like* it... but too many people here like it too..." His eyes direct over to Liam behind me.

Diverting the budding tension, I hop in and wade over to where Lexi is resetting the cups. "You got this, babe. Show him *no* mercy." She extends her fist so that I bump it.

Liam jumps in with my drink, sploshing through the water to hand it to me. "Figured you would be needing this." His smile broadens as he reaches me. Like he should get some sort of brownie points or something.

"Thanks." I take a nice sip and place it down on the floating table.

"Can I be your partner?" he asks, nudging my shoulder.

"No. This is between Madison and I," Diego answers for me. For once, I'm grateful for it.

Liam lifts his hands in surrender. "Alright. Con and I have next."

Liam, Lexi, and Con convene in the corner of the shallow end as a round of shots gets passed around. They eagerly accept, tossing them back with ease. When the waitress leans over the side of the pool to offer me one, I politely wave her off.

It's too early for shots. We have all night.

I grab a ball from the cup and toss it back and forth between my hands.

"Alright, *Mariposita*. Let's make this game a bit more interesting. How about a wager? You can set your terms first."

"Hmm...If I win, you have to give me anything I want." I cross my arms, pushing my boobs up and teasing the fuck out of him. *How about a dose of your own medicine, Bone Breaker?*

It works. His eyes zero in on them while his tongue darts out to lick his lower lip.

"You don't need to win a game in order for me to give you anything you want. So, if you win or lose, it makes no difference to me."

I can't help but smile at that. It really is the truth. He would *give* anything, *say* anything, *and do* absolutely anything for me.

"And if you win?" I raise a snarky eyebrow.

"If I win...I get to steal you away before dinner. And I think you already know what I want," he says pointedly, staring below my navel.

Goosebumps spring up along my skin.

"Deal." I reach my hand out to shake his extended one. His grip is firm, but his thumb is gentle, rubbing back and forth over the top of my hand. Those sapphire eyes are shaded by dark-tinted Oakley sunglasses. I don't need to see them to know they are swirling with lust.

Let the games begin.

"MADISON! How could you? Our winning streak is officially ruined," Lexi fake cries into her hands.

I pretend to console her, rubbing her back. "I'm sorry, Lex. No one told me Diego was a fucking beast at beer pong." My gaze darts over to my husband who is doing a celebratory shot with Liam.

Seems those two have gotten over the tension. Probably at the expense of me losing this game. *Men.* I roll my eyes.

"He is a beast and a brute." Lexi glares at him.

"I heard that, *Alexis*," Diego laughs, stacking the plastic shot glasses and leaving them at the edge of the pool.

"If Madison and I are late for dinner, you can blame her," Diego announces to everyone.

The grandest of smiles is spread across his face. He's so at peace, so carefree right now. I stare longingly at him.

This is exactly where I belong.

Diego swims up next to me, circling my waist and pulling me flush against him. "Are you mad?"

"No," I say, wrapping my arms around his neck.

"I bet you're just dying to know what I have planned." He lowers his forehead to mine.

"I am," I admit.

"A few more hours and you'll find out..." He waggles his eyebrows.

A little while later, we get out and dry off. I slip on a pair of black mesh pants and a camisole. Everyone gathers around the table set up by the pool. Drinks are served and salads are placed on each of our charger plates.

I dig in, enjoying the delicious flavors bursting on my tongue. Leafy greens and fresh fruit tossed in a Dijon balsamic dressing. Candied pecans and blue cheese crumbles top it off, adding a nice crunch.

Lainey may not be my favorite person in the world, but she is a damn good chef.

Diego gapes at me as my eyes practically roll. He silently chuckles when I look back at him innocently. *What?*

Liam's chair screeches back against the stone pavers as he stands. "I have an announcement." He uses his knife to tap against his beer bottle.

Everyone quiets down, turning their heads to look at him. "Tonight after dinner I have a special event planned. One I think you all may enjoy. My tattoo artist has agreed to fly out tonight and join us. He'll be doing tattoos at the main house for those of you who wish to add to your collection. Couldn't have a bachelor and bachelorette party without the availability of a drunk and impulsive decision to get inked." Excited chatter fills the space around us.

"*Wow*. That's fun," Lexi speaks up. "Maddy and I are deff getting inked."

"Yeah...we'll see..." I say wryly.

CHAPTER 30

DIEGO

WE SPENT the rest of the day playing sports on the beach—Madison, not so much. She, Lexi, and Selena tanned, gossiped, and played some raunchy truth-or-dare game. Lainey was supposed to join but never did. She's avoided Liam at all costs.

Madison and I just got back to the bedroom. Her skin is literally sparkling. The sunscreen she uses has a shimmer to it.

She plops her beach bag on the chair at the foot of the bed. "I can't believe Liam got his tattoo artist to come down," she says incredulously. "He never told me anything about that."

"Are you considering getting one?" I purr, hooking my chin over her shoulder and pulling her to me from behind.

"Maybe..." Which means yes. *I wonder what she'll get?*

"It is time to collect, *Mariposita*. I've been patient all day," I tut. I collect her hand in mine and guide her back out of our room and down the hallway.

I navigate her to the room next to my office. Pressing my thumb to the doorknob scanner, it unlocks, granting us access. I twist the metal knob and use my foot to open the door, all while watching Madison's reaction.

"I figured you wouldn't want to go down to the basement..."

She steps around me, looking around the room. Her eyes have grown wide as she nibbles on her lower lip.

"So *this* is what is hidden behind the mysterious door. In the six months I lived here, never once was I able to open it."

"You'll have access to it now. But I can't imagine why you would be in here without me..."

I walk over to the chains hanging from the ceiling and tug, bringing the cuff down and opening it. Madison steps closer. Her breathing accelerates as she looks at the fur-lined cuff.

"Give me your hand."

She does, placing her right one into the cuff. I secure the padded leather and walk behind her, pulling back her left elbow. My fingers trail down her arm to place her left hand in the other cuff. I circle back around to greet her exhilarated amber eyes.

"I love you, *Mariposita*. I've loved you since the first moment you gave me your blind trust." I caress her face with my hand, giving her the reassurance she can trust me once again. "Back when I had you chained up in my dungeon, I told you that you should see yourself from my perspective. You told me it was fear you were experiencing, but we both know it wasn't." I saunter over to the table and retrieve my laptop. I find the file and click play, bringing the laptop close to her face.

Her nostrils flare as the memories of that night replay on the screen. It was absolutely lust.

My little liar.

The video shows her hanging from the ceiling. I circle her, knife in hand. That pretty mouth of hers bound by tape. The edge of my blade slicing through her clothing like butter. Her nipples harden and her breathing becomes labored.

We watch until the end. My hand comes down to slap the laptop shut. She jumps, rattling the chains.

"I've been dying to reenact that moment. And I know you have too," I say, lust coating my throat in gravel. The black of her pupils expands as the gold threads explode around it.

I place the laptop back on the table before collecting my favorite pocket knife. Then I grab the remote for the electronic chains and hit the button to raise her a few inches off the ground. Her arms raise above her head as the chains go taut. Now she is at eye level with me.

The predator in me enjoys circling her, playing with her mind. "I thought about covering that pretty mouth with tape, but last time I made you bleed. In that moment, I vowed to never again have you bleed at my hand. So there will be no tape. Besides, I need that mouth accessible to hear you scream my name."

"So sure of yourself..." she pants, her breasts rising and falling beneath the thin camisole she has covering her bathing suit.

The tip of my knife starts at the neckline of her shirt. With precision, I glide it through, splitting the fabric in two. When I am done, all that is left are two spaghetti straps holding the fabric around each of her arms. Pulling the material taught, I slice into both of them. The scraps of fabric sink to the floor.

Madison's nipples harden, pressing against the purple bikini she has on. I want to run my tongue around them until she is moaning my name—but we have time for that. Instead, I slip the knife into the waistband of her mesh coverup.

The outline of her ribs shows as she sucks in a breath.

With steady hands, the knife descends, splitting the seam and recreating our first moment of heightened sexual tension.

I circle her again, guiding my other hand around her hip as I switch the handle of the knife into the other hand, running the blade up between her ass cheeks. She lays her head back to rest on my shoulder and my teeth find my new favorite spot on her.

Right over that tattoo she got for me.

Mariposita.

When my knife slices through the remaining fabric, both sides slide right off her. The pants have a drawstring at the top and are flared at the bottom. It pools on the floor with the remnants of her shirt. Next to go are her bikini bottoms. Careful as ever, I line the tip of my knife just above her pubic bone. It cuts into the material with ease. Adding a bit of pressure, I lower the blade and cut through the elastic, easing off when I reach the thin nylon.

Once more, I trail the pathway between her legs, tracing the slit she has beneath the fabric. A shiver rocks her, rattling the chains above us. I lean in to kiss her and she does the same. Needing to tease her, I lean back, continuing to circle around her back.

"*Asshole*," she sneers, all frustrated.

"I've been called worse, sweetheart." I chuckle.

I finish off, slicing through the backside of her bottoms. The purple scraps land neatly on top of the growing pile.

My heart beats erratically against my ribcage seeing her naked from the navel down. She could be naked all hours of the day, and I would still react the same exact way.

Every. Damn. Time.

Madison De La Cruz is a goddess among us. Even more so today. Her body literally shimmers, making her appear ethereal. It's as if she was dipped in gold, the color complementing her bronze skin perfectly.

Hard as stone, my cock strains against the confines of these board shorts. Her gaze goes right to the tent in my pants as she licks her lush lips. Lips I'd love to have wrapped around this cock right about now. But this moment isn't about me.

It's about her.

Leaving her dangling a few inches off the ground, I pad back over to the table behind her. She swivels her head over her shoulder trying to get a glimpse, barely able to see what I am up to. That is all part of the game I am playing with her. It heightens her senses, making this moment even more thrilling.

I collect the pliers I set out earlier. This wasn't in my original plan... but most plans need adjustments. When I noticed at the pool she was wearing a bandeau top with a nice metal ring in the center—I had to add a new tool to my inventory.

My bare chest presses against her back as my hands come up to fondle her breasts. The ridge of my cock lines up with her ass —that she desperately tries to push against me. I pinch a hardened nipple, siphoning a beautiful moan out of her.

The hand with the plier slides up her stomach, tracing a line until it reaches the circular ring holding the two pieces of her top together. Her shimmering chest is rising and falling so rapidly, that I swear she may hyperventilate.

"Calm down, *Mariposita*. Breathe, baby," I whisper.

The head of the plier slips underneath the metal, the teeth opening to accommodate the ring. Carefully, I close them, making sure not to pinch her skin. Adding pressure, the metal snaps, finally freeing her breasts. With a *clink*, the top falls to the floor.

Goosebumps spring up along her breasts as the chilled air caresses her sun-kissed skin.

I place the pliers back down on the table and kick the pile of clothes out of the way. Needing to raise her higher, I reach into my pocket and hit the button on the remote. Long, toned legs now dangle right at shoulder length. *Perfect.* Her fingers grip the chains as her body squirms, adjusting to the new height.

The remote bounces as I fling it onto the bed behind us. Dropping my shorts to the floor, I toss them with the rest of the clothes. Madison's eyes shoot straight to my jutting cock.

My hand reaches out to stroke it for good measure. "Like what you see, baby?" I purr.

She responds with a nod.

Not wanting her shoulders to strain too much, I make my way over to her with haste. I grip her thighs, firmly wrapping them around my shoulders before cupping her ass and bringing her glistening pussy to my face.

Christ, I've been wanting to taste her all day.

Like a starved man, I devour her, licking and sucking up her liquid sweetness.

"Mmm," we moan simultaneously.

CHAPTER 31

MADISON

I AM WRITHING on his face. My hips gyrating against him. Though my arms and hands don't hurt—thanks to his shoulders giving the chains slack—they itch to reach out and touch him. To tangle my fingers into his soft curls and pull his head closer to my core.

"*Ocean Eyes...*" I moan breathily.

His grip on my ass grows firmer as his tongue destroys me.

The walls of my pussy clench, sending shocks of pleasure radiating through me. My arousal drips down my thighs and over his chin as he continues his tongue's relentless assault. Stars cloud my vision as the chains rattle. The pads of my fingers burn from clenching them too tightly.

"Diego...please...*pleaaaase*," I weep. I don't even know what I am begging for... to come? For him to be inside me this instant?

His teeth scrape against my clit and I explode, crying out my release. If not for his strong hands supporting me, I would have gone completely slack on these chains.

"Holy... fuck." I am barely able to get the words out.

"Hold on, baby. We are just getting started," he apprises. The five o'clock shadow at his chin glistens with my release.

Supporting my trembling body in one arm, he reaches over

and hits a button on the remote. Instantly, I am lowered, my arms coming down to wrap around his neck. He kisses me hard. I taste myself on him as our tongues dance.

"If only you could see yourself when you come. It's quite the sight, *Mariposita*," he rasps.

He lowers me slowly, letting my Jell-O legs get reacquainted with the ground. When steady, he releases me to undo my bindings. His fingers rub at the places the cuffs dug into my wrists before bringing them up to his lips to kiss each one.

Bending over, he scoops me up and walks a few feet over to what appears to be a sex swing. If my cheeks weren't already bright red, they would be now. I have never seen a sex swing in real life. Looks like I am about to find out how this works...

Gently, he lowers my body so that my head rests against the cushioned pillow-like thing and my ass sits at the edge of it. His strong fingers grip my trembling calves.

"I will be the only one to ever tell you to spread those beautiful thighs, *Mariposita*. Are we clear?" he asks... *demands*... whatever... as he slides each of my legs into the stirrup-looking straps.

My head is spinning and my tongue becomes tied. I'm still in the process of recovering from my orgasm. I nod vehemently, prompting him to smile wickedly.

"Good," he praises as he pulls me forward by the straps and enters me. I'm so wet he slides all the way in, bottoming out.

I inhale sharply from the pleasure that vibrates through me. The sensation of fullness causes my walls to cave around him. He groans in appreciation.

Diego doesn't ease up, continuing to pound into me and sending me into a spiral of passion and ecstasy. I am already so sensitive. It doesn't take much for him to build me back up.

Our bodies are slick with sweat. A saltiness permeates the air between us from our swim in the ocean earlier. Hints of coconut and mint flirt with my heightened senses. Such a delicious and deadly combination.

Just like him.

The Bone Breaker is *mine.*

"Mine. Mine. Mine," I chant internally... or so I thought.

"You're mine too, baby. All mine. I belong to you and you only. No other woman will ever have my eyes, my cock, or my heart and soul. Just you. Always you," he groans. The sound of his anguish and how close he is to release has my eyes rolling back in my head.

So fucking sexy.

His voice alone could make me come on the spot.

Sensing my impending release, he increases his pace, thrusting into me at a rate I can only describe as manic. My walls grip him impossibly hard as he roars out his release, his cock twitching inside me as he empties himself completely. The sound he makes sends me over. And then I'm spiraling right along with him and screaming out my euphoria.

Our chests heave as we catch our breath. Diego grips the straps of the chair, his knuckles white. Sweat drips down his chest onto the trimmed hair he has at the base of his cock.

"That was fucking incredible," he says between breaths. He pulls out and I wince.

"I need a nap before dinner," I admit groggily.

"*We* need a shower. Unfortunately, there isn't much time before dinner. I'd say a shower is priority."

"You did say I would be late..." I argue.

He removes my legs from the straps and grips my hand to help me up, placing a sweet kiss to my lips.

"I did. But I'm sure Lexi would appreciate her Matron of Honor being there on time."

"I know, I know. I can't be late. You know that kind of stuff gives me anxiety."

He shakes his head back and forth in awe. "Blood, carnage,

and crime doesn't give you anxiety, but being late to dinner does. What am I going to do with you?" He chuckles while guiding my arms into a fuzzy bathrobe.

I tighten the belt as he steps back into his board shorts. Diego comes back over to me, offering me a hand and helping me stand. He raises my left hand to place a kiss over my engagement ring.

"I have another surprise for you. But you'll have to wait until later." He winks, leading me back to our room.

I gaze up at him, but his mask is back, hiding his true intentions or any hint of what's to come. When we arrive back at the room, I practically wobble my way to the en suite.

"Can't wait..." I say giddily.

He slaps my ass, ushering me into the shower. "Tick, tock, *Mariposita*. You've got sixty minutes to get ready. Fifty, if I make you come again."

Smug bastard.

"CAN you zip the back of my dress?" I ask as I collect my hair over one shoulder.

Diego comes up behind me where I stand in front of the vanity. He pulls me close by the waist and places a kiss on the back of my neck while zippering the dress. Swirling ocean eyes connect with mine in the mirror.

"You look beautiful," he whispers.

"Thank you," I reply, blushing.

He twines his fingers through mine, tugging me toward the door. "Shall we?"

TIKI TORCHES and lanterns surround the patio by the pool. A white runner lines the length of the table, along with fresh flowers and votives. It looks incredible—and this isn't even the rehearsal dinner. Diego kindly offered his yacht for that. I've gotten to see it from the beach, it's docked on the other end of the island. From what I can see, it is just as big as the original and twice as beautiful.

Everyone is socializing around the pool, snacking on hors d'oeuvres, and indulging in cocktails.

"I'll grab us a drink," Diego excuses himself, placing a kiss on my temple.

Liam spots me, drawn to me like a magnet. Grabbing a fresh bottle of beer from the bar, he cracks it open and heads my way. At least he's attempted to dress for the occasion, wearing a nice pair of slacks and a fitted collared shirt. The sleeves are rolled up and the top few buttons are open to reveal his tattoos. The man despises these types of events—the kind where he is required to dress up.

Killian, on the other hand, is wearing a crisp pair of dress pants and a navy blue sports jacket over his dress shirt. Hair slicked back and cleanly shaven—in typical Killian fashion. Sel is beside him, sipping a ginger ale and looking phenomenal in her red cocktail dress.

"Once again, Madison, you nailed it. The space looks incredible," Liam applauds.

"It really does look amazing. Good call on the tattoos," I commend, hoping we are back on semi-good terms.

His chocolate brown eyes light up with curiosity. He brings the bottle up by the neck to take a swig before asking, "What do you plan on getting? My guy finally has the chance to do your raven tattoo."

My heart sinks at that. I have considered getting one, but every time I bring myself to do so, it just doesn't feel right. And that's sad. Liam was once a huge part of my life. Ravens not only remind me of him and the love we shared but the journey of my transformation. The work it took to start getting over my past and discover the potential of my future.

Now, the raven is a reminder of death, of endings—specifically with Liam. Permanently inking my body with one would always be that painful reminder.

Liam once told me ravens meant the truth will set you free.

And the truth is... I'm not getting that raven tattooed on me tonight.

My face must give me away, which causes his lips to turn down at the corners. I catch it before he takes a larger swig of his beer.

"I get it. Ravens remind you of *me*. And that butterfly tattoo you have reminds you of *him*. You look gorgeous by the way." He looks over his shoulder at Conor and Lexi approaching. "I'm going to go chat with Con. I'll catch up with you later..." The disappointment and hurt are thick in his voice.

It kills me to hear it, that I am hurting him. We may have agreed to part ways, but acceptance is a whole different thing. I don't have a second to process my troubled thoughts. Lexi is already there hugging me.

"Madison De La Cruz! This dinner is everything and more... And it's not even the rehearsal dinner. You sure you don't want to find a career as an event planner?" she laughs, rocking me back and forth in her arms.

I pull back, collecting her hands in mine. "You've been through so many of my ups and downs, always the most amazing friend. This is the least I can do for you," I sigh.

"You don't owe me anything. You're my sister. Always." She pulls me in for another hug and whispers in my ear. "Liam treating you fairly? He's been a mess, Mad. Con and the guys were up with him all night on the beach. He didn't get much sleep, if any."

Once again, my heart breaks. I'm the reason he's hurting... and there isn't much I can do to fix it.

Only time can heal those wounds.

"I feel awful. I'm sorry this is all transpiring before your wedding."

"Don't be. I'm having the time of my life. And you should be too. Liam will be alright. He still has a lot of demons to work through. You can't be a healer for everyone—even though I know you want to be."

"I do. I wish more than anything that he can find happiness as I have in Diego."

She looks around, cautious of who is around us. "Lainey isn't it. I thought she was, but I'm starting to think she may have been a familiar rebound for him while you were away."

"Seems that way. I feel bad for her. She really cares about him." I can't help but wear a sour look on my face.

Diego, being the man he is, notices. He stops chatting with his sister and Killian and works his way over to us.

"Ladies," he announces himself, handing me my cocktail.

I lick the sugar off the rim and take a sip. Maybe the lavender will help me chill the fuck out. I'm tempted to eat the damn sprig garnishing the top.

Diego silently chuckles next to me, reading my thoughts as I eye the pretty purple flower.

"I thought earlier would have calmed you down," he states confidently. "Liam say anything to bother you?" he questions, his sapphire eyes shimmering with the need to protect.

"Nothing I didn't already know. He's upset. I can't really blame him." I shrug, taking a sip of my drink.

Diego does the same. "I can't fault him for his feelings, but he needs to stop making you feel guilty for your choice."

"I don't think he's intentionally doing it," Lexi defends him.

Diego doesn't respond with words, just raises an eyebrow as if saying, *"We'll see."*

CHAPTER 32

MADISON

DINNER WAS nice and the food was delicious. I'm absolutely stuffed. I ate way more than I should. Those might have been the best tacos I ever had.

It's imperative that I keep my wits about me tonight. Liam has effectively gotten in my head. It would be awful if I ruined another night with my emotions.

Next up is a game of *How well do you know your partner?* We are supposed to couple off around the fire and then go over the answers collectively. *This should be fun.*

Those not in relationships have decided to play some poker that is set up on the patio. They moved the dining table to give more space for us to use. Liam, hearing the title of the game, was the first to take a seat at the poker table. Colin, Kieran, and Ryan followed right behind him.

Lainey has been MIA all night. Honestly, I haven't seen her since our little blowout last night.

I take my seat on the oversized bean bag chair and dig my toes into the cool sand. There is a nice breeze tonight, making me snuggle in closer to Diego—who has his hand wrapped around my waist. He's running his fingers up and down my ribcage, which is oddly relaxing. I'm finally feeling a bit better.

Papers and pens are passed around.

Diego sits up, claiming his paper and pen from my hands. "Let's see here... Question one. What's your partner's favorite TV show?" he speaks aloud.

A ping of anxiety hits me. We are going to fail this game miserably. I may know this man's soul in and out, but I have no clue about aspects of his life like this. *Fuck.*

I jot down my answer as he moves on to the next question, having jotted down his answer almost immediately.

"Question two. Who said I love you first?" A smile forms on his face, knowing the answer, as do I. Sweet memories of our wedding night play on a reel in my brain. The two of us lying in bed together, him confessing his love for me, knowing it may be the last time he would get to say it.

"That was a special night." I go to press a kiss to his cheek, but he turns in time to claim my lips. Passion flows out of him, rousing me. It wouldn't be appropriate to straddle my man in front of everyone. *Would it?*

After taking my breath away, he releases me, shifting me so that I snuggle back into him. "It really was," he agrees, kissing the top of my head.

"Question three," I start. "What was your partner's first impression of you?" I laugh to myself. *This will be good.*

We jot down our answers, taking longer than the last response.

"Question four," he states, clearing his throat. "What is your partner's favorite drink?" We both look at each other before cracking up. Maybe we won't fail this game as miserably as I thought.

We scribble out our answers.

"Question five," I say. "What's your partner's favorite season?"

"Easy," he scoffs.

I smile inwardly. *Am I that much of an open book?*

Feeling pretty confident in my answer, I scrawl it down.

"Last question," he confirms. "Who made the first move?" The corner of his lip raises, that dimple in his cheek on full display.

We collect our thoughts, writing them down and folding the paper in half.

Perfect timing. Lexi's phone goes off signaling time is up.

Standing and dusting sand off her dress, she announces, "Okay, everyone. We are going to go over the answers now. I'll read off the questions and I want you to go in a circle and read them aloud to the group.

"I feel like I am in therapy," Killian murmurs beside us. Sel nudges him in the ribs.

The guys come over to us, chatting lively with each other. "Can we join? I'm sure these responses will be better than any reality TV show," Kieran chuckles.

Liam's eyes connect with mine as he takes a seat next to his brother.

Lovely.

The guys are laughing and rough-housing with Conor.

"Okay. Settle down!" Lexi hollers.

"Question one. What's your partner's favorite TV show?" Conor asks our little crowd.

"We'll start," Lexi adds. "Conor loves *Game of Thrones*," she says confidently.

"Correct. That is also hers."

"Us too!" Sel chimes in.

Killian chuckles. "We're a bit obsessed. Once Kian is down, we grab a glass of wine and enjoy a nice evening."

Sel smiles at her man, enamored by him.

"Aww!" Lexi sighs. "What about you, Dylan?" she asks, turning her attention to her brother and his husband.

"Guilty. We are both *Game of Thrones* fans as well. Right, babe?"

He turns to his partner, who nods and juts his thumb out. "He knows me well."

"Simon and John, you are up next," Lexi announces.

Simon speaks first. "Not to shock anyone, but *Game of Thrones* is not our cup of tea. We both love *Master Chef*. Don't we, John?"

John pats his belly. "We do. I've gained a ton of weight recreating all the recipes."

"Mad?" Conor looks at Diego and me.

I open my paper nervously and look around. All eyes are on me. Particularly, John and Simon—who just arrived this afternoon. They each wear an amused look. I'm thrilled to see them. We seriously need to catch up after the game.

"His favorite show is *Vikings*."

Diego cups my head and places a kiss on my forehead. "She's right. I love Greek and Norse mythology."

Yes! I was actually right!

"Madison loves *The Vampire Diaries*. Grey's Anatomy being a close second," Diego shares, as Liam mouths, "*The Vampire Diaries.*"

"He's right. I'm obsessed," I say uncomfortably.

Lexi notices and swiftly moves on to question two. *Who said I love you first?* When it comes back around to Diego and me, Diego goes first. Proud of himself.

"I did. It just so happened to be on our wedding night. This woman only recently told me she loved me…" He side-eyes me jokingly. "Even though I knew for a while that she did."

The crowd awes and jokes around—everyone except Liam, that is. He looks completely bewildered by that information.

I shift in my seat. *Whose idea was this game? Not mine.*

Question three rolls around. *What was your partner's first impression of you?*

It's our turn.

"Diego's first impression of me was that I was a means to an end," I laugh. I expect everyone to also, except no one does. They all are at the edge of their bean bag chairs like curious toddlers.

"The truth is, *Mariposita*, that was my intention when I first put that plan in motion. But then I collected you in my arms and felt you fight me, felt you give everything you had to protect my sister and yourself. In that moment, I knew you were more than just a chess piece. You were the match that lit my entire plan on fire. I mean, fuck the plans... The second you entered my life they didn't mean shit anyway. You, Madison, lit my whole life on fire, burning up the person I was, and from the flames, birthing the man I've always wanted to be. As I held your unconscious body in my arms, I sent a prayer up to Mamá that you would forgive me for taking you."

His sapphire eyes are on fire right now as he looks at me. The organ in my chest beats as if it ran a marathon. He knew before I even met him that I was his person. If that isn't a soul connection, I don't know what is.

I swipe at the tear floating down my cheek. "Wow."

"Wow, is right. *Holy fuckballs*, Diego. You're quite the poet," Lexi approves, wiping her own lone tear from her eye.

"And what do you think my first impression of you was?" I raise an eyebrow at him.

"Oh, you fucking *hated* me when I was taking you... then again, I was wearing a mask," he laughs deeply. "There was a moment you woke up on our flight to Miami. You looked up at me in my arms and mumbled, *'Am I dreaming? You are the hottest guy I have ever seen,'*" he mimics my voice then smiles while taking a sip of his drink.

I push myself off his chest, looking down at his large frame eating up the bean bag. Legs spread, relaxed. "I wouldn't lie about that..." he flirts.

"You're so full of shit, Diego," Liam argues.

"*Please.* Madison was probably scared shitless of you." Kil adds his two cents.

Feeling like *The Bone Breaker* is telling the truth, I feel the need to defend him. "I can't speak for what happened when I was semi-conscious and *drugged*—" I narrow my eyes at my husband, still bitter about that detail. "What I can confirm, is the minute he walked into my cell, I was smitten. He made me feel incredibly safe, even knowing he was the reason I was there as a prisoner. It was the days he sat outside my door talking to me or leaving me motivational quotes on sticky notes—before I even saw his face—that I knew he was someone I could trust."

Diego is satisfied with that. "I saved them, you know," he lowers his voice just for me to hear.

"The sticky notes?" I ask, dumbfounded.

"Yes. To me, they are love notes," he admits.

Swoon.

CHAPTER 33

LIAM

I WISH *these two would get a fucking room.* Then again, I am putting myself through this hell. I could be playing poker right now, ignoring this Godforsaken love fest. Yet, here I am. A fucking masochist, sitting on the edge of this awful bean bag chair, trying to get any scrap of information I can about their time together.

About what their relationship is really like when no one is looking.

I would say behind closed doors, but we all know what they do there. I run a hand through my hair, gripping the back of it.

Conor shoots me a sympathetic look. He was with me on the beach last night as I let it all out. Losing Madison and the finality of her decision is driving me mad. I agreed to let her go... but I can't. She and I had it all. *What the fuck happened to us?*

We reach the final question. The last two were easy. *Favorite drink. Favorite season.* You'd have to be blind and deaf not to know Madison's favorite drink. All she does is talk about how much she needs a coffee or how it gives her *'life'*. The same goes for Diego—except, he isn't as theatrical about it.

As for seasons, Maddy is a fall girl. Pumpkin being her favorite seasonal coffee. Those damn Ugg boots she loves so much are a dead giveaway. Beyond fashion and her studded leather jacket that she adores, Madison thrives when the weather turns crisp. Her mood always changes, like the leaves, adding a little spark of color to her personality. She's always smiling and headed out to a vineyard or farm. The princess loves a good bonfire.

Don't even get me started on Halloween. Anything spooky and spiritual has her name written all over it. I swear she and Lexi are some sort of witches with that telepathy of theirs. They are probably reading my mind right now—*get out of my head, ladies.*

The last question is who made the first move. Con did first with Lexi, asking her to save a dance at the New Year's Eve Masquerade Gala. Selena and Kil laughed at their turn, agreeing Killian made the first move by asking her out but felt pressured by their fathers to do so. Sel made the first *real* move, kissing him when he continued to stay a prude. Lexi's brother and his husband went in for a kiss at the same time at a mutual friend's party. And Lexi and Maddy's neighbors met at a cooking class. They were assigned the same station. Simon asked John out for drinks after class.

And now that we are all caught up...I've been anxiously awaiting Madison and Diego's responses. It'll put things into perspective for me about when Madison really fell for him.

"Maddy?" Lexi asks.

"I did," she states as my heart plummets.

What the fuck? I expected Diego to have made the moves on her first, considering she was his fucking *prisoner.* Did she lose feelings for me before he even laid on the charm with her?

Diego chuckles like a smug arsehole, rubbing a hand up and down Madison's back, encouraging her to tell the story. Jealousy like no other runs rampant through my body, heating it to the core. I take a healthy chug of my beer as I lean forward to hear this, resting my arms on my thighs.

Madison's eyes connect with mine for no more than a second before she begins. *Was that a flash of sympathy?*

"It was after Liam and I had broken up. Diego was consoling me while I was spiraling, questioning my worth and questioning my role in Liam and I falling apart. I knew deep down it was because I had grown feelings for Diego beyond attraction. I continued to mentally fight with myself, trying to convince myself this wasn't a case of Stockholm Syndrome. That night, I couldn't deny it any longer. This connection went far beyond attraction or forced proximity. He was someone who understood me almost better than I did myself. Diego, knowing Liam and I had just ended a few moments earlier, continued to respect my boundaries. I was the one who asked him to kiss me."

"Are you fucking serious, Madison?" I stand, unable to help my reaction to this new information. I knew about her having sex with him on their wedding night, but I chalked that up to her mind being in a haze with everything going on in her life.

She was the one to kiss him first? Did she ever really love me at all?

"*Liam*," Killian warns through his teeth. "Why don't you go take a walk and cool off?"

"You're not the leader anymore, Kil. I am. I don't need to listen to your commands," I growl at my brother. *Fuck him.* He's been in my shoes, he should know why I am reacting the way I am.

Diego looks like he wants to say something but remains quiet, allowing Madison to do his bidding. That's the difference between him and me; he'll bite his tongue where I wouldn't. *That's your girl, mate. Speak up.*

"You didn't let me finish, *Liam*." Madison sneers at me.

I'm pissed. What more can she say to break my fucking heart?

I hold my hands up in mock surrender, the neck of my beer

bottle held between my thumb and index finger. "The floor is all yours, *princess*."

"I asked him to kiss me. But he didn't. He knew I would likely regret it since my emotions were all over the place," she says calmly, looking me dead in the face.

As if her explanation makes it any better. So Diego stopped her from making a mistake. Good on him. The fact that she *asked* him is what is ripping my bleeding heart right out of my chest. The woman who claimed to love me *asked* him to kiss her right after I left that yacht, a broken man.

"So when did you finally kiss him?" I goad.

"Our wedding day." Diego growls. "I'd say this game is over, yeah?" He looks around at everyone. They nod their head in agreement, tossing their papers into the fire and dispersing.

Madison storms off as I struggle to get to my feet. *Fucking bean bag chairs.* I punch it for good measure.

It guts me to see her upset. I somehow always manage to find a way to fuck it up with her.

Godfuckingdammit.

When I finally get to my feet, I storm off after her, but Diego stops me, standing in my way. "I know that was hard to hear, but you are your own worst enemy, Liam. Quit inserting yourself into situations you know will bring you further pain. It fucking sucks. She moved on from you. But you have got to stop hurting her. She takes what you say so deeply. Not only that, but you are ruining your best friend's bachelor week."

He's right. He's always fucking right. *Christ.* I toss my beer bottle into the fire. This needs to stop. *I* need to stop with the bullshit. I just hope I'll be able to earn back Madison's friendship. If that is all I will ever get, that's what I need to preserve. That woman will always mean the world to me.

"I'd like to talk to her. You're right. I need to apologize," I concede.

"Start with Con and Lexi then come find us. If she is willing to talk with you, I'll give you guys privacy and time to talk. If she's not—you're not going to get very far," he threatens.

Noted.

I nod my head in understanding, trudging my way over to the couple.

"Sorry, brother. That was a lot to take in." Con squeezes my shoulder.

"It's my fault. I did it to myself. I'm sorry for causing a scene. I've been a shit friend and an even shittier Best Man."

"It's fine," Lexi consoles, touching my arm. "Just please give Maddy some grace. This decision wasn't easy for her either."

"I'm hoping to get the chance to apologize to her," I groan, hanging my head in shame.

"I'll talk with her," she offers.

I ENTER the living room of the main house in search of Madison. She was with Lexi at the beach a little while ago. Diego went off to check on something. I figured now would be the best time to offer her my apology.

The sliding glass door clicks shut behind me. The vibrating sound of the tattoo pen infiltrates my ears, instantly sending adrenaline coursing through me. Getting inked could be therapeutic right about now.

I am about to ask if I can be next in line when I discover who is in his chair.

Looks like I won't have to continue my search any longer. Madison is there, lying prone on the leather chair. Her purple hair cascades in waves over one side of her head, dangling to the floor. Danny, my tattoo artist, is bent over her, etching something that looks iridescent onto the back of her neck. The colors are similar to that of spilled oil.

Madison's eyes are scrunched shut. Her fingers clench the

leather headrest. She hasn't noticed me yet. Rhythmic breaths ease in and out of her as she attempts to soothe herself.

I plop down on the couch beside her and pry her hand off the leather. Gorgeous chestnut eyes stare at me, a mix of sympathy and anger wrestling there. I grip her hand more firmly, afraid she'll pull away.

She doesn't.

"Keep breathing, princess. It'll help." I offer her a small smile.

Her nostrils flare as she inhales deeply. Danny is working on some shading, which is always a bit more painful than line work.

I crane my neck over her to take a look at what she's getting.

Wow. A scorpion.

"It's a reminder to keep facing my fears while also owning them. Scorpions represent healing as well as... *fuckkk...*" she groans. "Self-discovery," she says through gritted teeth.

My other hand lands on top of hers, my thumb creating soothing circles on her soft skin.

"It looks amazing. You are going to love it. Look, I'm sorry, Mad. Jealousy caused me to lose my cool back there. The truth is, I still want you. You know this. Doesn't change how you feel, I know that. Saying it out loud feels good. I had to get it off my chest."

Danny whistles like this gossip is about to get juicy. I can't imagine the shit he hears from his clients.

My lips form a thin line. "I don't want to lose you from my life," I lean in and whisper.

"It's okay, Liam. I never meant to hurt you. Not back then on Diego's yacht, and not now. I don't want to lose you, either. But you need to focus on dealing with your anger. The drinking needs to slow down, it doesn't help you whatsoever. Take some time to heal," Maddy suggests gently, giving my hand a reaffirming squeeze.

I bring her hand up to my lips and kiss it. "I promise you. This time I will."

"All done, sweetheart," Danny announces, leaning back in his chair. He sprays the diluted green soap onto a paper towel and cleans up the leftover ink. The iridescent black scorpion comes to life, almost looking 3D. *Damn.* Danny's work is truly top-notch. He snaps a picture with his phone and lowers it down to show her before placing a Saniderm bandage over it.

"Oh my gosh. It's perfect. Thank you so much, Danny."

"You're welcome, darlin'. Hit me up anytime you'd like. Tattoos on the back of the neck are painful. I've had grown men ask for a break. You took it like a champ," he praises, patting her calf.

I help her sit up, monitoring her for any dizziness. On instinct, my hand drops to her waist, guiding her out of the chair. Just as she stands, Diego enters, his eyes immediately going to my hand. I remove it, valuing said hand.

"Baby, if I had known you were getting a tattoo, I would have stayed with you," he says remorsefully.

"I needed the time alone," she asserts.

The Bone Breaker eyes me, seeing as that is not the case. "Have you two made up?" He crosses his arms over his chest.

"We have. It's all good now," she insists, smiling reassuringly.

I can see why he's good for her. Why, perhaps, he is the better man. He knows how to compartmentalize his jealousy and anger —whereas I don't.

The front door slams open and my heart sinks into my stomach for a whole other reason. Half a dozen Feds enter the house, guns drawn.

"Diego De La Cruz. You are under arrest for the murder of Geraldo De La Cruz, the explosion of your yacht that killed fifteen others, faking your death, evading the law, and bribing a medical doctor. Everybody put your hands up where I can see them," shouts the lead female officer. The same lass I am quite familiar with. *Intimately.* She goes by the name Lindsay.

Diego slowly turns his back, hands raised. It doesn't go unnoticed that he shifts his body to stand in front of Madison. Her eyes are wide and her hands tremble as she stands glued to her spot.

Lindsay steps forward, lowering her gun and placing it back in its holster. A bulky male officer comes up behind her, aiming his weapon at Diego's skull. Blondy moves over, stepping between *The Bone Breaker* and Madison. She angrily tugs his arms back, cuffing him, and begins reading him his rights.

"They are all enjoying a friend's bachelorette weekend. Please leave them to continue the festivities," he requests calmly.

She ignores him. "Your wife is coming with us."

"She has nothing to do with any of this. I forced her to marry me."

The officer spins Diego around to face us. Madison has tears dripping down her face. "Is this true?" Lindsay asks her.

"No. He's trying to protect me. I will not say anything else without my lawyer present." Maddy crosses her arms over her chest and raises her chin. *Good girl.*

"We don't believe you are associated with his crimes. That means you are good—*for now.* Do not leave the country until we let you know you are in the clear." She turns to me, winking. "Liam, it's always a pleasure seeing you. Hope you're staying out of trouble."

"Sure am," I say, crossing my arms over my chest and flexing them. Her eyes immediately greet mine with lust.

"I'm not as heartless as the Bureau makes me out to be. I'll let you say goodbye. You have two minutes," she states sweetly, stepping back a few feet to talk to her peers.

"We don't have time for tears, *Mariposita.* I need you to trust me and I need you to be strong. You're going to have to face all the fears running through that pretty mind of yours. Just like

272

that scorpion tatt you got— which is sexy as hell, by the way," he jokes. "I'm fucking hard right now."

And he is. *Sick bastard.* Only *The Bone Breaker* would be turned on at a time like this, in a pair of cuffs with the FBI breathing down his back.

If he is feeling anxious, he hasn't given himself away. A mask of indifference is firmly in place.

"Someone sold you out," I growl, lowering my voice to a whisper. "I'll find out who, don't you worry," I vow. And I will. This will destroy Madison. I can't have that.

"Good. Liam, take care of my girl. I promised her father I wouldn't bring her down with me and I won't. If shit goes south and we don't come up with the evidence we need to wipe my case, I need you to look out for her." He pauses to glance over at Lindsay. "Looks like your little friend over there is coming in clutch. I suspect she is working on my release?"

"Damn, you and her father had a heart-to-heart? I'm impressed. He's not a man to be fucked with. And of course I'll take care of Madison. You know I will. Hopefully, you'll be out of there soon, brother."

"We did. He gave me his blessing. He also threatened my life if I got her involved with the Feds," he laughs, looking at his wife. "So if I do make it out of there, I'm not so sure I'll be around long enough to see my wife." He gives Madison the puppy dog eyes.

"Diego, stop joking. What am I supposed to do without you?" Her voice, now full of nerves, has crept up a few octaves.

"If everything works out the way Antonio, Liam, and I have planned, I will be back, baby. Then we can live the life you deserve—God willing your father doesn't put a hit out on me. But if I'm not...*Mariposita*, please listen to me. If I am not, you move the hell on. Let me rot in prison. Don't associate yourself with me. Do you understand?"

"Diego, I can't," she weeps.

He lowers his head close to hers. "You can, and you will. I love you, Madison."

"Times up, buttercup," Lindsay sings, pulling him back by the cuffs. "Oh, and by the way, be careful who you consider family. Some of the most beautiful snakes are venomous," she whispers.

It must click into place for all of us at the same time. Madison looks like she is ready to commit murder. Diego remains calm, but a look of understanding crosses his features.

As for me? My body trembles with how much red-hot anger is coursing through me... I am ready to tear this house up in search of a snake to behead.

CHAPTER 34

MADISON

"HOW AM I supposed to go back to the party and act like everything is okay, Liam?" I whisper-shout, pacing the deck of the bedroom Diego and I share. My hands have come up over my lips as in prayer.

What the fuck is going on? God, I hope he is able to get out of this. Those are some serious charges stacked against him. He'll be lucky if he doesn't get the death penalty. At the thought of a life without Diego's smile, his eyes, his sarcasm, or his hands all over me, my heart rate spikes. I continue to pace back and forth, lost in my spiraling thoughts.

Liam's tattooed hand grips my bicep, stopping me. "Mad. Stop. It's going to be alright. I swear on my life I will make sure of that. Diego, Antonio, and I have come extremely close to getting this case wiped clean."

His voice is softer than normal. This is the Liam I miss. The person I once fell in love with. The man I could still love, just not what it was before. Not *romantically,* that is.

Twisting my body to stare up at him, I ask, "Who was that woman? The female officer?" I cross my arms over my chest, forcing Liam to drop his hand. He in return, runs it through his hair before pinching the bridge of his nose.

"Diego isn't leaving you out of his plans, so let's get that clear before I start. I had mentioned to your man that I have an in with an FBI agent named Lindsay. She's helped my brother and me out of a lot of shit that could have been the end for us. She and I used to cross the line between business and pleasure...even though it felt like part of the business transaction. Anyway, I gave her a ring the other day, *strictly business*—so don't get ya panties in a twist—and she offered to hop on the case. Being associated with the notorious *El Rompe Huesos* case would help her career. Even if that outcome meant his name was cleared and it all fell on his uncle Geraldo. At the very least, she could keep an eye on him if and when he was taken into custody."

"He never told me that," I pout.

"He didn't know I called her. All Diego knew was that I was *going* to call. This is a good thing Madison, she's on our side. As for who is behind this... We need to discuss that. I will *never* kill a woman. So what the fuck do I do? She betrayed me, my family, and not one, but two syndicates. One of which is our ally." Liam's pained eyes stare down at me, asking me what to do here. He wants me to call the shots. *How refreshing.*

"*You* may not kill a woman... doesn't mean *I* won't," I growl, my anger boiling, dangerously close to causing an explosion. Someone is about to get burned.

"That's not a burden you want on your shoulders. Trust me. An angel like you wouldn't be able to live with yourself. Taking a life will always sit with you, no matter how evil the other may be. You don't want that blood on your hands," he rasps, his mind going elsewhere.

"So, you need me to go outside and act like none of this happened? Lainey probably watched the whole damn thing with a bucket of popcorn somewhere," I huff, throwing my hands in the air before letting them slap the sides of my thighs.

"She wasn't up here. I just saw her prepping the dessert station outside before I came up," he confirms.

"He can't be in prison forever, Liam." A fresh coat of tears pools in my lash line.

Liam pulls me to him by the back of my head, securely wrapping me in the safety of his arms. He soothingly pets my hair. "I know. It's gonna be alright, love."

I nod my head up and down as tears drip onto his tattooed forearm. "I'm going to collect myself and head back outside. You find Killian. Let's meet back here in an hour. If you don't get her by then, I am dropping this plan and *will* drag her by the hair back here," I promise.

Liam's deep chuckle vibrates my face. "You've always been too cute when you're mad."

"Shut up. Now's not the time." I smack his chest, using it as leverage to push me off and get moving.

I inhale deeply, centering myself before walking out the door. Taking the steps two at a time, I head back toward the commotion by the pool. Lexi is on Con's shoulders wrestling John, who is on Simon's shoulders.

"Winner has to run ass naked into the ocean," Lexi taunts.

"Bring it, Alexis," John shoots back. "I hope your wax girl was thorough," he snides playfully.

Normally, I would be joining right in on the banter. Right now? I can't help but scan the property for the little bitch that decided to ruin my whole world. *'Girl's Girl'* my ass. Jealousy drove her to betray her syndicate. The people she was raised with. The man she claims to love.

Puhhhlease.

Liam is right, I won't kill her. I want to—but that isn't something I think I could ever do. That doesn't mean we can't hash it out with our fists before Liam ultimately decides her fate. Maybe I'll even face my fears and revisit the dungeon.

Speak of the fucking devil. Lainey is over by Sel, chatting away with her—as if she didn't just stab her brother in the back with a butcher knife. She must have thought her anonymous call would stay anonymous. Or perhaps she didn't think they would come to the island today and take him away. Well, if she thinks she can play me, and my family, she has another thing coming....

I approach the bar, pretending to search for Diego. "Hey, Sel...Lainey," I nod at them. "Have either of you seen my husband?"

A look of concern crosses Sel's relaxed features. "He was over by the docks last I'd seen him..." She leans forward to whisper. "But you didn't hear that from me." She winks.

Now she has me curious. What was my husband up to? He told me we weren't sleeping in the room tonight... does that mean he was over by the docks because we were going somewhere? Did he know the feds were coming? Some sort of tip-off?

"You alright, Madison? You look a little pale." Sel begins to mother me by rubbing my arm.

"Yeah. Diego kept me up all night. I'm just a bit tired." I add in an obnoxious faux yawn.

"Love you, girl...but I don't need to hear about my brother's sex life with my best friend." Sel covers her mouth with her hand, pretending to gag.

I roll my eyes. "Lainey. I know the last few days have been a lot. Liam's been looking for you. I think he wanted to apologize and make things right with you." I make sure to lay the charm on thick.

Her eyes light up, looking hopeful. I almost feel bad for her. *Almost.* "I have been avoiding him. Maybe I should go find him. I'm sorry for the drama, Madison." *No you're not.*

Liam walks out of the sliding door, locking eyes with me. He nods subtly.

He stops by the edge of the pool. "Hey, Lainey? You want next?"

He pulls his shirt over his head, flexing his muscles. Next to go is his belt and then his pants. Lainey's tongue is practically hanging out of her mouth. *Go get him, tiger.*

"Excuse me, ladies," she announces.

Pulling her dress over her head, she walks towards him, swaying her ass as she goes. Lexi pushes John, causing Simon to step back exactly where the shallow end meets the deep end. John goes tumbling backward.

"YES!" Lexi shouts, throwing her arms above her head as Conor makes a victory lap. "Get moving boys...I wanna see hineys jiggling down towards the ocean." She points to the dark water.

Perfect timing. I don't need Simon and John witnessing whatever is about to happen. Lexi's brother and his husband jog after them, cracking up as they go.

As Lainey approaches Liam, he tackles her, knocking her into the pool. She comes up sputtering before he pulls her arms behind her back and pushes her head back down.

"Liam! What the fuck are you doing?" She coughs as she resurfaces before her head is submerged again—this time longer.

He cages her hands behind her back in one strong arm as his other grips her by the hair. Tugging her up by the scalp, he lowers his mouth to her ear. "Why did you do it, Lain?" he growls between clenched teeth.

"I already apologized to Madison," she lies.

Violently, he shoves her face back into the water as her body bucks against his. When he finally lifts her head back up, she's sobbing. "Fuck all of you. *Especially* Madison. She never deserved a spot in this life."

I get closer, drawn to the chaos. If this is karma, Liam is the justice.

"Here's what's gonna happen, Lainey. You are going to be dropped off in Ireland by one of my men. You will be monitored. So if you think for one second you'll find your way back here, you're *dead* wrong. A crime like this in our world is punishable by death. Since I won't kill a woman, and your mom was an angel, you're in the clear of that. However, you are going to wish for death with the life you'll live. You will *never* see another country again. You will live and breathe in Ireland. No traveling. No vacations. For as long as you live. You'll be lucky to find a job or ever love again after our family in Ireland hears about this. Best wishes to ya, lass."

"You're making a mistake!" she screams. "Madison is the toxic bitch here, not me! I hope her man rots in prison, and I hope he takes you all down with him."

Liam drags her up the pool stairs, tossing her into Ryan's arms. "Dry her off. Leave her in her bathing suit for all I care. Take the two recruits with you. I want eyes on her at all times. I'll call my family in Ireland and let them know of her arrival. Keep me posted. I'll let you know of your assignments when you get there."

"Yes, Sir," Ryan confirms his orders, collecting Lainey and slapping on some zip ties to keep her restrained.

"Fuck you, Liam Kennedy!" Her manic screams carry towards the house.

Lexi's mouth is hanging wide open. Con looks at her, shaking his head. Now wouldn't be a good time for a sarcastic remark.

Kil comes up to me, smelling of rich smoke. He wraps his arm around me protectively. "You alright, love? What the fuck happened? I was smoking a cigar with some of the guys in one of the cabanas."

"I'm fine. Liam will explain everything. Find me when you are ready to form a plan," I clip. Anxiety is starting to creep in.

Somehow my legs carry me over to the dock. I stare up at the gorgeous new yacht Diego purchased with the insurance money. It's all lit up, looking majestic. I need a place to look at the stars and be alone with my thoughts. As I approach the boarding platform, I notice a beautiful butterfly painted onto the bow of the ship. In an elegant script, *'Mariposita'* is positioned underneath the mural.

Tears prick the back of my eyes. Diego named his superyacht after me.

HE MADE ME A READING NOOK. Not that the word *nook* even gives this *room* justice. Where on *Pontus* the upper levels hosted a gym and spa, this upper level has that included along with this gorgeous space.

I tilt my head to stare up at the dome glass that is providing the perfect visual of the stars. My gaze travels lower to the rows and rows of bookshelves. Warm underlighting and comfy furniture fill the space, adding to the charm of the room. I find my way to the oversized couch and plop down, pulling a gray throw blanket over me. I lean my neck against the arm of the couch and once again look up at the glass dome, admiring the clear starry night.

This is incredible, and so thoughtful. Not only did he name his superyacht after me, but he added a goddamn library with a real-life planetarium. A fresh round of tears hits me as I curl up with the blanket. *What if he doesn't clear his name? Is it even possible for him to come out of this completely unscathed?* I can't see how...and I've always been an optimist.

Reaching behind me, I snag the brand new Kindle that is propped up on a stand on the end table. Another sweet gesture. It shows how much he has paid attention in our short time *actually* together. Sliding a thumb across the screen, I set it up and dive right into the last fantasy romance book I left off on. Nothing like a woman and her dragon defeating the odds stacked against her. Perhaps it will give me some inspiration in my own life circumstances.

I'm not sure when I closed my eyes, but I am stirred from

sleep by a deep voice calling my name. I brush the hair off of my face and sit up, disorientedly looking around for the source.

"Madison? Are you up here?" Liam shouts, his voice carrying from outside the door.

"Yeah," I call back.

The wood door slides open, revealing a disheveled Liam.

"Christ, sweetheart. I've been looking all over for you. Nice touch by the way on the space by the pool. Did you have the event planners do a trial run for the rehearsal dinner?"

That prompts me to sit up straighter. I tuck a strand of hair behind my ears and swing my feet over to stand. "No. I came straight up here. The dome was the first thing that caught my eye. What are you talking about?"

Liam raises his hand to rub the back of his neck. He looks around, silently in awe of the room Diego created. "You should take a look then. I just hope it won't upset you..." he trails off.

I walk over to him, still standing awkwardly at the threshold. "Why would it upset me?" I ask.

"You'll see. I guess that is where Diego went off to while you were getting tatted." He reaches a hand out to collect mine.

Needing the comfort, I place my hand in his and allow him to lead me out of my library and over to the elevator on the helipad.

We take the short ride down in silence. The doors open with a ding, revealing the reasons Diego said we wouldn't be sleeping in our room tonight. Flameless candles flicker, lining the entire deck that surrounds the pool. A table is prepared with a bucket of champagne and chocolate-covered fruits and pastries. The entire pool is filled with rose petals and floating candles in flower-like lily pad votives. String lights crisscross over the pool, warming the space and enchanting it. A white screen is set up with a projector facing it. The screen is blue, just waiting to be played.

I cup a hand over my mouth in awe of what is set up before

me. For a guy who claims he has zero idea of how to 'do romantic', he sure is good at it.

"So... this wasn't for the rehearsal dinner."

"Nope," I confirm, dropping my hand.

Liam whistles low. "Seems like he prepared a special night for the two of ya."

"Seems that way," I agree, unable to vocalize any real opinions. My mind is swimming with what ifs. He already proposed again. *So what was this for?*

A sniffle leaves me as tears rebuild. *God, I am an emotional wreck tonight.*

Liam pulls me into him. "It's gonna be okay, Mad. He's coming back," he soothes, rubbing gentle circles over my arm.

I wish I could be as confident as he is right now. I nod my head against his chest.

Liam's phone vibrates in his pocket. He releases me to grab it, placing the phone to his ear. "Ya?... I got her, she was on the yacht..." His dark eyes reach mine. There is contemplation there. "No, we'll come to you... Alright, brother. See you soon." Pressing a middle finger to the bottom of his phone, he ends the call before slipping the phone back into his pocket.

"That was Killian. He's been looking for you too. He wanted to know if he should meet us up here... but clearly, this night didn't go as planned for you and your man, I don't want to tarnish what he was surprising you with by bringing the drama up here. Let's head back?" he asks, stretching his hand out again.

I smile up at him. So hot and cold all the time. This is the sweet Liam I miss so much. I let my hand slide into his as we head back to the house.

CHAPTER 35

LIAM

MADDY'S HAND is clammy in mine as we reach Sel and Killian. They are sitting at the dining room table. A brown bag sits between them and two plastic cups are filled to the brim with Baja Blast.

"Taco Bell," Madison voices my thoughts.

"Thought you could use some comfort food," Sel says, patting the seat next to her.

Maddy joins her, leaning into her friend. "Thank you," she sighs.

Sel pulls her in for a hug before opening the bag and divvying out the goods. *Better be a Crunchwrap in there for my gir...for Mad.* I need to work on that. It's too easy to fall back into that feeling with her when we aren't angry with each other.

As predicted, a Crunchwrap and a Chicken Chalupa slide across the table towards her. A wide smile grows on her face. This woman is obsessed with Taco Bell. Smart move, guys. I wink at Sel in appreciation.

"Okay. I spoke to Lindsay. She has Diego being held at their new location in Miramar. So he's close, Madison. That's good," Killian announces before diving into his chicken quesadilla.

Madison takes a sip of her Baja Blast. "We need Antonio. I

285

need to know what information he has that will help Diego's case."

"Already done," I add behind a mouth full of steak burrito. "Antonio is en route as we speak."

A relieved sigh leaves Madison's lips before she goes in on her Crunchwrap. "Great," she mumbles over the food.

Killian killed his quesadilla in a matter of seconds. Crinkling fills the room as he crumbles the wrapper in his hands and tosses it into the brown bag. If you didn't know any better, you'd say we were all starved. *Far from it.* We've been eating well since the moment we got here Friday evening. Speaking of arrivals, Madison's family is due to arrive on Wednesday in preparation of the wedding. Lex and Con are getting married on the beach this Thursday. The rehearsal dinner is also Wednesday night. All while the Feds are up our ass and Diego is missing from the events.

Madison's father, Vincenzo Marrone, is a man of his word. If he told Diego he would end him if Madison was roped into his crimes, he *abso-fucking-lutely* will. He told Killian and me the same thing when we had a talk with him at Madison's graduation dinner. Maddy never knew we knew her Dad. He kept his involvement in the Mafia a secret from his kids—that is, until now. Perhaps Vincenzo will give Diego a grace period, knowing his daughter is quite captivated by the lad.

Captivated. Who am I kidding? She's batshit crazy over him.

Anyone can see that.

"Where is Lexi and the rest of the crew now?" Maddy inquires.

"Those still awake are in the hot tub at the pool," Kil confirms.

Sel pats her belly, pushing the rest of her food in front of her. "I'm stuffed." Kil covers her hand with his, smiling down at his unborn child.

"Mind if I eat that?" I ask, pointing to the rest of her quesadilla.

"All yours," she giggles, extending her hand to pass over the food.

I scarf it down in a few bites, eliciting a smile on Madison's tense face.

"*Savage*," she mouths, shaking her head.

"When am I not?" I laugh, licking the sour cream and nacho cheese off my thumb.

The front door opens and we all tense, directing our attention to it. A spark of hope enters Maddy's eyes. I assume she thought Diego was going to walk through that door. His cousin slams the door behind him, walking in our direction.

"We're in Miami, and you guys choose *Taco Bell*?" he jokes, taking a seat next to Madison and playfully nudging her in the ribs. "I love a good Crunchwrap, too—don't tell anyone," he whispers.

"Your secret is safe with me." Maddy cracks another smile while finishing up her meal.

Antonio laces his hands together, placing them on the wood table. "I've got some good news. The Greek Coast Guard agreed to testify about their recent findings. They believe the explosion was caused by a bomb Geraldo planted. He was there to sabotage the wedding, wanting to eliminate any *possible* threat to his reigning power. The officiant has also been kind enough to offer a statement saying Geraldo had threatened to take his life if he didn't lie about his involvement in the explosion."

"And the rest of Diego's crimes? How are we going to get past him lying to the world about his death?"

"On paper he did flatline. So that's the truth. We can spin it to look like he went into hiding after that, afraid his uncle was still alive after the explosion and he wanted to try and protect you..." Killian proposes.

"I already have my lawyer reviewing all our paperwork. He's

going to do a Skype meeting with us tomorrow afternoon to help solidify the angle we are taking," I state.

Madison's gaze reaches mine, full of appreciation. *You're welcome, baby.* Whatever I can do to help get that smile permanently back on her face, I will. I promised no matter our relationship status, she would always be mine to protect.

And that's what I am doing—*plus, I've come to enjoy the camaraderie Diego and I created.*

As we sit around this table, the last two days filled with nothing but unease and tension, I suddenly am overwhelmed by a strong sense of family. A blended family, but a family nonetheless. We have all come together, allies or not, to help out Diego and Madison. This is what has been lacking in our group for the last year or so. I turn to look at my brother who is likely feeling the same way. He shoots me an understanding grin.

"It is all going to get sorted out. Diego will be back here soon enough," I promise.

"I really hope so," Madison says wearily. "When did you become so positive?" she jabs playfully.

"It's called manifesting, Maddy." I wiggle my fingers in the air for a spooky effect.

"Wow." She crosses her arms over her chest, looking impressed with my use of spiritual jargon.

"You should get some sleep. We have our final fittings early tomorrow morning," I remind her.

She stands, tossing her garbage into the brown bag. "That's a good idea. I need to shower and attempt to sleep," she agrees sadly.

"Want me to walk you up?" I offer.

"No, that's okay. I'll be fine. Danny is still waiting for you." She nods to the living room where Danny is tattooing Lexi's brother.

I almost forgot about my tattoo. Before the crazy unfolded, I planned on getting the Tree of Life tattooed on my back. Right between my shoulder blades. The roots represent my past, my upbringing, and my romantic connections—specifically one.

Lifting my head, I spot Madison hugging Kil and Selena goodnight. She's taught me so much. She keeps me grounded. Her influence in my life has had a huge effect on my spiritual growth and desire to keep pushing for more for myself. Even though there is heartbreak and a shit ton of it, there's healing, there's maturing, and strength through all of life's unpredictable challenges. The Tree of Life is about accepting endings and embracing the new beginning.

How poetic is it that I have chosen to get it now, at this stage of my life? I have been planning on getting this tattoo for a while now. It's as if fate required the lessons Madison taught me to truly embrace getting this inked into my skin. So I can truly live by the meaning of it. Its place at my back is a gentle reminder that my past is behind me. It's time to look towards the future and stop looking back.

Stop looking at her to save me.

That doesn't mean Madison can no longer be a part of my future—but that chapter of 'us' is closed. I am hopeful we can create a new version of what that means to us moving forward.

MY PHONE RATTLES the nightstand next to me. I squint at the number on the screen.

Lindsay.

"Hello, love," I mumble.

The sheets screech as I lean up on my elbows. I slept on my stomach last night, allowing my new tattoo to breathe.

"If I told you I could get a phone call in with Diego *and* be in your bed in about an hour, what would you say?" she purrs.

My eyebrows raise at her boldness. She's always been like this, but today she's extra direct. I run a hand through my unruly hair and stare up at the white ceiling. Below this navy blue sheet, my cock throbs with the thought of a quickie. All this pent-up stress could use a good outlet. The problem is, she wouldn't be able to touch my back—*and she's a scratcher.* After a night with her, my back looks like a goddamn scratching post.

"I want the phone call to be with Madison. Then get your pretty arse over here so I can fuck you. On one condition...you promise to keep your hands on the headboard like a good little agent," I growl.

"Diego will call this phone after I hang up. I'll see you in an hour, handsome."

The phone disconnects, leaving me scrambling out of bed.

CHAPTER 36

MADISON

"MADISON, baby. I need you to wake up," Liam's calm voice stirs me. I finally fell asleep after tossing and turning all night.

I open my eyes, disoriented for the second time tonight. His fingers pet my hair as his ringing phone comes into view. The name *Lindsay* is glowing on the screen.

Lindsay. *Lindsay*–as in the FBI agent. I sit up, pressing my back to the headboard and frantically grabbing his phone.

"It's Diego. You probably will only have a few minutes," he warns sleepily.

I anxiously press the phone to my ear with shaking hands. "Diego?"

"Hello, *Mariposita*," Diego's whiskey smooth voice fills the line. My heart hammers in my chest hearing his voice.

"Are you okay? Where are they keeping you?" I need to know he's okay. That he hasn't been injured or strapped down somewhere.

"You gonna come break me out?" He chuckles deeply. I can almost see that dimple on his cheek and his ocean eyes swirling with humor.

"It would only be fair to repay you for breaking me out of my cell."

"You never belonged there in the first place," he growls.

"Antonio is here. He came over tonight to help work on a plan," I alert him, easing us into a new direction.

"Good, baby. I can't stop thinking about how you admitted I didn't coerce you into marrying me. And that scorpion tatt on your neck... *fuckkk*," he groans, prompting Liam to roll his eyes. "I can't wait to wrap my hands around it while I push you into the mattress... the thought has had me so hard all night..." he trails off and starts talking to whomever is with him—I am assuming Lindsay. "Oh, stop with those judgy eyes. You and I both know what you are planning to do after your shift."

I look at Liam with raised eyebrows. Now I am the one being judgmental. He gives himself away when his cheeks redden.

"I wish you were here. I wish this bed didn't feel so empty. Who am I going to dance with at Lexi's wedding if you are in a prison cell?" I attempt to joke but it only breaks my heart further.

"I'm sure Liam is more than willing to dance with you, beautiful." He laughs it off, but there is a hint of uneasiness in his voice. Even he doesn't think he'll be home for a while.

Liam sympathetically pats my leg. I'm sure he would dance with me—but that's not the point.

"Was our snake problem taken care of by the exterminator? I'm sorry it disrupted the bachelorette party." *Slick.*

"Yeah." I look up at Liam. "It was relocated. They will monitor it for a bit before releasing it."

"That's good news." He chuckles again at my use of code. Liam bites his lip, holding back his own laughter.

"Alright, Mr. De La Cruz. I've been more than generous," Lindsay's voice grows louder as she gets closer to my man.

"I've got to go, baby. Keep your head up. I'll be home as soon as I can. And if not you fly—this time for good." His tone is serious. Gone is my sarcastic husband.

"I'm not flying anywhere this time. Love you, *Ocean Eyes*," I vow.

I hang up before he has a chance to argue with me. I may have flown away from my fears once before, but regardless of what happens now, Diego is it for me. He could be in prison his whole life and I would still be his. I'd visit and call as often as I could. I would never move on.

This is the life I took on, the risk I accepted when I agreed to be his wife. *Especially* the second time. The first time was based on my desire to help out everyone involved. When we proposed to each other again, and I vowed to be his once more, I sealed this fate. We will forever be entwined—no matter what happens to either of us.

I am his and he is mine.

A prison cell won't stop the love I have for him.

THE NEXT MORNING is a shit show. Everyone in the bridal party, minus Lexi, is in a guest room getting our final fittings done. I stare at my reflection in the floor-length mirror as a seamstress works on my hem. The shoes I'll be wearing sparkle in the light as the sun trickles through the curtains.

"This color compliments your hair beautifully," the seamstress muses as she adds a pin to the bottom of my amethyst-colored satin dress.

She is right, it absolutely does. The dress is form fitting with a deep slit running up toward mid-thigh. Spaghetti straps hold the loose scoop neck up. My cleavage is tasteful, just enough to show off my bronzed skin—thanks to a fresh tan.

Liam is on the other side of the room. A tailor is working on the hem of his tuxedo pants. As usual, he looks uncomfortable. Colin and Kieran are making bets on how long it will take for him to ditch the jacket after the ceremony.

Ten minutes is my guess. He'll be asked to put it back on for pictures and then it will be off again, the top two buttons opened by cocktail hour.

His eyes connect with mine in the mirrors. A small smile builds on his face as he messes with the cuff link on his left arm. We haven't gotten the chance to talk after his night with Lindsay. She crept out of his room around 5 AM when I got up to grab a coffee and a scone.

She may be on our side, which I am grateful for, but I can't tell if she is using Liam for sex.... or if there is something more to it. The beautiful blonde actually looked shy when she shut his bedroom door behind her. We stood in the hallway for a brief moment. I expected her to grill me on Diego's case or throw jabs at me, but she tucked her hair behind her ears and wished me luck in dealing with a cranky Liam at the fitting. I surprisingly laughed, knowing that would be exactly the case.

Con looks dapper in his all black Armani tuxedo. He even made sure to trim up that wild beard of his. His shaky fingers grip the lapels of his tux, examining himself in the mirror. *Aw, he's nervous.* He wants to look good for his future bride-to-be.

"That tux might not make it down the aisle," I joke with him.

Colin, Liam, and Kieran all laugh at the same time. "She's gonna tackle ya, brother," Liam agrees, easing his best friend's worries.

"We are all done here," the seamstress announces, placing the last pin in my dress. "It will be steamed and ready for you on Thursday. As for your rehearsal dinner dress, I should have that up to your room and in your closet around noon today."

"Thank you, Mary-Ann," I say graciously.

She helps me down from the pedestal and over to the bathroom to get changed back into my swimsuit. We are spending the day Jet Skiing and boating. Tomorrow, Lexi and I are doing a spa day. My family comes in the day after that, as do the rest of the guests attending the wedding. Even my college roommate Leah will be here. Then Wednesday night, we are doing the rehearsal dinner on the yacht. It will be the first time it officially hits the waters for a night out.

Guilt gnaws at my insides. Diego won't even be here to entertain everyone the first time *his* yacht gets used. There is so much going on emotionally in my brain. I need to tighten the lid on it. My best friend is getting married to the love of her life. This is no time for me to wallow in my own sorrows. The weekend was already a drama fest. We don't need more of it.

"SLOW DOWN, LOVE!" Liam shouts over the hum of the Jet Ski engine.

He wraps himself around my waist, hanging on for dear life. I hit the throttle a bit more, increasing his chances of having a heart attack by tenfold. A deep chuckle emanates from him as he draws himself closer to my body. The warm air nips at my face as my violet hair whips Liam in his. I'd say from an outsider's perspective this moment would be comical at best.

Lexi and Con zip by us splashing water at us. *Fuckers.* As bad as these last few days have been, and as much as it's killing me to keep a smile on my face, I am finding this moment therapeutic. Lexi is having a blast—as she should be. She's been spending too much time worrying about me and not enough enjoying herself.

I ease up on the throttle, giving Liam a break from my hair beating him, then lean over my shoulder. Warm eyes greet mine.

"I'm glad you're enjoying yourself, love," he remarks.

"I'm trying," I murmur as I navigate us back towards the dock. "Are we going to talk about last night?" I peer at him over my shoulder.

He shrugs, backing up and loosely placing his hands on my

waist. "Nothing to talk about. We got what we wanted from each other. She left this morning."

"I'm aware. We ran into each other in the hallway."

"You were up at 5:30 this morning?" he asks, seemingly impressed.

"I was. I couldn't sleep. Figured a cup of coffee would start my day. I ended up sitting on the front deck and got to watch the sunrise."

The Jet Ski comes to a halt as Liam hops off to tie it up. He offers me a hand to help me up. Lexi and Con pull up behind us, followed by her brother and brother-in-law, then Simon and John. Life vests are abandoned and left to dry on the hooks. We collectively start making our way back to the beach for a casual barbecue dinner.

Simon slinks an arm through mine, pulling me away. "Sorry, I need to borrow her, Liam."

I wave awkwardly behind me as he tugs me down the beach towards the food and towels. John collects a stack, handing them out to Simon and I.

"Thank you," I say, wrapping it around myself and grabbing myself a plate with a cheeseburger. I add some ketchup and pickles and a nice scoop of potato salad on the side before making my way over to the lounge chairs.

Simon takes a seat after getting him and John some food and pats the space next to him.

"You and Liam seem to be in better spirits," he instigates. John sits down on the other side of me, sandwiching me between them. It feels like gossip sabotage. They are greedy for the details.

"We needed to give each other closure. I think the other night we were finally able to close the door on us for good."

"It's a shame. That is a whole lot of man," John snickers while taking a healthy bite of his burger.

"You two are insufferable. Yes, Liam is a catch." I shake my head, digging into the potato salad. *Mmm. This is delicious.* Love a good Dutch potato salad.

Liam notices my friends grilling me and chooses to make himself scarce. He takes a seat with the boys. Lexi, being the odd girl out, gives Conor a quick kiss before skipping over to us. She drops down on the chair across from us.

"What gossip did I miss?" Her blue eyes are wide and eager, waiting for the dirty details.

"We were just going over how Liam has been eyeing Madison's *ass* all day. And don't think we didn't notice his big paws gripping you right under your luscious breasts," John teases.

My jaw drops as I spin my head to look at him. "He was *not.* The poor guy barely fits on a Jet Ski by himself, let alone with me in the front. I'm sure he was afraid of falling off at the speed I was going."

"Sure. *Sure.* Keep telling yourself that," Simon chimes in.

"Have you guys been introduced to Madison's husband?" Lexi drops the bomb.

Audible gasps erupt from the two of them. John goes as far as to clutch his chest. "You're married?" he squeaks.

"*Alexis,*" I growl, narrowing my eyes at her.

"And not to Liam. So Diego, your mysterious billionaire boyfriend is actually your husband?" he ponders, pursing his lips and narrowing his eyes.

"Yes," I admit. No use lying to my friends now. "We didn't start off great as you may have heard the other night. I have filled you in on the minor details, but I think you can fill in the gaps with how we ended up."

"It's not our place to judge who you choose to love. As long as both you and Alexis are treated right and they make you happy, that's all we care about," Simon says, patting my leg reassuringly.

"They do. Trust me, Simon, those men would start a war for us. Diego already did for Maddy," Lexi chirps.

The guys look at me for confirmation on that and I just smile and shrug. He technically did. And he would do it again. Any of them would. Butterflies swarm my stomach and heavy emotion sits thick in my throat.

Diego should be here right now.

CHAPTER 37

MADISON

LIKE CHOCOLATE, I am practically melting into this massage table. My limbs feel ooey gooey and all that tension is finally gone. These Egyptian cotton sheets are extremely soft against my freshly scrubbed skin. *Note to self: Ask for the thread count. We need these for our bedroom.*

The salty, relaxing scent of the ocean wafts into the cabana that Lexi and I are getting our treatments in. *Now this is what I needed.*

Conor and the men went golfing. The rest of the guests are spending the day poolside enjoying some sun and mojitos. My sister Mikayla texted me earlier, excited to actually spend time getting to know Diego.

Little does she or my father know, he is currently in Federal custody.

She and my family should be arriving around dinner time tomorrow. The rehearsal dinner starts at 6 PM. Part of me is hoping to avoid that conversation until the wedding the following day.

"I'm thinking we need to schedule massages weekly, Madison. What do you think?" Lexi moans her approval.

I turn my head to look at her. Her blonde hair is cascading off the table and her eyes are closed. "I agree. This is heaven," I mumble as the masseuse works on a knot in my shoulder blade.

"Are you holding up okay?"

"As best I can be. Antonio and Liam spoke with Lindsay today. She believes things could swing in our favor, but it might be a while before then."

"Least there is hope. Hang in there, girly."

My eyes close and I relax back into the bed, freeing myself of the cage my thoughts are being held captive in.

I WAKE up with a feeling of coming off anesthesia, all disoriented and groggy. The masseuse gently taps me on the shoulder. "Mrs. De La Cruz. We are finished now. We hope you enjoyed your spa day."

"Loved it. Thank you, Charles," Lexi beams. She hops off her table and comes over to me, collecting my hand in hers. "Time to go see the boys. Con just texted me saying they are waiting for us by the pool."

When the Earth stops spinning, I join her, tossing on my bathrobe and sandals. We walk down the beach and back towards the house to discover not only the guys hanging there but my entire family.

Fuck.

"Maddy!" Mel shouts, running towards me.

Mik turns her head and directs her attention to us. Her designer shades mask what she is currently thinking—which could be a problem. Liam shoots me the eyes, letting me know she's onto us. When Mel reaches me, she pulls me in close for a hug.

"Hey, you! I thought you guys weren't coming until tomorrow night?" I ask anxiously.

"We were, but then Mik got a text from Liam who offered for

our whole family to fly down on his private jet. Holy crap, Maddy. I felt like a Kardashian," she gushes.

Irrational, ugly anger hits me like a ton of bricks. Why would Liam do that, knowing we are dealing with so much around here?

Liam joins us at the same time Mik does. "Does this guy fly everyone around on his private jet or just us?" She juts her thumb out at him.

"Hey now, lass. I just wanted to make Madison smile, so I thought bringing her family in a day early would help her."

"Why would she be upset? Her best friend is getting married..." She starts to tick off each point on her fingers. "They have been drinking and partying all week... She's *clearly* gotten some sun...And her *boyfriend* is here with her," she presses, moving that hand to her hip.

Liam scrubs a hand down his face as if he is at a loss. Mik can be a lot, but we love her. I raise an eyebrow at him, indicating he should answer her—because I sure as hell am not.

"We had a little argument this week that is now resolved, but it stirred up some old emotions." He smirks, seemingly satisfied with his proper response.

"Mhm," is all Mik responds with.

"Hey, Mel. Can you get us a drink? If you ask for two mojitos for your sister and the bride-to-be, I'll give you mine." Lexi winks at her. Mel is quick to oblige, jogging up the patio stairs towards the bar.

Teens. I roll my eyes and silently thank her.

"Let's just have a nice evening, please? Diego isn't here and I'm not sure when he'll be back. I really would rather not get into it right now. Hey, maybe you'll even find yourself a man while you're here." As I say that, Kieran and Colin look our way. Either of those two would get a kick out of my sister.

"Did you break up?" Her hand reaches out to clasp the sleeve of my bathrobe.

"No. If anything we are better than ever. Things just kinda, sorta, hit the fan and now we are dealing with the consequences of that. That's all I can say. I really don't want Dad finding out."

"Fuck, Mad. Okay, is there anything I can do to help?"

"No. Not really. Maybe if you can try and keep Dad from questioning where Diego is, that would help. Mom doesn't even know about Diego. I think she still believes I'm single after breaking up with Killian. Dad—well, you heard him that night. He's given us his blessing, but he told Diego that he'd end him if I got caught up with the law."

"So are you saying he's been arrested?" she asks cheekily.

"We are working on it." That will have to placate her for now.

THE NIGHT of the rehearsal dinner is here. Diego's yacht has been transformed into a candle-lit, intimate space that radiates the love the pair share. Lexi and Conor's family have arrived. Most are gallivanting around and chatting at the bar. Others are dancing on the plexiglass dance floor we had installed over the pool.

It reminds me of my wedding night, which triggers a wave of anxiety within me.

I haven't spoken to Diego since the night he was taken in. Liam has offered to ask Lindsay to arrange another call, but I know what that means for him. Whether he is willing to or not, I can't put him in that position for my own selfish needs.

A waitress comes by with a tray of champagne. I claim one, guzzling it down to soothe my nerves before collecting another one. The waitress' eyes widen, but she doesn't acknowledge my off-hinge behavior.

Lexi joins Conor front and center for a dance. The crowd surrounds them, admiring their love for one another. Liam comes up behind me and presses both of his palms to my shoulders.

"I'm happy for them. Those two are the perfect couple."

"They really are," I sigh.

"Sorry about earlier. I wasn't aware you hadn't told your family about Diego. I should have asked you first if it was okay to have them here a day early."

I angle my body to face his direction while still watching my bestie dance with her man. "It's fine. I was upset at first, but honestly, having my sisters here is exactly what I needed. So, thank you. I was a bitch earlier and shouldn't have reacted the way I did."

He presses a kiss to the top of my hair. "Anything for you, Mad. I just want this all to go away so you can be happy like them." He nods his head to the swaying couple.

"Any updates?" I clear my throat.

"Nothing other than your father asking me where Diego has been."

"Shit. Please tell me you avoided that as best you could?"

"Actually, your sister did. She interrupted us and pulled your father away for a family picture." He laughs, knowing how persistent my sister can be.

"Thank God. Okay, let's try and keep him off our radar," I sigh with relief.

He nods his agreement before extending a hand. "Dance with me?" I look around at the rest of the couples who have now joined our future, Mr. and Mrs. Hayes.

"Okay," I agree, accepting his hand and letting him lead me through the crowd. He finds a spot next to Lex and Con, bumping into them to grab their attention.

"How's it going? You guys enjoying your rehearsal dinner?" Liam asks.

"It's everything and more. We can't thank you both enough for all the work you've put into this," Lexi gushes.

303

"Seriously, thank you," Conor adds, slapping Liam's shoulder.

"It was our pleasure," Liam and I say in unison before laughing. *Always in sync—that hasn't changed.*

An hour later, dinner is served. Everyone is raving about it. Luckily, Diego's chef was able to rally her good friends—who are also experienced chefs—to help with the catering. Lainey fucked us over in so many ways.

So many ways that's had my blood boiling all night. Liam notices my shift in drunkenness and irritability and pulls up a chair next to me. When Diego isn't around to stir up old feelings and jealousy, Liam can be the sweetest man. I wish he was always like this. I hope that after the dust settles a bit, we can go back to being the way we were—minus the romance.

His tattooed arm lands on the back of my chair. He leans on the other one which he has propped up onto the wooden dining table. The white sleeves of his dress shirt are rolled up and the top two buttons of his shirt are popped open. I smile knowing he couldn't help himself. He brings his glass of water to his lips to take a sip. That's another thing I noticed since our argument. He's been drinking far less, sticking mainly to soda, water, or beer. I can't recall him having whiskey or any mixed drinks these last few days.

"I don't want to get your hopes up, but there is a chance you may get to speak to Diego tomorrow after the wedding. Lindsay asked when our next," he air quotes, "*get together*" would be. I told her after the wedding would be easier. Fewer prying eyes, more people drunk and not paying attention to who is coming back to my room with me."

I place my hand over his forearm and shift my body, leaning in closer to whisper. "You don't have to let her use you like that to help me out. I can't ask that of you." My eyes search his for the truth. But what I get in return isn't what I expected.

His smile grows as he takes another sip of his drink. "She's not using me. I've always enjoyed our time together. We are the no bullshit type. No emotions, no bullshit. Just straight up dirty sex. You wouldn't be asking this of me, I'm completely willing."

"Ahh. I see. Well, I hope she feels the same cut-and-dry way."

"Sweetheart, there isn't much *dry* when it comes to me...you should know that." He winks.

I roll my eyes dramatically. Seems things never really change, do they?

CHAPTER 38

LIAM

THE WEDDING DAY has officially arrived. The groom and I stand under the archway set up on the beach. Guests from both sides and organizations are seated before us on wicker chairs. Purple fabric and a mix of flowers coil around the wooden semicircle. Behind us, the sun is setting over the water, both appearing as if they were set on fire. The purples, pinks, and oranges add to the theme.

Stunning.

Con is fidgeting with his bow tie, cursing every time it is the slightest bit crooked. I approach him, smacking his hand out of the way and adjusting it until it's straight.

"Deep breaths, brother. The lass is obsessed with you. There is zero chance of her having cold feet." I grip his shoulders and lightly shake him.

He nods appreciatively. "I've never wanted anything more in life than I do her. I can't believe she is going to be my wife in a few short minutes."

His dark eyes desperately search the staircase leading down from the pool where the bridal party will start their processional. I follow his line of sight, spotting Madison at the top, waiting for the music to cue her descent. She looks insanely beautiful in her form-fitting purple gown. Elegant satin hugs her curves in all the right places while still remaining respectful. That iridescent hair of hers shimmers with the last rays of the sun on the horizon. Dark charcoal lines her eyes as a spiderweb of black lashes adds to her seductive look. Her long purple locks are styled wavy and collected to one side, the gentle breeze catching it.

I can't stop staring.

I. Just. Can't.

I will always find Madison in a room.

The soft melodic music of the orchestra starts, alerting Madison it's time to begin her journey down the stairs and down the aisle. She raises her bouquet, holding it out in front of her stomach, and smiles as she glides down them. There is murmured chatter, likely her family admiring her beauty.

I smile at her encouragingly, knowing behind that smile is a ball of nerves. *Can't blame her.* Her family is here, watching her every move. Her husband is in Federal custody. And her best friend is about to marry the love of her life. She's put so much into helping plan this. I know she wants this day to go off without a hitch.

When she finally reaches us, she shoots us another devastatingly beautiful smile. Honest to God, I think my heart stops for a minute.

Instead of a purple dress, I envision her in all white, walking towards *me.*

Fuck. Why is heartbreak such a bitch?

She takes her place on the opposite side of the officiant, then shifts her gaze to the staircase where the rest of the bridal party continues to pour in. They take their respective sides, joining us in waiting to greet the bride. Conor shifts anxiously back and forth on his heels. My hand comes down on his shoulder to ground him. *You've got this, mate.*

The song ends, transitioning into a new one designed for the bride.

"If everyone will please rise for our bride?" the officiant requests of the crowd.

Alexis comes into view at the top of the stairs with her father linking arms with her. He's teary-eyed as are many among us. Conor lets out an enamored sigh. His future wife looks stunning.

The white lace mermaid gown has her taking cautious baby steps down the stairs. Her father has a tight grip on her arm, making sure she'll never fall. A delicate cathedral veil slinks down the aisle behind her as she moves closer to us. An elaborate bouquet is held steadily between her hands. *This is a woman who knows exactly who and what she wants.*

Baby-blue eyes are locked in on her betrothed. I swivel my head to look at Con who has tears pooled at the rims of his. Lexi's father kisses her cheek and places her hand on Conor's, who then takes it and places a kiss to the top of it.

"You look incredible, angel," he whispers.

Lexi's Dad takes a seat as she hands off her bouquet to a waiting Madison. The couple situates themselves in front of the officiant as Madison gently lowers the massive bouquet and smooths out Lexi's dress and veil. The thin lace material covers the space like a sand dollar, curling around them.

The ceremony is short and sweet. No more than twenty minutes. Con and Lexi both agreed to remove a lot of the fillers that would cause the event to drag on. Our lovely couple recites their vows and places their wedding bands on each other's respective ring finger.

"By the power vested in me by the State of Florida, and in the company of your near and dear, I now pronounce you husband and wife. You may now kiss your bride," the graying man sings.

Conor grips her face and dips his wife in an elaborate kiss. The crowd hoots and hollers, whistling for our friends. Madison even cups a hand over her face and howls like a wolf. The excitement she is showing for her best friend is beautiful. Quite frankly, they are more like sisters than friends. The pair breaks apart and Madison hands Lexi her bouquet as Conor collects his wife's hand in his.

"It's my honor to introduce to you Mr. and Mrs. Hayes!" the officiant exclaims.

Claps and cheers ignite as The Hayes begin their walk back towards the pool area where cocktails and appetizers will be served. Flower petals are thrown into the air, falling on top of their ecstatic faces.

I couldn't be happier for them.

Madison approaches my right and links her arm through mine. The party planner signals us to go next, followed by the rest of our bridal party. Photographers snap pictures as we walk down the aisle. Sadness and regret try to inch their way into my chest as we continue walking. *How different things could have been.* Madison, always sensing my anxiety, taps her fingers on my forearm that she's gripping.

"I know what you're thinking. You'll have a moment like this, Liam. I promise you," she soothes.

Her sweet voice pushes the demons back down and places a lid on the box they came from. When we reach the stairs, I place my hand around her waist, supporting her and helping her up them. Those shoes she's wearing, although gorgeous, are not designed for this sort of environment.

"There is a sandal station for later. Don't worry. I won't be wearing these all night." And once again, the little witch reads my mind.

I run my hand up and down her back. "Do ya think they have my size?" I joke, glancing down at my shiny black dress shoes.

Sand has already found its way in.

Lovely.

"ARE YOU STILL COMING?" I ask into the phone. I'm over in the corner of the bar nursing a whiskey. I don't plan on getting out of control drunk with grief tonight. Quite the opposite, actually. I'm enjoying a celebratory bottle Killian and I got for Con. It's somewhat of a tradition in our family.

Madison comes out of nowhere, tugging my dress shirt. "We are going to miss speeches. Come on. Get your jacket on," she tugs me off the stool, sounding irritated.

She shakes out my jacket I had on the stool next to me and holds it out for me to slip into. "Text me when you get here," I clip into the phone before hanging up and depositing it into my pants pocket.

Madison raises a dark eyebrow as I begin buttoning the tux jacket. "Hot date?" she inquires.

"Something like that," I clip.

Maddy sighs heavily as she pulls me back towards the beach where the tent is set up. "Is it Lindsay? I don't want her stirring shit up at our best friends' wedding."

"There you are," Killian sighs with relief as he reaches us. "The band just announced speeches and of course, you two went missing."

"I was looking for Liam," Madison hisses defensively.

Without another word, she takes her place next to Lexi as I take mine next to Con.

Everyone balled their eyes out at Madison's speech whereas they nearly pissed themselves listening to mine. Con claps me on the back and Lexi snags Madison closer by the waist as we take a group picture.

The flash of the camera has my eyes all fucked. Madison starts to walk away, heading towards the bar. I start to follow her when my phone vibrates in my pocket. I take a peek, smiling at the person lighting up my screen. Quickly, I type out a response before sliding my phone back into my pocket and catch up to Madison.

She is leaning a hip against the bar and slowly sipping a glass of Prosecco. Her eyes slowly scan the crowd that is now making their way to the dance floor.

The music picks up speed at the same time the band requests for everyone to join the couple. Madison downs her drink and walks off towards the tent's exit. I snatch her arm, pulling her into me and spinning her into the crowd.

Her gasp turns into a smile, then a giggle as I place my hands on her hips, getting her to sway them. "Come on, Mad. Loosen up. Don't go sit on the beach and wallow. Diego would want you to enjoy tonight."

"It feels selfish of me to. He's doing God knows what in a cell and I'm supposed to be over here drinking and being merry?"

"Yes. Life is too short to stay miserable. You taught me that. Now let me see what you've got. Cause I've seen you dance and this is pitiful," I provoke her.

Mikayla comes over to us as well as Lexi and Con. We all throw our hands in the air and sway to the music, letting all our worries slide off our shoulders.

At least for tonight.

CHAPTER 39

MADISON

DINNER PLATES ARE REMOVED from the tables as more and more people head for the bar. Liam slides his chair back, tossing his napkin down. He stands abruptly, extending a hand towards me. *Not this again. I can't take any more dancing.*

"The photo booth is open. Let's take a picture. Maybe I can get Lindsay to send it to Diego."

"That's cruel, Liam," I reprimand, even though I smack my palm into his.

His fingers curl around mine, guiding us to the table in front of the booth. All different props and signs are spread out. Liam grabs a sign that says 'I'm here for the drinks'. I decide on #MatronofHonor. Simple but classic. All the other ones are for couples...

The guy working the camera gives us a quick overview. We step into the booth—which is more of an open space with lights and a giant tablet that captures the pictures. Liam presses the button and the front-facing camera begins counting down from ten. Liam throws his arm over my shoulder and holds up his sign. I smile and hold up mine. As we get to five Liam jumps out of the frame.

In complete confusion, I turn to look at him, wondering what the hell he's up to.

A hard body replaces Liam's from behind me. A body I know *oh so well.* I spin around in shock. Ocean eyes full of triumph greet mine as the timer chimes. His smile broadens as my eyes widen in disbelief.

"Told you I'd be back, *Mariposita*," he purrs, the words dripping off his lips like honey.

And then his lips are on mine.

Devouring me. Consuming me. Thrilling me.

Clicks go off around us as the pictures are snapped. Diego raises his hand, seemingly holding a sign. I can't bother to tear my lips from his to see what it says.

It has to be at least a minute later that Liam's chuckles interrupt us. We break away, still clinging to each other as he approaches us. His tattooed hand extends to offer us the picture. *The Bone Breaker* and I lean forward to look at the sequence of my reactions in each frame.

Props to Liam for planning this. *That's who he was talking to earlier.*

"I must say improvising this worked out perfectly. I originally had him meeting us on the dance floor. This one definitely takes the cake," Liam muses.

My eyes linger on the last frame. Diego is proudly holding a sign that says 'MINE'. The feral part of me stirs at those words. *His.* In this lifetime and those that follow. This man truly is all mine. He reaches into his pocket and pulls out my wedding ring. Gentle fingers grip my left hand as he slides it onto my finger.

"Back where it belongs," Diego states proudly.

"You are back where you belong," I croak through the tears, pulling him back to me.

I lay my head on his chest as his arms come out to rock me back and forth. Liam looks down at us. The proud smile he is sporting says *everything* about who he really is. He put his pride and hurt aside to get Diego back for me.

"Thank you," I tell him.

"Anything for you, princess."

Lifting my head, I look up at my husband, my eyes searching his. "Are you back for good?" Hope fills my voice. *Is this nightmare really over?*

"He is," Lindsay answers for him, looping an arm through Liam's. "Unfortunately, the evidence we had against him has been destroyed. We believe an extremely experienced hacker wiped our servers clean. Lucky for Diego, that meant we had no physical evidence to charge him with. Beyond that, the witnesses who have come forward to make a statement have all proven Geraldo De La Cruz was to blame for what Diego was being charged with. Between us, the faking of his death is considered fraud. I was able to pull a few strings and we were able to work out a deal—assuming he did it to protect his loved ones from any possible retaliation. With that being said, we still have him on a watch list, but there isn't enough reason to keep him," she explains to me before looking at my husband all amused. "Stay out of trouble, Mr. De La Cruz."

Liam winks at us before he guides her to the bar, giving us a minute to process this.

Holy. Shit.

Diego's hand comes up to cup my face and I lean into it. "You look ravishing...and downright fuckable," he groans, lowering his forehead to mine.

"I have a feeling we won't be sleeping at all tonight," I giggle.

"I have a feeling you won't be getting any sleep for a few days," he smirks, slapping my ass.

His lips find mine once more before the band requests that everyone join the couple in a slow dance. Diego breaks away to lead me to the dance floor. He places my hand on his shoulder and tugs me forward by the hip. I place my hand in his as the familiar melody of our wedding song fills the speakers. The lead singer sounds identical to Michael Bublé. I stare at my husband longingly, knowing he requested this song play for us.

Mikayla and Kieran surprisingly join us. Mik doesn't say anything, just winks her approval. Kieran looks nervous as he awaits my reaction. When he notices Diego, a look of elation fills him. Where once *The Bone Breaker* was a person who created tension amongst the Tri-State Syndicate, he now is looked at with mutual respect.

My roommate Leah bumps into me from behind, giggling as Colin haphazardly spins her around in a circle. He too, smiles widely at Diego and me. "Welcome back, mate," he says enthusiastically.

"So this is your man. I've heard all about you," she gushes, extending a hand. "I'm Leah."

Diego reaches out and shakes it firmly.

"I don't care that your nickname is '*The Bone Breaker,*" she air quotes with her fingers. "Hurt my friend again, and I will *end* you," Leah menaces before resuming her dance with Colin like she didn't just threaten the underworld's most dangerous mobster.

An unladylike snort leaves me, prompting Diego to break out laughing. We quickly gain attention, a few heads turn our way. Two of them being my father and his girlfriend. He dances his way over to us, all suave.

Diego manages to get his laughter under control. "I like her." His smile grows wide as my father approaches.

"I didn't expect to see you here, son." My father lands a hand on Diego's shoulder.

Diego reaches out a hand. Dad takes it, firmly greeting my husband as Diane kisses me hello.

"Everything sorted out?" Dad questions. He hasn't released Diego's hand.

"Yes, Sir. I'm free of all charges," my husband affirms confidently.

Dad pats Diego's shoulder and releases his hand, curling it around his girlfriend. "Good. I'm glad. You two are glowing. Madison went from timid and anxious tonight to radiating excitement and happiness. I'm sure your arrival had a lot to do with that."

My face hurts from smiling so widely. Not to mention all the pictures we took today. It really does a number on your facial muscles. *Perhaps that is why celebs have such snatched jawlines.*

Liam and Lindsay approach and Dad nods at us before slipping back into the throng of people dancing. Diego releases me for a second to embrace Liam. They pat each other's backs and Liam grips the back of Diego's head, shaking it.

"Thank you," Diego expresses.

"You guys deserve a happy ending. Whatever I could do to help," he states simply, aware of Lindsay next to him.

Lexi squeals as they approach us. She leaps forward and pulls Diego into a hug. "Holy crap. He's back. Oh, Madison. Today truly is the perfect day!" she sobs.

I rub her back as she continues to cling to my husband. When she finally releases him she hugs me, swaying me back and forth. The song eases to an end and the band announces the Viennese hour is now open.

Lexi and Con head off to join their guests at the chocolate fountain.

Lindsay smiles up at Liam, who wraps an arm around her waist as they follow the crowd. She seems to be more involved with Liam than I had thought. The way she looks at him is way more than lust. *Definitely* more than a crush.

Diego breaks my reverie by tucking a strand of violet hair behind my ears. His fingers trace the butterfly tattoo I have there.

"Care for an espresso, *Mariposita*? You're gonna need it with what I have planned for you..." Mint and coconut swirl around me as he leans over and lowers his lips to where his fingers once traced.

Goosebumps spring up on my skin as a low moan leaves my lips.

I will always have this reaction to this man.

"With you, I don't need espresso. Your presence alone awakens every nerve ending and synapse inside of me," I admit breathlessly.

"Well in that case..." He scoops me up and carries me the opposite way of the crowd, snatching a slice of wedding cake off a nearby table.

The Bone Breaker carries me all the way down the beach and up the dock. He boards his yacht and takes the elevator up to the top floor. When the doors open, he strides over to my reading room with minimal effort. Using his elbow, he nudges the door open and gently lays me down on the fur rug beneath the dome.

"Dessert for you," he says, handing me the plate while scooping up a piece of decadent chocolate cake. The metal of the fork hits my teeth as he feeds it to me. His lips press against mine, stealing a kiss as his tongue licks the chocolate mousse off them. Firm hands start to bunch the satin fabric of my dress, impatiently pushing it up over my thighs. He hooks a finger into my panties and slides the matching lace to the side.

"And dessert for me," he murmurs between my thighs.

I lie back and stare at the stars as pleasure washes over me.

For once, they don't make me question everything.

I am *exactly* where I should be.

EPILOGUE
MADISON

THEY SAY: 'LIGHTNING NEVER STRIKES TWICE'...

Apparently—based on a quick web search–it can.

Multiple times. Usually, with things that are isolated and tall. Like me.

This fact has me wondering if love can also strike you multiple times, changing the beat of your heart each time.

It couldn't be possible to love two men at the same time? Could it?

COLD JELLY HITS my stomach as the white paper sheet crinkles below it. Diego squeezes my hand tighter, anxious about what will happen next. A wand is pressed down onto my swollen abdomen as the doctor spins the screen in our direction.

"Are you ready to know the gender of your baby?" she asks us, smiling from ear to ear.

Our doctor has been absolutely incredible. She has helped us through every heartbreak. Every loss. This entire IVF journey has been one stressor after another. Just when I thought I couldn't take it any longer and stopped all treatment, Diego and I fell pregnant naturally. We actually found out on our fourth wedding anniversary. *Fifth,* if you count our first wedding.

The second wedding was everything I could have ever wanted and more. We did it on the yacht again, this time surrounded by the love and support of our family and friends. I wore a similar dress and hairstyle, wanting to preserve the sweeter memories of that first night. Diego did the same, wearing a navy blue tuxedo and a smile that drove me wild.

We decided to marry off the coast of France and celebrated a week-long honeymoon on a vineyard Diego purchased for us. Our guests enjoyed the yacht and its amenities as we indulged in each other and plenty of wine.

I had my first positive pregnancy test when we came home. The two of us were over the moon excited. Unfortunately, a few weeks into the pregnancy I started to spot—ultimately leading me to the ER.

That was the start of our long fertility journey.

Ocean Eyes squeezes my hand as the mouse hovers over the anatomy of our child growing inside me.

"It's a boy!" our doctor cheers.

Tears drip down my face as I sob into Diego. He hugs me tightly, placing a kiss on my lips before pressing kisses all over my belly. I stare at the screen, my eyes blurry from the salty tears. I rub the palms of my hands against them, clearing them.

"Hi, sweet boy. Mommy and Daddy love you so much. We can't wait to meet you," I coo.

Diego presses a tender kiss on my forehead. "We are going to have a son," he says in awe.

"Congratulations you two," the doctor says, before printing out the sonogram pictures. She cleans the jelly off my stomach and gives us privacy so that I can dress.

I dress quickly. I need to get back to the coffee shop to

decorate it for Halloween. Tonight, a costume party is being held at our New York location in honor of our growing family. Everyone has been texting me all day placing their votes on the gender.

Diego lowers himself to one knee, placing my Uggs back on my feet. His hand slides up my calf as he rises. He leans over me, sliding those hands over my thighs before grabbing my waist. Soft lips connect with mine as my hands come up to tangle in his hair.

Pregnancy hormones have made me extremely horny. It doesn't matter where we are, the need for my husband has been amplified—*as impossible as that sounds.* I tug him to me, opening my mouth and granting his tongue access to tangle with mine. He moans, setting me off. My hands slide under his t-shirt and over his delicious abs.

He places his hands over mine, stopping me. "As much as I'd love to take advantage of these stirrups right now, *Mariposita*, we need to get moving. Our family is just as eager to know the gender as we are. Plus, I'd like to speak with your photographer about adding some new pictures to my book. You'd look incredible with flour all over you and your belly swollen with our child."

I pout, removing my hands, knowing he's right. My staff and I have a lot to prepare for tonight. I still need to bake those pumpkin scones.

"Maybe later?" I ask hopefully.

He smirks, gripping my head between his hands and kissing me briefly.

"Definitely later. That's a promise," he vows, helping me off the table and handing me the sonogram photos.

I once questioned if it was possible to love two men at the same time. As I smile at my husband and look over at the black-and-white pictures in my hand, I can now confirm—

You absolutely can.

The End

ACKNOWLEDGMENTS

Wipes tear drops off computer keyboard

We did it, friends. We made it to the end of The Triskelion Trilogy. *Three.* That number in numerology was always significant to me. All to do with self-expression, using your creative abilities, and overcoming personal challenges. In a way, all the signs and symbols encouraging me to write the series played such a larger role within the books. That is where The Triskelion Series was born. Our past, our present, and our future. Mind, body, and soul. Those ideas truly inspired this story.

And what a wild ride it was.

I went into this book series as a brand new indie author with a tiny idea. I knew I had a story to tell, I just wasn't expecting it to grow and evolve into a completely different story. I never anticipated the hold these characters I created would have on me. My past had inspired some of these crucial moments— loosely of course, but the rest was up to the magic of my mind. A place I love hanging out in. A place where I can daydream and plot what comes up next in a chapter. Ending the book the way I did was a full-circle moment. Madison has come so far since we first met her. She's experienced heartbreak and loss at such a young age. Along her journey, she's met incredible individuals who helped guide her on the path she was on. Friends, if you have those people in your life, hang on to them. They are precious and rare.

I hope that you forgive me for throwing your heart around as Madison navigated her feelings. Ultimately, I think she chose someone who not only supported her but gifted her the patience and distance to do so on her own. It also didn't hurt that that person worshiped her spiritually—and physically 😉. As for Liam's happy ending, I just may write another book for him one day. I plan on moving on to new characters and new projects, but I will always find my way back to this series. It's what made me love being a writer.

Thank you, the reader, so much for giving these books and a baby author like me a try. Your kind feedback continues to encourage me to write. And where there is writing there is healing. It's been an incredible journey.

Now, the thank-yous for those who, without their expertise, my books would never have gotten off this laptop:

Emily, my amazing cover and interior artist at Quirky Circe Designs. Thank you so much for these gorgeous covers. You took exactly what I had visualized and turned it into a reality. Even more than making my books look beautiful, your expertise in the field and mentorship have helped me immensely. I started this journey with no clue how to write a book or what it required when I first reached out to you. I had a vision and story. Your advice and direction were exactly what I needed to get started. I can't wait to work with you again on my next adventure.

To my family and friends who have supported me on this journey. Thank you. Thank you for promoting the books, reading them, editing them, and offering advice. They say it takes a village to raise a baby—well these books are my babies and *you* are the village that has supported me. So, thank you.

Last but not least, to my beautiful daughter. Seeing your cute little face light up when I am reading you a book has Mama all sorts of proud. I loved reading as a kid and obviously still do. I hope that as you get older, you can see that anything you love and put your mind to, you will achieve. I have always wanted to write a book, and now I can say that I wrote a series. Never let fear of failure prevent you from chasing those dreams; those goals. I love you, sweetheart.

Until the next adventure...
Xoxo,
Luna Everly

ABOUT THE AUTHOR

Luna Everly is an indie romance author who would like to share the fantasyland she has in her mind with the world. This dream world consists of strong sarcastic men, who are grounded by their smart sassy heroines. Add a bit of suspense, impossible decisions, and amazing besties to the lives of these characters-- and you've got yourself quite the adventure to go on. Grab the tissues for emotional ups and downs and a fan for some seriously steamy moments.

As a Pisces, Luna often gets lost daydreaming. When she's not lost in thought, she's spending time with her daughter, family, two rescue dogs, and her clingy cat Loki. Luna enjoys cooking, game nights, getting lost in a good book, self-care bubble baths, and even the occasional marathon of Call of Duty. You'll never find her far from her cup of coffee--or multiple cups for that matter.

Luna Everly is a pen name. She currently resides in New York with her family.

GET SOCIAL

authorlunaeverly.com

Facebook
https://www.facebook.com/profile.php?id=100088486166891

TikTok
https://www.tiktok.com/@authorlunaeverly

Instagram
https://instagram.com/authorlunaeverly

info@authorlunaeverly.com

* Subscribe to my newsletter to stay up to date on new releases and giveaways.

* Follow along with my blog to keep up with me and my wild adventures.

SPOTIFY PLAYLISTS

I don't know about you, but I love listening to music while reading and writing. It makes the story even more intense and emotional for me. I hope these songs make you feel those emotions the same way!

Follow Luna Everly on Spotify for music inspiration!

Book 1: Tomorrow's Never Promised

Book 2: If Tomorrow Never Comes

Book 3: A Promise For Tomorrow

www.ingramcontent.com/pod-product-compliance
Lightning Source LLC
Chambersburg PA
CBHW051233260626
47162CB00002B/404